COMPANY OF STRANGERS

COMPANY OF STRANGERS, BOOK 1

MELISSA MCSHANE

Night Harbor Publishing

Dedicated to the cast of Critical Role,
for helping to keep the dream alive

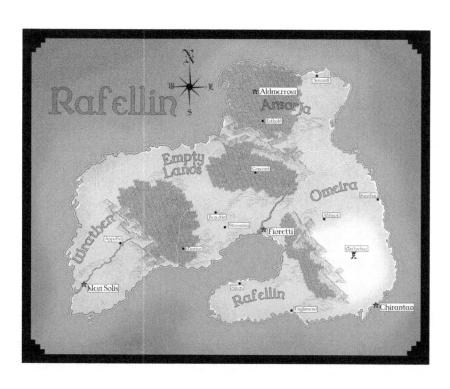

PART I

1

The playful west wind, threading its way through the narrow streets, brought the briny smell of the harbor and the fainter, sweeter scent of clematis growing up the wall of the Lucky Coin tavern to Sienne's nose. More scents, those of barley soup and roast chicken, tangled with the wind, free advertising for the tavern's wares. The umber stone of the pavement, slick from an early shower, gleamed dully in what little morning light found its way through the high walls that made a brown brick canyon of the little street. The Lucky Coin's heavy wooden door was banded with iron as if the owner expected to have to defend against bandits here in the capital. It hung slightly ajar, inviting Sienne to step inside.

It was as good a place as any for a last meal.

Sienne pushed the door open and squinted into the dimness. The tavern lay tucked between an apothecary on one side and a chandler on the other, so no windows lit its interior. Instead, dozens of frosted glass bulbs, each containing the steady gleam of a magical light no bigger than a button, lined its walls. The cold white glow made the few people within look sickly, consumptive, though they were no more gaunt than anyone else.

A man sat at the long oak bar, cradling a mug in his large hands and staring at its contents as if willing them to reveal the future. Four or five people sat at a table in the corner, playing crack-stones, with another two people standing nearby watching the play. A woman about Sienne's age leaned against the wall in a chair near the hearth, empty this fourth day of true summer. Fine dark blonde hair was braided in a crown around her head, wisps of it escaping its bonds and standing up in all directions. Her eyes were closed, and the remnants of a meal lay on a nearby table. By noon, the place would be packed with laborers seeking a quick, cheap meal, but at nine o'clock in the morning only the desperate had found their way to the Lucky Coin. Sienne wondered what their stories were. It was unlikely any of them were as desperate as she.

She took a seat at the bar, several stools away from the quiet drunk, and shifted the spellbook that lay nestled against her stomach. A short, stout woman, probably less than five feet tall, came out of the back room, wiping her hands on her apron. "What'll it be, miss?"

Sienne mentally checked the contents of her purse. It didn't take long. "Soup," she said, opting for the cheapest thing she could think of. "And half a pint of the house brew." She probably couldn't afford it, but she had to eat, didn't she? And then—she stopped herself thinking about "and then."

The woman nodded curtly, took Sienne's coin, and bustled away. Sienne shifted the spellbook again. It would have been more comfortable to carry it in her pack, but this was the big city, and who knew what cutpurses were capable of? Losing the book would be the worst fate she could think of, worse than what awaited her if she couldn't find a job, and soon.

She glanced at the man nursing his pint, then swiftly looked away before he made eye contact. He had the look of someone who wanted to share his sad story with a compassionate listener, and the way she was feeling, she didn't want to be that person. She wanted to get drunk and feel sorry for herself and maybe cry a little, not in that exact order, and being a listening ear didn't fit with that plan.

The mirror over the bar was cracked and blistered at the edges, sign that it was a real mirror and not a magical effect. Well, a place like this probably couldn't afford that kind of wizardry, the light globes notwithstanding. Sienne pushed her chestnut brown hair back from her face and examined herself. Was it the mirror, or did she have spots on her cheek? She rubbed at the offending mark, but it didn't go away. The mirror, then. She closed her eyes and pinched the bridge of her nose against a headache. If she knew the right spell, she could offer to replace the spotty mirror with magic, pay for her meal that way. But she didn't know the spell, and that was the problem, right there. Not knowing enough.

The woman came back and set down a pottery bowl with a shiny red finish. Soup slopped up the sides as if she'd slammed the bowl on the bar. Sienne accepted a spoon from the woman and smiled half-heartedly. The shiny, almost oily finish told Sienne the bowl had been treated with the same magical invulnerability that protected her spellbook and the glass lights, though invulnerability frosted glass rather than giving it an oily sheen. Maybe she was wrong about the relative prosperity of the tavern.

The woman turned her back on Sienne and lugged a short stepstool out from under the counter. Sienne took a careful bite of barley soup. It was almost too hot to eat, which suited her just fine, because it meant she could spin this meal out indefinitely. She watched the woman climb to the top step and reach for a wooden box on the highest shelf. Her fingertips just brushed its lowest edge as she strained for it. The stool rocked, and the woman froze, her other hand gripping the shelf.

"Here, let me help you," Sienne said, unable to bear the suspense. She nudged the box tentatively with a brush of magic she always thought of as invisible fingers. Not too heavy. The box slid forward, then floated down to rest on the bar. The man with the pint ignored it. This was the big city. People could afford to be blasé about magic.

The woman stepped off the stool and wiped her brow as if she'd run a mile. "My thanks," she said. "You a scrapper?"

"Sort of," Sienne said. Could you call yourself something if you'd utterly failed at becoming one? It was the only identity left to her, which was a depressing thought all by itself.

"Never do know what to say to a scrapper," the woman said. "Might well get yourself killed in the Empty Lands if I wish you luck, you know?"

"I'd settle for a nice boring job somewhere close to home." Sienne took a long pull on her pint. It was good, if not nearly strong enough. But getting drunk was a bad idea for a wizard, especially an unemployed one, so she reminded herself to be happy with what she had.

She drained the bowl, careful not to spill on herself. Invulnerability sounded like a good idea, but it made pottery surfaces virtually frictionless, and unless you wanted your food to come off your plate a good deal faster than was healthy, you treated unbreakable dishes with care. Then she turned around and watched the crack-stones game for lack of anything better to do while she nursed her pint. The players, all men, were nearly silent, telling Sienne it was a serious game for high stakes. She was terrible at crack-stones, or so Rance—

She closed her eyes and cursed herself for her momentary weakness. She was never going to think of him again, not even so much as think his name. *Some people* had told her she was bad at crack-stones, which she knew; she was too straightforward a thinker, always looking at her own throws and not at the other players'. She preferred to watch, trying to guess the tosses before they fell.

From where she sat, she couldn't see the lead's stones, because he had his back to her, but she could see three of the other five. One played daringly, tossing his stones almost too high to be legal, but the other two kept their throws close to the scarred surface of the table, its finish so dark as to be nearly black. It was a fine contrast to the pale ovals of the crack-stones.

Sienne watched as the bold player once again tossed his stones high. They seemed almost to hover at the apex of the throw, quivering with excitement. Her eyes narrowed, and she took another look. That wasn't normal behavior. Something else was going on.

She set her mug down and slid off her stool, crossing the room to stand beside one of the observers. The short man looked up and flashed a smile at her, which she returned absently. The other watcher, a slender woman with prominent front teeth like a rabbit, ignored Sienne. Her eyes were fixed on the stones in play. It was mid-game, half the stones scattered in front of the players, the others still in hand. A pile of coins and a few forfeits lay in the center of the table.

Sienne examined the bold player. He had the fairer coloring of a Wrathen, his hair light brown and braided halfway down his back, and his eyes were half-lidded as if he were, despite appearances, falling asleep. "My luck can't last," he laughed, and tossed the three stones he held. They spun lazily in the air, first cracked faces up, then smooth. Then they landed, bouncing across the table until coming to rest, one of them striking the coins in the center. All three landed smooth face up.

The other men groaned. "Your luck will cost me everything," one of them said, flicking a coin into the pot and rubbing his other hand over his beard. "Which avatar did you sell your soul to? Or did all of them get a cut?"

"He's cheating," Sienne said.

Everyone turned to look at her. Out of the corner of her eye, Sienne saw the woman leaning against the wall sit up. "What was that?" the bold player said. "You calling me a cheat?"

"Yes, actually." Sienne pointed at the rabbit-faced woman. "Or, rather, she's cheating for you. Is she your sister? Lover? Or just a partner in crime?"

The man shoved his chair back and stood. "I won't be slandered by some chit of a girl got nothing better to do than stick her nose in where it's not wanted."

"You have been awful lucky," the bearded man said. "Miss, what proof have you?"

"She's using magic to turn the stones," Sienne said. "It's a simple trick. I can feel her touching them with magic every time."

"You have no proof," the woman snarled.

"You've all been watching him play." Sienne included the other players in her gaze. "The stones land neatly on the table no matter how high he throws them. If magic didn't keep them in place, they'd bounce all over the room, thrown that high and hard. Have him make another throw like those and you'll see."

The other players looked at each other. "I...think I want to see this," the bearded man said. "Make the toss."

The bold player scowled. "I got nothing to prove."

The scrape of steel against leather sounded loud in the suddenly quiet room. The bearded man rested his hand, holding a wickedly sharp dagger, on the table next to the heap of coins. "I say you do."

The bold player cursed and shoved back from the table. "I'm no cheat," he said, "and I won't play with people as think I am. Come on, Latrice, we're leaving." He made as if to scoop up the coins from the table, then froze as the bearded man reversed his grip and drove the point of the dagger deep into the table beside the man's hand. He snatched his hand back, snarled wordlessly at Sienne, and stalked away, the rabbity woman scurrying to keep up. Sienne let out the breath she hadn't realized she was holding.

"Our thanks," the bearded man said. "You didn't have to say anything. It's not your problem."

Staying silent hadn't occurred to her. It never did. "I don't like cheats," she said, and went back to her seat.

"You didn't make friends today," the barkeep said in a low voice. She picked up Sienne's empty bowl, but stood there holding it. "Seen those two before. They're not the nicest of characters."

"I can take care of myself," Sienne said. She realized she was fingering the edge of her spellbook through her shirt and made herself stop.

The woman shrugged. "Wizards usually can. Don't suppose you can teach me that lifting magic?"

She smiled to show it was a joke, and Sienne smiled back. Nobody who wasn't born a wizard could do anything the least bit magical. "No, but I could give you an extra twenty inches of height," she joked back.

"*That* I could do with. I suppose it'd slim me down some, too?"

"Not this spell. But it only lasts six hours, and I likely won't be here this afternoon to repeat it."

"Too bad." The barkeep winked and went away into the back room with the bowl and spoon. Sienne drained her mug, too late remembering she'd intended to make it last. She set it down on the counter and sighed. One last time at the market board, and then—

"Pretty girl," the drunk beside her said. "What's a pretty girl like you doing here, all alone?"

Sienne rolled her eyes. "Leaving," she said. She stood and strode to the door, adjusting her pack and shifting the spellbook.

Outside, the bright sun of true summer blazed in a cloudless sky, only visible as a sliver from where she stood at the bottom of the brick canyon. Women carrying bundles over their shoulders walked past in both directions, some of them hauling huge jugs of water drawn from the communal well. Sienne headed that way. The market lay past the well, and at the center of the market lay the board where people posted scrapper jobs they wanted filled. They were the lowest of the low, grunt work or jobs too dangerous for any sane person to take on, and Sienne had disdained them when she first came to town. As the weeks passed, she discovered she wasn't as picky as she'd believed. This time, she'd take whatever was offered, anything but—

A hand grabbed her by the back of her collar, yanking her sideways into a tiny alley that stank of turds and piss. "Think you can ruin our game?" a deep, harsh voice said.

The bold player shoved her up against the wall, making her pack dig into her spine. Sienne opened her mouth to scream and felt the prick of a knife blade between her ribs. "Scream, and I knife you," the rabbit-faced woman said. "Where's your spellbook?"

Sienne felt the book shift under her shirt and said nothing. The man transferred his grip from the back of her collar to the front of her shirt and tugged it aside, revealing the pouch she wore there. "Back country girl, thinks her money's safe between her breasts," he said, yanking on the cord around her neck and making it cut into her skin before it broke. "Call this a painful lesson, country girl." He opened the pouch and shook its contents. "Hah. Nothing but a couple of centi."

"I want her book," the woman whined. "That ought to make up the difference."

The man spun Sienne around and pulled the pack off her back. She lashed out with her foot and caught him hard on the knee, making him curse and stumble. She wrenched free of his grip and tried to run, but found the woman and her knife in the way. "Mistake," the woman said, thrusting at Sienne's midsection.

The knife struck the concealed spellbook with a sharp crack. The woman's eyes widened, and she smiled, her prominent front teeth gleaming. The man wrenched Sienne's hands behind her back, painfully tight. The woman lowered the knife and approached, hand outstretched to take the hem of Sienne's shirt.

"Now, is this the way Fiorettans welcome strangers?" said a new voice from the alley's mouth. It was a woman, backlit by the scant light hitting the street, and she held a slim blade as if she knew how to use it. The rabbit-faced woman half-turned to look at the newcomer, the hands gripping Sienne's shoulders loosened, and Sienne took advantage of their distraction to twist away from her captor and snatch up her pack from where it had fallen.

"This is none of your business, woman," the man growled.

"Oh, I think I want it to be my business." The woman advanced, flicking the tip of her blade toward the rabbit-faced woman. "Back away. Slowly."

"You can't take both of us at once."

"You want to bet on that? I think this woman just proved how bad your luck is. Besides—" The woman gestured with the sword. "I can certainly take *one* of you, and I don't much care which one it is. So you might want to think about the odds of it being you."

The man swore and took a step backward, raising his hands. Sienne darted forward, past the rabbit-faced woman, past her rescuer, and turned, clutching the spellbook to her stomach. The woman raised her sword in mocking salute and said, "Good day to you both." She lowered her sword and walked away, out of the alley and down the street.

After a couple of quick steps, she turned back to face Sienne and cocked her head inquiringly. "Well?"

Stunned, Sienne hoisted her pack and hurried after her rescuer. They walked rapidly down the street, surrounded by bundle-toting women and hurrying men, taking turns at what to Sienne was random. Finally, when Sienne couldn't bear it any longer, she said, "Why did you do that?"

"I don't like bullies," the woman said, not pausing. "You're an idiot, but you don't deserve to be robbed just because of that."

Sienne took a closer look at her. It was the woman who'd been leaning against the wall in the Lucky Coin. "So I shouldn't have called them on their cheating?"

"You shouldn't have done it so publicly. But it doesn't matter. Here, come in and I'll buy you a drink."

"Thanks, but—" Sienne's heart sank as she reached up to clutch a coin pouch that wasn't there anymore. That was it. The end. No money, no prospects, and after this morning, nowhere to sleep. "All right," she said. She might as well have a drink, if she was facing the end.

The tavern the woman had led her to was near the port and as unlike the Lucky Coin as a tavern could be. The low-ceilinged taproom was ringed with expensive glass windows letting in the clear morning light. Brightly varnished pine tables stained a dark red invited a customer to draw up a chair and settle in for a companionable drink. It smelled of the ghosts of a hundred thousand kegs, an oddly comforting smell that soaked into Sienne's bones and made her think of fireplaces on a chilly night, so far from this sun-drenched coastal city.

They had the place to themselves. The woman rapped sharply on the bar. "Two pints, Giorgo," she called out, then pulled a chair away from a table near the center of the room and gestured to Sienne to join her. "I'm not trying to get you drunk," she said.

"I doubt a couple of pints of new beer is enough for that," Sienne said.

The woman shrugged. "Everyone's got their limit. I'm Dianthe."

"Sienne," Sienne said. She'd learned early on that no one was offended if she didn't offer her surname, which she absolutely was not going to do. No money, no prospects, but she wasn't that desperate.

A round little man, presumably Giorgo, bustled out to the bar and drew off a couple of pints, then brought them to their table. Dianthe took a healthy swig and set her mug down. "Good stuff," she told the man.

"It always is," Giorgo said, bustling away.

Sienne took a rather smaller drink. It was good, smooth and light. "Thank you for rescuing me."

"I had selfish reasons," Dianthe said, leaning back. "You're a wizard?"

Sienne nodded.

"Were you serious when you told May you could grow her twenty inches in height?"

"Who?"

"The barkeep at the Lucky Coin. You said you could give her twenty inches."

"Oh. Yes, that's true."

"Can you do it the other way? Shrink someone?"

"Yes, it's—yes." This woman wasn't interested in the details of the spell.

"Damn." Dianthe took another drink. "And you're a scrapper?"

Sienne felt she owed Dianthe the truth. "Trying to be. Nobody's hiring."

"That's not true," Dianthe said. "I am."

2

"You...want to hire me?" Sienne said. Her heart sped up, and she had to make herself breathe slowly.

"As it happens, I need someone who can make people smaller. It's a fairly quick job, assuming we have that spell. Three days into the wilderness, to a well-charted ruin, in and out and Jack-a-dandy. You get fifty lari and an equal cut of any salvage, not that I expect there to be much. You interested?"

"I—" Her instinct to leap up and beg Dianthe to hire her warred with common sense that said she ought to play at least a little hard to get. "Why me? It's not an uncommon spell."

Dianthe smiled. "Surprisingly, all the wizards I've found who know that spell aren't interested in traveling into the wilderness to raid a ruin from the before times. And...let's just say not a lot of scrapper wizards are interested in working with me and my partner, even for the promise of learning a new spell for free."

"Why not? Is there something wrong with you?"

Sienne regretted her words immediately, but Dianthe only smiled wider. "My partner doesn't like wizards. We generally don't work with them. This is a special case."

"Oh." It still sounded too good to be true. "Is it dangerous?"

"Anything worth doing is." Dianthe shrugged. "It's known territory, and the ruin has been explored thoroughly. So it's not like we'd be facing wereboars or carricks or anything like that."

"If it's been explored, what's the point of going in?"

"Our client is convinced there's unrecovered salvage there. In our initial attempt, we discovered a concealed section of the keep. We're pretty sure no one's been in it since it collapsed four hundred years ago. There's always a chance we're wrong, but my partner is willing to take the risk."

"So do I still get paid if there's nothing there?" She hoped she didn't sound too eager, but the absence of her coin purse burned against her chest.

"The fifty lari is yours no matter what we do or don't find. So, you in?"

Sienne didn't have to think about it again. "I'm in."

"Great." Dianthe swilled down the last of her beer and stood, slapping some coins down on the table. "This time of year, we sleep outdoors, but you can share a tent with me. You have supplies?"

Sienne didn't answer quickly enough, and Dianthe smiled again, amusement lighting her brown eyes. "You really are new to this, aren't you?"

Sienne's chin went up. "I'll learn."

"Even so, you'll go to the market with me. Lots of people try to cheat the babes in arms—the new scrappers—and you don't need to be burdened with the crap they'll want to foist on you."

The missing coin purse burned hotter. "I don't—I can't," she began, her face hot with embarrassment.

Dianthe eyed her. "The money is paid up front," she said, "if that's what's worrying you."

Sienne eyed her right back. She might be rubbish at crack-stones, but she knew when someone was telling a whopper. *And how were you going to pay for your gear otherwise?* she chided herself. "Oh," she said. "All right."

Dianthe reached into a pouch hanging from her belt and drew out five gold coins. "Here," she said, handing them to Sienne. "I'll show you where to shop, then I'll take you to meet my partner. I should warn you, he's rather...abrupt...in his manner."

"That's all right." She wasn't sure that was true. If this mysterious partner didn't like wizards, it was unlikely he'd be very friendly. Sienne didn't have any romantic illusions about scrapper teams being like family, but she was sure the successful ones weren't at each other's throats. And if Dianthe was willing to pay her out of her own pocket, that suggested a level of desperation not evident in her speech. So what wasn't Dianthe telling her?

Sienne stood. It didn't really matter. Even with having to buy supplies, the payment for this job would keep her going for a while longer, and if she did well, that was the beginning of building a reputation that would get her more jobs, and ultimately, independence.

They left the tavern and walked side by side down the broad streets leading from the port to the market. It was going to be another hot day, tempered only by the constant cooling wind that blew in off the harbor. Sienne drew in a deep breath of salty air and felt a knot of tension loosen at the base of her spine. Which avatar, she wondered, was responsible for her last-minute reprieve? She wasn't a very religious person, paying her devotions to each on their name-days, but otherwise not troubling them with requests. Her mother, a devout worshipper of Kitane, would say God never considered Her petitioners a trouble. Sienne scowled. Her mother had lost the right to meddle in Sienne's life, even in memory.

The din grew louder as the streets narrowed, until Sienne and Dianthe were walking between the semi-permanent booths and stalls that made up Fioretti's world-famous market. Here, everything was for sale, from ordinary household items to luxury goods and everything in between, even humans, if indentured servitude counted as sales. Sienne hadn't paid much attention to the things people sold before, because she'd had her sights set on the jobs board at the market's center. Now she slowed to match Dianthe's leisurely pace and openly gawked at the kind of things people were willing to buy. The noise of hundreds of merchants hawking their wares and hundreds of buyers arguing price with them ebbed and rose like the distant tide, soothing to her soul.

Dianthe slowed to look at a stall whose tables held bits of tarnished metal studded with dull, sometimes cracked cabochon stones, jasper and onyx and a couple of garnets. "What do you think?"

Sienne scanned the table. Artifacts from the before time, none of them complete enough to hint at what they might have been for. "Nothing," she said. "Trinkets."

"I beg your pardon?" the stall owner said. He'd been hovering nearby in the attitude of someone who knew how to strike a careful balance between selling too hard and letting a sale slip away. "My wares are of the highest quality, miss."

"Without any trace of magic left," Sienne said.

The man drew himself up to his full outraged height. "I have never claimed otherwise!"

"Thanks anyway," Dianthe said, taking Sienne's arm and pulling her away. Sienne caught the amused look in her eyes. That had been a test, hadn't it? Dianthe knew perfectly well there was nothing magical about those things and wanted to see if Sienne would claim otherwise to make herself look more skilled. Well, there wasn't any skill in lying when the other person knew the truth. And it wouldn't have occurred to Sienne, anyway. She wondered how many wizards would have fallen for it.

They turned down one of the narrow paths that passed for streets in the market, and Sienne smelled warm leather and metal heated by the sun, climbing toward its apex. All the booths in the market were arranged according to what they sold. And this, apparently, was where scrappers went to be outfitted. Booths selling outdoor gear, tents and bedrolls and blankets. Booths selling pots and pans and all manner of cooking supplies. Booths selling fishing equipment, traps, and snares. One place that sold nothing but rope and rope-related items. Booths selling things Sienne had never seen before and couldn't imagine a use for.

She stopped to admire a knife vendor's wares and was hustled along by Dianthe. "Not there," she said. "If you're interested in weapons, there's a shop my partner and I use. She'll give you a good deal."

"I can use a knife," Sienne said, trying not to sound defensive. Dianthe's expression had suggested she didn't think a wizard was any good with weapons. Which wasn't true, in general. Sienne had had plenty of classmates who excelled at swordplay. It was just coincidence she wasn't one of them.

"You won't need a tent, as I said," Dianthe went on, "and we've already got cookware. Bedding, definitely, a mess kit, and a compass, just in case—"

"There's magic for that," Sienne said.

Dianthe raised her eyebrows. "Really? You'll have to demonstrate. I'm afraid I don't know much about a wizard's capabilities." She stopped at a stall displaying bundles of canvas and cloth. "Don't overburden yourself. We've got a pack animal, but anything beyond the basics, you have to carry yourself. Though I suppose if you can shrink things, that would help."

"Not things, just people. They're different spells. I don't know the other."

"Too bad." Dianthe picked over the rolled-up bedding tied with hemp rope and handed one to Sienne. "Take an extra blanket, too."

"It's true summer. Won't it be too hot?"

"You never can tell. Besides, you can use it as a pillow if you want."

Sienne chose a woolen blanket that didn't feel too heavy, woven in a pattern of dull greens she thought wouldn't stand out in the wilderness. She could have chosen the bright red one that appealed more to her, disguising it however she liked with one of the many confusion spells she knew, but that felt like showing off. Dianthe didn't comment on her choice, so it was probably a good one.

"You probably want one of these," was all the woman said,

handing Sienne a leather belt pouch. "Seeing as the last one was stolen. Sorry about that, by the way."

"It doesn't matter," Sienne said. The new pouch was larger and had an abstract design impressed on it. She self-consciously hung it around her neck and tucked her money into it. Back country girl— she could almost laugh at the irony of that.

Her arms full, she followed Dianthe to a larger booth hung with shirts and trousers. "I already have clothes," she said.

Dianthe looked her over. "Are they all as fancy as what you're wearing now?"

Sienne flushed in embarrassment. "These aren't that fancy," she said, though she was conscious as she hadn't been before of the fine linen of her shirt, the soft woven cotton of her trousers.

"You need new clothes," Dianthe said firmly, and proceeded to choose plain shirts of ivory cotton, suede leather sleeveless tunics that laced up the sides, and twilled cotton trousers considerably heavier in weight than what Sienne was currently wearing. "You know how to sew? You'll probably want to alter these to fit closely."

"I will," Sienne said, not saying that most of what she'd been taught was embroidery. Sewing a seam couldn't be that hard, could it?

Dianthe cast a glance at Sienne's feet. "Boots," she said. "Let's hope we can find some ready-made that fit. We don't have time to wait around for a bespoke pair."

They left the market after stowing Sienne's new clothing in her pack. It hadn't cost as much as she'd feared—not even a full ten lari. Sienne's relief lasted only as long as it took to enter the bootmaker's shop, where a wizened old woman took one look at the pair of them and said, "Dianthe. For you, or for the babe?"

"The babe," Dianthe said. "You'll give us a good deal, right?"

The woman sniffed disdainfully. "That ox of a partner of yours still hasn't paid me for his last pair."

"I'm sure Alaric is good for it."

The woman folded her arms across her narrow chest and tapped her toe impatiently.

"You're going to refuse this woman service because of something someone else did?" Dianthe exclaimed.

"It's what he didn't do I'm miffed about."

Dianthe rolled her eyes. "How much?" she asked, rummaging in her pouch.

"Eighteen lari."

Sienne choked and turned it into a cough when the woman turned her impatient gaze on her. She'd never spent that much on shoes in her life! Maybe if she were her sister—she scowled and shut that line of thought down. Rance, Felice, her mother...there were a lot of people she'd sworn never to think of again.

Dianthe pulled out a handful of coins. "Here. Now, what can you do for my friend?"

The old woman looked at Sienne's feet with an expression that made Sienne want to hide them. "You don't want bespoke?"

"We're leaving in the morning. No time."

"Well, lucky for her she's got nice small feet. Not like some oxen I could mention." The woman turned away and disappeared into the shop's back room. Sienne took the opportunity to look around. For all the shop was small and dark, it displayed remarkably few wares, just like the high-end, brightly lit shoemakers Sienne was familiar with—models hinting at what was possible rather than ready to wear. But that was a lifetime away, and Sienne busied herself turning a red leather boot over in her hands, warding off memories.

"Those aren't at all suitable for the wilderness," Dianthe said.

"I know. I was just looking. Her craft is good."

"It's why we're willing to pay eighteen lari for her wares. That, and Alaric has sodding enormous feet. Yours won't cost nearly so much, if you were worried."

"Not really," Sienne lied.

The old woman returned with a pair of knee-high boots in her hands. "This should do," she said, extending them to Sienne. "Try them on."

Sienne did. They were a lovely dark brown leather, supple with the slightly greasy feel of good waterproofing, and they fit her almost perfectly. Too bad she didn't know the *fit* spell for objects, or she could have perfected them, but slightly too loose was better than slightly too small. "Very nice," she said.

The old woman sniffed disdainfully again. "Don't insult me. You want them? Eight lari."

Dianthe laughed. "She may be a babe, but I'm not. Five and five."

"You think I can survive by giving my wares away? Seven, and that's because I like you."

"You've got a funny way of showing it. Six, then."

"What, you can't let your friend do the talking for herself?" The old woman turned on Sienne. "Seven's reasonable."

Sienne pursed her lips. "Six and two," she said. "That's the best you'll get."

"Oh? You're so sure?"

Sienne raised her foot and ran a finger across the top of the toe. "These have been sitting in your store room for a long time, to get this dusty," she said. "I'll wager you haven't been able to find anyone they'll fit, since I have, as you said, nice small feet. So you can either let them go on taking up space, or you can make a nice little profit. Six and two."

The woman's wrinkled face split in a smile. "And here was me thinking you were just a pretty face. All right. Six and two. And come back when you're ready for a pair made for you."

Sienne handed over the coins and received her change. On the street again, Dianthe said, "That will teach me to underestimate you, just because you're new to this."

"I like haggling. It keeps me sharp." She couldn't tell Dianthe she'd grown up never needing to ask the prices of the things she bought. "Where next?"

"Knife, right?" Dianthe gestured. "It's a bit of a walk. You want to stop at your rooms and drop some of this off?"

"I, uh, I'm not staying anywhere at the moment," Sienne said, desperately clinging to what was left of her dignity.

"Really?" Dianthe gave her a sharp look. "That's probably just as well. There are rooms at the hostel where we're staying—makes it easier to gather in the morning. This way."

They crossed Fioretti by the broad streets paved in pale yellow stone that gleamed like gold in the sunlight, reminding Sienne why they called it the City of Golden Ways. Nobody looked twice at them, though Sienne was laden like a common worker and most of the people surrounding them rode horses or shining lacquered carriages. Their clothes were fine silks and linens, lightweight and perfect for true summer, and their voices and trilling laughter trailed them as they passed. Sienne watched them and felt not a trace of envy.

The road they were on terminated at one of the vast bridges spanning the Vochus River. Its white stone looked as if it had been scrubbed clean by an efficient housewife, though Sienne was sure it was magic that had done the cleaning. She looked upriver toward the royal palace, spread out on the isle that split the river in two. Arches and spires like a stonemason's dream gave the palace a classical appearance, though it had been built only a hundred years ago. By day, it looked unreal, faded and misty as if it were only half there; by night, lit by ten thousand white and ruby lamps, it seemed the only real thing in the world. Sienne had never been inside and had never wanted to, but it was hard not to be awed by its beauty.

She realized Dianthe had gotten ahead of her and hurried to catch up. Dianthe seemed oblivious to the architectural beauties of the city. "Are you from Fioretti?" Sienne asked when she was once again beside her guide.

Dianthe didn't look at her. "No," she said with such finality Sienne swallowed her next question. *Don't pry if you don't want prying in return,* she reminded herself.

The broad streets gave way to narrower ones until Sienne once again felt herself to be at the bottom of a tall canyon, though unlike the street outside the Lucky Coin, these walls were plastered white and felt much brighter. Signs hung above the doors displaying pictures that indicated what might be bought or sold inside, suggesting to Sienne that the typical clientele might not be literate. The street was also quiet, with few people passing by. It was so quiet

Sienne was afraid to talk, afraid of disturbing the unnatural calm that might well be due to someone's funeral.

Dianthe pushed open a door above which dangled a wooden dagger. "Not a smithy?" Sienne asked in a low voice.

"Smithy is for repairs, in Fioretti," Dianthe said. "Not sure what it's like where you're from, but unless you want something made particular, this is where you come for weapons."

"How do you know I'm not from Fioretti?" Sienne said.

Dianthe gave her a knowing look and a smile, but said nothing. "Zen?" she said as she opened the door. "It's not too early, is it?"

Sienne followed her into the shop, which was, counter to her expectations, brightly lit—lamps, not magic, she noted. Light glinted off the metal which hung on every wall, more swords and knives than she'd ever seen in one place except her father's armory. Polearms leaned together like a deadly sheaf of wheat stalks in one corner; weapons she didn't recognize lay displayed under glass. It was awe-inspiring even to her, whose martial career had begun and ended when she'd nearly taken her instructor's ear off with a wild swing.

"Zenobia?" Dianthe said. She let the door close behind them. "Go ahead and look around. I'll see where Zen is. Might still be abed."

"But the door wasn't locked. Isn't that inviting thieves?"

"Zenobia pays a priest of Kitane a pretty sum to keep this place better protected than the palace." Dianthe smiled, a reflective expression that made Sienne wonder whether she had firsthand knowledge of this fact. It occurred to her to wonder what Dianthe's skills were. She carried a sword, but she moved like someone used to passing unnoticed in a crowd.

Dianthe disappeared through a door, beyond which Sienne could see stairs going up. She turned away and went to the nearest display cabinet. Rows of knives lay spread out on purple velvet, light gleaming along their sharpened edges. One in particular caught her eye. It was plain, with a three-inch blade sharpened on both edges to a nice point. The hilt was wrapped in leather the same color as her new boots, and it had just enough of a guard to make the grip look solid.

Sienne examined the cabinet's glass lid. There didn't seem to be a way to open it, but she really wanted to try its heft. Well, she could test its weight another way.

She reached out with her invisible fingers and let the magic wrap itself around the knife, lifted—and an ear-shattering blast of sound so loud it was almost tangible cracked the air.

3

S ienne dropped the knife and covered her ears. The sound blasted out again, shrill like a horn, and she stumbled backwards, squeezing her eyes closed as if that would block the sound.

"*Thief!*" came a cry that cut over the sound of the horn. "Drop it, now!"

"I didn't take anything!" Sienne cried out. "I'm sorry!"

The sound cut off mid-blare. "You're damned stupid to try magic in this place," someone said. Sienne opened her eyes. Dianthe had returned behind a fat woman with red hair and a complexion to match it. She wore a dressing gown of figured Chysegaran silk, and the nails of her bare feet were lacquered gold. "What did you do?"

Sienne lowered her hands. "I—wanted a closer look at a knife. I didn't think...I'm sorry, I should have realized. You're right, that was stupid."

The woman pursed her lips in thought. "New in town?"

She clearly thought Sienne was a back country hick, too. Sienne didn't care. "Yes."

"I hired her for a job," Dianthe said.

The woman's eyebrows went nearly to her hairline. "Alaric agreed to that?"

"He didn't have much choice."`

The woman turned her attention back to Sienne. "You poor thing," she said. "I'm Zenobia. Which knife did you want to see?"

Sienne pointed, though it was obvious which knife she'd picked up because it had fallen across two of the others. Zenobia reached beneath the case for a hidden latch, and the lid popped open. She removed the knife and handed it to Sienne, hilt first. "Good choice," she said. "Nice utilitarian blade, full tang, though it's really not meant to be a weapon. Still, it will do some damage if you need it to."

Sienne gripped the hilt loosely. It was beautiful, and though she was no fighter, it spoke to her. "How much?"

Zenobia peered at her, and Sienne realized the woman was very near-sighted. "For you, ten lari," Zenobia said.

"I'm sure you can do better than that," Dianthe protested.

"That's my best price. I'm knocking five lari off because she's a friend of yours."

"It's fine," Sienne said, "but...what about trade?"

Zenobia frowned. "I doubt you have anything I want."

"I don't know. How much is your eyesight worth?"

"My...eyesight?"

Sienne untucked her shirt and pulled out her spellbook. At about nine inches high and a little more than half that in width, it was an average-sized book, if odd-looking for being bound in wood that, being indestructible, flexed like fine leather. The binding was stained a rich russet color, unadorned save for a linked pair of initials burned into the cover: S V.

"I have a spell that improves sight or hearing," she said, holding the book in both hands as if poised to open it. "It's not very common here in Fioretti—I've found most people go to a priest for healing if their eyesight is poor. But it's more effective, though it doesn't last forever, I'm afraid."

Zenobia stared at the book the way someone might a burning brand too near the bed. "How long?" she said.

"A year, maybe? It fades rather than simply reverting, so you'll have plenty of warning. What is that worth to you?"

Zenobia pursed her lips. "Do it," she said, "and I'll tell you how much it's worth."

"That's not very fair," Dianthe said.

"You know I'm honest," Zenobia said. "I wouldn't cheat anyone. But I won't know what it's worth until I see—if you'll allow me a little humor."

"All right," Sienne said. She focused her will on the book and let her knowledge of the spell press inward with her fingertips on the edge of the pages. The book sprang open where she wanted it. That little piece of magic was something she was better at, faster at, than anyone else—something she hoped might be an edge as a scrapper, fighting wild animals or worse.

She'd been trained to name spells in Ginatic, the language spoken before the wars and the plagues that followed, but among the scrappers, that had earned her a reputation for being uppity. So she'd learned to say, for example, *sharpen* instead of *na'astreta*. *Sharpen* was a spell she wasn't supposed to have learned; a woman of her social position should have focused on confusion spells, not transforms. But she loved the honey-sweet taste of a transformation, loved the challenge of speaking the words at just the right speed and the feel of the many vowels rolling perfectly off her tongue.

She held the book in both hands, just below the level of her chin, and read off the spell. The syllables tugged at her mind, the first slipping away from memory before she got halfway through. The human mind wasn't made to encompass magic, which was why Sienne's spellbook was her most precious possession; no one could memorize a spell any more than they could lift themselves by their bootlaces.

As she reached the end, she focused her attention on Zenobia, shaping the words to encompass the woman. A glassy blue sheen passed over Zenobia's eyes, and she gasped, then blinked several times. She looked wildly around the room, looked back at Sienne, and said, "By Kitane's right arm. You were right."

"Are you satisfied?" Sienne said.

"I didn't know how blind I was," Zenobia said. She blinked again as if clearing water from her eyes. "The knife's yours. No, wait." She reached below the cabinet and brought out a slim silver boot knife, no more than four inches long from tip to hilt, and extended it to Sienne. "Now we're even."

"Are you sure?" Sienne hesitated.

"I know the worth of my wares. And I know the value of yours. Take it. You never know when you might need that edge."

Sienne took it and tucked it into her boot. "Thanks."

Back on the street, Sienne said, "What?"

"Nothing," Dianthe said.

"You weren't looking at me like it was nothing."

"All right. I just haven't been that close to wizardry in...well, ever."

"Does it make you uncomfortable?" *Sienne* felt uncomfortable, like a fly caught in honey watching the swatter descend.

"No. It's astonishing." Dianthe fell silent for a few steps. "I should warn you," she said finally, "Alaric can be...he *really* doesn't like wizards."

"Yes. You said."

Dianthe shook her head. "Just...it's nothing personal, understand? He has his reasons. But you shouldn't look to wizardry as a way to win him over. And *never* cast a spell on him unless he asks for it."

"I wouldn't. It's impolite."

"Good." Dianthe strode a little faster. "Let's get you a room, and then it should be time for a meal. Haggling always makes me hungry."

The inn where Dianthe and her partner were staying was halfway across the city from Zenobia's shop, in a shabby-genteel part of town that was mostly homes rather than shops. In fact, Sienne realized, it wasn't an inn, it was a large house whose owner rented out rooms, something she discovered when Dianthe led her around to a side door rather than entering by the front. It was built of the small brown bricks typical of Fiorettan construction and was at the end of a row of similar houses, all three stories tall with steeply slanting roofs of pale gray slate. Blue curtains waved at its many small, square windows like handkerchiefs fluttering in greeting.

The hall beyond the side door was short, leading to steep narrow stairs on one side and a kitchen on the other. It smelled deliciously of roast pork and honey. A man, tall and gangly, poked his head out of the kitchen. He held a wooden spoon that dripped brown juice slowly onto the flagstone floor. "Master Tersus isn't in," he said, in a voice accented with the broad vowels of a Wrathen.

"She needs a room now," Dianthe said, jerking a thumb in Sienne's direction. "Will he mind?"

The man shrugged. "Not if she can pay." He ducked back into the kitchen.

"I guess you're in," Dianthe said. "Mind the stairs, some of the treads are loose."

They went up two flights to the third floor, where the narrow stairs let out on an equally narrow hall lined with white-painted wooden doors. "Used to be servants' quarters," Dianthe said. She pushed open the second door on the right. "There are six rooms up here and just Alaric and me, so you can take your pick if you don't like this one."

"It's fine," Sienne said hastily. The room was small but clean, with whitewashed walls and a varnished pine floor. An iron frame bed, bare of sheet or blanket, stood beneath the open window where the blue curtains fluttered in the brisk sea breeze. There was a chest of drawers opposite the bed, of the same pine as the floorboards, and that was all the furniture there was.

"Sorry it's so bare," Dianthe said. "We never stay long, so we don't care."

"It's nicer than the last place I stayed," Sienne said. The last place had had rats. She dumped her pile of gear on the bed, grateful now for the extra blanket, since it was clear she was expected to provide her own bedding.

"Dianthe?" A man's voice, deep and commanding, came from somewhere down the hall.

"In here," Dianthe said. "Let me introduce—"

Quick steps sounded outside the room, and then the biggest man Sienne had ever seen in her life came through the doorway. He was at least six and a half feet tall, certainly tall enough that he had to duck his head as he entered. His arms were corded with muscle, his broad shoulders filled the doorway, and he had thighs like small tree trunks. His blond hair, bleached by the sun to near whiteness, was cut shorter than was fashionable. A blue-eyed gaze swept the room and came uncomfortably to rest on Sienne. She swallowed and hoped her stunned amazement didn't look like fear. He gave her the beginnings of an idea of why they might need the *fit* spell.

"Who's this?" the man said. He had a slight Sorjic accent, though the hair and eyes were enough of a hint that he was Ansorjan. His voice had a pleasant rumble to it, but his expression was, if not unfriendly, certainly not cordial.

"Our wizard," Dianthe said. "This is Sienne."

"*Our* wizard?" the man, who had to be Alaric, said. "Sorry to waste your time. We don't need you, after all."

Sienne's heart lurched. The new boots, the knife hanging at her hip, even the pile of gear on the bed seemed to turn a blazing, pulsing red. She couldn't return the fifty lari and she'd never be able to pay all that gear back. She might as well fling herself off one of the bridges and let the river take her. It was a cleaner death than the slow torture of indentured servitude, and far, far better than what she'd left behind.

Dianthe's lips compressed tightly. "Oh? You've come up with a better solution?"

Alaric didn't look at her. "We'll hire out the labor. Plenty of children—"

"*Child labor?* Are you out of your damn mind?"

"Teens, then. It won't cost—"

"Sienne, would you excuse us?" Dianthe said, her voice dangerously placid. She took Alaric's elbow and steered him into the hall, shutting the door behind her. Sienne whipped her spellbook out and opened it. She knew eavesdropping was wrong, but that had never stopped her before. And she had a feeling this was a conversation she needed to hear.

As quickly as she dared, she spoke the rolling syllables of *sharpen*, giving it the flick at the end that limited the duration to five minutes.

The noise of the breeze grew rapidly until the flapping of the curtains sounded like the crack of a whip. She pressed her ear against the door and covered the other with her hand.

"—been through this," Dianthe said, as clearly as if she were in the room with Sienne. "The shrinking spell, or whatever she calls it, is the only way we're getting into that keep."

"We don't need a damn wizard," Alaric said. He was clearly trying to keep his voice down, but to her heightened hearing, it rumbled like an oncoming storm. "And that one—you're one to talk about child labor! Has she ever been outside Fioretti in her life?"

"She's no younger than we are, you fool. Don't let the big eyes fool you. And I've seen her do wizardry. She's competent. *And* she's the only one I could find who has the right spell and is willing to make the trip."

"This is a mistake."

"You want to go back to Master Fontanna and tell him we failed? We can't afford to return the money."

"We shouldn't have taken the job in the first place."

"We can't afford to be picky. You know that. I trust your instincts, yes, but unless you've learned something I'm not privy to, this is still the best opportunity we've had in weeks. And that means hiring a wizard."

Alaric let out a sigh that to Sienne sounded like a gale. "Fine. But I'm not interested in making friends. Make sure she understands that."

"It's not the same, Alaric. You can't possibly think—"

"You don't know what I'm thinking."

"I have a good idea. She's a nice person, and she doesn't deserve to be damned for the sins of another."

"As if it were that simple."

"I know it isn't. Just...give her a chance."

Another gale tickled Sienne's ears. "Let's just get this over with."

Sienne backed away from the door and busied herself rearranging her pack, so when the door opened, she could look up with a credible expression of innocence.

"Sorry about that," Dianthe said. Alaric had disappeared. Sienne tried not to wince at how Dianthe's voice echoed painfully in her ears. That spell couldn't wear off soon enough. "Everything's fine. I told you he didn't like wizards, but he'll get used to you."

"I understand." Her own voice thrummed through her head like harp strings tuned to near breaking. "Do we eat here?"

"They feed us in the kitchen. Part of the arrangement." Dianthe kicked the door idly, making a dull booming sound. "Go ahead and finish putting away your things, then come downstairs. You can store anything you don't want to take into the wilderness here—it's part of the fee. Of course, the deal is, if we don't come back, Master Tersus will sell whatever we leave behind, but it's not like we'll care, right?"

Dianthe flashed a smile and headed toward the stairs. Sienne waited, teeth clenched, for the booms of her feet to fade, then swiftly changed into her new clothes and folded her old ones into the chest of drawers. Best she begin as she meant to go on.

The kitchen was modern and open, with a large iron range filling one side of the brightly-lit room. The table, on the other hand, was as battered as if it had seen generations of diners. Alaric and Dianthe sat at one end, eating pieces of roast chicken with their hands. Sienne sat next to Dianthe and picked up a drumstick, tearing into it awkwardly. Five weeks in the big city as a nobody hadn't been enough to cure her of the manners she'd learned back in her home dukedom of Beneddo, but she didn't think she stood out quite as much as she once had.

She cast covert glances at the big man sitting at the head of the table. Alaric showed no sign that he knew she was in the room. He ate steadily, with a tidy economy that made him look impatient with his food. So, some wizard had done ill by him? At least, that was the impression her eavesdropping had given her. Well, she'd just have to prove wizards weren't all bad. She wasn't sure why she cared about winning him over, except that it struck her as a challenge, and she liked challenges. Besides, she needed him to spread the word of her good reputation, if she wanted to turn this job into the start of a career.

"Did you find anyone else?" Dianthe said between bites.

"Kalanath Oushikdali," Alaric said.

Dianthe whistled. "I thought he was with the Giordas."

"They had a difference of opinion. Specifically, Alethea made advances and Kalanath turned her down cold. You can imagine how popular that didn't make him."

"You think he'll work well with us?"

Alaric shrugged. "He's a professional, for all he's young. He'll do. It's just the one job, after all."

"What about a priest? Did Bernadetta—"

"*Not* Bernadetta," Alaric said with finality. "We're going to talk to someone else this afternoon."

"We?" Dianthe said, casting a glance at Sienne. Sienne sat up and tried to look helpful and competent, but with chicken grease running down her chin, she didn't think she was successful.

Alaric assessed her with his eyes. Sienne couldn't put her finger on what made them so unsettling. The color, maybe, so light a blue as to be almost gray. "All of us," he finally said, in a neutral tone that unnerved Sienne more than outright dismissal would have.

"Sienne, does that eyesight spell work to improve normal vision?" Dianthe said. It was so casual Sienne was certain she'd said it to point out to Alaric how useful Sienne's wizardry could be.

"It does," she said, "but there are limits to what the human eye or ear can be shaped to do. The further you push those limits, the shorter the duration. Most people want it for seeing in the dark. If I tried to do that in daylight, it would just blind you."

"Sounds like quite the weapon," Alaric rumbled.

"It isn't—" Sienne stopped mid-sentence. "I guess it could be. I'd never thought of it that way."

"You ought to know by now what wizardry is capable of." Alaric washed down his chicken with a huge swig of whatever was in his cup. His tone of voice was dark, like someone predicting a great evil.

"Good things, as far as I'm concerned," Sienne said.

"That attitude won't take you far as a scrapper." Alaric set his cup down and turned his gaze on Sienne again. "You need clever thinking and a willingness to look at things sideways."

"You don't know anything about me," Sienne said, stung into a sharp retort. "I may be new to this, but I'm good at what I do."

"Alaric," Dianthe said, her voice a warning.

Alaric shrugged. "Maybe so. But it doesn't matter. We're bringing you along for the shrinking spell, nothing more. You can leave the fighting to us."

Sienne's face warmed with indignation, but she said nothing. This arrogant bastard thought so little of her, did he? But he wasn't wrong, either—she knew almost no offensive spells and had no practical experience in the field. Even so, his dismissive attitude rankled.

"Let's not quarrel before we've even left the city," Dianthe said. "Who are we meeting?"

"His name is Perrin Delucco, and he's new to the priesthood," Alaric said.

"New is bad, where we're going," Dianthe said.

Alaric scowled and was silent.

"You couldn't get anyone else, could you," Dianthe said. It was not a question. "Alaric—"

"It wasn't my fault. All the scrapper priests are either affiliated or...not interested in this job."

"Because there's no chance of salvage, you mean." Dianthe sighed. "All right, that's not your fault."

Sienne almost said *What, your winning personality didn't charm them?* but decided that was too rude for such a new acquaintance. Instead, she said, "Is salvage more important than a flat fee up front?"

"Up front?" Alaric said. "*All* up front?"

"Yes, *all up front,*" Dianthe said, glaring at him. "Most scrappers like the gamble of finding salvage that will make their fortunes. The place we're going, well, I told you it was thoroughly explored already. So not a lot of scrappers will see the appeal."

"But if there's a secret area—"

"You told her about the secret entrance?" Alaric demanded.

"I had to, to explain why we needed that spell," Dianthe said, unruffled by his outburst. "As you can see, we're not telling people about the secret entrance, for fear they'll go off and try to discover it themselves. So we can't offer it as an enticement."

"I understand." Sienne wiped her mouth and chin and looked around for a napkin. She wasn't about to wipe her greasy fingers on her new trousers. A pile of folded cloths near the sink looked perfect. Without thinking, she used her invisible fingers to lift the top one and whisk it across the room to her hand. She cleaned off her hands and gave her chin one final swipe. Then she saw her companions' expressions. Alaric looked like she'd just wiped her hands on his shirt. Dianthe's eyes were fractionally wider than they had been. Sienne dropped the cloth on her plate and willed herself not to blush. Magic was perfectly ordinary, and she wasn't going to pretend to be other than she was just because the big ox was afraid of it.

Dianthe cleared her throat. "Shall we go?"

4

Sienne trailed slightly behind Alaric and Dianthe as they set out for their mysterious rendezvous. It was like following in the wake of a battleship. Crowds parted for Alaric, who behaved as if he didn't notice. Maybe it was his size, maybe it was his white-blond hair, so different from the darker Rafellish, but whatever it was, he was always going to excite notice. What would it be like to draw the eye that way? Sienne knew she was pretty enough, but she'd never been the kind of beautiful that caught people's attention. She was average in height and build, her coloring was typical of the Rafellish, and she didn't dress outrageously. If she'd lived a different life, she might have been a sneak thief rather than a wizard. She might even have been happier.

They crossed the Vochus again, this time by a different bridge, and Alaric led them past the palace and through the high-class parts of the city into what might as well have been a different world. Sienne had never been to the slums of Fioretti, and she drew closer to Alaric, grateful now for his forbidding presence. Streets dark even at midafternoon wound crooked paths between buildings of crumbling brown brick, their upper stories jutting out over the streets not by design, but from age and neglect. Where the sunnier streets of Fioretti were thronged with passersby, men and women walking or riding purposefully from one place to another, these streets were stagnant with loiterers. Hard-eyed men watched them pass, calculation evident in their eyes as they looked at Alaric and assessed their chances at him. The constant murmur of the city took on a menacing tone that made Sienne wish she'd stayed behind.

"It's here somewhere," Alaric said. "Not a lot of sign markers in this place."

"Yes, because they don't want to give the city guard even passive assistance," Dianthe said. "What kind of man have you found us?"

"He's a priest of Averran," Alaric said curtly. "I imagine one bar is as good as any other as far as he's concerned."

"You want to take a drunk priest into the wilderness with us?" Dianthe exclaimed.

"The priests of Averran aren't drunks," Sienne said. "They say drink is a different path to wisdom, and drinking to excess is just another way of approaching God."

"What do *you* know about it?" Alaric said.

"I had—I know a little bit about religion." She wasn't going to tell them religious instruction had been part of her studies during her fosterage to Stravanus; that would certainly out her as noble.

"Well, it's true," Alaric said, and to her surprise Sienne heard grudging approval in his voice. "Perrin Delucco was perfectly lucid when I spoke to him earlier. It's why I agreed to meet him again—he said he wanted to meet the companions he'd be risking his life with."

"Sensible," Dianthe said. "Can we get this over with? Those men are looking at me like they're wondering what kind of price they could get for my dead body."

Alaric stopped and looked around. "That way," he said. He ducked down a side alley and pushed open a wooden door that was scorched from some long-ago fire. Sienne sniffed as she followed him, and could still smell smoke, acrid and cold. Maybe not so long ago.

The room beyond was dimly lit by lanterns, not magic lights, and to the acrid smell of old smoke was added the pungent aroma of cheese gone off and the stink of unwashed bodies. The tavern was packed full of men and women engaged in eating, silently and without paying attention to anyone else, not even the blond giant who'd appeared in the doorway. Morose drinkers occupied the bar stools, drinking as steadily as the diners were eating. It all made Sienne profoundly uncomfortable, like she'd interrupted a divine service. To Averran, naturally.

The woman behind the bar caught Alaric's eye. "What'll you have?"

"Beer," Alaric said. "For all of us." He pushed through the crowd to a table in the corner. Unlike the other tables, which were packed shoulder to unwashed shoulder, this one had only one occupant. The man was in his mid-thirties, or so Sienne guessed from what was visible of his face, curtained from the world by a fall of untidy brown hair. He sat sprawled in his chair with his back to the wall and saluted Alaric with his pint mug as the three of them approached. "Mountain of an Ansorjan," he said, "you have found me." His words slurred enough to tell Sienne he was fast on the way to serious inebriation.

"I have," Alaric said. "Can we sit?"

"Can you?" the man said, and took a long drink from his mug. "I presume you have the capability."

Irritated, Sienne was about to say something rude when Alaric interrupted her with, "Thanks." He pulled out a chair and sat across from the man. Dianthe and Sienne followed. Sienne wished she could put her back to the wall. Having the whole tavern behind her made her neck itch.

"This is Dianthe and..." Alaric looked at Sienne without a trace of embarrassment at having forgotten her name.

"Sienne," Sienne said.

The man gave them all a lazy wave of his hand. "Perrin," he said. "Delucco as was."

"What does that mean?" Dianthe said.

Perrin shrugged. "It means, fair lady," he said, "my family has taken steps to dissociate themselves from my embarrassing presence."

Dianthe glanced at Alaric. "Embarrassing, how?" she asked.

Perrin took another long drink and signaled the barmaid who was just then approaching their table with three pint mugs. The girl set the mugs on the table and took Perrin's empty one without comment. "They took exception to my conversion and priesthood," he said. "Gavant is an avatar any blue-blooded aristocrat might credibly worship. Averran is rather less so. But you aren't interested in my sad story."

"I—" Sienne began, but fell silent when Perrin's eye, sharp and not at all fogged with drink, fixed her in place. *No prying*, she reminded herself.

"This is most of us. See everything you want?" Alaric said.

"I asked to meet all of you."

"Kalanath Oushikdali will join us in the morning. No doubt you've heard of him."

"Ah." Perrin nodded. "All right. It's acceptable."

"So have you made a decision?"

Perrin accepted a fresh mug from the barmaid and drained half of it in one gulp. "I have. I will join your merry crew on this journey into the hinterlands. I ask only that we leave as soon as possible. I find the air of Fioretti uncongenial."

"Tomorrow morning," Alaric said.

"Then—let me see." Perrin sat up straighter, as straight as he was capable of; he still listed to one side. "You are clearly the muscle," he told Alaric, who to Sienne's surprise gave a tiny half-smile at this. "You...slim build, graceful walk, and so self-effacing you might as well be invisible," he said to Dianthe. "I take it you are a picker-up of unconsidered trifles belonging to other people?"

"I'm no thief," Dianthe said. "That doesn't mean I couldn't be if I wanted."

"Point taken," Perrin said. He turned his attention on Sienne. "And you are...what? Not a swordswoman, not with the way you walk. Not a priest, because then you would not have approached me. Hired help?"

"I'm a wizard," Sienne shot back, irritated.

Perrin's eyes widened. "Of course," he said. "My apologies."

"Meet us at the western foot of the Storm Wind Bridge at eight a.m. tomorrow," Alaric said. "If you're not there, we leave without you."

"I'll be there," Perrin said, saluting him with his pint.

Alaric took a drink from his mug, grimaced, and put it down. "How can you stand to drink that piss?"

Perrin tilted his mug and stared into it as if reading the future. "Averran taught that many roads may lead to a single destination, and sometimes the journey is irrelevant. But Averran was a crotchety old drunk, so I wonder how much of what he said was inspired by dyspepsia." He smiled. "And I happen to like the taste. A reminder of the good old days."

Alaric rose, followed by Dianthe and then belatedly by Sienne, who had been wondering if she could get away with not drinking the sour-smelling stuff. "See you in the morning," he said, tossing some coins onto the table. Perrin smiled again and leaned back, rocking on the hind legs of his chair like an acrobat preparing for a complex trick.

On the way back through town, Sienne said, "Why did we have to be there? We sat down, he said yes, and we left again."

"He told me he wouldn't agree to join us unless he saw the rest of us," Alaric said. "No doubt it was some mystical thing or other. Priests have divination magic; maybe he wanted to search our souls for compatibility."

"You don't really believe that," Dianthe said.

"No, I don't. But it makes as much sense as anything."

"I don't know," Sienne said. "Priests of Averran aren't supposed to get as drunk as that. Are you sure—"

"He's the only option available," Alaric said. "You, ah, Cinna?"

"It's Sienne," Sienne said irritably.

"You have everything you need? You know we'll be gone most of a week, what with traveling there and back again."

"I do," Sienne said, though as she did so she was assailed by doubts that she'd forgotten some key item Alaric would no doubt mock her for not having. "Don't worry about me."

Alaric hmphed. "No one's going to carry your load for you. Don't go looking for special treatment."

"Alaric," Dianthe said, "turn around."

He glanced down at her, startled. "What?"

"I need to pull the stick out of your ass."

Sienne laughed and swiftly covered her mouth. Alaric glowered at the two of them, but said nothing, just walked faster.

"*Holla! Ham-fist!*"

Alaric came to an abrupt stop in the middle of the street. Sienne took a few involuntary steps past him and half-turned to see what he'd stopped for. Dianthe had her hand on his arm. "Just keep walking," she said in a low, urgent voice.

"If it isn't Ham-fist and...who's the babe in arms?" A short, compact man came toward them, smiling in such a friendly way Sienne was confused at the discrepancy between his demeanor and the dismissive, obviously insulting words he flung at Alaric. *Holla.* It was a greeting, but it was also Sorjic for "fool."

The man was dressed much as they were, but over his scrapper's ensemble he wore a cloak far too heavy for the true summer weather, something a wizard in a child's story might wear. He came to a stop in front of Alaric, still smiling, unconcerned at forcing other pedestrians to step out of his way. "Hmm. Have you run through the list of scrappers in this city willing to work with you, that you're robbing the cradle now?"

"Back off, Conn," Dianthe said. Alaric said nothing, just closed his enormous hands into fists. Sienne could guess how he'd gotten the insulting nickname Conn had flung at him.

Two other scrappers, both taller than Conn, sauntered up. All three, two men and a woman, had narrow faces with elegant noses and complexions fairer than usual for Rafellish. A family of scrappers, perhaps? Sienne looked to Dianthe for a clue as to how to behave. Whatever bad blood existed between Alaric and the trio, Sienne didn't want to make it worse in her ignorance.

Conn looked at Sienne. "You're not with these two, are you? I didn't know they were making them so foolhardy these days."

"She's none of your concern, Giorda," Alaric said. "And I think I warned you what would happen if you tried to interfere with me or mine."

"Oh, yes, do take out that oversized toothpick of yours—but you're not wearing it, are you?" Conn sneered.

"I'd hardly waste it on the likes of you, when I've got two perfectly good fists, as I'm sure you know." Alaric took a step forward, and Conn took an involuntary step back, fear flitting across his face for the briefest moment before the sneer settled back into place.

"Throw a punch," the second man said. "I'm sure the city guard will understand. No, wait, they told you if you started one more fight, you'd be banned from the city for a week."

"I wouldn't start a fight," Alaric said, "but you can be damn sure I'd finish it. Now, get out of my way."

"I want to be introduced to the young lady," Conn said, stepping to one side. "Conn Giorda, wizard and famed raconteur. And you are...?"

Sienne cast a desperate glance at Dianthe, who widened her eyes trying to convey a message Sienne couldn't understand. "Sienne," she said. "Wizard."

"Really? And you're with Ham-fist?" Conn's smile mocked her. "You must be very new to the city. Let me give you some advice, one wizard to another." He stepped closer. Alaric put out a hand as if to ward him off, but stopped short of touching the man. Conn cast his mocking smile at Alaric, then nodded to Sienne. "He's poison. No one works with him for long. And if he's grown desperate enough to abandon his principles and work with a wizard, whatever plan he has cooking will probably get you killed."

"That's enough," Dianthe said. She grabbed Alaric's outstretched arm and put herself between the big man and Conn. "I didn't realize your ego had grown bigger than your head. Or am I wrong, and the Berschelli job paid off for you?"

Conn's smile disappeared. The woman said, "That's none of your business. At least we've never lost a companion."

"Let's ask Kalanath Oushikdali what he thinks about that, Alethea." Dianthe smiled. "Does it count as 'lost' if you disgust someone into leaving?"

The woman raised a fist and advanced on Dianthe, who stood her ground, grinning. Conn spun and grabbed her arm, pulling her away. "No, go ahead and pick a fight," Alaric said. "I'm sure the city guard will understand. No, wait, they told *you* if you started one more fight, you'd spend a week in lockup."

"This isn't over," Conn snarled.

"There is no 'this,'" Alaric said. "But if we meet outside the city limits, we'll see about changing that."

The Giorda siblings circled wide around him, Conn still snarling. Sienne watched Alaric instead of them. He looked calm enough, but his hands were still clenched and he was breathing heavily. "Bullies," Sienne said.

Alaric looked at her as if he'd forgotten she was there. "What?"

"Trying to make you angry enough to start a fight. I take it this isn't your first run-in with them?"

"No." Alaric relaxed his hands and let out a deep breath. "We've competed for the same salvage a few too many times. Conn thinks that makes us rivals."

"You know, if you want to leave..." Dianthe said to Sienne.

"What?" Alaric exclaimed.

"She has a right to know we're not the most reputable pair. That might make a difference." Dianthe cocked an eyebrow at Sienne. "Well?"

Possible answers choked her. *I don't care about your reputation. I've already spent your money. I don't have a reputation at all.* And, most telling, *I've got nowhere else to go.* She went with, "I don't let bullies dictate my actions."

Dianthe let out an exaggerated sigh of relief. "Good, because the city is fresh out of scrapper wizards who are willing to work with us."

Alaric shook his head and walked on. "Not to discourage you," he said, "but let's hope you don't regret it."

5

Sienne woke at the first light of dawn and lay looking out the window and thinking of nothing in particular. To her surprise, she didn't feel anxious the way she had the night before, when she'd lain sleepless from nerves and excitement about the coming day's adventure. She'd packed all her gear neatly, folded her nicer clothes into the chest of drawers, and tried not to think about the possibility that Master Tersus might sell her things. That would mean she wasn't coming back. It was still better than indentured servitude or returning home in disgrace.

She'd met Master Tersus the night before, and he'd turned out to be an old man, probably in his seventies, but spry and agile like a man twenty years younger. When Dianthe had introduced them, saying only that Sienne was her new companion and in need of a room, Master Tersus had said only, "Five soldi a week, two for meals, more than that if you want me not to rent the room out while you're gone, no subleasing," and turned away. It comforted Sienne to know he was mercenary-minded. So long as she paid, he'd keep his word.

She rose and dressed, then shouldered her pack and her bedroll and hesitated in the doorway. She was too excited to feel hungry, but shouldn't she eat something anyway? If only to keep Alaric from rolling his eyes at the inexperienced wizard passing out from hunger at midmorning.

She went down the stairs to the kitchen where Leofus, the cook, was already hard at work preparing Master Tersus's meal. "Porridge," he said, pointing with the wooden spoon that might be permanently attached to his hand. Sienne took a bowl from the sideboard and helped herself, adding a scattering of golden raisins. She set her pack in the corner and took a seat. It was good, for porridge.

Heavy steps on the stairs alerted Sienne to Alaric's arrival. In his left hand he carried a sheathed sword, the biggest weapon Sienne had ever seen that wasn't meant for siege warfare. It was almost as tall as she was, and Sienne had to admit it was more appropriate to Alaric's size than a more ordinary weapon. How did he carry it? If he slung it at his side, he'd spend all his time kicking it out of the way. But could he draw it easily if it were strapped to his back?

Alaric nodded to Leofus, scooped himself a generous bowlful of porridge with the smallest grimace, and was halfway to the table before he noticed Sienne. Sienne bristled inwardly at the way he stopped in his tracks, then made a decision to sit anyway that was plain on his face. She smiled pleasantly, but said nothing. Her earlier resolve to win him over was eroding fast.

They ate without speaking for a few minutes, Sienne feeling increasingly uncomfortable. She reminded herself of the fifty lari and potential reputation building and tried to ignore her dining companion. At least he wasn't being openly antagonistic.

Alaric shifted in his seat. "You're not from Fioretti?" he said, startling her.

"No. Beneddo," she said, then cursed herself silently. All right, he probably wouldn't guess her identity just from that, but she needed to be more cautious.

"That's far north." He wasn't looking at her, but at his bowl.

"Not as far north as you come from."

"No."

Silence fell again. Sienne tried, "Have you lived in Fioretti long?"

Alaric visibly tensed. "Six years," he said, with a finality that suggested Sienne not pursue that line of questioning. Well, that was fine by her.

"Do you...like it here?" she said.

"Sometimes. It's where the best jobs are."

"What kind of jobs do you prefer? Dianthe said, not the typical salvage kind."

Alaric raised his eyes from the bowl. "You really are a babe in arms, aren't you?" he said. "You have no idea who I am."

"Just what that Conn Giorda insinuated yesterday. Should I?"

He actually smiled at that. "Not if my reputation will scare you off. I don't have time to find another wizard with the shrinking spell."

Now Sienne felt nervous. She'd dismissed Conn's remarks as spite, but if Alaric said the same...he had a reputation that might scare her? "Is it the kind of reputation where you get your teammates killed?"

It came out more sharply than she'd intended. Alaric's eyes narrowed. "No," he said. "And I don't take unnecessary risks or lead my companions into ambushes. You have nothing to fear. I may not like wizards, but I won't let you come to harm."

"Then I don't care what your reputation is," Sienne declared. She wanted to ask him why he didn't like wizards, but was certain he wouldn't answer.

They were nearly finished with their porridge when Dianthe ran in, looking disheveled. "I overslept," she said. "You let me oversleep."

"It's not my place to wake you," Alaric said, making Sienne wonder for the first time if Alaric and Dianthe were lovers as well as long-time companions. Probably not, she concluded. They didn't look at each other or touch each other the way two people in love would. She scowled into the last scrapings of porridge in her bowl. As if she knew anything about it. She was the last person who'd recognize real love when she saw it.

She waited outside with her gear for Dianthe and Alaric to finish packing, then followed them down the waking street to the market, which was just stirring to life on this beautiful day. Alaric's destination was a stable just outside the western edge of the market. It sprawled between two large streets, big enough to house at least a hundred horses, and busy even at this early hour. The familiar smell of horses and manure overrode the scents of the harbor, making Sienne feel suddenly homesick. She blinked away stupid tears and focused on Alaric's broad back.

Then awareness struck. "Are we *riding*?" she asked Dianthe.

"Just as far as the first outpost," Dianthe said. A look of dismay touched her eyes. "You do know how to ride, don't you?"

"I—yes, of course," Sienne said without thinking how that must sound. It wouldn't be "of course" for most of the people in Fioretti. "I just thought taking horses into the wilderness was supposed to be a bad idea."

"Which is why we aren't doing it," Dianthe said. "We'll ride until we have to leave the road, and then we'll take just the donkey to carry our gear. This stable has a deal with the scrappers—rent a horse here, return it at any of the outposts within twenty miles. You like horses?"

"I don't hate them." She'd never been horse-mad, not like her older sister who she was *not going to think about ever again*, but she was a competent rider.

The stable had a low ceiling and was full of horses, most of them just waking up and poking their inquisitive noses over their stall doors. Sienne and Dianthe waited while Alaric negotiated for the rent of five horses. The donkey, it turned out, belonged to Alaric outright.

Negotiations complete, they led the horses into the yard to saddle and bridle them. Sienne put tack on a bright chestnut mare while Dianthe loaded the donkey. The donkey was a spry little thing, as quick-stepping as the mare, and Sienne wondered how long Alaric had had it, and whether it had gone on many adventures with them.

The mare butted her hand as if chastising Sienne for not giving her her full attention, and Sienne petted her nose. "The stable owner says your name is Spark," she murmured. "It's a good name. I can make a spark myself, though I doubt Alaric wants me to do so. He'd probably say flint and steel is as good for starting a fire as magic."

"It is," Alaric said, startling her. "Do you have your gear stowed?

These horses are pack animals rather than warhorses, but you can't overload them and not see them get wearier than they should."

"I do know how to saddle a horse. And it's not as if settling my gear is all that hard."

"Even so." He checked over her work. Sienne thought he looked disappointed that he couldn't find anything to correct. "Mount up. We have to meet the others at the Storm Wind Bridge."

Sienne mounted easily, hoping to show him she was competent in this, at least, but Alaric had already turned away. Irritated, Sienne wheeled Spark in a smooth turn and followed the others out of the stable yard.

The whispers and covert glances began almost immediately. The first time she noticed someone pointing at her, fear shot through her, fear that she'd been discovered and would have to leave Fioretti. But no one shouted her name or accosted her horse. After the fifth time she caught someone staring, she realized she wasn't drawing attention for being her father's daughter. It was because, dressed the way she was, mounted on Spark, and in company with Alaric and Dianthe, she was, for the first time, clearly a scrapper. Not just a scrapper, but one headed off for the wilderness and who knew what kind of adventure.

Sienne relaxed and fingered the edge of her spellbook, nestled between her shirt and her suede vest. There had to be a better way to carry it, one that kept it on her person while still making it easily accessible. Maybe there was, and she was just too ignorant to know about it. Something to look into.

Traffic on the Storm Wind Bridge was already brisk by the time they reached its western foot. Sienne didn't recognize Perrin at first, because he'd pulled his long dark hair back from his face, which was pinched as if the light were too bright. He wore the kind of clothes Dianthe had told Sienne were too fancy, a fine linen shirt and a vest embroidered with silver and copper threads, and his thigh-high boots looked too shiny for anything but indoor wear. A ring on a silk cord hung around his neck, a man's heavy ring set with a bright red stone. As they drew nearer to him, Perrin saw Sienne looking at it and casually tucked it into his shirt.

"I give you good morning, fair sir, gentle ladies," he declared, pressing one hand to his heart. "I'm sure Averran would smile upon our journey if he were at all inclined to be pleasant before eleven o'clock in the morning." He swayed, and Sienne realized he was already a little drunk. Despite what she'd said about the priests of Averran, she couldn't help wondering why he couldn't stay sober at least until afternoon.

"Just so he grants your prayers for our protection, he can be as cranky as he likes," Alaric said. "And there's the last of us now."

A young man was crossing the bridge toward them. He was very good-looking, with dark red hair and strong cheekbones that, combined with his umber skin and narrow eyes, declared him to be Omeiran. Sienne watched him with great curiosity. She had seen Omeirans in Fioretti, but never met one. Kalanath Oushikdali moved as gracefully as a cat, never stepping out of anyone's way, simply managing not to be there when they were. He wore plain, well-worn clothing that on his exotic form looked totally out of place, as if he were meant to wear flowing silks and the desert robes of his distant home. His boots, Sienne noticed, came only to his ankle, not his knee like hers did, and he carried a steel-shod staff in his left hand.

"Kalanath. Good morning," Alaric said, raising a hand in greeting. "This is Dianthe, Perrin, and...Sienne."

Sienne was starting to get tired of Alaric pretending not to remember her name, and she was dead sure it was pretense. The next time he did it, she would call him on it.

"Good day," Kalanath said. His speech was precise, almost clipped. "I am glad to meet you. It is good that we fight together." His accent turned *that* into *zat* and *together* into *togezzer*, but otherwise was perfectly intelligible.

"Let's hope there's not a lot of fighting," Dianthe said. "Wastes resources."

"As you say," Kalanath said, bowing slightly. He mounted the horse whose reins Alaric handed him, not very gracefully, which surprised Sienne. Well, he couldn't be good at everything.

Alaric waited for Perrin to boost himself into his saddle, which he did in a competent way that was completely at odds with the drunken fool he appeared to be. "We ride for the first outpost," Alaric said, "which we should reach by noon. Then we'll strike out into the wilderness. When we're safe from prying ears, I'll explain this job more fully. Any questions?"

"Any chance of a drink when we stop at noon?" Perrin asked.

"Probably."

"I have no other questions."

"Then ride out," Alaric said, and heeled his horse around to head westward.

The hushed pointing and commentary continued all the way through the market district and into the streets where the various crafter guilds were located. There, the men and women transacting business barely glanced at them, only seeming to notice them when they had to step out of the horses' way. Even then, it was generally to stare at Alaric and Kalanath, visibly foreign. Sienne was grateful for the anonymity, though it would be a fluke if she were recognized. Still, she didn't relax until they passed through the Dexter Gate and were well and truly on their way.

Long grasses burned gold by the hot sun of first summer waved languidly in the light breeze that blew off the coast. From where they rode, the ocean was distantly visible as a bright patch of reflected light, dimming occasionally as high, wispy clouds passed in front of the sun. They rode in a loose bunch, not quite single file but not abreast, with Sienne near the middle of the pack. She didn't know how that had happened, and wondered if there were some kind of protocol for how scrapper teams rode or walked. Putting the non-combatants in the middle made sense, but they were on the highway, which was well traveled and not prone to bandit attacks, so what was the point?

She looked at Alaric, who rode immediately before her with Dianthe on his left. That put him free to use his sword, which he had, in fact, strapped to his back. Its hilt gleamed dully, the finish matte-silver with hundreds of fine scratches covering it, speaking to years of hard use. Did it have a name? Scrappers could be sentimental about their weapons, but somehow Sienne couldn't picture Alaric naming his sword.

A pair of birds swooped by, silent but for the sound of their wings. Sienne followed their flight and saw them disappear into the trees some hundred yards ahead that surrounded the highway. A gaily painted caravan emerged from their shelter, headed toward Fioretti. The sound of laughter and song floated toward Sienne on the breeze. Traveling performers, come to try their luck in the big city. Sienne edged her horse to the side, though the highway was big enough for their group to pass the performers without inconveniencing anyone.

The woman driving the lead wagon stood up on her seat as they neared. "Scrappers, ho!" she shouted. "Where fare thee?"

"Yonder and far," Dianthe said. It had the sound of a ritual greeting.

"Good luck to ye," the woman said. "Boys, let's sing them along, shall we?"

A couple of men in the wagon behind the first waved and laughed. One of them held an instrument made of pipes of varying lengths to his lips and blew a merry trill that brought another pair of men—boys, really—swarming out of the back of the wagon to perch on its flat wooden top. The three men hummed a note that the pipe player mimicked. Then they sang out in a three-part harmony those birds might have envied:

As I went walking down to sea,
(Sing tirra-la, hey, lay,)
I met five travelers, two and three,
(Sing tirra-la, la lay!)
The men were bold as scrappers be,
The ladies loveliest to see,
All five to fight courageously,
Dread bandits, run away!

The man playing the pipes winked outrageously at Sienne with the line about "lovely ladies," and she blushed and laughed. Perrin applauded when they reached the end of their song and bowed, one of the boys nearly falling off the wagon in his enthusiasm.

"A cheery start to the journey, don't you think?" he said when the caravan had passed.

"I'd rather not begin by eating dirt," Alaric said. The wagons had kicked up large puffs of dust as they passed.

"Averran said a man must eat a peck of dirt before he dies, but it is generally agreed he did not mean all at once," Perrin said. "Though he might have done. There is, after all, the story of the stone biscuits."

"Is that a legend of your avatar?" Sienne asked.

"There are many stories of Averran, some of them likely not true. I am told Averran takes credit for all the best ones regardless."

"What are stone biscuits?" Kalanath said. He was riding at the rear of their procession, and Sienne looked over her shoulder at him. He wore a scarf pulled up to cover his mouth and nose that he lowered now that the dust had settled somewhat.

"As the story goes, Averran was traveling to Marisse when he met a young woman going the same way. They fell into company, as one does, and the young woman revealed that she was low on supplies and very hungry. Averran confessed that he was in the same situation, as he chose to depend on the kindness of strangers. But he had some stone biscuits he was willing to share with her. The biscuit he gave her was round, like a stone, and when she tried to eat it, it was as hard as the same."

"Sounds like my cooking," Dianthe murmured.

Perrin smiled. "When she complained, Averran told her that he could never go hungry so long as he had stone biscuits, because all he had to do was contemplate eating one, and the prospect of doing so was so unappetizing he was able to control his hunger a little while longer."

Perrin fell silent. After a moment, Sienne said, "And?"

"There is no more. That is the story."

"I do not understand," Kalanath said.

"Neither do I," Perrin said. "I hope someday to comprehend its meaning. For now, I take it to suggest that anything can be endured when the alternative is more terrible. The priest who taught me, though, claimed there was more to the story—that the stone biscuits could be eaten if one knew the secret. But he did not tell me what it was."

"Your beliefs are odd," Kalanath said. There was an unexpected note of derision in his voice.

"You are, of course, entitled to your opinion," Perrin said stiffly. "I would not expect an Omeiran to understand."

"We worship God in Her pure form, not through go-betweens," Kalanath said.

"Please let's not get into a religious debate," Dianthe said. "I'm sure God is understanding of all our human weaknesses."

"I should not speak of God," Kalanath said. "I am sorry I was rude." He didn't sound very sorry.

"Perfectly understandable," Perrin said, still a trifle coolly.

Alaric, who'd been silent this whole time, said, "Is Averran as hard to communicate with as everyone says?"

"He is known for being ill-tempered and impatient," Perrin said. "One must approach him carefully and with great humility, for he may reject a supplicant's plea simply because he is irritable at that moment. Praying for Averran's blessing is rather like coddling a crotchety old man."

"Then...forgive me if this is rude, but...why would anyone worship him?" Dianthe asked.

"When one might pay one's devotions to a simpler avatar?" Perrin shrugged. "Averran is still one of the faces of God—" Kalanath made a grunting sound, but Perrin ignored him—"and we should not ignore one of Her aspects just because he is unpleasant. Averran was wise, for all he was difficult to get along with, and he was, and still can be, generous and giving. Though it is true that his generosity is sometimes of the sort you are not certain you wanted."

"This won't be a problem, will it?" Alaric said.

"I do not take your meaning, sir."

"I mean, if Averran is so testy, how does that affect your prayers for divine blessings? We depend on those protections."

"Ah. If I may be permitted an immodesty, I understand Averran well enough to know how to approach him. I assure you there will be no problem."

"Let's hope not," Alaric said, in a tone that suggested the discussion was over. Sienne cast one more glance at Kalanath, who'd retreated behind his scarf again. What would it be like to worship God face-to-face, or however it worked for Omeirans? Sienne might not be very religious, but she knew God was too powerful for humans to comprehend. That was why She had come to earth in the form of Her six avatars, to give humans a way to approach Her. Sienne wished she dared bring up the subject with Kalanath, but he hadn't sounded as if he wanted to discuss it.

They passed another group of travelers, these on foot, with the look of people who'd come a long way, and then they were in the forest. The cool shade of the oaks was a welcome relief from the sun's rays, which had become uncomfortable once they'd gone far enough inland that the ocean breezes didn't reach them. The oak trees grew less densely than the pines of Sienne's northern home, and there were places where the road was exposed to the full sunlight, but for the most part it was beautifully shady and smelled of green leaves. Sienne hadn't been out of Fioretti since she'd arrived five weeks earlier, and she'd forgotten how big the world was outside the city walls. And they hadn't even really begun their journey yet.

They rode along in silence for a few hours as the sun climbed higher in the sky. Sienne watched for wildlife, squirrels mostly, but also birds that called to one another and, once, a fox, its dusty red coat slipping between a couple of overgrown bushes. If she were home, she might see litters of tree-cats in the branches, their gold or black fur touched by sunlight as they glided between trees. It was too bad they were so hard to domesticate, because they were soft and purred when they were happy. In the before times, people had had them as pets, or so legend had it. It was a nice idea.

Just after noon, when Sienne's stomach had begun complaining,

Alaric said, "We're here," and urged his horse into a faster gait. Ahead Sienne saw a sprawling building with several horses hitched to a rail out front. Smoke rose from the stone building's chimney, bringing with it not only the smell of a fire, but also the scent of roasted meat. Sienne's complaining stomach growled.

"We'll eat here, then strike off north," Alaric said. He dismounted and looped the horse's reins over the post, then began pulling his gear off and making a neat pile on the ground. Sienne did the same, then followed him up the hard-earth path and through the door.

The outpost was lit only by the sunlight coming through its many windows, and Sienne blinked in the dimness. Vague shapes loomed, gradually resolving into chairs and tables like an ordinary tavern. About half of them were occupied. People looked up when they entered, then looked away, uninterested. The smell of roast pork and cooked vegetables filled the air, mingled with the scent of warm beer.

Dianthe nudged Sienne. "Sit," she said, indicating a nearby table, and Sienne sat. The others joined her, all but Alaric, who headed for the bar that occupied the whole left side of the room.

Sienne watched him lean down to speak to the very short man behind the bar. "Aren't we going to eat?"

"Alaric will order meals and drink. There's no menu. Trantius cooks something and you eat it or you go hungry." Dianthe smiled. "But it's not like outposts are known for hospitality. A meal, a place to sleep, and somewhere to pick up the latest gossip or a fresh horse, that's pretty much it."

Alaric returned. He was glowering. "Something wrong?" Dianthe said.

"It's nothing." He leaned back in his chair and stretched out his long legs. "Trantius says some Ansorjans came through here two days ago. Seems they were poking around our find."

"They won't find anything. *We* were barely able to find anything."

"Maybe."

Alaric straightened as the short man appeared at his side. He was balancing plates on his arms and gave them all a friendly smile.

"So this is your new team," he said. "Two of you I've never seen before. I'm Trantius."

"Perrin Delucco as was," Perrin said, bowing from his seated position. "A pleasure."

"I'm Sienne," Sienne said.

"Well, you can't ask for better companions," Trantius said with a wink to Dianthe. "Drink's coming up."

"We took care of a little problem for him, a year or two ago," Dianthe said as the man bustled away, "and now he thinks highly of us. Refreshing, really."

"Because your reputation lacks the star-like luster of the typical scrapper team?" Perrin said. "Why is that, I wonder?"

"You didn't seem to mind when you took this job," Alaric growled.

"And I mind even less now. I am simply curious."

Dianthe looked at Alaric, who shrugged, still scowling. "We take... unusual jobs," she said. "The kind that don't always pay off in coin or artifacts. Some of our past associates took exception to our unorthodox approach to scrapping."

"But this is not one of those," Kalanath said.

"We don't discuss our business in public," Alaric said.

"No, it's not," Dianthe said. "But if you want to back out, now would be a good time. If you're concerned about your profit."

Kalanath looked from Dianthe to Alaric. "I would not have agreed if I did not wish to join you," he said. "And my reasons are not the common kind either."

"So why—" Sienne said, then shut her mouth. No prying.

Kalanath glanced at her, and to her surprise, he smiled. It made him look even younger than he was. "Anyone who will black a Giorda's eye is one I will call friend."

"I can accept that," Alaric said. Sienne longed to ask Kalanath why he disliked the Giordas that much—that had sounded like much worse than fending off unwanted advances from whatever her name was—but Kalanath turned his attention to his food, and the moment was lost.

Trantius returned with a handful of mugs, which he distributed. "On the house," he said.

"You're losing money on us," Dianthe said.

"I can afford it. You heading out?"

"Going east," Alaric said, shooting a warning glance at Sienne. How he'd known she was going to say something, she had no idea, but he'd said before they were going north, not east. He must think the easygoing Trantius too loose-lipped for safety. Smart.

She took a bite of pork roast, which was juicy and delicious, and washed it down with some beer. Kalanath took his mug in both hands, bowed his head, and whispered a few words over his drink. Sienne tried not to stare. She'd heard Omeirans had dietary restrictions and unusual religious beliefs, but she didn't know the details. So far it didn't seem to be an issue.

Perrin drained his mug and waved for another. "It's not as strong as I like, but quite delicious," he said, and let out a belch. "Ah. Much better."

"It's noon," Alaric said.

"It is indeed, sir, but I think your meaning is other than your words declare." Perrin put down his mug and leaned forward. "I enjoy my drink, but I assure you it will not interfere with the performance of my duties. Averran's blessing falls upon his priests regardless of their state of inebriation."

Alaric raised an eyebrow, but said nothing. Sienne felt filled to bursting with all the questions she didn't dare ask. Prying into their business would give them tacit permission to pry into hers.

The rest of the meal passed in silence, uncomfortable and wearing as if they were all strangers who happened to share a table. That was mostly true. Sienne didn't know any of them well, and here she was proposing to travel into the wilderness with them. She wasn't afraid of them—well, Alaric made her uncomfortable, a little—but they would face danger together, and that was the sort of thing she'd always believed she'd do with friends. *How do you think you get those kinds of friends?* she asked herself. She looked at each of them in turn, Alaric still glowering, Dianthe rapt in her own thoughts, Perrin getting solidly drunk, Kalanath reserved and silent, and had to admit she couldn't imagine ever being friends with any of them.

6

When the meal was finished, they handed the horses over to the outpost's ostler. Sienne shouldered her pack and picked up her bedroll. It wasn't heavy, but still weighed too much for her invisible fingers to manage. With the donkey laden with the tents and cookware and supplies, she'd have to carry it on her back. The trouble was, she didn't know how to strap it on. She hoisted it over her shoulders to rest above her pack. It slid and rolled, and she had to twist to catch it before it hit the ground.

Hands took the bedroll from her. "This way," Alaric said, positioning it comfortably and fastening it across her shoulders. "Balancing the load will let you walk for miles carrying it."

"Thanks." He hadn't sounded at all dismissive or scornful. Maybe—

"Try to keep up," he added. "Nobody has the means to carry you."

"I'm not weak," Sienne retorted, entertaining a brief fantasy of slapping him across the face. He probably wouldn't even notice, the big oaf. "Stop making assumptions about me. Not all wizards are the same, you know."

Alaric crossed his arms over his massive chest and regarded her dispassionately. "You don't know enough wizards," he said, "and I don't think I'm wrong in assuming you've never traveled rough. It's a difficult transition, and if you slow us down, we'll all suffer."

"Then why aren't you nagging Perrin? He's probably never traveled rough either. And his boots aren't made for it. He's the one you should worry about slowing us down."

Alaric scowled. "Worry about yourself." He turned away, leaving Sienne fuming and wishing she'd thought of a better retort. Likely one would come to her at three in the morning.

They walked eastward along the highway until they were out of sight of the outpost, then Alaric turned off the road and headed north. The rough terrain, uneven and covered with dead grass and low scrub, forced Sienne to walk carefully to avoid tripping. It took her some minutes to get the hang of stepping lightly, lifting her feet rather than shuffling along. The unusual gait was tiring, but she gritted her teeth and held back complaints, which wouldn't make the journey any easier.

"Our destination is about two and a half days from here," Alaric said, not sounding the least bit winded from the pace he set. "It's what's left of a city from the before times. Most of it is long since crumbled to dust, but it had a fortress built of stone that's still mostly standing. That's our goal."

"And we seek...what?" Perrin asked. He did sound winded, but his voice was strong.

"Our client, Vincentius Fontanna, studies the history of Rafellin —or, more accurately, the part of the old world that Rafellin now occupies. He's learned that fortresses like this one were part of a line of defense stretching from the southern coast through what's now the Empty Lands to the eastern sea. Apparently they were worried about an Omeiran invasion. No offense."

"It is in the past," Kalanath said.

"At any rate, these fortresses were equipped with distance-viewing magical artifacts, some of which have been recovered elsewhere. Master Fontanna has identified this fortress as belonging to the defensive line, something no one knew before, and believes the artifact is still there. The fortress has been raided, but the keep, the inner structure, is intact."

"That seems a trifle unlikely, good sir," Perrin said. "The rapacity of scrappers, which I say recognizing that I am one of that rapacious bunch, should surely mitigate against anything remaining."

"You'll understand when you see it," Dianthe said. "It looks utterly destroyed. But we found a way in—*if* we were half our size. Or a third our size, in Alaric's case."

"We're being paid to retrieve the distance-viewing artifact, and we can keep anything else we find," Alaric said. Sienne looked at him sharply. He'd sounded unusually eager just then, as if he were more interested in the "anything else." But hadn't he said they weren't interested in salvage? She was sure there was something he wasn't telling them.

"What else might there be?" she asked.

Alaric glanced over his shoulder at her. "The ancients created magical artifacts as readily as breathing. It's impossible to say what they might have created. But even broken artifacts have a market."

And now he sounded too casual. Sienne couldn't think of a way to call him on it when she had no clue what he might be hiding. She resolved to watch him carefully when they reached the ruin. If he intended to cheat the rest of them by concealing whatever artifact he was after...but he hadn't struck her as the duplicitous type, so what else might he want out of this journey?

The trees continued sparser than Sienne was accustomed to, giving the five plenty of room to spread out. Sienne was able to pretend she was alone in the wilderness, which made her uncomfortable. She hated being alone, but the company of these people...all right, she was just in a bad mood because of what Alaric had said to her when they set out. They were all, with one notable exception, probably nice people. More to the point, they were her companions, and she would depend on them for her survival. Making friends was the smart course of action.

But as the hours passed, no friend-making opportunities presented themselves. The sun slid down the sky and disappeared behind the trees, leaving behind a welcome coolness that dried the sweat rolling down Sienne's back and neck. Her legs were limp and her feet burned with fatigue, and she had a blister on the little toe of her left foot where the poorly-fitted boot rubbed it. She kept putting one foot in front of the other out of sheer willpower and the ardent desire not to give Alaric the satisfaction. She wasn't weak and she wasn't going to make him carry her.

Someone stepped in front of her. "Sienne," Dianthe said, "you can stop. We're pitching camp here."

Sienne looked around. It didn't look like an ideal campsite, more like a spot where the trees grew less closely together than an actual clearing, but Alaric was clearing ground for a campfire and Dianthe had turned away to unload the donkey, whose name had turned out to be Button. "You can help me pitch tents, if you like," Dianthe added, and Sienne shed her burdens and went to join her.

She hadn't realized how heavy her gear was until she wasn't carrying it anymore. Her whole body was going to ache come the morning. The tents, on the other hand, were surprisingly light. Dianthe showed her how to erect the poles and hammer stakes into the ground, and between the two of them they got the first tent up before Alaric had finished lighting the fire. Sienne, still annoyed at his condescension, thought about striking a spark to start the fire before his efforts with flint and steel could bear fruit. But pitching tents was more important, and Sienne didn't want their animosity to degrade into childishness. She, at least, could be mature.

Perrin was gathering wood for the fire Alaric had started. Kalanath had disappeared. "Where did Kalanath go?" she asked Dianthe.

"Hunting," Alaric said. "Setting snares, I think. We try to live off the land so we don't have to carry much food." He made it sound like something she should have known, and she flushed red with irritation.

She helped Dianthe with the second tent, which was only a little larger than the first. If the three men intended to share it, they'd find it tight quarters. She spread her bedroll in the smaller tent and arranged her pack at its foot. It looked so...official. The reality of her situation struck her as it hadn't before. She was a real scrapper. Her parents would be appalled. Good.

She emerged from the tent to find Dianthe setting out cookware, a heavy pot and frying pan. "We need to find water," Dianthe told Alaric. "I think the stream we passed about five minutes ago is the closest source. We probably should have camped nearer it."

"There wasn't anywhere good nearer it." Alaric hefted the pot. "I'll be back."

"Wait," Sienne said. "You don't have to go anywhere. I can create water."

Alaric shook his head. "Not necessary."

"It will be fresh and pure, not mucky like the stream."

"I said, that's not necessary. I don't want to put you to the trouble."

Like that's the reason. "It's no trouble. Give me the pot."

Alaric said nothing.

"Give her the pot, Alaric," Dianthe said. "It saves time and she's right, it's probably better water."

His lips thinned, but he handed over the pot. Sienne set it on the ground at her feet and concentrated. A head-sized glob of water appeared in the air above the pot, hovered for half a breath, then fell neatly into it, splashing a few drops on the ground. Dianthe picked up the pot and sniffed deeply.

"It smells like spring water," she said. "Is that what it is?"

"It comes out of whatever's in the atmosphere," Sienne said, "but stripped of impurities. It tastes a little bland, I'm afraid, because it lacks minerals, but it's clean and good."

Dianthe smiled broadly. "That's amazing. Don't you think that's amazing?"

Alaric grunted and turned away, ducking to enter the larger tent. "Sorry," Dianthe said in a low voice. "I warned you—"

"He doesn't like wizards, I know. Why not?" It was prying, but Sienne was exhausted and frustrated and annoyed at being so thoroughly dismissed by the big man.

The smile fell away from Dianthe's face. "That's not my story to tell. Sorry. He'll get used to you." She didn't look very sanguine about the possibility.

Kalanath returned after another ten minutes with a brace of rabbits, big ones, dangling from his hand. They'd been cleaned and skinned already, and he offered them to Dianthe, who cut the meat neatly from the bone and into bite-sized pieces. Sienne's water was already boiling, and Alaric had chopped carrots and potatoes into it with a handful of aromatic herbs. Dianthe added the rabbit meat, and the soup began to smell very good.

While they were waiting for it to cook, Sienne summoned more water for washing up. Alaric continued to scowl, but washed his hands like the rest of them. "Very civilized," was all he said. Sienne gritted her teeth and said nothing.

They ate rabbit soup, with hard biscuits—not stone biscuits, thankfully—to dunk in the broth, and drank more of Sienne's water, all but Perrin, who had a flask he took swigs from. Sienne was having trouble not feeling critical of him, and never mind what he'd said about Averran. How could he possibly be effective if he was that drunk? She drained her bowl and mopped up the drops with the last of her biscuit. It was hard not to think of it as her business, given that his condition might well mean the difference between life and death for her. But she couldn't think of any way to broach the topic without sounding judgmental.

The sun had just set when the last of the soup was eaten. Alaric rose to his full height and stretched. "Since you seem equipped for it, why don't you wash up tonight," he told Sienne. "We take turns watching once it gets dark so none of us are exhausted come the morning."

"Sienne helped cook," Dianthe said.

"No, I don't mind," Sienne said. In fact, she was pleased Alaric wasn't going to coddle her—and that he'd accepted her magic at least as far as washing dishes went. She gathered the cook pot and the bowls and took them to the edge of the campsite, where she made a couple of floating lights to illuminate her work. She was awkward at washing up, having little experience with cooking or cleaning, but the work soothed her nerves, as did the pleasure of summoning water in globs of different sizes and heating them just enough to be comfortable. Finally, she scrubbed the last of the spoons and dumped them all in the pot to carry back. The others were settled in around the fire, silently staring at the flames, though Dianthe smiled at her when she returned.

Sienne put the dishes near the fire, where they'd dry before morning, and asked, "Do we...should the fire burn all night?"

"It depends on where we are," Dianthe said. "Some places, you want a fire to ward off animals. Others, you don't want to draw human attention. Tonight we'll bank it before we go to bed. We don't need it for warmth, after all."

Sienne took a seat near her and as far from Alaric as she could manage, which put her next to Kalanath. She drew her legs up and hugged her knees and let her eyes go unfocused as the warmth of the flames eased her aching muscles. She'd survived her first day as a scrapper, and it hadn't been too bad. Someday, she'd do this with real companions, and the end of the day would mean talking and laughing around the fire, not this morose silence.

Kalanath stirred. "What can you do?" he asked.

"I'm sorry?"

He waved a hand. "Your magic. What can you do?"

"Oh. Lots of things. Summon water, start a fire, make light. Then I know about a dozen spells."

"I do not know what is the difference. In Omeira we have no wizards."

"No wizards?"

He shrugged. "It is not our way."

That didn't make sense. Surely Omeirans weren't so different from the Rafellish or even Ansorjans that they didn't have people born with magical talent? "Well...wizards are born with the ability to do small magics. You just think it and it happens, more or less. But stronger magic, wizardry, requires spells, and for that you need a spellbook." Sienne pulled her book out of her vest and offered it to Kalanath.

He leaned away from her. "I should not touch."

"No, there's no magic in it, it can't hurt you. Well, that's not entirely true. I mean, no, it can't hurt you, but it does have magic on it. It's been treated with invulnerability so it can't be destroyed." She opened the cover and flexed it back and forth. "Invulnerability makes thin wood pliable and unbreakable, and it makes paper rigid like metal. Go ahead, hold it."

Kalanath gingerly took the spellbook from her and turned the pages. "It is as you say. Like metal. And these lines...they are not Fellic."

"No, they're in the four magic languages."

"May I?" Perrin took the book from Kalanath and turned it over, tracing the letters burned into the cover. "And any wizard knows these languages."

"Yes, but only I can cast the spells in my spellbook."

"Why is that?" Dianthe asked.

"Because I wrote them myself. In...my own blood, actually." She braced herself for a rude comment from Alaric, but he was silent, eyeing the spellbook as if it were a live snake. "I can copy a spell from someone else's book, but I can't just, well, steal some other wizard's spellbook and use it. Wizards need the connection their blood gives them."

"Pity," Alaric said. "I'd love to see Conn Giorda's face if we snatched his precious spellbook."

Dianthe reached across Alaric for the spellbook and turned its pages. "These look like different alphabets, even."

"They are. The alphabets give form to the language. That is, a transform spell like *fit*—the shrinking spell—is round and flowing, and the script matches that." She accepted the spellbook from Dianthe and ran her fingers down its smooth, warm spine.

"If it's invulnerable, how do you write spells in it?" Dianthe asked. "Wouldn't the ink...the blood...slide right off?"

"I write the spell before I make the page invulnerable. It—here." Sienne worked the complicated clasp at the base of the spine, and the back cover popped open. She slid the last page free and waved it. It made a *whopwhopwhop* sound as it flopped back and forth, just like a thin sheet of metal. "It's made to expand. When I gain a new spell, I write it on paper, put the invulnerability on it, and add it to the book. Some wizards arrange their spells by language, or by difficulty, but I find it easier to remember where they all are if I just put them in as I get them." She returned the page to the book, careful not to cut herself on the sharp edge, and latched it shut.

"Can you cast a spell now?" Perrin said. "I find myself quite curious about your capabilities."

Sienne glanced swiftly at Alaric. He looked irritated, but he'd looked that way from the moment she sat down, so it was unlikely she could make him more annoyed. "All right," she said. She pressed her fingertips to the page edges and willed the book open. *Cast*, that would be dramatic and not frightening. She let the polysyllables of the confusion spell roll off her tongue, blinked away the haloes they left around the dancing flames, and felt the back of her throat tingle. She closed the book and said, "Listen."

"Listen," her voice said again, this time coming from behind Alaric. He jumped and half-turned in his seat. "I can cast my voice anywhere I like," she said without moving her lips, making it sound as if the flames were speaking. "It's a fun party trick," she said in Kalanath's ear, "and some wizards," high in the trees behind the tents, "make a good living at it, entertaining the wealthy," echoing from inside the cook pot.

Dianthe laughed in delight. Perrin slowly applauded. "Marvelous," he said, "though I admit the usefulness seems limited."

"Fooling your enemy," Alaric said. "Giving yourself invisible allies."

"Exactly," Sienne said, surprised that Alaric had seen the potential in something he despised. Though he'd come up with the idea of blinding someone using the *sharpen* spell...for someone who hated wizards, he'd have made a good one. She decided against saying this.

Perrin yawned. "I'm for bed," he said, "unless you wish me to watch first."

"I do," Alaric said. "If you're like the other priests we've worked with, you'll rise early to make your prayers."

"Actually, Averran tends not to respond to prayers made before dawn. But I will take whatever watch you desire."

"Then you'll go first." Alaric stood and stretched again. "Then Kalanath, me, Dianthe, and Sienne will take the last watch."

Sienne nodded, though by the look on Dianthe's face there was something wrong with her taking the final watch. It would give her a good night's sleep, and maybe that was the problem—maybe it was just another way in which Alaric assumed she was weak, that she'd need a good night's sleep. But that was an assumption she couldn't call him on, so she simply went to her bedroll and removed her boots and vest. Sleeping in her clothes wouldn't be comfortable, but she'd known going into this that comfort wasn't important to scrappers.

The firelight dimmed as someone banked the hot coals. She heard people moving around outside and in the neighboring tent. Footsteps sounded outside her own tent, then low voices. "...not weak..." she could barely hear Dianthe say. "...last watch is..."

Alaric's rumbling voice said, "...exhausted...could use the rest..."

"...treat her...companion..."

"I said I would, didn't I?" Alaric's voice came through clearly, tinged with impatience, and Dianthe shushed him. "She's doing better than I thought."

"Told you...good idea."

"...right..." Alaric murmured, and Dianthe laughed. Then the tent flap parted, and Dianthe entered, dropping heavily onto her bedroll and pulling off her boots.

"You don't snore, do you?" she asked.

"I don't think so. No one's ever complained." Sienne wished she hadn't said that. For one thing, most ordinary people grew up sharing a bedroom with siblings, and for another, she'd only ever had one lover, even though she'd just implied she had plenty of experience. If she had it to do all over again, she'd have stayed a virgin.

"Well, I do, so I apologize in advance." Dianthe set her boots just inside the tent flap and lay back on her bedroll. "Still glad you came along?"

"Absolutely," Sienne said with a fervor that surprised her.

Dianthe chuckled. "Don't worry about starting breakfast at the end of your watch. You didn't seem experienced at cooking, if you'll pardon me saying, and porridge is harder than it looks."

"Maybe you could teach me."

"Sure. Wake me at dawn. I never sleep well after a pre-dawn watch, anyway. Good night."

"Good night," Sienne said, lying down and stretching out her legs. They already ached from all the walking. Well, she wasn't going to complain and give Alaric something to criticize her for. Though... he'd said she was doing better than he'd thought, so maybe he wasn't as critical as she believed. Even so, she didn't want to be a burden.

At night, in the darkness of the tent, the forest noises were louder than they'd been when the five of them had been tramping through the undergrowth. The high-pitched chirruping of crickets and the rushing of the wind in the leaves made a steady background against which Sienne heard the distant hooting of owls on the hunt and, even farther away, the cries of an animal she didn't recognize. Some-one, probably Perrin, walked past, his footsteps rustling the dry grass. Beside her, Dianthe let out a gentle snore. Sienne smiled. She'd never felt so at peace.

Between one thought and the next, she drifted into sleep.

7

She woke to Dianthe's gentle hand on her shoulder, shaking her. "Time to watch," she whispered. "Wake me when it's bright enough to see, and we'll wake the others when the food's ready."

Sienne nodded, then added, "All right," when she realized it was too dark for Dianthe to see the motion. Sitting up reminded her of all the walking she'd done the day before. Every muscle ached, especially her calves and thighs, and her shoulders were stiff from carrying that load. She gritted her teeth against a moan of pain. She wasn't going to complain, even to Dianthe, who would probably be sympathetic. She pulled on her boots, but left her vest lying where it was.

The night was cool, but not chilly, and high, thin clouds obscured the stars in the moonless sky. The banked fire glowed red, and she crouched to feel the heat radiating from it. Then she made a circuit of the camp, listening for anything out of the ordinary. Nothing but the crickets, who went silent as she neared and took up their shrill song again once she'd passed.

She thought about making a light, but decided against it. If she heard anything big approaching, that would be the time for it. She circled the camp again. What exactly was she supposed to do? Could she sit by the fire and watch from there, or should she continue pacing the camp's perimeter? She thought about asking Dianthe, but decided the woman was probably asleep already and shouldn't be disturbed. Besides, walking eased the aches as she stretched and warmed her muscles.

The blister on her toe was more annoying than it had been the day before. She needed to pad her boot with extra socks or something, or it would be awful during tomorrow's journey. Today's journey. She pulled out her pocket watch and squinted at its face. Just after four o'clock. These early days of true summer, dawn would come around six. With five people to split the hours of night between, standing watch wasn't so hard. She'd probably have been all right taking an earlier watch. What had Alaric said? Something about being exhausted? She hadn't been *that* tired.

And yet...he'd grudgingly complimented her, though not to her face. Maybe she stood a chance of impressing him. She scowled. She didn't care about impressing him. It wasn't as if she was likely to work with him again.

A crack rang out through the darkness, someone or something stepping on a dry branch. Sienne froze. It had come from her left, some distance beyond the camp. She strained to see movement in that direction. What now? At what point did she sound the alarm? If she woke everyone over nothing, how humiliating that would be.

Another crack, this one closer. Sienne took a few steps in that direction and made a light. If something out there was coming for them, seeing it coming was worth the risk of giving it something to aim for. The wan light, not much brighter than a half-moon, lit up the campsite and cast odd shadows on the tents. It played over the nearest tree trunks, steady and cold as winter.

Sienne covered her mouth to hold in a shriek. Eyes, several pairs of eyes, gazed back at her from the scrub beneath the trees. They were low to the ground and gleaming green-yellow with the odd reflective glint of a cat's eyes. She took a step forward. They didn't move.

Sienne swallowed. It might just be animals. Or it could be something worse. She knew about the creatures who lived in the Empty Lands north of Beneddo, how some of them were ordinary animals altered by the magic thrown around during the wars of the before time. More frightening were the ones that had been deliberately made by wizards of that time. This wasn't the Empty Lands, but it was unlikely those creatures knew or cared about human-drawn boundaries.

She reached out with her invisible fingers and rustled the bushes. The eyes blinked out, and she heard the movement of half a dozen small bodies running away, rustling the bushes harder than she was. She let out a relieved sigh. Just animals. She wished she knew more about wildlife to make a guess as to what kind.

She went back to circling the camp. It took her a moment to realize why everything was so bright. Swiftly, she extinguished her light and blinked as her eyes adjusted to the darkness.

Far in the distance, another light gleamed.

It winked out almost immediately, but it was unquestionably a light. Not a lantern or a flame, but a magical light like her own. Sienne stood still, waiting for it to reappear. Nothing happened.

She hesitated, then made for the larger tent. A magical light in the forest might be anything, but it was certainly cause for alarm. She thought briefly about waking Dianthe, but that was the cowardly way, and Dianthe would almost certainly wake Alaric anyway.

The men were shadowy lumps inside the tent. She grabbed the feet of the biggest lump and shook them. "Alaric. Wake up."

The big man sat up swiftly. "What?"

"I saw a light. A wizard's light."

She backed up as Alaric emerged, barefoot and bare-chested, from the tent. His skin was almost as pale as the light dun canvas tents. "Where?"

She took his hand and pointed him in the right direction. "It's gone now, and it was a ways away, but it was bright enough that I saw it through the trees."

"You're sure you didn't imagine it?"

His straightforward inquiry somehow didn't offend her. "Positive."

He released her and stood with his hands on his hips. "And you saw no other motion."

"Just some...I don't know what they were, but ordinary animals."

He was silent so long she began to be impatient. She managed not to say anything. Finally, Alaric said, "It might be a wisp. Those shed a cold light like yours. Or it might be another scrapper team."

"Is that bad?"

"It's not good. If someone's following us...we don't need another team sniffing around our find. Dianthe can check it out in the morning."

"Not right now?"

"She'd just stumble around in the dark."

"I could adjust her eyes."

"*No.*"

The curt, short syllable startled Sienne into saying, "Shouldn't that be up to her?"

Alaric let out a long breath. Then, in a tense tone that told Sienne he was hanging on to his temper with both hands, he said, "Even if she could see in the dark, it would take her at least an hour to investigate, probably more, and if she did find something, she might not be able to tackle it on her own. By that time, it would be full light, and we'd lose the element of surprise, since none of the rest of us are capable of moving silently. And *don't*, for the love of Sisyletus, tell me you have a spell that will let us move silently. Not everything can or should be solved by magic."

His face was a pale smudge high above her. Biting back a harsh retort, she said, "You brought me along to do wizardry. Why won't you let me help?"

"We need the shrinking spell. That's help enough."

She was either going to hit him or burst into tears. "Fine. I'll keep an eye out for that light, and if it gets closer, I'll scream. That should be enough, don't you think?"

"Go back to bed. I'll finish your watch."

"I'm perfectly capable of staring into the darkness, thanks."

"I'm not going to fall back asleep."

"Then lie on your back and stare at the tent roof. I don't need your pity."

"It's not pity. You can use the rest."

Sienne summoned the light directly in Alaric's face, making him squint. "All right," she said. "You can either avoid me because I'm a wizard, or you can treat me like a liability because I'm inexperienced, but I'll be damned if I'll put up with both. So take your pick."

Alaric glared down at her. "Last night when we made camp, you looked like death on two legs," he said. "You're no good to any of us if you wear yourself to collapse. It's my job to make sure everyone in this team is at their peak, and in your case, that means getting plenty of rest while your body adjusts to the demands you're putting on it. I told Perrin the same thing before he took his watch—or did you think it was coincidence he also got an uninterrupted night's rest?"

Sienne gaped at him. "For what it's worth," Alaric went on, "you're doing much better than I thought you might. You didn't need to ride Button, for one, and you haven't said one word of complaint. I'm hard on you because anything else is an insult to your capabilities."

"I...thank you," Sienne said, stunned.

Alaric turned away. "Go ahead and finish your watch. Let me know if you see the light again." He ducked into the tent, and she heard him rustling around, then there was nothing but the crickets and the wind.

Sienne walked slowly around the campsite. So Alaric wasn't as disdainful of her as she'd thought. True, he still hated wizards, and he didn't fully trust her magic, but he thought of her as...what? Not an equal, but someone with the potential to become such. It embarrassed her that his approval warmed her heart. *He's bigoted and full of himself*, she thought, but it was hard to stay angry with him when he'd so straightforwardly complimented her. If she could get him to overcome his prejudice against wizards, they might even become friends. It wasn't an unpleasant thought.

When there was enough light that Sienne could see her fingers in front of her face, she woke Dianthe, and the two of them stirred up the fire and began making porridge. With Alaric not present, Sienne felt comfortable using magic to light the fire and summon water. Dianthe showed her how to measure out the grain and stir it in a little at a time so it wouldn't get lumpy. Sienne considered accelerating the cooking process by heating the water herself—she could warm or cool water, just not to boiling or freezing—but decided not to risk ruining breakfast until she was more comfortable with cooking. She contented herself with producing water for coffee, which she didn't care for but seemed, as far as Dianthe was concerned, to be essential.

Alaric emerged from the tent a few minutes before the porridge was done, pulling his shirt on over his head. "Did you tell her about what you saw last night?" he asked Sienne.

"No, I was distracted. Sorry."

Alaric shrugged this off. "We might have some hangers-on," he told Dianthe. "Off that way—is that right?"

Sienne nodded. "I saw a wizard's light last night, but—"

"I'll take a look," Dianthe said, and headed off into the trees.

Alaric picked up the spoon and gave the porridge a stir. "I hate porridge," he muttered. "But eggs don't travel well, and bacon goes bad in this heat." He paused. "That was to give you time to tell me how there's magic for that."

It startled a laugh out of Sienne. "Not to my knowledge," she said. "But there might be wizardry to keep bacon fresh. If I cast invulnerability on an egg...well, you see the problem."

"I do."

Kalanath ducked out of the tent, looking much fresher than Alaric, whose short blond hair was mussed and whose eyes were a little puffy. He nodded to the two of them, picked up his staff from where it leaned against the tent, and headed off into the forest to the left of where Dianthe had gone. "Morning exercise," Alaric said. "I wish he'd do it where we can see. His fighting style is supposed to be unique."

"Is it a religious thing?"

"I don't think so." He gave the pot another stir, then picked up a bowl, filled it, and handed it to Sienne before taking another for himself. Startled at his courtesy, Sienne found a spot on the ground and ate. It was a little gluey, but otherwise not bad for a first attempt.

Alaric sat nearby, almost companionably. If he noticed the glueyness, he didn't bring it up. Still, Sienne felt uncomfortable at the silence. She wished Dianthe had waited long enough to eat.

A loud yawn from the men's tent made them both look back. Perrin stuck his head out, his dark hair flopping forward into his face. "I will sacrifice any limb you like for coffee," he groaned.

"The water's boiling," Sienne said. Perrin crawled forward, the very picture of a man dying of thirst. She took pity on him to the extent of showing him where the coffee was, and caught Alaric looking at them both, a wry smile on his lips. She felt a moment of perfect amity with him. No doubt it wouldn't last, but for the moment, they were in harmony.

Perrin fumbled about with the coffee, which was pre-ground—Dianthe had said something about how only effete snobs brought coffee grinders into the wilderness—and finally produced a steaming cup, which was so aromatic Sienne had to remind herself that the taste was too bitter for her unless it was seventy percent cream. Perrin drank his black and unfiltered with a generous measure of brandy mixed in, which disgusted Sienne, but to each his own.

Alaric made a cup of coffee too, but didn't drink it, just left it sitting beside the fire to steep. Just as he was draining off the dregs, Dianthe appeared and dropped heavily to sit beside him. "My hero," she said as Alaric handed her the cup. She drank deeply, sighed, and added, "I can quit any time I want."

"Sure you can," Alaric said. "What did you find?"

She took another drink. "Not much. I didn't see evidence of another team camping anywhere near, but there also weren't any wisps in the vicinity. If I had to guess, I'd say it's slightly more likely it was a wisp, but that could just be me not wanting to admit someone's following us."

"Maybe I was wrong," Sienne said. "It might have been my imagination."

"That's possible, too," Dianthe said. "But we want to err on the side of paranoia, in this business. If someone's following us, we'll want to take precautions."

"I might be able to do something about that," Perrin said. His eyes were closed and he had his coffee cup close to his face, but his voice was strong. "Seeing what is hidden is by way of being a specialty of Averran's. I will petition him for a blessing of that nature."

"Then the rest of us will begin striking camp," Alaric said, setting his bowl down and rising. "Take your time."

Sienne quickly finished her porridge and went to pack her things. It didn't take long. With a glance for permission at Dianthe, she rolled up the other woman's bedroll and tackled the tent poles. The tent came down more easily than it had gone up, in a tangle of canvas and rope Sienne was sure she'd never get untangled. She dragged the poles away and stepped back to look at the canvas. How had Dianthe done it?

"That's a good start," Alaric said. Sienne looked up to find the big man watching her. His tent, naturally, was already neatly collapsed and bundled up. "If you clear away the ropes first, it leaves the canvas half folded already. Then you just keep folding."

"Oh," Sienne said. She lifted one side and carefully brought it to meet the other. Alaric turned away. She felt a moment's irritation that he wasn't going to help her, but it didn't last long. She wanted him to treat her as an equal, didn't she? And she was beginning to see the value of his approach. She already felt more confident doing it herself.

She left the bundled tent for Alaric to load onto Button—that was something she really was bad at—and saw Kalanath had returned and was placidly eating porridge, and Perrin had finished his coffee and was sitting cross-legged beside the fire, his hands resting on his knees and his eyes still closed. His hair hung down in strands concealing his face, but his chest rose and fell in a peaceful, meditative rhythm. Sienne noticed a loose pile of thin, square papers in his lap, translucent white and crossed with fibrous lines. Rice paper.

"Oh most cantankerous Lord," Perrin said in a conversational voice, exactly as if he were addressing Sienne, "it's that time again. Hear my plea, and forgive my pestering you."

Kalanath had stopped eating with the spoon hovering inches from his mouth, his narrow eyes wider than usual. Casually he set his bowl down and rose, backing away from Perrin. Sienne wanted to do the same, but she was too fascinated to move.

"I realize it's early," Perrin went on. "But did you not in your wisdom say, 'Time waits for no man, especially when there is a drink to be had'?" Still with his eyes closed, he took a long swig from his flask and smiled. "That's better. Now, it seems my companions and I may have been followed, and I would like to take a look around. There's also the chance we will stand in need of your curmudgeonly protection. And I sincerely hope it is unnecessary, but should we stand in need of healing, I'd like to think your ill temper would not prevent you from aiding us. As always, I leave it to you to determine the form your assistance will take."

He went silent. Sienne became aware that Alaric and Dianthe had come to stand nearby, staring at Perrin with as much astonishment as she was. Perrin's brow furrowed, and his lips quirked in a smile. "My Lord, I realize how much I ask of you," he said. "You are generous and —" He stopped speaking and cocked his head as if listening. "No, I had no intention of toad-eating you, merely of showing my respect for your many blessings upon me. You are certainly entitled to grant or withhold your blessings as you see fit, o querulous Lord of drunks and vagrants." Another pause. Perrin's face went still. "I should not have to remind you that drink is a sacrament unto you, my Lord, and your objection is—"

Sienne heard a hiss, like the sound of water on a hot pan. A thin stream of smoke rose from the pile of papers in Perrin's lap, scented like jasmine mixed with a sharp, minty odor. It was like a splash of cold water to the face, making her feel alert and awake.

"My thanks, o Lord," Perrin said. He opened his eyes and began sorting through the papers on his lap. "Hmm," he said. "Interesting."

"Are those...blessings?" Dianthe said.

"Indeed. Though Averran has an interesting sense of humor

when he is petitioned before noon. I have no idea what this one does." Perrin displayed one of the papers, holding it by one corner like a dead mouse. It now bore a scorch mark in the shape of a complex sigil.

"I thought you made specific prayers, and the avatar granted them," Sienne said. "That's how—I mean, I've only seen a priest of Kitane do it." No need to say it was her mother's personal priest, since only a noble would have one of those.

"It may well be different for other avatars. The priests of Gavant —" Perrin's lips went tight, and he shook his head slightly as if warding off bad memories. "Averran in his wisdom sees farther than mere mortals, and his priests have found that allowing him to bless them as he sees fit carries with it advantages beyond a slavish adherence to one's own intellect and wisdom."

There were quite a few papers left blank. Perrin sorted these from the scorched ones and set them aside. The scorched ones, he scrutinized carefully, one at a time. "This is the one that will allow me to scry out the locality," he told Alaric, displaying a paper with a slightly less complex sigil than the first. "And I think we are in for an interesting day."

"How so?" Alaric said.

"Three of these are healing blessings. In general, I am given only one or perhaps two of these in a day. If Averran sees fit to grant me more, I can only assume we may need them. These two—" He teased out papers with a different sigil. "These are for protection, specifically to ward off attacks. And, as I said, this one might do anything."

"How does your god give you spells you cannot use?" Kalanath said.

"First, he is an avatar of God, not God Herself, and second, they are not spells, they are blessings. I realize the distinction is meaningless to you." Perrin sounded more irritated than Sienne had ever heard him, and Kalanath, hearing a rebuke, scowled back at him. "We grow as priests of Averran in many ways, not least of which is being given the opportunity to stretch our minds and our understanding. I will study it as we go and attempt to interpret it, and then when it is given me again, I will know how to use it."

"Then let's finish breaking camp, and before we move on, you can invoke that scrying blessing," Alaric said.

They were mostly done already. Sienne put out the fire by first kicking dirt over it and then soaking it with a couple of gallons of water. It made a muddy mess that satisfied her. She prodded it gently with her toe, having padded her boots with her spare socks to make them fit better. No spark remained.

Alaric and Dianthe were finishing loading Button and tightening a few straps. "All right," Alaric said, "let's see what's out there."

"You said you believed there were others following us?" Perrin said. "This blessing will reveal the presence of other sapient minds. It will exclude any animals, which means if there are dangerous creatures out there, we will not know of them unless we encounter them personally. Is that acceptable?"

"We can deal with beasts," Alaric said.

Perrin nodded. He took a long, thin branch from what was left of their firewood and drew an awkward circle in the mud where the fire had been. Tossing the branch to the side, he removed a bundle of papers from his vest—the papers with scorched sigils on them. He had stitched them together at one corner and daubed color that had the matte brightness of pastels on the opposite corners, two red, three green, and one violet. The paper he tore from the bundle had no color. Perrin put away the bundle and gripped the loose blessing in both hands, bowing his head over it. His lips moved soundlessly, making Sienne wish she dared enhance her ears and listen.

A blue glow radiated from within the circle, growing gradually brighter until it was painful to look at. The sigil on the paper burst into flame, consuming the paper in an instant and licking at Perrin's fingers. Perrin didn't react as if he'd been burned, just transferred his attention to the blue glow. Sienne squinted at it. It didn't seem to be doing anything but glowing. It flickered twice, and then it was gone.

At the center of the circle, five sapphire dots glowed in the mud, grouped tightly together. The rest of the circle was empty. "No one but us," Perrin said.

"How wide is the scope?" Dianthe asked.

"Two miles, possibly two and a half."

"That's definitive," Alaric said. "Anyone following us would likely be closer. At least, anything that's an immediate danger."

"I did see a light," Sienne said.

"No doubt, but it was likely a wisp," Dianthe said. "Those are harmful in large numbers, so we should watch out for them as long as we're in the forest."

"Let's march," Alaric said, slapping Button's rump.

8

S ienne's various aches increased for the first mile, then gradually
subsided. She already felt stronger, more capable of walking the
long miles, and she was able to look around and appreciate her
surroundings as she had not the previous day. True summer was not
yet advanced enough to have burned the forest pale, and the oak
leaves were a verdant, glossy green that smelled fresh and wet. They
slogged through the undergrowth, which was dewy and shed showers
of droplets wherever they trod. Squirrels skipped away from their
procession, waving their furry tails like banners that dipped and
swayed as they disappeared up tree trunks. Sienne followed the path
of one with her eyes as it ran across a branch that hung low over her
head. Its scampering movements reminded her of the voles that lived
in the field where she used to ride her horse, how they would dart
into their holes at a human's approach. She felt no anger or sorrow at
the memory.

Around mid-morning, they left the forest behind for wide, grassy
fields, the blades tall and tipped with white tassels. It was easier
going than the forest had been, but without the shade of the trees,
Sienne was soon sweaty and exhausted. She drank deeply from her

waterskin and thought about summoning water not just to refill it, but to drench her head against the terrible heat.

When Alaric called a stop for a noon meal, Sienne was more than ready to sit on the lumpy ground, cushioned by matted grass she tromped down in a circle, and eat salted meat and drink more delicious, chilled water. Cooling the contents of her waterskin was something to do against the monotony of the walk. She caught Alaric looking at her and smiled pleasantly. He had the look of someone contemplating a problem, and she had no intention of giving him the opportunity to patronize her or coddle her. She could keep up as well as anyone.

"I see now why the ruin we seek might yet contain a fortune," Perrin said. "No casual traveler would come this way, with neither inn nor tavern to provide shelter and sustenance. I mean no criticism, simply a comment on human nature."

"We take advantage of that every time we go out," Dianthe said. "That, and the fact that humanity's no longer clawing for survival. It's only been maybe sixty years that anyone could make a living as a scrapper. Sixty years out of four hundred...there are too many ruins for them all to be cleaned out already."

"How long have you been at it?" Perrin untied his hair and pushed it back from his face, retying it more securely.

"Alaric and I have been partners for eight years. Scrappers for six." Dianthe glanced at Kalanath, who had not sat, but remained standing, leaning on his staff. "What about you, Kalanath?"

"Two years," the young man said. "It was not on purpose."

It was the most he'd ever said about himself. "How so?" Sienne asked.

He scuffed the ground with his toe. His ankle boots were surprisingly clean for someone who'd walked as hard as anyone. "I do not come to Fioretti to fight," he said. "Only to work. I took work as a porter with scrapper teams. With a team of *chaitani*—it is not a word you have. It means, lovers of comfort. They travel with many horses, not light as we do, and many servants. But this does not protect them from attack. Werebears. I fought for my life and theirs, and they noticed." He smiled one of his rare smiles. "It is a truth that scrapper fighters make more money than porters. So I became a scrapper."

"Your skills are certainly legendary in Fioretti," Alaric said.

Kalanath shrugged. "When I am the only of my kind, I am legendary. There are many like me in Chirantan, in Omeira's capital city."

"Don't take this the wrong way, but I hope we don't need your skills," Dianthe said, rising. "I prefer the jobs where I don't have to fight."

"As you say," Kalanath said.

An hour or so after their noon rest stop, Sienne saw a dark smudge on the distant horizon. Another forest. She tried not to walk faster, to outpace the long-legged Alaric in her desire for the cool shade. Half an hour's walk brought them beneath its canopy, and Sienne sighed with pleasure. This one was denser than the last, with less undergrowth, and Sienne thought they were making good time.

She noticed the quiet about the same time Dianthe said, "Wait. Something's wrong."

Alaric halted and signaled the others to do the same. "What is it?"

"Don't know. But the birds have stopped singing."

Alaric drew his sword and held it loosely in one hand, a feat that impressed Sienne. "Everyone be on your guard. We may have a problem."

"Not humans," Sienne said. "Wouldn't we see humans?"

"No. Wild creatures. This is their home, and we're trespassers, which means some of them might take violent exception to our presence."

Sienne's heart beat faster. She fingered the outline of her spell-book under her vest. Alaric saw the movement, and his eyes narrowed. "You won't need that. Stay in the middle and you'll be safe."

Sienne nodded, but didn't stop touching the book. Alaric might be confident in his ability to kill or at least maim anything that attacked them, but Sienne didn't like the idea of waiting helplessly to be protected. Though she had no idea what she might do. She only knew one offensive spell, and it was a weak one, not fire nor ice nor even stone. She would have to think creatively, because if Alaric was wrong, she might need to defend herself or the others.

They moved more slowly now, watching carefully in all directions. Sienne, for her part, looked up as best she could, noticing that the others seemed not to be aware of this potential avenue for danger. There were no more squirrels. The birds, as Dianthe had pointed out, had stopped singing. Even the wind had died down, and the leaves were still. It felt as if the world were holding its breath.

Sienne became aware of patterns in the branches. They were like clouds that way, making pictures that changed as her position did. Only these were angular patterns, not soft and fluid like cloud pictures: stairs leading to nowhere, chairs without backs and tables missing legs, rooftops with cut-off chimneys. And faces, odd ones with too-short noses and too-long chins. It was funny how the human mind tended to turn any loose grouping of two dots and a line into eyes and mouth.

The eyes blinked. Then they dove.

Sienne screamed a warning and flung herself flat on the ground, scraping her cheek against the ground beneath the scrub grass. The thing landed on her back and grabbed her hair, pulling her head back painfully. It was about three feet tall and made of splintered wood, with leaves woven into its limbs and around the short stump it had for a head. Its claws tangled in her hair.

More of the creatures dropped out of the branches, leaping to attack. Sienne rolled over, groping for her spellbook. The thing let go with one hand and raised it to strike at her face, chittering viciously at her.

Silver flashed, and the thing shattered into a dozen pieces. Alaric stepped past Sienne, not offering to help her up. He thrust his massive sword and spitted two of the creatures at once. They squealed, but otherwise seemed not to notice, crawling up the blade they were impaled on and reaching for him. Alaric swung and sent them flying into a nearby tree.

They were everywhere, Sienne saw, at least twenty of them,

swarming toward their little group screaming in high-pitched voices like rabid squirrels. Dianthe had her slim sword out and was slashing valiantly at them. Kalanath spun his staff and flicked creature after creature out of the way. Neither of them seemed to be making progress. Kalanath's victims, in particular, shrugged off his blows. Perrin had his riffle of blessings out and snatched one free, holding it high and once more muttering under his breath. A dome of faint gray light sprang up around him, encircling all of them but Dianthe, trapped outside with her back to the dome.

"What are you doing?" Alaric shouted. He pounded on the dome, which gave slightly. Outside, two of the splinter creatures flung themselves at him and were repulsed by the gray light.

"I...she was too far away," Perrin stammered. "I didn't know. My apologies."

Alaric swore violently and swung his sword at the protective dome, again and again. Finally the light parted around his sword's blade, and he dove out, followed by Kalanath. Sienne gripped her spellbook with both hands and exchanged despairing looks with Perrin. She had to help. There must be *something* she could do.

She watched the other three fighting. Alaric's sword appeared to be doing the most damage; any creatures he sliced in half stayed down. Dianthe was chipping away at them, her smaller sword not capable of cutting them in two. Kalanath was mostly successful in batting the creatures away, or toward Alaric or Dianthe. They didn't have any vital organs that Sienne could tell, had no weaknesses except being extremely brittle—

Sienne gasped and shoved through the protective dome where Alaric had sliced it open. The gray light seemed to have driven the splinter creatures mad, because half of them flung themselves at it, scrabbling with their sharp clawed hands and peeling away thin, translucent strips of gray. The other half surrounded Alaric, Dianthe, and Kalanath. Sienne willed her spellbook open. *Break.* She'd never used it on anything so big, but it would work, she was certain.

She ran to where she had a clear view of the splinter creatures, braced herself, and read off the sweet syllables of the transform, not rushing though she desperately wanted to. She knew it took practically no time to cast, but it felt like forever as she stood there defenseless, watching her companions fight for their lives. As she read, she felt power building in the back of her throat, felt the words pushing themselves out of her, until the final sounds emerged as a shout that cracked like a whip across the space between.

Seven of the splinter creatures shattered, spraying shards of dry wood in every direction. Sienne heard Dianthe cry in pain and drop her sword, but she was already turning toward the dome to repeat the spell. Again, the creatures exploded, and this time Sienne was close enough to feel a fine spray of wooden splinters on her face and arms that stung like sand whipped by a windstorm. She wiped her face and raised the spellbook to try again, but the remaining creatures fled, diving into the branches and disappearing. Only the rustle of leaves moved by their passage showed where they'd gone.

Sienne found she was breathing as heavily as if she'd run a mile. She closed her book and looked around. Kalanath was leaning heavily on his staff. Perrin had emerged from the dome and was advancing toward Dianthe, who had her hands over her face. Blood streamed from beneath her fingers. Alaric, who had a long, deep gash along his arm, had his other arm around her and was trying to pry her fingers off her face. Sienne ran to them.

"It's not bad," Dianthe was saying. "No, don't touch it."

"Allow me," Perrin said, gently removing her hands. Sienne gasped. A two-inch splinter had driven into the flesh beside Dianthe's eye, making a bloody mask of her face. "I will have to remove the splinter before invoking the healing blessing."

"Be careful. Her eye—" Alaric said.

"I will be most gentle." Perrin reached up. His hand was shaking. Alaric grabbed it before he could touch Dianthe.

"I'll do it," he growled. "Don't close your eye."

Sienne winced as he plucked the splinter out, making the blood flow more freely. "I don't think there's anything else in there," Alaric said.

"Thank you," Perrin said. He tore off one of the blessings, one with a green smudge in the corner, and crushed it in his hand, muttering words too low to make out. His hand erupted with fire that burned brightly and then went out, leaving him untouched. Green-tinged light radiated from the wound for about a second, and then vanished. Dianthe blinked several times.

"I didn't feel anything," she said. "The last healing I had hurt like molten iron. What happened?"

"I know not, save that all avatars grant their blessings differently," Perrin said. "I think we should get you cleaned up. Alaric, you require healing as well."

"Let me—" Sienne began.

Alaric rounded on her. "That is *enough* 'help' from you," he shouted. "I told you to stay out of the fight!"

"But I—you were overwhelmed, I could see that!"

"We had everything under control. You nearly cost Dianthe her eye! You think blinding her was a good idea? That's not something an ordinary healing can fix!"

Sienne involuntarily stepped back from the looming figure. "It was an accident. And she wasn't blinded!"

"By sheer good luck. No thanks to you." Alaric took his waterskin from where it hung at his waist and lifted Dianthe's chin with his other hand. "Close your eyes."

"Alaric, I can do this myself," Dianthe said, taking the waterskin. "And you're being unfair. Sienne's spell routed those splinterfolk."

"It was nothing we weren't already doing." He wouldn't meet her eyes.

"That's not true. Kalanath couldn't hurt them, not with only a staff. My sword took too long to finish one off. And Perrin—"

"I offer my apologies for my carelessness," Perrin said, sounding not at all as carefree as he usually did. "I did not realize the limits of that blessing. I will be more careful in the future. And you, good sir, if you are to scold Sienne, I believe you should reserve a portion of your bile for me."

"I was useless," Kalanath said. "We were lucky."

Alaric swore and strode off toward the trees, sheathing his sword as he went. He kicked the remnants of the splinterfolk bodies, sending them flying. Sienne watched him, her hands shaking with anger and humiliation. Now that the fight was over, she could think of ways she might have used that spell without hurting her companions. If they'd all been behind the protective shield...if she'd warned them what she intended to do...it had been effective, yes, but she'd been careless. Alaric had overreacted, but he was right about that.

She stuffed her spellbook violently into her vest. Her first battle. She hoped someday she'd be able to forget it.

"Sienne." Dianthe stood at her elbow. Most of the blood was gone, and there wasn't a mark to show where the splinter had gone in. "Let's go."

Sienne nodded and once more took up her now-customary place at the middle of the group. Above, birds sang in the branches, but she couldn't find it in her to be happy about it. This had been a huge mistake. They weren't a real scrapper team. They were just five people who happened to have the same goal—maybe not even that, if she was right that Alaric wanted something other than the distance-viewing artifact out of this trip. Well, it didn't matter. She'd finish the task, cast the *fit* spell, go in, get out, and get back to Fioretti. And she'd never have to see these people again.

The forest dwindled as they walked northward until they were once again in open land. Now, however, instead of flat, grassy plains, low hills spread out as far as Sienne could see. The five trudged up and down the gentle slopes as the sun sank in the western sky and their shadows pointed eastward like sundial gnomons. Sienne's legs ached worse than they had the day before with all the up and down movement. She tried not to look at Alaric, which was difficult because he was enormous and right in front of her. The hilt of his sword bobbed over his right shoulder. She wished it would smack him in the head. He needed a good head-smacking, and she was too short to do it properly.

The spot Alaric chose for that night's camp looked no different from anywhere else, but it was at the bottom of a slope between hills and concealed from any prying eyes, or so Dianthe told Sienne.

"There's no water anywhere nearby," she added, "so we'll need your magic."

"Are you sure about that?" Sienne said bitterly.

"Sienne, he's just...we're protective of each other, and he has good reason to hate magic."

"That's irrational. Magic is as good or as bad as the wizard using it. It's not inherently evil."

"Still." Dianthe handed her the cook pot. "Try to feel some...I don't know. Compassion?"

Sienne glared at her. "Did you give *him* this lecture?"

"Yes, actually. His version had more swearing. And...thanks. In case nobody else said it. You really did save our lives."

Sienne turned away and set the pot on the ground, trying to hold onto her resentment as she summoned water. That was unfair. It wasn't Dianthe's fault. She lugged the pot over to the fire where Alaric crouched, laying on sticks Button had been carrying all afternoon, and set it over the flames without a word. Alaric ignored her. That was fine by her.

They found no fresh meat for the pot and had to make do with the dried stuff they'd eaten at noon, soaked in boiling water until it was almost tender. The rich broth it produced was salty, but delicious, and Sienne drank hers down and felt invigorated. She drank her fill of water, then produced a thin stream that poured into her waterskin until it was fat and sloshed pleasantly. Nobody paid any attention to this minor piece of magic. That, too, was fine by her.

"Sienne, you'll take first watch," Alaric said. He was staring at the fire, not looking at her, and she felt a moment's irritation that he couldn't even bring himself to address her directly. "Then Kalanath, me, Dianthe, and Perrin."

Nobody said anything. Alaric rubbed his face with one enormous hand. "Sienne," he said, startling her, "I owe you an apology. You made a decision that turned out to be the right one. The truth is, I failed to get us to act as a team, and I blamed myself, but I took it out on you. I'm sorry."

Sienne gaped. "I, uh, accept," she said. "But you were right, I was careless, and Dianthe—"

"Accidents happen," Dianthe said. "Once a fight begins, it can be over in a matter of minutes, sometimes seconds, and it's hard to keep track of the enemy, let alone four other people all trying to defeat them. But we could have been better coordinated."

"I do not know what I could have done differently," Kalanath said. "Not without a blade." He sounded very distant.

"There's a reason I wanted you along," Alaric said. "Every fight is different. Different strengths, different weaknesses. There will be fights in which swords are useless. The important thing is to recognize what else you can do that isn't a direct attack. You flung those splinterfolk in Dianthe's and my direction so we could destroy them, and those ones were too stunned to effectively fight back. And Perrin —that defensive shield was extremely effective. You just need practice in where to put it."

"Very true," Perrin said, sounding a little more cheerful than he had earlier. "I am afraid some of these blessings are ones I have never been granted before. But I will not always have the luxury of testing them before they are urgently needed. I will find ways around that."

"I was thinking," Sienne said, "if we'd all been behind the shield... I'm pretty sure I could cast that spell outside it, and we would have been protected from the blast."

"I can picture it," Alaric said. "What in Sisyletus's name was that? I didn't think—sorry—you were that experienced."

"I'm not. It's just a simple *break* spell. It really only works on fragile things, or things that are intended to break. It wouldn't damage your sword, or the cook pot, but those splinterfolk were made to shatter, I think. So it was luck that it worked so well."

"I'll take that kind of luck," Alaric said with a wry smile, and to her surprise, Sienne returned it.

"The truth is, we haven't been behaving like a team," Dianthe said. "We ought to understand each other's abilities and know how to work with them under pressure. This won't be the only challenge we face, even if the keep is unprotected."

"Is it?" Kalanath asked.

"It was when we were there before, scouting. But you never know what creatures might come calling." Dianthe stretched, and her back gave out a long string of staccato pops. "Kalanath, is there any reason you can't do your morning exercise where the rest of us can watch? To get a feel for your fighting style?"

Kalanath nodded. "It is not private. It is just easier to focus without a watcher. But I think you are right."

"I anticipate the show with great enthusiasm," Perrin said.

Kalanath reddened and ducked his head. "Is something amiss?" Perrin said.

"I do not understand your words many times," Kalanath said. "What is 'anticipate'?"

It was Perrin's turn to blush. "That had not occurred to me," he said. "You speak Fellic so well...it simply means to look forward to. Is that why you never speak to me?"

Kalanath shrugged. "I have little to say."

"Well, that can't be true," Dianthe said. "I don't want to pry, but you've had an interesting life, as a foreigner in Fioretti, and you've had two years' experience as a scrapper. Scrappers always have stories to tell."

"I choose not to speak of myself," Kalanath said. Then he sighed, and added, "But if we are to work together, we must know each other. It is simply not my way."

"Nobody's going to pester you for your secrets," Sienne said.

"As we all have secrets of our own, no doubt," Perrin said. He cast a quick look at Sienne that startled her with its calculated appraisal. Surely he didn't know *her* secret? He was Fiorettan, not Beneddan, and not noble...and Sienne wasn't an uncommon name...probably it was nothing.

"But trusting each other begins with understanding," Alaric said, "and Kalanath's right, we need to know each other."

"Just not tonight, all right?" Dianthe said. "I'm exhausted."

"Fair enough," said Perrin. "Good night to you all."

Sienne banked the fire while the others disappeared into their tents. She was bone-weary, but her mind was sharp and excited. Alaric had actually apologized to her. They'd all talked frankly about the battle—encounter? It hadn't seemed big enough to be called a battle. For the first time, she felt like part of a team.

A brisk wind had come up, and she rubbed her arms. Her shirt was thin enough to be comfortable during the day, but right now it didn't feel warm enough. She paced the outer perimeter of their camp and watched the stars in the cloudless sky, black and distant as the lidless eye of a serpent. She had studied astronomy during her fosterage at Stravanus, but with ready access to a little magic that let her find true north, she'd never needed to know more than the basics about the sky. She could identify constellations, though. There was the Sailor, just coming up over the eastern horizon behind the Lovers, and the Bull, poised to gore his neighbor the Queen of Stars.

The men's tent rustled, and a large form emerged. Sienne turned her back in case Alaric intended to relieve himself—there wasn't any privacy on the hills—but instead heard him approaching her. "You know when to wake Kalanath?" he said.

"I have a pocket watch."

"Good." He stood silent for a moment, and Sienne thought he might be watching the sky. "Try to sleep soundly. We'll reach our destination tomorrow afternoon."

"I will."

There was another long silence broken only by the hiss of the wind over the grass covering the hills. Finally, Alaric said, "I don't like how easy it is for wizards to cause untold harm with their magic. I've seen it happen—oh, it doesn't matter how often. Enough to make me wary. And you're enthusiastic about it—no, I'm sorry, I don't mean that as a criticism." He sighed. "I mean the possibilities for evil inherent in your magic don't seem to occur to you. That's dangerous."

"Isn't it a good thing, though? That I would never do evil with magic?"

"It only means you wouldn't *intentionally* do evil. If you aren't aware of the possibilities, you can't guard against them."

"I...think I understand. But I don't deserve to be blamed for other people's sins."

He laughed, a low, deep chuckle. "That's what Dianthe said. She's smarter than I am."

"You make a good team."

"We've had many years to get used to each other. This team will come together. It just takes time."

Sienne tried to see his face in the gloom, but the moonless night made even his fair skin dark and unreadable. "I didn't think you wanted a team. Not the kind where it matters if we come together."

Alaric was silent for a moment. "Maybe I was wrong about that."

She didn't know what to say. It had sounded too honest for her to challenge him on it, to point out that he had a policy of not working with wizards, that Kalanath never stayed with one team for very long, that Perrin was only sober because he'd run out of liquor. "Maybe," she managed.

Alaric clapped her on the shoulder briefly, a comradely gesture. "I am sorry for what I said to you," he said. "You'd be within your rights to belt me across the ear."

"If I thought you'd feel it, I would," she retorted, making him laugh.

She watched him return to his tent, then went back to pacing. He was nothing like she'd thought. Maybe they could be friends, after all. If she could be sure his change of heart was permanent.

She walked until she began feeling sleepy, then checked her pocket watch by the glimmer of a magic light. One of her teachers at Stravanus had had an artifact, a watch whose dial gleamed in the dark with a light that never faded. What a useful thing that would be. It was a pity no one today knew how to create magic artifacts. Of course, if they did, scrappers would have no purpose.

She put her watch away and woke Kalanath, then climbed into her bedroll and fell deeply asleep.

9

The next day's journey took them through the hills and up onto a grassy plateau, from which Sienne could see for miles. At their noon rest, she walked up a short rise and surveyed the landscape. The forests they'd left behind were dark smudges against the pale gold of the grasses. Far to the east lay other dark smudges, these barely visible as mountains. The Bramantus Range, dividing Rafellin from the eastern desert and Omeira.

"What do Omeirans call those mountains?" she asked Kalanath.

Kalanath looked where she was pointing. "Ikhshuvaan," he said. "Though each mountain has its own name. I do not know them. When I crossed them, I cared just that I did not die."

"They're dangerous?"

"Very steep. There are many...I do not know the word. Ditch? But very deep."

"Crevasse," Perrin said.

"And many creatures," Kalanath said with a nod, acknowledging Perrin. "Most of them not friendly."

"They're higher than the Pirinin Peaks in Ansorja," Alaric said. "Or so I've heard. The Pirinins are also dangerous."

"You must have crossed them, coming south," Sienne said.

Alaric frowned. For a moment, Sienne thought he wouldn't answer, and she wondered what had disturbed him. "I came south in the summer," he finally said. "In winter they're nearly impassable."

"They make a good natural border for Ansorja," Dianthe said, "just enough of a deterrence to make sure people who go there really want to."

"There's probably a lot of unexplored ruins, too," Sienne said.

"They can stay unexplored, as far as I'm concerned," Alaric said, his eyes grim. "Let's get moving. We'll be at the keep in a couple of hours."

Sienne felt rebuffed at his abruptness, but she shouldered her pack and fell into line behind him. Whatever had brought him south, through the hazards of the mountains and the Empty Lands, had been serious enough that he didn't want to discuss his past life. Well, she didn't want him to know her secrets, so she wouldn't pry into his.

She fell into a routine of trudging along with her eyes on the ground ahead of her, watching for anything that might trip her up. The alternative was looking at Alaric's back, which was familiar after two days of travel. He had shoulders like an ox, and the back of his neck was burned a reddish tan where it wasn't covered by his short hair. Watching him made her uncomfortable, so she went back to looking at the ground. The plateau was covered with short, fine grass like a dusty green carpet. Occasionally their passage disturbed a small animal, a mouse or a rabbit, that went bounding away into the distance, and she watched that until it disappeared.

The ruins, when they came upon them, were almost invisible. Sienne only realized they'd reached their destination when her foot came down on cracked stone rather than earth. The grasses had taken over there, too, growing up through the cracks in the flagstones and making odd humps where houses might once have been. Anything wooden was long gone.

She looked past Alaric and saw the large, irregular shape of a stone building some half a mile ahead. "That's it," Alaric said. He turned to Perrin. "You have another one of those scrying blessings?"

Perrin tore a scrap of paper free from the riffle of blessings. His morning prayers had been similar to those of the day before, though it seemed without alcohol he had more trouble getting Averran's attention. The unused blessings from the previous day had burned to nothing, prompting Dianthe to say, "It seems like such a waste, when you went to all the trouble of petitioning for them."

"Each day is a fresh start," Perrin had said, "and Averran, at least, dislikes looking to the past. And as his blessings are in part a promise of what is to come, it is better not to hold on to a past that did not come to fruition."

Now he scuffed the surface of a large flagstone with his toe and knelt to draw a circle with one of the pastels in the packet he carried. Once again, a blue light filled the lopsided circle, and the blessing flared to ash. When the blue light faded, five glowing specks clustered at the center of the circle. "No one," Perrin said. "But I should caution you that the limit of this blessing means we cannot know for certain that we have not been followed."

Alaric adjusted his sword. "We'll keep that in mind. Let's move on."

Sienne kept a careful eye on her surroundings. The humps of former buildings were too low to obscure her vision, and she could easily see to the horizon, but the place unnerved her. Possibly it was the knowledge that the people who had lived here had had lives so unlike her own she could barely imagine them. The wars that had torn the world apart four hundred years ago had destroyed almost every vestige of that civilization, erasing knowledge both magical and mundane. The one thing everyone was certain of was that the ancients had used magic for *everything*. Cooking, cleaning, fighting, even travel. Stravanus was an isolated dukedom, but even there Sienne had heard of the carriage that moved without horses, a rare find by a lucky scrapper team. They'd sold it to the duchess of Marisse, who'd made a present of it to the king. Sienne had occasionally daydreamed about finding something as extraordinary as that.

Alaric cursed, and Sienne stopped, pulling out her spellbook. "What?" Perrin asked.

"That's fresh," Alaric said, pointing at one of the humps. Unlike the others, its smooth green sides were torn open, revealing black earth and dirt-covered stones. "Someone's been here recently."

"They are not here now," Kalanath said.

"And it's unlikely they found anything," Dianthe said. "If they were still here, the scrying would have revealed them."

"True." Alaric turned to look in all directions, his head held stiffly alert like the world's biggest pointer hound. "We should move quickly."

They hurried, not quite running on the uneven terrain, until they neared the stone structure. Sienne slowed to look at it, trying to picture what it had looked like when it was intact. It had once been surrounded by a stone wall, remnants of which still lay here and there, enough to mark out its outline. Beyond the wall, the fortress rose two broken stories into the air, its dark gray stones weathered from centuries of neglect. The wind chose that moment to pick up, threading through the gaps in the fortress wall and making a whistling sound that rose and fell in pitch like a wailing lover. Sienne shivered. It was the kind of place ghosts would love. *No such thing as ghosts*, she told herself, and followed the others around the side of the fortress.

The wall to the right had a huge gap where a door should have been. Like the rest of the town, the wood had long since rotted or been weathered away. Dianthe took the lead and waved the others to stay back. "Checking for any surprises," Alaric said.

"Hasn't this place been thoroughly searched?" Sienne said. "What surprises could there possibly be?"

"If other scrappers have been here since we last visited, they might have left traps for people like us." Alaric took up a resting position Sienne tried to mimic. It looked comfortable, something a person might maintain easily for hours. "Stupid, really, because it tells other scrappers there's something worth guarding. But that's cold comfort if you're crushed by a rock someone rigged to fall."

Dianthe was waving to them. Alaric nodded, and they proceeded through the gap into what had been the fortress's courtyard.

The grass hadn't taken quite as much control here as in the rest of the town. Enormous flagstones made of some material Sienne didn't recognize fit so closely together there was barely room for blades of grass to squeeze between. She knelt to touch the stones, which were rough like coarse sandpaper. "I wonder why these have lasted when the others didn't?"

Kalanath scraped the steel-shod end of his staff across one. "They feel different."

"I bet someone in the city would pay for these."

Alaric glanced back at her. "The transport would be far too expensive."

"Not if you could shrink them. A *fit* spell would make them pocket-sized."

"Huh," Dianthe said. "But you don't know it."

"No."

"Something to consider for another time," Alaric said. "We need to worry about getting into the keep."

One look told Sienne why Alaric and Dianthe had been so sure no one had gotten into it. The front of the keep was caved in, as if someone with a battering ram the size of a mountain had gone to work on it. The rest sagged alarmingly at the back. The ruins of two towers stood ominous watch over two corners of what was left of the keep; their mates at the other corners were nothing but piles of shattered stone. One wall had crumbled, leaving a hole big enough to climb through. "That cannot be our method of ingress," Perrin said. "Surely anyone might have entered there."

"It's why we're sure the rest hasn't been breached," Dianthe said. "That's the obvious way in, but it leads only to a dead end. It was stripped clean years ago."

"What about the tower?" Sienne said, pointing at the one at the left rear corner, on the northwest. "It's mostly intact. Couldn't someone have gone in that way? Flying, possibly?"

"They have," Alaric said. "They reported the interior blocked. And none of us can fly—" He paused, and Sienne shook her head. "No, where we want to go is around back."

Sienne followed him, carefully picking her way across the rubble.

The back of the keep, which was about eighty feet long, wasn't as destroyed as the front. It was still a wreck. Worse, it looked as if it might come down if she breathed on it the wrong way. "I don't see anything."

Alaric walked over to one of the larger pieces of rubble, a man-sized stone of green-streaked granite. He squatted, got his arms around it, and heaved it out of the way, revealing a three-foot-tall hole leading deep within the collapsed building, narrow enough that anyone entering would have to sidle through to pass. "Clearing away any more of the stones will collapse the roof, or whatever it is that's holding the thing up," he said. "It's stable for now."

Sienne passed him and knelt by the hole. It smelled of dust and dampness but not, she was relieved to discover, of animals. "How long will we be inside?"

"A few hours," Alaric said.

"We should be all right, then." She stood and opened her spellbook to the *fit* spell. "I'll have to cast it five times, so be patient. I don't think any of us should go in there alone."

She had only cast *fit* a few times before, and then only as a joke she'd played on a fellow student. Now she let the words spill out of her as she focused on Dianthe. *Fit* was a true magical transformation, not one that conserved mass the way a were-creature's did, so there were never any worries about finding clothes in the right size or getting hugely fat or skinny. Dianthe's eyes widened as the transformation took effect. One moment, she was eye to eye with Sienne, and the next she was a little over two feet tall and staring up at her in astonishment. "This is so strange," she said, her voice squeaky. She drew her sword, which was now less than a foot long. "It altered everything."

"Kalanath, you're next," Sienne said.

"It should be me," Alaric said.

"You're going to be last except for me. I'm not sure how small the spell will make you, and it may be...complicated."

Alaric's lips thinned in displeasure, but he only nodded.

First Kalanath, then Perrin underwent the transformation, both of them exclaiming in surprise. Sienne had never had it cast on her and didn't know how it felt, though she assumed if it were painful, their exclamations would be different.

She turned to Alaric, who had his arms crossed over his chest. "You may still need to duck," she said.

"Just do it," Alaric said, his voice gruff and impatient. To her surprise, Sienne realized he was afraid. She'd known he hated magic, but fear was unexpected and out of character—at least, out of what she'd interpreted his character to be. She wished she could reassure him, but that would only embarrass him. She read off the spell as quickly as she dared without ruining it. The taste of honey had turned cloying after four castings. Alaric gasped, and then he was barely three feet tall and breathing as heavily as if he'd been running.

"Is it enough?" Sienne asked.

Alaric walked to the hole and touched its roof. "Barely," he said. Sienne bit back a giggle at how his normally deep, booming voice was suddenly an octave higher.

"Good, because if I had to cast it again, you'd be *really* short," she said. "Give me a minute." She closed her eyes and spat out the sweetness. She felt only a little unbalanced, which meant she hadn't tapped her reserves deeply yet. If she had to do many more of those, she'd start to feel the effects, which were similar to illness—body aches, vomiting, dizziness. If she had to do a *lot* more of them, she'd eventually lose consciousness. Fortunately, she was unlikely to need to.

She read the spell a final time, focusing on herself. Nausea swept over her, followed by the feeling of falling, and then everything looked different. Her companions were back to being the right size, but the keep was suddenly much taller, and the hole looked the right size to walk through. She juggled her spellbook, which was the only thing she was carrying that hadn't shrunk. It was now the size of her torso and felt much heavier. She tucked it under her arm and hooked the bottom edge over her hip, like carrying a toddler.

"We take this slowly," Alaric said. "Dianthe goes first, to look for any pitfalls or traps. I back her up. Then Sienne and Perrin, you stay

in the middle. Perrin, you should be as close to the actual middle of
the group as you can, so the defensive blessing will cover all of us if
you have to invoke it. Kalanath, you bring up the rear. Keep your eyes
open for anything that might come up behind us. Any questions?"
His voice was back to being booming and deep again.

Sienne shook her head. Alaric nodded at Dianthe. "Sienne, could
I have a light, please?" Dianthe said. Sienne glanced at Alaric, who
was expressionless. She summoned a pale light and set it to bobbing
above Dianthe's left shoulder. Dianthe cracked her neck, a swift
movement to each side, then walked forward.

Sienne waited for Alaric to squeeze through the hole, then
followed him, sucking in her breath in a futile attempt to make
herself thinner. It wasn't as tight a fit as she'd feared, not nearly so
tight as it was for Alaric, whom she could hear breathing heavily and
scraping along the stones. She prayed his passage wouldn't disrupt
anything and bring the roof crashing down atop them. The smell of
old stone filled her nostrils, and she breathed shallowly, hoping not
to sneeze. Then, like pulling the cork from a wine bottle, she was
through and gasping for breath.

The hole led not to a room, but to a sort of triangular tunnel
formed by fallen stones and beams protected from the elements. No.
Sienne brushed her fingers across one of them; they looked and felt
slightly greasy. Protected by an invulnerability spell. Invulnerability
didn't work on wood more than about half an inch thick, or so she'd
thought. It brought home the existence of the ancients more than did
a moldering old keep that could as easily have been two hundred
years old as four. No wonder the roof hadn't fully caved in. The
beams could be dislodged or even pulled out of their foundations,
but not broken.

Alaric's broad back blocked most of the light from Sienne's
magic, so for her the tunnel was lit only by the scraps of daylight
coming through the hole. That faded quickly as they proceeded,
until Sienne was walking virtually blind. She resisted the urge to
take the hem of Alaric's shirt for guidance and summoned another
light. It cast wan shadows over the triangular space, with the wall of

the keep on her left and the fallen remnants of half the roof on her right. The dirt she kicked up as she walked smelled not of fresh, fertile loam, but of dead things, of a place that had lain dormant and sterile for centuries. It made her feel frightened as the darkness had not, and she tried to breathe shallowly, fearing irrationally what might happen to her if she breathed in too much of the dead soil.

Soon Alaric, who was walking bent over, stopped, and Sienne nearly ran into him. "Door," he said over his shoulder. Sienne peered past him and saw Dianthe on her tiptoes peering into a lock slightly above her eye level.

"This may be a problem," she said. "My lock picks shrank with me. I should have set them aside before you performed the spell." She drew out a roll of soft suede and unrolled it, revealing a number of slim silvery rods and hooks. "On the other hand, I might be able to fit my fingers inside the lock."

"My mother always told me never to put my hands anywhere I wouldn't put my nose," Perrin said. "I never understood that saying."

Dianthe smiled and inserted a metal rod into the lock, twisting it to one side so a second rod could fit beside it. It bent alarmingly, and Dianthe swore, removed the first rod, and stuck her finger in its place. After a few moments of jiggling, there was a grinding clank, and Dianthe pulled her finger and the rod out and pressed down on the door handle. "That's just unnatural," she said.

"Just so we're inside," said Alaric.

Beyond the door lay a kitchen that in Sienne's current size looked cavernous, the ceiling high enough to be beyond the reach of her magic light. One corner of the room was collapsed on itself, with a broken table rotted nearly to sludge under a fall of stone that blocked most of a doorway. An iron stove, pitted and orange with rust, took up half the opposite wall. Another door, this one untouched, stood dark and forbidding directly opposite them. It was black with age and its iron hinges, unlike the stove, were grimy but not rusted. The entire room smelled sharp with rust and decay.

Alaric stood with his hands on his hips surveying the stove. "We need to find a way up," he said. "There's at least one intact section of roof, and the distance viewer should be up there."

"Well, there's the door," said Dianthe, pointing.

Perrin, who was standing beside the door, touched it. "The wood is weak," he said. "Punky, I believe is the word."

"Let's see if the frame is solid," Alaric said. Sienne watched as the three men felt along the arched stone of the doorway. She directed her light to give them more illumination and looked around the room. Something gleamed beneath the broken table. Curious, she crossed the room and knelt beside it.

"Sienne, what are you doing?" Dianthe said, sounding alarmed.

"Just exploring." Whatever it was had a coppery sheen to it. She worked her fingers under the rubble and felt something soft and damp surrounding what felt like metal chips. Cringing, she pulled out her find. A coin, impressed with a sheaf of wheat on one side and the profile of a woman on the other. She showed it to Dianthe, who'd joined her. "I think there are more. But they're just copper."

"Yes, but in excellent shape. There's high demand for ancient coins regardless of metal." Dianthe held out her hands as Sienne pulled five more coins out of the rubble.

"We need to move on," Alaric said, coming up behind them. "This spell won't last forever."

"It will last for six hours," Sienne said.

"Look what Sienne found." Dianthe displayed the coins. Alaric picked one up and examined it.

"Very nice," he said. "A little salvage, at any rate."

Once again Sienne felt warmed by his approval and had to remind herself that his good opinion wasn't any more important than anyone else's. She might not hate him, but she certainly wasn't going to idolize him.

Dianthe handed the coins to Sienne. "Your find, you hold onto it," she said.

Sienne put the coins into her bag and followed Dianthe to the door. The wood was indeed punky, and the men had opened the door by way of simply breaking off chunks of wood until only bits of it hung from the black metal hinges. Dianthe stepped through, Sienne's light bobbing along after her.

The vastness of the empty space beyond the door swallowed up the tiny magic light. Dust and debris covered the stone floor, made of the same material as the flagstones outside. Sienne gaped at the ceiling, which looked like a night sky, complete with bright stars. It took her a moment to realize the light specks were gaps in the collapsed ceiling through which sunlight shone. It would have been enormous even had she been her correct size.

Perrin and Kalanath had drifted past her toward the fall of beams and slates that was the wrecked front of the room. "It is like a tomb," Kalanath said, his voice hushed.

"I notice there are no cobwebs," Perrin said. "If even the spiders dare not live here..."

"It's just an old ruin," Alaric said. "Don't let it get to you. Sienne, we need more light."

Sienne created a few more lights so each of them had one hovering near their ear. Alaric gestured. "It's this door," he said. "We'll see how accessible that tower really is, then go from there."

The door in question was heavy oak banded with iron, its hinges rusted and its doorknob fallen off. It was unlocked and made to open inward, inconveniently given the lack of handle. Alaric wedged one finger in the hole left by the missing knob and pulled. The door swung open, and a groaning creak echoed through the room. Everyone froze, looking up at the ceiling. It groaned again, then was still. No one moved. Finally, Dianthe said in a low voice that wasn't quite a whisper, "Move carefully," and went through the doorway.

This room was much smaller and, to Sienne's relief, had an intact ceiling. Rotted leather covered a collapsed chair behind a table whose contents Sienne was currently too short to see. Empty lantern cages rusted quietly on every wall. The faint wind generated by their entry made the remnants of tapestries hanging on the walls shift, sending up eerie shadows when the magic light fell upon them. What might once have been a carpet had turned black over the centuries.

The thought that she might be the first to tread this carpet in four hundred years left Sienne breathless.

Alaric gestured to Dianthe, knelt, and cupped his hands together near the floor. Dianthe stepped into his cupped hands and balanced effortlessly as he lifted her to look at the table. "Nothing," she said. Alaric lowered her to the floor and dusted off his hands. "Looks like there might have been something once."

Alaric looked grim. "That could mean the tower was accessible, after all."

"Let's keep looking," Sienne said. The reality of being in the keep had finally sunk in. Despite what Alaric and Dianthe had said about the place being cleaned out, she couldn't help imagining what it would be like to find something remarkable. She'd found the coins, hadn't she? Which meant there might be other overlooked things.

There was another door, much smaller, adjacent to the one they'd entered by. Dianthe opened it easily. "Damn," she said, stepping aside for the others. "It's clear."

Sienne followed Alaric and Perrin through to a narrow, cramped space filled with broken stones and splintered wooden boards. A progression of holes wound its way up the stony sides of what had to be the northwest tower. Chunks of wood sticking out from some of those holes told her they had once been stairs, and when she peered up into the dimness, she saw intact steps circling the tower's interior, starting about eight feet up. A square of light brightened, then dimmed, then brightened again the way a door slowly opening and closing with the wind might do.

"That's it," Dianthe said. "We're too late."

10

"We cannot be certain of that," Perrin said. He tilted his head far back to look at the tower's nearly invisible roof. "Just because it is possible for a wizard to fly does not mean one gained access to the keep that way. We should not give up."

"Alaric?" Dianthe said.

The big man was staring at the steps, which would have been well above his head even if he had been his normal size. "No," he said, "no, we shouldn't give up. If someone had found the distance viewer, Master Fontanna would have heard about it. So either it's not there to find, or no one's found it, and either way, we need to continue the search. Which means getting into one of the other towers." He turned around and left the room.

Back in what was left of the keep's great hall, Alaric said, "Spread out. Let's see what other doors we can find."

Sienne trailed after Kalanath, who moved with swift confidence to the far side of the hall. "There is one here," he announced.

"And another here," said Dianthe.

Alaric paced the perimeter of the room. "Neither of those leads directly to the other intact—mostly intact—tower. Let's see which is more accessible."

One of the doors was locked. "Give me a minute," Dianthe said. "Damn, but I wish I had a box to stand on."

Sienne watched her go to work on the lock, adding her light to Dianthe's, though it didn't seem lock picking depended much on light. Dianthe said, "Still glad you came along?"

"This is so exciting!" Sienne said. Dianthe laughed.

The others came to join them. "It was another kitchen," Perrin said, "and the blocked door in the first presumably led to the pantry that lies between them."

There was a soft click. "Let's see about this one," Dianthe said, pushing the ancient door open.

The room beyond was totally bare, without even the remnants of furniture. Another door across from the first hung slightly ajar. Something about the room struck Sienne as odd, but she didn't realize what until Alaric said, "No dust."

Perrin scuffed his toe across the floor, which unlike the great hall was made of heavy, well-smoothed flagstones that were, in fact, free from dust. "What do you suppose it means?"

A deep creak sounded from somewhere high above, making them all go still. "I have no idea," Alaric said, "but I think that other door leads to the tower. Let's find out."

He was right. This time, the stairs were intact, though a few of them had rotted out of their sockets. "Can we climb that?" Sienne asked.

Alaric settled his sword more securely across his shoulders. "We'll have to crawl, but none of the gaps seem too wide. It's a good thing we're small, because I wouldn't trust my full weight to any of those. Be careful, and make sure only one of us is on a given step at a time. I'll go first."

Sienne ended up nearly at the rear of the procession, with only Kalanath behind her. Once Alaric, Dianthe, and Perrin had clambered up, she put her hands on the first step and hauled herself up. The treads were too far apart for her now-short legs to stretch, but not so far that she couldn't use her hands to boost herself high enough for her knee to reach the next one. The wood felt soft and splintery under her hands, not quite damp, but unpleasantly moist. She gritted her teeth and kept climbing, carefully not looking down even to see how Kalanath was doing. She heard Perrin's heavy breathing ahead of her and the scrape of Kalanath's staff across the stones of the wall. How far had they come? A full story? The ceiling of the great hall had been so high up...but it might have risen the full two stories, if it was like the one in her childhood home.

She dragged herself up another step and realized she was at the top, or at least had reached a landing. She stood and moved out of Kalanath's way, looking around curiously. The stairs continued some distance up before—Sienne swallowed and looked away. The roof of this tower had partially collapsed and looked close to completing the job. If it had come down on them while they climbed...! She reminded herself that it had been in the process of collapsing for a long time, and it was unlikely it would choose to collapse further just because they'd arrived.

Dianthe had her arms stretched out above her head, unlocking a door to one side of the landing. "I think we've come high enough that we've bypassed the broken stairs in the other tower," Alaric said as Kalanath came to join them. "We're going to see if we can make our way across to it."

The door creaked open. "Good news," Dianthe said. "It occurred to me that if anyone had come through here, these doors wouldn't be locked."

"That is good news," Kalanath said. "But we still have seen nothing worth taking."

"Patience," Alaric said.

The long, low-ceilinged room they entered next was untouched by the elements—and occupied.

Sienne gasped. Alaric put himself between her and the enemy, then stopped and gave an embarrassed laugh. "Mannequins," he said.

The wood and cloth mannequins looked much as they must have four hundred years before, the sealed room preserving them against the elements. All but a few were bare, and those few held pieces of leather armor as if patiently waiting for their owners to claim them. Alaric examined one. "These could be worth something to the right buyer," he said, "if we could get them out of here."

Frustrated, Sienne said, "I know what spell I'm trading for as soon as we get back to Fioretti."

The others laughed. "It's not important," Dianthe said. "We'll make far more if we find the distance viewer and get it to Master Fontanna."

Across the room, Kalanath rapped on another door. "This one sounds rotten."

"Another good sign no one's been here," Dianthe said, pulling out her lock picks again.

The door led, as Alaric had surmised, to the northwest tower. "It looks like the stairs go all the way to the tower roof," he said. "Time to climb."

Once more Sienne ended up near the back. This close to the tower's open top, she smelled the sweet odors of fresh grass and sunlight carried by the wind that blew constantly around the tower. It heartened her, reminding her that this dead keep wasn't all there was to life. When she reached the flat top of the tower, she took a few steps out of Kalanath's way and went to look over the short wall surrounding the tower's perimeter—short by normal standards; in her current state she had to pull herself up on the stones to look out. It was a marvelous view, all the way back to the plateau's edge.

"Sienne. Take a look around," Dianthe said. Sienne turned and saw the others scanning the rooftop and the collapsed roof of the main keep. Wall-walks extended out from two sides of the tower, one terminating abruptly about three feet toward the destroyed southwest tower, the other going all the way to the northeast tower they'd climbed up to the second story by. Sienne walked in that direction. The sun had gone behind some high clouds, dimming its light enough that Sienne could see without squinting. The northeast tower was definitely impassable, half of it collapsed inward so the remaining top of the tower looked like a cake someone had taken an enormous bite out of.

A gap in the clouds lit the keep briefly. Sienne gasped. "There's something over there," she said. "Something metal."

Dianthe came to stand at her shoulder. "Where?"

The clouds covered the sun again. "Near where the stones crumbled, on the far side—the east side."

"What did it look like?" Alaric said.

"It didn't look like anything. But I was thinking of the coins I found, so light on metal is what I was looking for. It—"

Another break in the clouds made something gleam dull silver. This time, they all saw it. "Dianthe," Alaric said.

"I'll be right back," Dianthe said, and started off across the wall-walk.

Sienne held her breath until she felt dizzy. The wall-walk did not look safe. It was open on one side, toward the collapsed center of the keep, and even though Dianthe was shorter than the outer wall, that wall had huge gaps where enough stones had fallen over the years to make it look like lacework. Dianthe moved lightly, like a dancer leaping from stone to stone across a rushing river. Then her foot came down on a loose stone, and she slipped, sliding toward the open edge.

Sienne clenched her teeth on a cry, afraid of disturbing Dianthe's concentration. Dianthe pushed off from the falling stone and flipped backward, landing neatly on the wall's edge, then bounded forward to safety as the second stone rocked and fell three stories to the ground. Sienne's fingernails were cutting crescents into her palms. She forced her hands open and let out a deep breath.

Dianthe stepped onto the northeastern tower's flat top and hesitated. "It's really insecure," she said. "Wait there while I investigate this."

Alaric was poised on the balls of his feet, his eagerness to cross the gap palpable. Dianthe edged closer to the crumbling stone, crouched, and crawled the last few feet. She picked up a few loose stones and tossed them past the broken edge of the tower, then swept something away with the palm of her hand. "I don't know what it is, but it's metal, and it's big. It could be the distance viewer. I can't imagine anything else they'd keep at the top of these towers."

"I'm coming over," Alaric said.

"You're too heavy. Kalanath and Sienne can come. One at a time."

Kalanath looked at Sienne and inclined his head, indicating that she should go first. Sienne set her spellbook down in a secure place and tried to ignore how her fingers were shaking. She swallowed her nervousness and edged out onto the wall-walk. It helped that she was too short to see over the outer wall to the three-story drop just inches from where she trod. Unfortunately, that meant she was perfectly capable of seeing the collapsed slanting roof of the keep, studded with beams jutting skyward and cracked stone perched precariously on other stones.

She kept her eyes on her feet, looking for loose stones and debris that could trip her. The wall-walk was about three feet wide, but bits of it were missing, giving its inner edge a jagged appearance. Between that, and the shaky outer wall, the available walking space narrowed to just under a foot wide. It felt much narrower, like walking a rope strung between the towers. At least it didn't sway in the wind.

She tried to think of other things, like what she would do when she returned to Fioretti as a successful scrapper. She'd have money to support herself while she found another job, and this time she'd have a reputation—surely Alaric and Dianthe would say good things about her? The idea left her feeling hollow, and she wasn't sure why. It was a bad idea to get attached to her current companions, since Alaric had made it clear this was a temporary commitment. Even so... no, it was just sentimentality talking. This was her first experience as a scrapper, so of course she thought of it fondly. Except that wasn't true, was it? She'd started out—

Someone grabbed her arm. "Careful," Dianthe said. "It gets slippery past here."

Sienne looked over her shoulder. Perrin looked like he was praying. She wondered if it was the kind of prayer that might receive divine intervention, and if so, what kind. Alaric's face was set like a statue, unmoving, but even at this distance she could tell he was willing them to be careful.

Kalanath was about two-thirds of the way across and using his staff to balance, exactly as if he felt it was a tightrope, too. He had his eyes closed, but his face was relaxed, not at all afraid. When he stepped onto the tower, he opened his eyes and blinked twice. "I did not think I would do that ever again," he said. "I am glad I still can."

Sienne wanted to ask him what he meant, but Dianthe said, "Take a look. It's embedded in the rock fall—the wall collapsed on it. We can dig it out, but we have to be careful not to collapse the wall further." She had brushed away the loose scree that concealed the object, and more of it was visible: about a hand's breadth of dull silver, scoured to a matte finish by the elements.

"If we lie flat, we will not be so heavy," Kalanath said.

Dianthe nodded and got to her knees, then prostrated herself like a worshipper of Lisiel coming before the avatar in her temple, her hands flat to show they were empty. She scooted forward to the edge of the pile of rubble. Kalanath followed suit. Sienne knelt, and said, "There's not enough room for all three of us."

"I'll scoot over," Dianthe said.

"No, don't. It might not support our weight." Sienne sat back on her haunches. "I can lift the lighter stones from here."

"Lift—you mean, by magic?"

Sienne nodded. A fist-sized stone drifted off the top of the pile and floated far out past the intact side of the tower, then dropped. Moments later they heard the thud of stone striking bare earth. "They can't be very heavy. I can only lift weights of about six and a half pounds. But it's something."

"Perfect. Let's do it."

After a minute or so of getting in each other's way, they fell into a rhythm. Kalanath had a sense for which stones needed to be moved, and he directed Dianthe and Sienne's efforts, pointing with the tip of his staff at each stone. Sienne sat cross-legged behind the other two and fell into the meditative state that made working low-level magic easy to do for long periods of time. She started flinging the stones away, far from the walls so they wouldn't land on anything and destabilize it further. Part of her wondered if she might not hit a creature, but she reminded herself they had seen hardly anything living and kept on doing it, enjoying the feel of releasing the stones to fly far.

Gradually, the thing became visible. When Alaric and Dianthe had talked about a distance viewer, Sienne had pictured a telescope, only one studded with semiprecious gemstones that gleamed with magical light. This was more of a flat box, about three feet long and half as wide, with no visible seam, and heavily dented. Possibly the distance viewer was inside? Sienne heaved another stone free and reached for one more. "I'm surprised no one who could fly found this before."

"I bet it was more thoroughly concealed five years ago, when everybody and their dog was out here sniffing around," Dianthe said. "Wait. That's enough." She carefully took hold of the box and rocked it free of the remaining stones. One fell rattling to the tower roof, and they froze, waiting for another collapse. But nothing happened. "Back across," Dianthe said in a low voice, as if she feared a loud noise would bring the tower down around their ears.

Sienne waited for Kalanath to cross before making her halting way back along the wall-walk. It was hard to move carefully when she wanted to run and skip with excitement. It felt like forever before she stood beside Alaric again. He had his gaze fixed on Dianthe, who was using the box for balance as Kalanath had his staff. "Come on, come on," he murmured under his breath. Sienne was certain he didn't know he was doing it.

Dianthe handed the box to him before stepping off the wall-walk and letting out a deep breath. "I could use a stiff drink right about now," she said.

"As could I," Perrin said, "though as I did nothing but watch and petition Averran for your safety, my need is rather less pressing than yours, I imagine."

Alaric ran his fingers along the sides of the box. "This could be anything," he said. He closed his eyes and brushed the smooth, flat surface. "I don't want to go back to Master Fontanna with something that turns out not to be what he—" A smile spread across his face. "Hah," he said, pressing down with his index and middle finger on a blank spot near the center of what might have been the box's top.

A chime of two notes like birdsong rang out, and the top of the box opened like an iris, revealing a sheet of gold and two silver styli on either side of it. Amber light flickered along the perimeter of the gold sheet, clear and bright one minute, dark the next.

"Is that...it?" Kalanath breathed.

"It's what he described. When it's activated, the gold sheet shows a picture of whatever another distance viewer sees," Dianthe said. "And it's still mostly working. By Kitane's eyes, this is an incredible find."

Alaric shifted the awkward load and felt around its edges. "There should be...there it is," he said, and the iris closed, returning once again to a blank, flat silver surface.

"We found it!" Sienne exclaimed.

Alaric and Dianthe exchanged an unreadable glance. "That we did," Alaric said. "But I think we'll make sure we're not leaving anything else behind."

"You said nothing else of value was here," Kalanath said.

"I said *probably* nothing. It doesn't hurt to look around. Those doors were locked, after all." He set the box down and removed a coil of rope from around his waist. "I'll tie the box to my back so we can get it down those stairs."

Sienne watched silently as Alaric and Dianthe secured the box. There was definitely something they were keeping secret, but what? It made sense to explore the keep, just in case. Not knowing the *fit* spell for objects annoyed her. Carrying the armor out was impractical even if they hadn't been two feet tall. The same might be said for anything they found. So why weren't Alaric and Dianthe satisfied with what they'd come seeking?

Climbing down from the tower was far more terrifying than climbing up had been, if only because Sienne had to look down at the bottom, covered in rubble. She could imagine how much it would hurt if she fell, though it was far enough that she likely wouldn't feel pain for long, because she'd die shortly thereafter. When she reached the second story landing, she was shaking, and had to take a moment to calm herself. Perrin noticed, and put a hand on her shoulder. "Almost done," he said quietly. Sienne nodded.

There was a third door in the armory, not locked, that led to the remains of a gallery overlooking the great hall. They followed it as far as they could in both directions, but found only one other door, so blocked by stone and crumbling wooden beams it was impossible for them to break through. "It's probably whatever's on the other side of that hole in the wall we saw," Dianthe said. "Not worth worrying about."

They clambered down the last flight of stairs in the northeastern tower, barely averting disaster when a stair Perrin had just put his weight on snapped and forced him to cling to the one above, panting and swearing. When he reached the ground, he was as pale as a Rafellish ever got, and sweating visibly. "Averran is accustomed to hearing his name taken in vain," he said, panting, "but I believe no priest of his has ever been so creative in his profanity as I was just now. I think I will avoid stairs in the future."

"How much time before the shrinking spell wears off?" Alaric asked.

Sienne consulted her pocket watch and discovered it had stopped running. She'd forgotten *fit* could have that effect on machinery. "I think another two, maybe two and a half hours," she said. "But if it does before we leave, I can just cast it again to get us out."

"Let's try to be done before that happens," Alaric said.

"But are we not done?" Kalanath said. "We have seen all there is on this bottom floor."

"Maybe," Alaric said. "I want to look at that empty room again."

It wasn't any less empty the second time, but it was darker. Sienne realized the magic lights were fading and summoned more of them. Now the room was as bright as a full moon, and still completely empty. Alaric and Dianthe circled it, probing the walls with their fingertips. "What is it you seek?" Perrin said.

"Nothing," Alaric said, too quickly.

It irritated Sienne. "If you tell us, we can help," she said. "Or is it a secret?"

"I'm not looking for anything in particular," Alaric said. "Just... this room is mysterious, don't you think? So...secret doors, trap doors, anything like that."

Kalanath tapped the floor in a sweeping pattern, listening for an echo. "This is not about your quest?"

Alaric stopped. "What quest?"

Kalanath shrugged. "It is not a secret. Mad Alaric Ham-fist looks for lost knowledge. Impossible knowledge. I was told this when I said I would join you."

Alaric's hand closed into a fist. "So why are you here?"

He shrugged again. "Rumor is the bastard child of lies. I do not care for it."

Sienne stared at Alaric. "Lost knowledge?" she said.

Alaric grunted and went back to searching the walls. "Don't worry about it. I'm mad, remember? And this whole search is for nothing. Just stand there until I prove I'm insane for looking for things that don't exist."

"I can hardly think you're mad if I don't know what you're searching for. What's wrong with wanting to find lost knowledge?"

Alaric stopped again and threw his head back, closing his eyes as if trying to keep his temper. Dianthe cleared her throat, an obvious warning. Without opening his eyes, Alaric said, "I'm looking for rituals. Does that satisfy you?"

"Rituals?" Too late Sienne realized how appalled she'd sounded. Alaric turned his gaze on her. His mouth was a tight line, angry and tense. "I'm sorry. I didn't mean it that way. Just...rituals are evil. Why—"

"No, all the rituals anyone knows about are necromantic," Alaric said. "There are—were—other kinds of ritual in the before times."

"No wonder they think you're mad. There's never been any evidence of that."

"Fine. I'm mad. Now let me finish searching, please." Alaric turned his back on her.

Sienne persisted. "I didn't say you were actually mad, I said I could understand why people thought so. Why do you believe in non-necromantic ritual?"

"That's not something I feel like sharing." Alaric finished his circuit of the room. "I can't find anything."

"Neither can I," said Dianthe, "which is rather more telling, given that you aren't always the most perceptive person."

"Thanks. I haven't been insulted enough already." Alaric glared at Sienne, who reddened. "Is the floor hollow?"

Kalanath shook his head and tapped his staff on the floor again, making the steel ring out against the stone.

"Then I suppose that's it. Let's head for home, shall we?" Alaric left the room without waiting for them.

Dianthe grabbed Sienne's arm and held her back when she would have followed. "Don't press him on this," she said in a low voice. "I mean it."

Startled, and a little hurt by the sharpness in Dianthe's voice, Sienne said, "I didn't mean to. I won't."

"Good." Dianthe released her and stalked away. Sienne trailed behind, feeling lost. She *didn't* think Alaric was mad, and she *wasn't* interested in prying. She just loved a challenge. And if Alaric thought there was such a thing as ritual that didn't involve raising the dead, she wanted to know why. Except the topic was clearly off limits. Fine. If he wanted to be aloof and stand-offish, that was his business.

She hurried to catch up to the others as they passed through the kitchen. That reminded her of the coins she'd found, which memory cheered her. It didn't even matter how much money they brought. They represented her first find as a scrapper. Maybe she ought to ask if she could keep one.

The open mouth of the tunnel wasn't as bright as before. More cloud cover, probably. Sienne couldn't see much of it anyway, given that Alaric was at the head of the group and blocking her view. She sped up again until she was right behind Kalanath, then had to back up a few steps to avoid being jabbed by the end of his staff.

The light brightened as Alaric left the tunnel. An instant later, thunder boomed, making Sienne cry out and cover her head instinctively. That had been right on top of them. The sky hadn't looked like rain, so what—

Someone shouted, and Kalanath surged forward. Sienne followed him, clutching her spellbook close to her chest and sidling as rapidly as she dared. She emerged from the tunnel and had to dodge so as not to run into Kalanath, who'd stopped right outside the entrance.

Alaric lay face down on the ground, his arms and legs splayed out limply. The rest of them stood very still, facing four strangers. Two were armed with swords, one guarding Dianthe, the other Perrin. One, an Ansorjan, held a short knife. The last held a spellbook he was in the act of closing. Sienne took another look, and gasped. They weren't strangers, after all.

"Thanks for retrieving our prize," Conn Giorda said.

11

"You *bastard*," Dianthe said, her voice choked with tears. "How did you find us?"

"Guess you weren't as careful as you thought." Conn's triumphant, sneering grin took all of them in. "Ham-fist leaves a trail a mile wide. You were easy to follow."

"He'd better not be dead."

Conn shrugged. "Maybe, maybe not," he said. "Osfald, get the artifact."

The Ansorjan with the knife came forward and crouched to cut the ropes tying the box to Alaric's back. Dianthe took a step forward and hissed as the Giorda woman—Alethea—pressed her blade closer to Dianthe's throat.

"*Fit*, eh?" Conn said, ostentatiously looking down at Sienne. "Clever. I would have used *fly*, myself. Oh, but you probably don't have that spell, right? A beginner like you?"

Sienne said nothing. She calculated how quickly she could get her spellbook open. Faster than they could slit her companions' throats? She was fast, but not that fast. And there wasn't anything she could do in any case. The one offensive spell she knew would catch all her friends in its effect. She was helpless.

"Let's see what else you found. Empty your pockets," Conn said. No one moved. "Don't make me kill one of you as an example to the others," he warned.

Sienne set her spellbook down and reached for her pack. It was a mistake. Conn's eyes lit on the book. "I'll have that," he said. "There's probably nothing worthwhile in it, but it's worth looking." He stepped toward her with his hand outstretched.

Kalanath leaped forward, bringing his staff around in an arc at Conn's knees, which was all he could reach. Conn jumped back, cursing. With a flick of his staff, Kalanath knocked the spellbook out of his hands and then thrust the staff high with both hands, catching Conn under the chin and knocking him on his back. Dianthe high-kicked Alethea in the knee and vaulted backward, rolling away and coming to her feet. The Giorda with his sword pointed at Perrin's heart stepped back in astonishment at Kalanath's attack, leaving Perrin free to turn and run toward Alaric. He ducked between the legs of the man with the knife, who held the box in his hands. The man danced awkwardly backward, but Perrin ignored him, crouching to roll Alaric onto his back.

Sienne scooped up her enormous spellbook and ran to join Perrin at Alaric's side. Kalanath went for Alethea, who brought her sword up in time for Kalanath's staff to sweep it out of the way. Faster than Sienne could follow, he spun, hooked her left ankle with his foot, and knocked her down. She yelped, parried his next blow awkwardly, then had to roll out of the way of the staff that slammed toward her chest. The other Giorda approached from behind, sword raised. Without even looking at him, Kalanath whipped the staff around and caught him square in the stomach with the steel-shod end, making the wind whoosh out of him with an audible gasp. The Giorda folded and fell to his knees.

Conn let out an enraged scream and sat up. His spellbook flew into his hand, springing open with a force that made the wooden cover slap his skin with a loud crack. He spat out angry, hard-edged words that sounded cut with acid. Sienne recognized an evoking spell when she heard it. "*Everybody duck!*" she screamed, flinging herself to the ground half atop Alaric's unconscious body. Another enormous thunderclap split the sky, this one louder with an echo that shook Sienne's bones. She braced herself for the impact of whatever *force* he'd flung at them, strong enough to break bones, turn organs to jelly, knock a man unconscious. Instead a loud grinding, crashing sound filled the air, and then the pounding of a thousand hammers, and the lights went out.

When she was sure she wasn't going to die, Sienne raised her head. Gray light filled the air from a hemisphere of glowing energy surrounding all of them, even Kalanath, who was close enough to the edge of the dome Sienne winced at the thought of him being caught halfway in. Stones and invulnerable beams pressed in on it from all sides. Perrin sat nearby, looking up at the dome with a slack jaw and wide eyes.

"Oh, my lord Averran," he whispered, "you are generous beyond measure."

Kalanath, who had a protective arm across Dianthe's shoulders, helped her to sit up. "It is a surprise," he said.

"To me more than anyone," Perrin said. "I did not know protective blessings were so strong. But we should move. It will not last, and then the rock fall will resume."

"Alaric," Dianthe breathed, and scrambled to his side. "Alaric!"

Perrin stood unsteadily and knelt next to Alaric's head. "He is breathing," he said, "but I believe healing is in order. Let us remove to a safer location."

The rock fall, and the dome, had extended the tunnel some five feet. With some effort, Dianthe sliced the protective dome open, making the rock fall sag in a way that propelled them all into action. Sienne made more lights for Kalanath and Perrin, who carried Alaric down the tunnel and into the kitchen. Once he was safely on the floor, Perrin waved the rest of them aside. He removed one of the healing blessings from his riffle of paper.

"What is it you say?" Kalanath asked.

"Beg pardon?"

Kalanath made a fluttering motion with his hands. "When you make the...blessing...work."

"Oh." A ruddy flush visible even in the pale light crossed Perrin's cheeks. "If you must know, it's... 'Stop being a cranky bastard and be useful for once.' It is not exactly respectful, but I think it amuses him."

Kalanath laughed. Sienne had never heard him laugh before. "I like your avatar," he said. "Though I still do not understand how God can be other than God. But it is for another time."

"Indeed," Perrin said. He muttered his invocation under his breath. Green light shone from Alaric's half-open mouth and beneath his eyelids, making him seem to be wearing a flesh mask. It was so unsettling Dianthe cried out in horror, and Sienne covered her mouth to hold in her own cry. The paper blessing burned to ash. Then the light was gone, and Alaric lay still on the ground, breathing slowly but otherwise not moving.

"It didn't work," Dianthe said. "Why didn't it work?"

Perrin's eyes were wide and fearful. "I know not. It should work. That is, the light means it worked, but...I fear he may be injured in ways my healing cannot mend."

Dianthe grabbed Alaric by the collar and slapped him. "Wake up!" She slapped him again, but Kalanath took her wrist when she would have done it a third time.

"He breathes, so there is hope," he said. "Let us wait."

Outside, a thunderous crash heralded the end of Perrin's protective dome. "I'm going to look at that," Sienne said.

No light shone from the mouth of the tunnel. Sienne picked her way along by the light of her magic until she reached the end. Conn had knocked part of the keep's wall down, what was left of the northeast tower based on how it had fallen. It was a good thing they'd rescued the box first... the box that was now in the Giordas' hands. Sienne swore until she felt better. The way Conn had looked at her, so dismissive... she wished she had him there right now to punch him in the face, or hit him with her spellbook.

She took a closer look at the rubble. She could see slivers of light beyond it, which meant there wasn't much between them and freedom. They could probably break through, and then hunt down the Giordas and get the box back. Sienne grabbed a stone to test her theory.

A painful shock went through her, stopping her heart for one terrifying moment and making her eyes water. She let go of the stone and breathed heavily. Her heart, once it started beating again, fluttered erratically for a few beats before settling down. The *force* spell was still tangled up with the stones. There was no way they could move them. They were trapped.

Sienne ran back down the tunnel. "We can't get out," she said.

Dianthe looked up at her. Tears streaked her face. "It doesn't matter," she said. "If he's dead—"

"He's still breathing, isn't he? He's not dead." Sienne hoped she wasn't giving the woman false hope.

"He's not moving. What did that bastard hit him with?"

"*Force*. It's concentrated magic, sort of magical lightning. He used it to bring the tower down on us, and now the stones are charged with it and we can't get out."

Movement caught her eye. Alaric shifted one arm and turned his head. Dianthe cried out. "Too loud," Alaric said in a whisper. "I can't move."

"I think it will come back to you," Perrin said. "I fear I have no medical training, just the blessings Averran bestows upon me. Are you in pain?"

"No. But everything feels heavy." Alaric opened his eyes. "What happened?"

Sienne looked at Dianthe and raised her eyebrows in a "you tell him" gesture. Dianthe said, "The Giordas ambushed us. Conn hit you with a...a magical lightning bolt, and then he stole the box and dropped a tower on us."

"Stole the box?" Alaric's shoulders quivered, and Sienne guessed he'd tried to sit up. "How did they find us?"

"The scrying showed no one within two miles of us," Perrin said.

He closed his eyes and cursed. "But scrying can be deceived, if another priest knows he may be thus observed."

"Why didn't you mention this earlier?" Alaric said.

"Why did you not tell me our putative followers might have a priest at their disposal?" Perrin shot back.

"I—" Alaric closed his eyes again. "You're right. It didn't occur to me. Dianthe, should we have guessed the Giordas would be on our trail?"

"How could we?" Dianthe said. "They've never followed us before, and there was no reason to believe they'd do so this time. Besides, last I heard, they didn't have a priest working with them. Kalanath?"

Kalanath shook his head. "They had no priest when I worked with them."

"There's no point in blaming anyone. What's done is done," Alaric said. His shoulders quivered again, and this time he sat up. "We need to follow them, quickly."

"Then we have to find another way out," Sienne said. "The tunnel is impassable."

When Alaric was capable of standing, they all walked back down the tunnel to look at the rock fall. Sienne had to grab Alaric's hand to keep him from touching the stones. Being *force*-blasted twice in half an hour couldn't be good for anyone. Alaric crouched to examine the rock fall, putting his hands behind his back as if he needed help remembering not to touch. "There's not much there," he said, standing to look at the top of the pile of rubble. "We could dig our way out in a couple of hours if not for that damned magic."

"There must be another way out," Perrin said. "It is simply a matter of finding somewhere that will not collapse the building upon us."

"We could try climbing down the outside of the tower," Dianthe said.

"We'd need rope for that," Alaric said. "I used mine to tie the box to my back, and that's in pieces."

"The rope we were carrying shrank with us, and the rest of it is on

Button," Dianthe said. She grimaced. "Poor Button. I hope they didn't hurt him."

"What about the hole to the outside?" Sienne said. "Didn't you say that door on the second story led to it?"

"I said it probably did. And it was solidly blocked." Dianthe shook her head. "It may still be our best bet."

"It means ascending once more," Perrin said, frowning. "And then climbing down from there."

"Let's just see if it's possible," Alaric said.

They ran back through the keep to the base of the northeast tower. Alaric pushed on the door. It didn't budge. He put his shoulder to it and heaved, but the rotten wood moved not even a quiver. "Break it down," he said. He and Dianthe and Kalanath went at it with their weapons, prying away huge chunks of wood.

"I could use *break* on it," Sienne suggested.

"We've almost got it," said Dianthe. Sienne shrugged and turned away. Perrin was standing in the middle of the empty room, staring at nothing. Sienne joined him there.

"I wonder what this room was used for," she said.

Perrin said nothing. She was about to walk away and leave him to his boring reverie when he said, "There must be something here we are missing."

"But what? We've already searched it."

Perrin bent, licked his fingertip, and drew a short line on the flagstone where he stood. "There is no residue of any kind," he said, displaying a clean and slightly damp finger. "I find that goes beyond unlikely into the realm of the impossible. There is something unusual about this room, and I believe—" He took out his riffle of paper and plucked out one with a violet smudge on one corner. "Averran granted me this same unfamiliar blessing two days in a row. I believe it may be useful here."

Alaric swore, and Perrin and Sienne turned to see what was wrong. They'd broken down the door to reveal a solid mass of stone blocking the space beyond. "Those are too big for me to move even at my normal size," he said. "We're not getting out that way."

"Sienne, will that magic effect wear off the stones eventually?" Dianthe asked.

"I don't know. Probably. But we're talking a matter of weeks before it does."

"By which time we all die," Kalanath said.

"There may be an alternative," Perrin said. "If this room holds secrets as I believe." He held up the scrap of paper. "I have worked out the meaning of part of this sigil. It hints at...revelation, I believe, is the most accurate word. To show what cannot be seen."

"Are you sure?" Alaric said. "What about the part you don't understand?"

"As to that, I simply lack the knowledge. I am yet new to the priesthood and I acknowledge that is a drawback. But I am certain it will not do us harm."

"Let's do it. We're about out of options," Dianthe said.

Perrin nodded. "I suggest the rest of you stand outside. My faith in this blessing does not extend to taking unwarranted risks."

They all moved into the corridor and clustered close together, watching Perrin. He backed up to the blocked doorway, shook his head, and moved forward again until he stood near the center of the room. He held the paper blessing high above his head, and in a clear voice said, "O Lord, we are in a bind, so if you would be so generous, stop being a cranky bastard and be useful for once."

Violet light flared, filling the room with a blinding radiance matched only by the white fire consuming the blessing. Sienne cried out and covered her eyes, and heard the rest of her companions curse or exclaim as well. The black inverse of the light pulsed behind her eyelids. Jasmine and sharp mint filled the room, making her gag at its overpowering sweetness. "Dear Lord," she heard Perrin say faintly, "I did not expect *this*."

Sienne lowered her arm. The room, which had been so bare before, now radiated pale violet light from hundreds of lines scribed all over the walls, ceiling, and floor. Some were curved, some straight, but all were done in a bold hand that made Sienne think of a master calligrapher scribing lines of text across a clean white sheet of paper.

She realized why she'd had that image when her eyes fell on a word written along the curve of a line. As she looked more closely, she saw more words, all written in a clear half-uncial script familiar to her from her studies. She walked forward and touched one of the words that fell at about eye level to her. "Sienne, be careful," Dianthe said.

Whatever medium the words and lines were written in, it didn't come off on her hands. She sniffed the wall and smelled wet stone where the word was. "It's in Ginatic," she said. "I've never seen the script so easy to read, though."

"You can read it?" Alaric said, coming to stand beside her.

"Not really. I know about a hundred Ginatic words, mostly spell names, so I can make out simple phrases, but it's not a language anyone speaks but a few scholars. This—" She brushed her fingers across the word again—"this is *adpriti*, open."

Alaric stepped back and tilted his head to look at the ceiling. "What other words here can you read?"

Sienne circled the room, then walked down the center of the floor gazing at her feet. "*Adpriti* is all over the place. So is *silla*, force, and *premma*, shift." She came to a stop near Perrin, still standing at the center of the room, and craned her neck back to look at the ceiling. "They're all spell names."

"Spell names?" Alaric's alarm was evident in his voice.

"Just the names," Sienne reassured him. "I can't cast *force* by saying *silla*. The spell itself is in the evoking language. But I wonder..." She returned to Alaric's side and contemplated the word *adpriti*. "I wonder if this isn't instructions of some kind. For example, stand in this place and cast *open*."

"You mean a ritual," Alaric said.

Startled, Sienne said, "I didn't—" She stared at him. His face was expressionless, but his eyes were fierce in a way she'd never seen before. "That's...you're right. That's what a ritual is."

"So what does this ritual do?"

"I have no idea. The only rituals I've ever seen written out are necromantic ones, and that was only to warn us students what to watch out for."

"Then make a guess."

Alaric's intense gaze was starting to make her afraid. Sienne swallowed and turned away, pretending to examine another section of wall. "With *open, force,* and *shift,* I guess you could…alter something. Something big. *Shift* is a confusion spell that lets you change your appearance in small ways. Hair color, face shape, things like that."

"So could you do this ritual?" Dianthe said. She sounded as eager as Alaric had not.

"No. For one thing, there's no clue as to when each spell has to be cast, or on what. For another, I don't know *force* or I'd have used it on Conn Giorda." She turned to face Dianthe, who was chewing her lower lip in thought. "And even if I could do all that, I'd be nervous of performing wizardry when I didn't know what it was for."

"It doesn't matter," Alaric said.

"What?" said Dianthe.

He turned to look at her and shook his head slightly. Dianthe subsided. "Why doesn't it matter?" Sienne demanded. "You were looking for ritual, and you found it."

"It is not the right one," Kalanath said. He was standing quietly in one corner, where a series of lines came together in a complex knot.

"How do you know that?" said Dianthe.

He shrugged. "It is clear you look for one kind of ritual. This is not it."

Alaric's lips were compressed with frustration. "No, it's not," he said. "And we're no closer to finding a way out."

"I do not think so," Kalanath said. He set the tip of his staff on the corner of the nearest flagstone and pressed down. There was a click, and the flagstone's opposite edge rose two inches. Dianthe gasped. Alaric and Perrin stepped forward at the same time, then stopped as Kalanath bent and pulled up on the flagstone. It rose, swiveling around an invisible axis, until it stood at right angles to the floor, revealing an opening blacker than midnight. Stale air that smelled of char and smoke drifted out.

"How did you know that was there?" Perrin said.

"The lines here all point to that spot," Kalanath said. "It is a sign."

"Sienne," Alaric said, "make a light."

Sienne conjured a light above the hole. Alaric knelt and looked down. "Stairs," he said, "and a room."

"Not a tunnel?" Dianthe asked.

Alaric shook his head. "There's not much space down there." He took hold of the flagstone and pulled. "And I can't remove the stone. Whoever this place belonged to must have been tiny."

"Or knew the *fit* spell," Sienne said. "How better to protect something than to make it impossible for anyone to get at it?"

Alaric sat on the edge of the hole and swung his feet down to rest on the stairs. "Sienne, can you make me fit through here?"

"Only by making you a *lot* smaller. You'd be less than a foot tall. But I bet I can fit in there."

She could see him marshalling objections behind his eyes. Dianthe said, "She is the smallest of us, Alaric."

Alaric grimaced and pushed himself up. "Be careful," he said.

Sienne nodded and set her spellbook to one side. She knelt by the edge of the hole and looked down. The magic light revealed very little beyond some angular shapes that might have been a cupboard and table. She swiveled around and lowered her feet to rest on the second step down. The stairs were steep enough they might have been a ladder, and after a moment's thought Sienne turned and climbed down them that way. The spaces between the steps, or rungs, were small enough that she was convinced her theory about *fit* was correct.

She reached the bottom and made a few more magic lights. The floor was bare earth, as were the walls. The smell of old smoke was stronger here, and when her eyes adjusted to the light, she saw why. A fire had ravaged the place long ago, blackening the cupboards leaning against the walls and mostly destroying the narrow table filling the center of the room.

"It's been burned," she called up to her companions.

"On purpose?" Alaric said.

"I can't tell. But I think the air ran out before the fire could completely destroy everything." Books with soot-stained spines filled a bookcase opposite the stairs. Sienne circled the table—there was no sign of chairs or stools, not even heaps of ash that might once have been chairs or stools—and drew one of the books out. The spine came away from the pages, blackening her fingers. She wiggled the pages free, dropping the rest of the cover on the floor. The book was small, which meant it was average-sized to her current form, and the pages were burned on the edges that had been facing out into the room. She carefully turned a few pages. Pictures of flowers and plants she didn't recognize met her eyes, their lines as bright as if they were new.

"I found books, but they're mostly ruined. I can't tell how old they are," she said. She checked a couple of other books, but they were in worse shape than the first, all of them apparently botanical reference books. Histories, those might have been worth salvaging, but these struck her as ordinary and worthless to collectors.

She turned her attention to one of the cupboards. It held a row of soot-blackened lumps too regular to be chunks of coal or burned wood. She removed one and brushed it off with her fingers, felt smooth glass and cold metal, and rubbed harder. It was a palm-sized disk of heavy two-inch-thick glass in an engraved metal cuff studded with grimy pearls. She lifted it to her eye and saw through the glass not the opposite wall, but black nothing. A weak trail of white light outlined the engraving and grounded itself in one of the pearls. The black nothing shivered, then lay still again.

Sienne set the glass disk down and picked up another soot-encrusted lump. It proved to be the twin of the first glass disk, but with cabochon tiger's eye stones instead of pearls. "I found artifacts," she exclaimed. "Six of them!"

"Do they still work?" Perrin asked.

"I don't know. Some of them still have traces of magic." She carefully stowed them in her pack, brushing as much soot off as she could before wrapping them in her spare shirt.

"Time to figure that out once we're free," Alaric said. "Do you see any sign of another exit? A secret door?"

Sienne crossed to the last cupboard, whose upper shelves were empty. "Just a minute." She opened the cupboard doors and sucked in a horrified breath, stumbling backward. The body in the cupboard was small, smaller than she was, and curled in the fetal position so it would fit inside the cupboard. It was shriveled and dried out, resembling nothing so much as a withered apple. Its sunken eyes were closed, its lips peeled back to reveal yellow teeth, and its clothing had disintegrated. In its nakedness it looked pathetic, like a child hiding from the darkness of a thunderstorm.

Sienne's breath came in heavy, gasping pants. "There's a body," she said.

"Sienne, be careful," Alaric said.

"It can't hurt me. I think there's no other way out of here, or it wouldn't have hidden from whoever burned the place down."

"That's a pretty extreme leap of logic," Dianthe said.

"I know. And maybe that's not how it happened. But..." Sienne couldn't think how to end that sentence.

Feeling obscurely that she ought to dignify this person's death with some kind of acknowledgement, she approached the cupboard and knelt beside it. The small hands were clasped together as if in prayer. Sienne swallowed and reached out to touch its head in farewell. Something glinted in the shifting lights around her head, something clutched in the tiny hands. Hesitant, Sienne took hold of one of them and pulled. It snapped off in her fingers, making her cry out. "Sienne!" someone shouted.

"It's all right, I was just startled," she said. She withdrew a pendant the size of a fat pea pod from the remaining hand. It was a dark blue stone set in silver, faceted rather than smooth, and it glittered in the lights like goldstone. Its shape was irregular, twisted, and reminded Sienne more of ancient wood worn smooth and hard by time than of a gemstone. If it had hung from a chain once, the chain was long gone.

Despite her increasing belief that there was no way out of this room but the one she'd gotten in by, she circled the space, checking the walls for secret doors, even tugging one of the cupboards down after removing all the books. Finally, she clambered up the stairs and sat, breathing heavily, on the edge. "I'd be more excited about this," she said, handing the pendant to Alaric, "if I thought we were in a position to sell it. It has a magical...I guess you could say 'residue' on it, like someone cast a spell on it once, but it's not inherently magical. Even so, I'm sure someone will want it."

Alaric turned it over in his hand, then passed it around for the others to handle and examine. "I agree," he said. "We seem to be out of options."

Dianthe turned abruptly and walked across the room, then back again. "Sienne, can you explain more about that spell Conn used on the rocks?"

Mystified, Sienne said, "Um...it's pretty much what I said. It shapes magical energy and directs it into a target. A person, or a building...any one thing. I think there's a version that can strike multiple targets at once, but none of my teachers knew it. If you cast it on something that breaks, it becomes sticky—meaning it persists, clinging to the pieces like a web. That's what happened to the tower. It broke apart when it fell, so the magic is still there."

"So it's a single piece of magic? Not a lot of little pieces, each attached to a stone or beam?"

"No. It's all one thing."

Dianthe stopped in front of Alaric. "There's a way out."

Alaric's face went expressionless again. "No."

"It's that or starve to death in here."

"Why did you not tell us this before?" Perrin demanded. "If you know a way out, why would you not take it?"

Alaric was silent. "This is no time for secrets," Kalanath said.

"We'll stay here," Dianthe said. She put her hand on Alaric's cheek and made him look at her. "I swear it."

"What is going on?" Sienne asked.

Alaric let out a deep sigh and bowed his head. "No," he said again, but this time he sounded resigned, as if he were facing the gallows.

"We've risked our lives together, and now we're facing death together. You've trusted me to bring you this far. I should be able to return that trust." He took Dianthe's hand and squeezed it. "Let's go."

Sienne caught Perrin's eye. He looked as confused as she felt. Trust them with what?

They followed Alaric back to the tunnel. "Stay at this end," he said. "It's going to be a tight fit. Sienne, is there any chance of the shrinking spell wearing off in the next fifteen minutes?"

She checked her non-functional pocket watch again out of habit. "Um...no. We have at least half an hour, I think."

Alaric nodded. He unstrapped his sword and leaned it against the stone wall of the keep. "Stay back," he repeated, and walked toward the collapsed stone. Dianthe had her hands clenched into fists. Sienne wanted to ask her what Alaric intended, but the look on her face, as if she'd said a final goodbye to her oldest friend, dissuaded her.

Alaric stopped about a foot from the end of the tunnel, just before he would have had to crouch to keep from hitting his head. He stood with his back to them, his shoulders flung back and his stance wide. Sienne's eyes watered from staring so hard at him. She wiped her eyes and blinked. The watery sensation was still there, only now she realized it was coming from the air around Alaric. A low hum purred through the ground, vibrating her bones until she had to clench her teeth to keep them from rattling. His outline blurred as if seen through water, stretched—and the world blinked, and he was gone.

Sienne covered her mouth to hold back an astonished gasp. In his place, formless in the low light, was something much bigger, four-legged and massive and dark brown that became black where the shadows struck. Sienne took in the powerful hindquarters, the long, muscular neck, and the black tail that switched impatiently at nonexistent flies. It was a stallion, filling the end of the tunnel almost to capacity. Then it turned its head to look back at them, and this time she did gasp. Rising from its forehead, scraping across the stones overhead, was a horn that shone like black oil in Sienne's magic light.

12

D ianthe's hand closed on Sienne's arm like a vise. "Don't," she said, and went silent. Sienne didn't know what Dianthe thought she was about to do. She couldn't stop staring.

The unicorn turned away and lowered his head. The bulk of his body prevented her from seeing what he was doing, but after a moment, yellow-white light traced the outlines of all the stones at that end of the tunnel. A rumble like thunder echoed, and the stones shifted. Sienne and Perrin shouted a warning, and Kalanath took a swift step forward. The unicorn's hindquarters shifted, and he backed toward them, gradually raising his head. Sienne caught one more glimpse of the impossible black horn.

Then it vanished, and there was only Alaric, striding toward them without meeting anyone's eye. He picked up his sword and slung it across his back. "The magic is gone," he said. "Let's clear a path."

Sienne looked at Perrin and Kalanath. Perrin's eyes were wide and stunned behind the hair that was once again falling in front of his face. Kalanath's face was a still mask of astonishment. She was sure she looked like she'd been struck by *force* herself. She turned toward Alaric, opened her mouth, and shut it again. Too many questions thronged her brain. Alaric the shapeshifter. Were-creature? And how had he removed the magic, just because he was a... Her brain refused to process the concept of "unicorn" linked to the man she was coming to like despite herself.

Dianthe had already gone to join Alaric. Kalanath shrugged and followed them. Perrin whispered, for Sienne's ears alone, "My eyes were not deceived, were they?"

"No."

"Then how—never mind. But I do not think I can look him in the face again." He went to join the others at the rock fall. Sienne picked up her spellbook and followed.

Alaric worked in grim silence, daring anyone to speak to him. Dianthe divided her attention between shifting rocks and glancing sidelong at Alaric. So, Dianthe had known. Sienne didn't waste time wondering why neither of them had mentioned Alaric's secret. If she didn't want anyone to know who she was, how much more must Alaric want to keep that secret? It was astonishing that he'd revealed it at all. Dianthe had been right, Alaric could have made them all stay away while he did whatever it was, and they never would have seen his transformation. It was a mark of trust that made Sienne feel horribly uncomfortable. She wasn't sure she deserved it.

She shifted small stones from the top of the pile with her invisible fingers, not wanting to disrupt the pile into falling on someone, and tried to think of other things. Six artifacts, some of them possibly still working, and the pendant, and the coins...she had no idea if it was good salvage or not, but she was sure it wasn't worth nearly what the distance viewer was.

She'd lost track of time, so she didn't even know if it was possible to catch up to the Giordas. To her surprise, she discovered she hated the thought of letting them win, not just because of the money, but because they didn't deserve to triumph over her team. Amazing how she'd come to think of them as "her team," where just days ago they'd been nothing but awkward strangers.

She moved another rock, and a beam of watery light shot through the hole it made. It energized all of them, and they redoubled their efforts, tearing down the wall and ignoring the loose stones that fell occasionally. Finally, there was enough of a hole for them to clamber through, and Sienne urged everyone out, certain the *fit* spell should have ended minutes ago.

The clouds had rolled in and threatened to open up at any moment. Filthy and drenched in sweat from their exertions, they stood outside the tunnel and surveyed the ruin of the tower. "Averran deserves great praise," Dianthe said. "That was a miracle." Then she gasped, and the next moment, she was a giant towering over them. Moments later, each of them were their correct size.

"We need to find Button, and then follow the Giordas," Alaric said. He still wasn't looking anyone in the eye. "It's not too late."

"It *is* too late, Alaric," Dianthe said. "I can't track anyone across this ground, and they might have gone anywhere."

"They're going back to Fioretti, though, right?" Sienne said. "If we head that way..."

"They'll conceal themselves," Alaric said. "That priest can no doubt continue to protect them from scrying."

"I have an idea," Perrin said.

"You don't have any blessings for detecting them, do you?" Dianthe asked.

"No, I do not. But what I have in mind is rather more subtle, and depends greatly on Averran's good humor. I wish I knew what avatar their priest served, and wish even more my flask were full of aged brandy, but I believe it is worth trying. We will need a map."

"Button," Dianthe said as if she'd just remembered the donkey. "Those bastards had better not have hurt him."

They circled the fortress and found Button hobbled where they'd left him, on the far side. Dianthe patted his nose in welcome. "Do you need the map now?" she said to Perrin.

"Immediately, yes. Though if this fails, urgency is no longer our companion."

Dianthe dug around in one of the packs until she found a water-proof scroll case, tightly capped. She handed it to Perrin. "There are two that show where we are now."

Perrin extracted the roll of maps and scanned them until he

found one he liked. "Where are we?" he asked. He hesitated, then held out the map to Alaric.

Alaric took it and jabbed his finger at a spot to the left of center. Perrin took out one of his pastels and scribbled a dot where Alaric's finger had landed. Then he sat cross-legged and spread the map before him, pinning the corners down with some loose stones. He closed his eyes and threw his head back as if addressing the heavy rain clouds. Kalanath took a few steps back. "Ah...I thought you already prayed to Averran, this morning," Dianthe said.

"That is true," Perrin said. "But one may petition for blessings at any time, if one is willing to expend the effort and take the risk."

"There's a risk?" Sienne said.

"The avatars of God take exception to being treated like dispensers of divine power, as if they were pumps one might tap at one's leisure. And they each have opinions as to what is important. If a priest's opinion differs from theirs...let us just say they are not shy about expressing their displeasure." Perrin's tone was light, but his eyes were squeezed tight shut as if the light was noonday bright instead of wan and gray with impending rain.

"Maybe we shouldn't do this," Dianthe said.

"If it means tracking the Giordas down, it's worth the risk," Alaric said, his deep voice startling Sienne. "And Perrin knows what he's doing."

Perrin smiled. "Thank you. Now, if you please, silence, and perhaps you might all step back farther?" He rested his hands loosely on his knees. Sienne stepped back and nearly bumped into Alaric. She managed not to recoil. She wasn't afraid of him, or disgusted; it was just that his continuing silence was unsettling, and she didn't know what to say to break it. Time enough for that when they knew if the Giordas were out of their reach.

"O most cantankerous Lord," Perrin said. Strands of hair blew into his face, but he didn't swipe them away. "I realize we have spoken once already today, and my importunities must annoy you greatly. I have a request that you are of course free to deny, but I hope you will demonstrate the generosity you are renowned for, as when you granted the desires of the Lady of the Fens."

He paused, his head tilted as if listening, and shook his head minutely. Drops of sweat rolled down his temples. "O great and irritable Lord, my plea is entirely selfish. My companions and I seek an item that was stolen from us, and we know not where to look for it. I will not ask you to scry for us, as I am certain one of your fellow avatars has granted our enemy the blessing of conceal—" A look of horror flitted across Perrin's face before he controlled himself. "Of course I do not suggest that you are weaker. You are, after all, gifted with wisdom, which allows you to see what is hidden far better than anyone else."

He went silent. Sienne made herself breathe. "I beg of you, turn away your crankiness," he finally said. "If you will show us where our enemy will be at...seven o'clock tomorrow morning...we may overtake them, and you will not come to blows with one of your fellows." Another silence. "I respectfully disagree, my Lord, my sobriety is not an improvement—" His breathing was labored and rapid. "Of course it is entirely up to you, o Lord of choler and irritability, but I assure you we would all be very grateful."

The clouds parted, and a beam of light no bigger around than a copper centus struck the map. Perrin opened his eyes and swiftly marked the spot with his pastel. "Thank you, my Lord Averran," he said, and collapsed.

The others exclaimed and surged forward, but he was already sitting up and waved them off. "I have never done that before," he said. "It is far more wearying than I imagined." He dropped the pastel into its packet, stood, and brushed off his rear end. "Please tell me you can find this location."

Alaric took the map. "We'll have to move quickly, and we won't be able to sleep long," he said. "Though at seven o'clock they might be on the move already."

"They will not," Kalanath said. "The Giordas like to sleep late. They will be in camp at that hour."

"We might actually be able to surprise them," Dianthe said.

"Let's march," Alaric said.

Sienne wound her watch as they went and set it to her best guess at the time, based on the sun she could barely see. They were going to be very wet in about half an hour, she judged. She looked at Alaric's back, so familiar and now so strange. What magic was hidden inside him? She couldn't bear it any longer.

"Alaric," she said.

"He doesn't want to talk about it, Sienne," Dianthe said.

"Well, he can't just change shape and expect us to not be curious!"

"She's right," Alaric rumbled, but said nothing else.

"So...what was that? How can you be a...a were-unicorn? Unicorns are mythical!"

"Clearly, they are not," Perrin said.

"He is not were," Kalanath said. "He is too big. The unicorn is too big, I mean."

"Right," Alaric said. He sounded weary, as if he'd been beaten soundly and then forced to march fifty miles. "Were-creatures always mass the same whichever form they're in. My...other self...weighs more than a ton."

"So if you're not a were-unicorn," Sienne said, "what are you?"

"Not quite human," Alaric said. "My people are called Sassaven."

"Faithful," Sienne said automatically.

Alaric turned to look at her, though he didn't stop walking. "What was that?"

"Sorry. I meant...the Ginatic word for 'faithful' is *sa'asava*. It was just coincidence."

Alaric let out a bitter laugh. "Probably not," he said. "It would make sense. We were created, hundreds of years ago, by a wizard who wanted utterly loyal servants. He tried breeding humans with dogs, reasoning that dogs have an inherent bond with men, but the dogs were too small to contain the amount of magic it took. So he used horses instead."

"But that was no horse," Perrin said.

"No." Alaric shook his head. "Most of the Sassaven are horses in their other form. Only a few of us, maybe one in ten, take...unicorn shape." He said the word reluctantly, as if it tasted bad.

"It must be a true magical transformation, like *fit*," Sienne said.

"Must be. I know very little about it."

A horrible thought struck her. "Are you...hundreds of years old?"

Alaric laughed, and the sound made her relax, because it was genuinely amused and not at all distant or bitter. "No, I'm twenty-five. We only live as long as the average human, though the unicorns live a little longer."

"But you are Ansorjan," Kalanath said.

"We were, originally. The wizard who created us lives in the Pirinin Peaks. He took Ansorjans for the root stock."

"How long ago was that?" Perrin asked.

"We're not sure. Maybe five hundred years?"

"That predates the wars," Sienne said. Then Alaric's words caught up with her brain. "What do you mean, he *lives* in the Pirinins?"

"He's still alive." The way Alaric said it made Sienne wish she could hide, anything not to have to face him in his anger. "At least he was when I fled. He stays young by taking the heart of a unicorn, a new one every year or so, and making that unicorn a vessel for his own heart. It...corrupts its host body, eventually killing it, and then he repeats the process. Someone that evil would naturally be expected to live for a thousand years."

"The Sassaven are under his thrall," Dianthe said. "We're looking for a ritual to counter that, to free the others. It's why we know non-necromantic rituals are possible. Alaric's seen them performed, to bind his people to the wizard."

"But you knew the ritual in that room was not the one you sought," said Perrin.

"The one I'm looking for has things in common with the binding ritual," Alaric said. "I'll recognize it when I see it. Then I'll use it to free my people. And I'll kill the monster with my own hands."

That left them all with nothing to say. Finally, Sienne dared, "How did you break the *force* spell?"

"The horn has magical properties," Alaric said. "It can break certain spells, ones that persist. The hooves, too, but there wasn't enough room in there to kick the wall."

Sienne noticed how impersonally he spoke of horn and hooves, as if they didn't have anything to do with him. Maybe that was how he felt about his other form, like it was a separate creature. "So...are the Sassaven the source of unicorn myths? Because I would have sworn unicorns were mythical."

Alaric shrugged. "Probably. Very few people see the Sassaven in their other form, horse or unicorn. But the imagery had to come from somewhere."

Sienne thought of the pictures of unicorns she'd seen, delicate and slender, and compared the images to the reality of Alaric in unicorn form, huge and muscular like a draft horse. She wanted to ask how it felt to transform, what it was like being a horse, but that felt uncomfortably like prying, and they'd already intruded on his privacy enough. "Thank you," she said instead.

"For what?"

"For trusting us."

"Dianthe was right, you might well have performed your transformation in private and left us none the wiser," Perrin said. "It is an honor."

"We will not tell," Kalanath said. "I am certain of this for all of us."

Sienne, watching Alaric's back, saw his neck redden. "I don't want anyone to know about it, because I don't want to be treated like a monster, or some unnatural creature. But I think you all have enough secrets that you understand how important it is to protect them."

"I hope that was not a hint that we must all share, to be even," Perrin said.

"No. But I hope you realize Dianthe and I know how to keep a secret."

They walked on. A fat drop of water landed on Sienne's arm, then another. Soon enough, the rain went from a sprinkle to a deluge, soaking them all. It wasn't a cold rain, but it was uncomfortable enough that Sienne wished she'd thought to provide herself with rain gear. It hardly ever rained in the summer, so it hadn't occurred to her. She wrapped her arms around herself and shivered.

Ahead of her, Alaric's blond hair turned dark with water, and his thin cotton shirt plastered itself to his back. What was it about calamity that sharing it with others made it easier to bear? Dianthe had pulled out a floppy hat from her pack, but the rest of her was as wet as everyone else. Sienne's spellbook lay warm across her stomach. It was as impervious to water as to everything else, but she felt compelled to protect it from the rain anyway.

They entered the forest after a few minutes, where the rain no longer fell so heavily, but the rattle of the drops on the foliage made it impossible to carry on a conversation, had they wanted to. The rain dwindled to a persistent drizzle after about thirty minutes and stopped entirely after an hour. Dianthe brought out the map and examined it. "We're about an hour away from where the Giordas will be in the morning. I don't get it. We shouldn't have caught up with them so quickly."

"They probably camped when the rain started, and decided not to pack up just for another hour's worth of travel," Alaric said. The clouds were heavy in the west, but it was still possible to see the sun hanging halfway below the horizon. "Cocky. They don't think we can find them."

"So should we camp? Or try to attack them?" Kalanath asked.

"Camp, and rest, and rise early," Alaric said. "We'll ambush them before first light."

"I am utterly grateful to you," Perrin said with an exaggerated sigh. "My weariness knows no bounds, and I would prefer to dry off before sleeping."

"This is as good a spot as any," Alaric said, and lowered his pack to the ground.

There was no dry wood for a fire, so they made do with dried meat and some apples for their dinner. Sienne went behind some close-growing trees to change into her other clothes, which were not perfectly dry, but much better than the alternative, even if her shirt was hopelessly stained with soot from the artifacts. She sat on a log outside her tent and pretended there was a roaring fire, and hot soup. Even coffee would be welcome now.

"I wish I knew a spell for evoking fire," she said idly.

"We could use it to burn the Giordas' camp," Alaric said.

Sienne eyed him warily. "Or we could use it to dry this wood and start a campfire."

Alaric shrugged. He was seated on the damp ground near her and engaged in cleaning and sharpening his sword.

"You have given much thought to the offensive uses of magic," Perrin said.

"Being nearly enslaved to an evil wizard will do that to you."

"I am not certain one's upbringing determines one's destiny. Take Sienne, for example. Being her father's daughter—"

Perrin stopped, a look of chagrin crossing his features. Sienne felt the blood drain from her face. "Wait, whose daughter is she?" Dianthe asked, her brow furrowed.

Sienne glared at Perrin. "Pray, forgive me," Perrin said. "I forgot myself."

"Is it important?" Kalanath said.

"How do you know?" Sienne asked.

Perrin said, "Messages were sent to many in the capital, from the...an important man seeking his daughter Sienne. It is not an uncommon name, but when I saw the initials on your spellbook, I drew the right conclusion. You need not fear, Sienne. No one here will give you away."

"*Whose daughter?*" Dianthe demanded.

Sienne closed her eyes and drew out her spellbook. She traced the letters on the cover, S V. She blinked away unexpected tears, and said, "This seems to be a day for revelations."

"If it turns out you're secretly half carver, you're sleeping outside," Dianthe said.

"No. It's just that my father is the duke of Beneddo. I'm Sienne Verannus."

Dianthe mouthed the word *Verannus*. Kalanath said, "A duke is important, but I do not know how important is Beneddo."

"Fairly important. It's the largest city before you reach the Empty Lands, so it's almost the northern frontier. My father and mother have influence even in Fioretti, with the king. I didn't think they'd enlist the nobles of the capital in searching for me." She heard the bitterness in her voice and didn't try to stop it. "Didn't think they'd search hard for me at all."

Dianthe took a seat on the log next to Sienne. "That sounds like a story."

"One that doesn't make me look good." Sienne sighed. "I don't know if you know how noble families work. Perrin might. It's common for noble families to send their children to foster with other noble families, to make political connections and so forth. For me, because I was a wizard, my parents arranged for me to foster in the dukedom of Stravanus, which has one of the best schools in Rafellin. I liked it okay. I'm not much of a student except in magical things, so I excelled at linguistics and magic and was utter crap at maths and geology. And then I met Rance Lanzano."

"I know of the Lanzanos," Perrin said. "They are quite wealthy." His voice sounded tight, as if there were things he wasn't saying. Sienne thought about pursuing that line of inquiry, anything to avoid having to talk about Rance. But she already felt better not carrying this burden of secrecy.

"Beyond wealthy," she said. "But Rance never behaved as if money mattered. He was a wizard, like me, and...we fell in love. At least, I loved him." Loved him enough to sleep with him, which memory burned humiliation inside her.

"At any rate, Rance might not have cared about the Lanzano fortune, but other people did. Specifically, my parents. There are eight of us children, you see, and for all Beneddo has power and connections, it's never been terribly wealthy. Sending me to school was a financial struggle. So my parents made an offer to the Lanzanos, a marriage alliance. Between Rance and...my older sister Felice. Heir to the dukedom."

Dianthe opened her mouth to say something, but Sienne held up a hand. "I was so sure Rance would refuse, or propose that he marry me for the alliance instead of Felice. But he didn't. He said he couldn't go against his parents' wishes, and what we had wasn't that serious, anyway. The truth is, he liked the idea of being duke of Beneddo someday. And Felice is more beautiful than I am, so there's that."

She let out a sigh. "I should have let it go, but I was stupid and in love, so I went to my parents and begged them to alter the arrangement so Rance would marry me. I told them I loved him. I completely humiliated myself. And they said—" She swallowed, and tasted tears. "They said they couldn't insult the Lanzanos by offering them the lesser sister. They actually called me that. I walked out of the palace and didn't look back."

Silence fell, broken only by the sound of the million crickets in the scrub surrounding them. Dianthe said, "And you became a scrapper."

"It was the only way I could think of to earn a living where my parents couldn't find me. I know they looked for me at first, because I had to use a lot of confusion spells to get away." Sienne smiled bitterly. "I bet they regretted giving me that expensive education then. I am *very* good at confusions. At any rate, I figured I could lose myself in the big city, go out on some jobs, find a team..."

"Which you did," Kalanath said. She looked at him, surprised, and he smiled. "Though I do not think this is what you intended."

"It's not," Sienne said, "but I don't regret it. Any of it."

More silence. Alaric set down his sword and stretched. "You say you're good at confusions," he said. "Why don't you show us how good?"

13

The pearly gray pre-dawn light reflected off the mist rising from the ground, turning it into a silver sea thigh-deep on Sienne. It swirled with every step she took, chilling and dampening her legs. Wading through fog was not something she'd ever pictured herself doing as a scrapper, but she'd found these past three days were nothing like she'd expected.

Ahead, Dianthe's dark form blended with the tree line. Perrin and Kalanath were already gone to their positions. Only Alaric was visible to her left, huge and hulking and as quiet as it was possible for him to be, which wasn't very.

Of the many plans they'd discussed and discarded before settling on this one, the one she least regretted losing was the one where she used *sharpen* to enhance everyone's eyesight. It wasn't as good as *cat's eye*, which allowed genuine night vision, so the advantage it gave was dubious. And this close to dawn, there was no guarantee it would wear off before the sun rose. Blinding them as they entered the Giorda camp would ruin everything and possibly cost them their lives. She'd only used *sharpen* on herself, as their plan depended on her being able to read her spellbook, and hoped she wasn't taking too big a risk.

"We don't kill unless it's their lives or ours," Alaric had said when Perrin had tentatively broached the subject. "And they'll likely feel the same way, if only because Conn Giorda can't lord it over a dead man. We want the box, and that's all." Sienne had privately determined to make Conn look like a fool if she could. The memory of how dismissively he'd treated her still rankled.

Dianthe came to meet them when they neared the tree line. "I've positioned the others," she said. "Alaric, wait here while I show Sienne where to go."

"I can find my own way."

"In the dark? Without making a tremendous racket?"

Alaric scowled, but said nothing. Dianthe said, "Stay close to me, and watch where you step. That priest is on watch, and he looks half asleep, but no sense taking chances."

The mist dwindled as they went deeper into the forest, then vanished entirely. Sienne regretted its loss, though it hadn't given her any real concealment; it had simply been a comfort. The trees grew close together, their branches tangled, which meant no light reached the forest floor and there was very little undergrowth. There were, however, plenty of fallen branches, and Sienne had to step carefully so as not to noisily break any of them. Her breathing seemed painfully loud in the silence, rough and raspy though she wasn't exerting herself. Dianthe, by contrast, was so silent Sienne wouldn't have known she was there if the woman hadn't been a moving shadow right in front of her.

Dianthe stopped and held up a hand, and Sienne obediently stopped walking. Dianthe leaned in close to her ear and murmured, "The camp is just a few paces ahead. Do you need to see it?"

Sienne nodded. Dianthe gestured, and they moved forward at half speed until Sienne could see three tents pitched around a banked campfire. Sienne froze as someone passed between her and the fire. The priest. Dianthe whispered, "Ten minutes, then you start the confusion spells."

Sienne took out her pocket watch and flipped open its cover. It still didn't tell the right time, but now her watch, Perrin's, and Alaric's all showed the same wrong time, which was just as good. Dianthe squeezed her shoulder and vanished the way she'd come. Sienne put the watch on the ground and lowered herself to sit near it, setting her spellbook in her lap. The Giordas' camp was on a very gentle slope, and she sat at the top of the rise, which gave her an excellent view of the tents, the fire, and the pacing priest. He stopped occasionally, once very close to her, and she saw him yawn. If he was sleepy, so much the better.

She checked her watch. Another three minutes. Quietly she turned the pages of her spellbook, stuck her finger in to mark her place, and turned more pages to a different spell. She was fast, but preparation was better than speed.

She could think of a lot of ways this plan could be better. First on the list was if all of them could communicate with each other somehow. That was the sort of thing divine magic was for, but Perrin had said Averran would definitely not communicate with him at this time of the morning, and anyway it was a blessing it took practice to use properly. Failing that, she wished she could alter Dianthe's vocal cords, let her speak with Alethea's voice, but she needed physical contact with Alethea for that. Dianthe was taking a tremendous risk without it. But she'd said "It's not the first time" and shrugged when Sienne pointed out the danger.

Finally, she wished she knew the *force* spell. If Conn was capable of it, he likely had other offensive spells at his command, and if this ruse didn't take him out immediately, he could turn them on her and her companions. Her friends. She hoped her inexperience didn't betray them all.

The pocket watch showed twenty-four past five. Sienne glanced at the priest. His attention was on something across the campsite. Quietly, she read off the first confusion spell, blinking away the rainbow haloes it left across her vision. She looked again, beyond the priest, and focused on a group of three trees that would be perfect for someone to hide behind.

A loud crack cut across the night. The priest froze, then turned toward the sound. A scuffling sound, like someone walking not too cautiously across dead grass. The priest trotted toward the sound, not very rapidly. Sienne thought he looked reluctant. Then Alaric's voice said, "He's seen us! Go!"

Heavy footsteps pattered from left to right in the distance. The priest shouted a warning, then said, "It's a raid! Hurry!"

Dark forms emerged from the tents, two tall, one short and compact. The footsteps grew closer, and Alaric again shouted, "Stand your ground!"

"After them!" Conn shrieked. "Osfald, stay here and protect the camp!"

The three Giordas pounded off into the distance, following the sounds of retreating footsteps. Stealthy movement next to Sienne heralded Dianthe's arrival. She was laughing silently. "That was good," she whispered. "I almost believed it myself."

"Stand behind the tree," Sienne said, flipping the pages of her spellbook to the next marked place. This one was more difficult. In a whisper, she read out the complex phrase, then had to close her eyes to keep her balance against the dizziness. With her eyes still closed, she let memory give shape to the image she wrapped around Dianthe. The height was right, the hair and eyes should be darker, narrow face, elegant nose… She opened her eyes and found herself face to face with Alethea Giorda.

"Did it work?" Dianthe's voice came from the thin-lipped mouth.

"Except for the voice, of course." Sienne glanced past her. "Be careful."

Dianthe/Alethea smiled. "I'm always careful," she said in a passable imitation of Alethea's voice. She turned and sidled along out of sight. Sienne sat, clutching her spellbook, then realized she might need to run and stood up.

The priest had a loose handful of white things Sienne identified as blessings after a moment and was sorting through them. Perrin's way was more efficient. He withdrew one, opened his mouth to speak, then shut it again when Dianthe/Alethea stumbled forward and swayed as if exhausted.

"They got the drop on us," she said. "We have to hide the box."

The priest, Osfald, waved the blessing at her. "I'll ward the camp—"

"That's no good. They'll have all the time in the world to break through. No, Conn says get it hidden and we'll come back for it later."

Osfald stared at her, his eyes narrowed. "Conn said that?"

Sienne whipped her book open and whispered the *echo* spell again. Footsteps sounded in the distance, drawing nearer. "Hear that?" Dianthe said. "They're coming *now*. Go get the box. I'll hold them off."

The priest gave her one last considering look, then ducked inside one of the tents. Dianthe drew her sword and paced in front of the tent, looking for all the world like someone watching for her enemy's approach. Sienne held her breath. The sound of fighting, a real sound now, broke out in the distance. That was bad. They weren't supposed to engage with the Giordas. Sienne bounced on her toes and bit her lower lip, mentally running through the spells she knew.

The tent flap opened, and Dianthe turned toward Osfald, her hand outstretched. "I'll take—"

"*Our Lady of Light, bless your servant,*" Osfald intoned. A blast of orange light exploded from his hand, taking Dianthe square in the chest. She dropped her sword and stepped back, almost losing her balance. A ripple passed over her, like heat radiating off hot stone. Alethea's illusory image vanished. Osfald stared in horror at Dianthe, his hand drifting down to his side. Dianthe shook off her momentary dizziness and charged at him, bowling him over.

"Get the box!" she shouted.

Sienne startled. That had been meant for her. She shoved her spellbook into her vest and ran for the tent, dodging the thrashing forms of Dianthe and Osfald wrestling for the upper hand. The tent was a wreck of disturbed bedrolls and loose clothing. She kicked someone's boots—whoever it was would be miserable running around in the forest barefoot. She picked up and flung aside a bedroll, kicking at the ground cloth underneath, though it was clear the box wasn't there. She tossed clothing out the open door, wondering why it was going so dark. She blinked to clear her eyes and realized the *sharpen* spell was wearing off. She was running out of time.

She made herself work methodically, pushing the contents of the tent to the back as she moved from side to side. Someone's sword tripped her, and she kicked it half out the door and kept looking. The box wasn't there.

Cursing, she hurried out of the tent, saying, "It's not—"

Dianthe and Osfald were gone. She was alone in the camp. Distantly, she heard the sound of shouts and more fighting, though not the clash of sword against sword. She pushed her hair out of her face, wishing it was long enough to braid it the way Dianthe always did, and ran to the next tent. They'd bought her some time, and she wasn't going to waste it.

The next tent belonged to a single person, and after an initial search Sienne deduced it was Alethea's, given the small boots and leather jerkin shaped to a female form. She went through it thoroughly and again didn't find the box. She rejected the idea that they'd already hidden it and ducked out of the tent.

"You," Conn Giorda said. "I didn't think they'd send you."

Sienne froze. Conn stood about ten feet from her. He cradled his spellbook in the crook of his arm and stared her down. "Interesting tactic," he said. "I suppose it's you we have to thank for sending us scattering through the forest chasing echoes? Very clever for someone who's a raw beginner."

Sienne said nothing. "Let's have you drop your knife—just let it fall, then kick it away," he continued. Sienne drew the knife from its sheath and dropped it to land point-first on the ground, where it teetered and then fell over. She gave it a hard nudge with her toe, watching her freedom go skittering away.

"Now, hand over your spellbook." Conn extended his hand. Sienne slowly began extracting it from her vest, frantically casting about for something she could do. He was alone, though she couldn't hear any more fighting, so who knew where his companions were.

"Faster," Conn said.

Sienne concentrated on the air above his head. For half a breath, a giant glob of water hovered there, then fell, drenching him and making him shout in anger. Sienne turned and ran for the trees.

A hammer the size of a hay wagon smashed into her back, propelling her forward ten feet to slam into a tree trunk. Gasping for air, she clung to the tree, scrabbling with her fingers to keep herself upright. She'd never felt such pain in her life. She tried to lift her head, but her neck seemed to be broken.

Footsteps approached. "That was *truly* inspired," Conn said. "You've pissed me off, but I can admit it was a bold move." He wrenched her left arm behind her back and dragged her off the trunk. Her knees wouldn't support her, and she feared they were broken, too, except surely they'd hurt more if they were. They were just numb, a terrible gaping numbness that extended everywhere she didn't hurt. A spasm ran through her, and she tasted bile just before she vomited on her boots.

Conn waited while she threw up, then resumed dragging her back toward his camp. "You know, I underestimated you. I thought, because you allied yourself with Ham-fist, you were a fool. I can see now you just didn't know any better. Not your fault, if you were new to Fioretti. And it's not too late for you to correct that mistake."

He dropped her next to the dead campfire like a bag of old clothes and walked away out of her sight. Sienne tried to turn her head to follow him, but *force* had left her incapable of more than the tiniest movements of her fingers and toes. She tried to be grateful her neck wasn't actually broken, but panic had set in, and her heart was beating fast enough she could hear it.

"Where's Milo?" she heard Conn say.

"On his way back," said Alethea. "He went far afield chasing what turned out to be an echo, the idiot."

"And Osfald?"

"No idea. They must have lured him away somehow. But the box is still here."

Conn grunted an acknowledgement. "So, we're left with the question of what to do with you." It took Sienne a moment to realize he was talking to her. "You're not the best hostage in the world, since I imagine Ham-fist doesn't care much about the fate of a wizard." He came to stand in front of her, then crouched to put himself at her eye level. "He hates us, you know. Kitane knows why. Maybe a wizard killed his mother, or something equally heart-wrenching. Whatever the reason, getting you back will only matter to him insomuch as it lets him score against me. So I have a proposition."

Sienne blinked at him. The feeling was coming back into her face and hands, but blinking was all she could manage. "Join me," Conn said. "You have potential. With me as your mentor, you could go far, maybe even end up with a team of your own someday. You've got a couple of spells I don't know, so I'd benefit as well. It's more than Ham-fist can offer you, that madman looking for magic that doesn't exist. What do you say?"

He looked utterly sincere. Sienne spat in his face.

Conn cursed and struck her a powerful blow across the face that made her ears ring and tears spring to her eyes. He stood and wiped his face. "Tie her," he told Alethea. "Leave her where she's visible. I want them to know we've won."

Alethea flung Sienne on her face and wrenched her arms behind her back. Sienne closed her eyes as scratchy rope went around her wrists. She told herself the others wouldn't abandon her, reminded herself that it was Alaric who'd wanted her magic to play a key role in the plan, that he didn't hate her. But she'd never felt so alone as she did just then, bound and with her face pressed into the mucky coarse grass. Her only comfort was that Conn appeared to have forgotten her spellbook; it still pressed hard against her stomach. Not that it did her any good now.

Alethea finished binding Sienne and rolled her onto her back. "You're going to regret trying to trick us," she said.

Sienne worked her mouth, found it dry but capable of speech. "Didn't try," she whispered. "Succeeded."

Alethea kicked her in the side, making her whimper. The pain was just one of many, but the effects of *force* were subsiding. It still made Sienne reconsider the idea of taunting her captors. She rested her head on the ground and looked up at the canopy of leaves. Pale light filtered through them in places, telling her dawn had come. Where was everyone? They had failed to get the box, but they were free, so what was the next plan? Sienne couldn't believe Alaric wouldn't have a fallback plan.

Loud footsteps made her tense, hoping it was one of her companions come to rescue her, but then she heard Milo Giorda's voice. "They disappeared. You sure they didn't get the artifact?"

"Sure," Conn said. Sienne craned her neck to look at him. He held the silver box in one arm and his spellbook casually in the other. "Where's Osfald?"

"Don't know. Do you think they captured him?"

"No great loss if they did."

"We should pack up and go," Alethea said. "You plan to take the whelp with us?"

"She's just misguided," Conn said. "And there's still a chance she can be a deterrent to them attacking us again. Ham-fist may not care about her, but Dianthe Espero probably does, as soft-hearted as she is. She won't want to see the girl's pretty little throat slit."

"*Hoy! Giorda!*"

It was Perrin's voice. Sienne's heart pounded with equal parts fear and joy. "We have something of yours," Perrin went on. "As you have something of ours. An even exchange seems in order, do you not think?"

Conn grinned at his siblings, a nasty expression Sienne wished she hadn't seen. "You mean Osfald?" he shouted. "He's nothing to me. Keep him, or throw him out, it's all the same."

The three Giordas had turned toward the spot Perrin's voice had come from. Nobody was watching Sienne. She flexed against the ropes binding her, but Alethea had done her work well, and they gave not an inch. If only she had a knife!

The thought had barely crossed her mind when she remembered Zenobia's boot knife. She'd carried it for so long its hard, angular hilt no longer registered. She strained, pulling up her feet behind her, but the thing had slipped deep into her too-large boot, out of her reach. That was probably a good thing, since Conn hadn't seen it to take it with her belt knife, but it might as well be gone for all the good it did her. She closed her eyes and breathed out through her nostrils. She had one last hope, which was that her invisible fingers could fetch it out for her. The trouble was, she'd never tried to lift anything she couldn't see. But she could feel the knife pressing against her shin, and she had absolutely nothing to lose.

Breathing out slowly again, she pictured the boot knife, the slim blade, the smooth hilt, and imagined her invisible fingers wrapping around it, tugging it free. She felt a smooth movement against her leg, like a snake sliding over her skin. Excited at her success, she pulled harder, and the thing slipped out of her grasp and slid back a fraction of an inch. She gritted her teeth and made herself relax, told herself this was nothing, it wasn't life or death, just a simple exercise—

The knife slid smoothly up her leg and into her hand.

Carefully, she reversed it and laid the knife's edge against the ropes. She prayed she wasn't about to slit her wrists, and began the agonizing process of cutting herself free.

She'd heard a conversation going on between Conn and Perrin, but hadn't had the attention to spare to listen to it. Now she heard Conn say to his siblings, "She's more of a bargaining chip than I thought. We'll have to keep her until we get back to Fioretti."

"I don't know," Milo said. "That's an awful burden, caring for a hostage. Maybe we should just exchange and be done with it."

"And give Ham-fist the satisfaction? Not a chance," Conn said. "Still not interested," he shouted. "You should give up and go home. You can have your little friend back when we return to Fioretti. If she wants to go back." He laughed. "I've got three days to convince her where her fortunes ought to lie."

The last strand of rope parted, and Sienne was free—but free to do what? Gingerly, making very small movements, she slipped her spellbook out of her vest. She had one offensive spell, and she'd never tried it, but the Giordas were grouped together as neatly as if they'd set themselves up for her to make her first test. She willed her book open to the right page and waited for her moment.

"That sounds like a threat," Perrin called out. "I warn you, threatening our companion will bring you nothing but misery."

"I won't hurt her," Conn began, but Sienne wasn't listening. With his words as cover for her own so he wouldn't realize what she was doing, she read off the evocation *scream*.

It was sharp, hard-edged, and it burned her mouth like acid. It poured out of her, building to a terrible climax, until the final syllables emerged from deep within her as a shrill, skull-piercing shriek that rattled her already muddled brain.

The Giordas screamed and threw up their hands to cover their ears, but it was too late. All of them dropped, Milo landing on his side and curling up into the fetal position, Alethea with her head pressed to the ground like she was trying to burrow into it, Conn retching and gagging on his knees.

Sienne lowered her spellbook and let her head fall. Someone was running toward her from the other direction, someone who dropped to their knees and supported Sienne's head. "Kitane's left arm, what was that?" Dianthe exclaimed.

Alaric came into view, standing over the convulsing Giordas. "Sorry that took so long," he said. "We had to be careful, working our way around while Perrin had their attention."

"She has rescued herself, I think," Kalanath said. He prodded Milo with his staff. "What is that?"

"*Scream*," Sienne whispered. Her mouth was still sore from the evocation. "Are their ears bleeding? Their ears are supposed to bleed if I did it right."

"I think bleeding ears are the least of their troubles," Alaric said. He crouched beside Sienne. "Can you walk?"

Sienne could barely shake her head in a "no." Alaric grunted, then scooped her up in his arms as easily as if she'd been a kitten. "Grab the artifact," he said, "and let's get moving. How long will they be out?"

"Don't know," Sienne whispered. "Half an hour?"

"More than enough." Alaric smiled down at her. "Did Conn try to recruit you?"

"Yes."

"You could have told him yes. He'd have resources—"

"I spat in his face."

Alaric and Dianthe laughed.

"Besides, he abandoned that priest, didn't he? Didn't want to trade me for him. I don't think he cares about loyalty."

"It is true," Kalanath said. "You did well."

"I didn't want anything he had to offer," Sienne said. "And I certainly wouldn't betray my friends."

Silence fell. Finally, Dianthe said, "I'm really glad I went into the Lucky Coin that morning."

"So am I," Sienne said.

PART II

14

The copper bath was barely big enough for Sienne to stand in. She focused briefly on the water, heating it to just above body temperature, then scrubbed herself vigorously before it could cool. Probably it was a bad idea, bathing when all she had to wear were her own filthy clothes, but it felt so *good* to be clean. Even so, she wasn't going to wash her hair, which would take forever to dry even in this heat. She'd put up with an itchy scalp until tomorrow, when they returned to Fioretti.

She stepped out of the tub and dried herself off. The outpost only had rudimentary facilities and no private bedrooms, just men's and women's dormitories, and the bed she'd been given was hard, but it was softer than the ground and Sienne wasn't going to grumble. She pulled her shirt on over her head—oh, it was worse than she'd imagined, the shirt stiff from its immersion in rainwater and grimy to boot! She gritted her teeth and finished dressing. Tomorrow, a real bath, a real bed, and clean clothes.

She'd been the last to bathe, at her own request, and now as she exited the bathing room she saw no one in the short hall that connected the dining hall with the dormitories. She deposited her things on her bed and followed her nose to the delicious smells of baked ham and fresh greens.

The dining hall was about two-thirds full. She found her team seated at one of the round tables, already eating. She was about to protest when Dianthe nudged a full plate at the place next to her. Sienne sat and dug into rich, salty ham, mashed yams, and an unexpected pile of green peas, out of season and therefore probably the result of magic.

"So what next?" she asked. "We'll be back in Fioretti by noon tomorrow, right?"

Alaric nodded. "Dianthe and I will deliver the artifact to Master Fontanna. Then we'll see about a buyer for the rest of the salvage."

"And you will deliver us the remainder of our money?" Kalanath said.

"Yes, if you'll give us a way to contact you. It shouldn't take long."

"I meant," Sienne said, "what about scrapping? What comes next?"

"We'll be happy to vouch for you with other employers," Dianthe said. "We may have a poor reputation among scrappers, but clients know us to be reliable. That should help you find another job."

"Oh," Sienne said, trying not to sound as disappointed as she felt. Sure, it had been a rough start, but they'd worked so well together, she'd thought maybe that meant—

"I, for one, am looking forward to a few weeks with nothing much to do," Perrin said. "I am not entirely certain I want a future as a scrapper. Though I admit this time together has been rewarding, and not just in a fiduciary way."

"I, too, have enjoyed this," Kalanath said. "You are not as I was told. I am glad I did not listen to rumor. I will remember this for future jobs."

Sienne pushed her remaining peas around her plate. So she was the only one who thought they should be a permanent team. She caught Dianthe looking at her in concern and smiled brightly. Had she said anything to indicate her feelings? She needed to keep her naïve sentimentality to herself.

After dinner, she and Dianthe walked to the women's dormitory together. The full meal and the relaxing warmth of the bath had made Sienne tired, and she found herself actually looking forward to the hard bed.

"Are you all right?" Dianthe said.

"Just sleepy."

"You seemed a little down. That's normal, you know. When a job's over, there's a bit of a letdown. But everything feels bright again when you get a new job. Don't worry about it."

"Oh. That's...good to know."

Dianthe nodded. "You did good work. Maybe someday we'll work together again."

Sienne made herself smile. "I'd like that."

———

SIENNE SWIPED HAIR OUT OF HER FACE WHERE THE WIND HAD BLOWN IT. A storm was coming in off the ocean, and the wind smelled of brine and sand. She realized her horse was crowding Dianthe and reined her in. Nobody on the streets paid any attention to them; everyone was heading for home, and shelter against the storm. Sienne felt disappointed. They'd returned to Fioretti as successful scrappers, and she thought *someone* ought to acknowledge that, even though reason told her no one could possibly know they'd been successful just by looking at them.

She spat a loose strand out of her mouth and made herself sit up straight instead of hunching to make herself a smaller target for the storm. Now she could look forward to a real bath in a real bathing house, a launderer, and a good meal. Once they brought the artifact to Master Fontanna and found buyers for their salvage, they were free to go their own ways. Sienne wondered if she should find other lodgings. It would be awkward if she were living in Master Tersus's house, but not going out on jobs with Alaric and Dianthe. But they were good lodgings, and...damn it, she wasn't going to let them make this uncomfortable! Even if she *was* the only one who thought they all worked well together.

They were passing through a district where wealthy men and women lived. Their houses resembled Master Tersus's, but bigger, with hedges surrounding pleasure gardens and fountains and horse paths. Sienne couldn't imagine keeping a horse in the big city just for fun, it would be so hard on the animal, but clearly people did. She was used to riding on the open downs, with the wind in her hair as it was now, but scented with green grass and the roses from her father's gardens at their country estate. She patted her horse's neck in apology for having to ride her over the hard cobbles.

Ahead, Alaric was turning in at the stables, which were busier than when they'd left. Did he think it strange to ride a horse when he was able to turn into one? Sienne wouldn't be able to manage it. She followed and dismounted, handing her reins to a stable hand and removing her gear. The stable hand led the chestnut mare away without saying a word, leaving Sienne feeling bereft and denied a proper farewell. Which was ridiculous, because she'd only ridden the animal for two halves of a day. Even so, it was one step closer to saying farewell to her companions, and that depressed her.

"We're going to drop our things at the hostel, then go straight to Master Fontanna's to deliver the artifact," Dianthe was telling Kalanath. "You're welcome to come along, but it's not necessary."

"Why not offer the other artifacts to this Master Fontanna?" said Perrin. He tied his hair more securely out of his eyes and added, "He certainly sounds as if he can afford them."

"We have a dealer we trade with. She gets first crack at what we find with the understanding that she'll give us the best possible deal. But if she doesn't want them, Master Fontanna will be the second we talk to."

"Very well. You may leave word for me at Pasotti's tavern, and Pasotti will know how to reach me." Perrin bowed low to each of them in turn. "It has been a genuine pleasure."

"That is so," Kalanath said. "You know how to find me. I would choose to work with you again."

Sienne was sure this was the highest praise he could give. She wished she dared suggest they work together again immediately, but that was stupid. There was no job, not even the possibility of a job. This was just loneliness talking.

"Thanks again, and good luck to you," Alaric said, offering his hand to each man. With a wave and a nod respectively, Perrin and Kalanath left the stable yard, turning opposite directions at the gate and disappearing into the crowd.

Alaric turned to Sienne. "What, you're still here?"

It hurt, and she wasn't sure why, since his smile showed he wasn't serious. She flashed a smile of her own and said, "I'm staying at Master Tersus's too, remember? And I'm curious about Master Fontanna. I want to see this through to the end."

"It was a joke, Sienne," Alaric said, one huge hand resting briefly on her shoulder. "Let's stow our gear, and get cleaned up, and then we'll satisfy your curiosity."

Relieved, Sienne followed Alaric and Dianthe through the streets. Fat drops of rain fell occasionally, spattering her face, but the clouds failed to let fall their burdens, and they made it to Master Tersus's house without getting drenched.

"I'll show you where the bath house is, Sienne," Dianthe said. "Don't take too long. His cistern isn't more than average sized."

"Oh, then you should go first. I can warm the water myself."

"No, I want a quick nap. I'll go last."

The bath house was actually a stone-walled room that backed off the kitchen's enormous fireplace. It would be comfortable in winter, when the storms howled off the harbor. At the moment, it was stuffy and damp, and Sienne's filthy scalp itched from the moisture in the air. It had a tub big enough for her to sit in, and she scrubbed herself clean and rinsed thoroughly, conscious of the need to hurry. She'd had a bath like this at home, only porcelain instead of copper, and no one used it but her. It was a luxury she didn't mind giving up.

She dried herself, dressed in the clothes she'd left behind, which were beautifully clean, and ran into Alaric in the hall. He had a bundle of clothes in one arm and a towel over the other. "Sorry," she said.

"That was fast."

"I—yes. I didn't want to dawdle."

"Master Fontanna's not going anywhere." He scratched his head. "I never appreciate bathing so much as when I get back from the wilderness. And to think I used to fight my mother over it."

Sienne had never thought of Alaric as having a mother. It was ridiculous, everyone had a mother, but he always seemed to have sprung fully-formed out of the earth itself. "I think most children do that."

"Probably. Though I—" He laughed, somewhat self-consciously. "I haven't thought of that in years."

"You must..." Embarrassed, she let her words die away.

"Must what?"

"I was going to say, you must miss your family, but that's presumptuous of me."

"I miss them. But I'd rather not talk about it. It's..." His eyes focused on something far distant from this narrow corridor, damp with condensation from Sienne's bath. "There's a possibility they were punished for my running away. I can't remember them without remembering my guilt."

"I understand. I mean, I can't possibly understand what you've been through, but I do understand having good memories tangled up with bad ones."

"Right." He blinked, and turned his attention on her. "You sure you want to come with us to see Master Fontanna? It's not really your responsibility."

It wasn't the first time he'd said something like this, and she now wondered if this were a hint she wasn't getting. "If you don't want me to, I'll stay behind."

"No. It's just that he's a busy man, and we're likely to have a long wait."

"I don't mind."

He smiled and shook his head in mock despair. "Suit yourself, but

I know I'd send Dianthe on her own if I didn't like having both kidneys in working order."

Sienne laughed. Alaric shouldered past her and shut the bath house door.

Back in her room, she emptied her pack and put her dirty clothes into it. She might find a launderer somewhere close, and get that taken care of before it was time to leave. Dianthe's door was partly open, and Sienne could hear her snoring, so she probably had time. She hurried down the stairs and into the kitchen, where Leofus sat leaning against the wall, his ubiquitous spoon on the counter next to him. He was reading a book and acknowledged her entrance with the barest flick of his gaze toward her.

"Ah...do you know where I can find someone to wash my clothes?" she asked.

"Three streets west, seventh door on the right," Leofus said. "You'll see the sign."

"Thanks."

The storm was blowing hard, carrying leaves and loose papers with it. It blew Sienne westward, ruffling her shirt like a banner and whipping her hair, pulled back in a short, damp tail, around her cheeks. The sky was the color of sand, the gray clouds tinged with yellow where the sun tried to shine through. It gave the brown bricks of the buildings an odd glowing bronze tint, making them look as if they'd been polished to a high gloss.

She found the launderer by his sign, a washboard hanging over the door by a single chain. The other rattled loose in the wind. "You're going to lose your sign," she told the round, rosy-cheeked man inside. The laundry smelled of hot water and soap, a comforting, homey smell, but the man's nose was pinched as if he smelled something else. Something nasty.

"You want something?" he said, his words biting.

"Um...laundry?" Under his scowling eye, Sienne felt her request was something unsavory.

The man rolled his eyes as if she'd asked him to do something impossible. "Pick up tomorrow," he said. "Payment in advance."

"Half in advance, so you'll do a good job."

"That's insulting!"

"It's good business."

He scowled so hard she was afraid he'd rupture something. "Fine. Six centi now, six tomorrow."

Sienne paid him and smiled pleasantly, not that she thought it would make a difference. She opened the door and the wind nearly took it out of her hands, blowing dust and rain into the laundry. *"Shut the damn door!"* the launderer shrieked. Sienne hastily pulled it shut.

Fat, hot raindrops pelted her, making her cover her head with her hands, which were inadequate to the task. She ran down the street and took shelter in the arched doorway of a little shop at the end of the lane. It wasn't much protection against the rain that was falling practically horizontally, but it was better than nothing. She'd seen these storms twice before in her short time in Fioretti and knew they never lasted long. She'd wait out the worst of it, then hurry back to Master Tersus's.

The lane ended at one of the main streets, paved in golden stone that shone with a bright slickness as the rain poured down. Rainwater filled the gutters, carrying with it trash and dog turds. Sienne felt a moment's gratitude for her waterproof boots, though not enough to want to stand in the rushing stream. A couple of men in broad-brimmed hats ran past, splashing through the street. Sienne watched them go and wondered how waterproof their shoes were. Probably not very.

She looked the other direction and saw another man approaching. This one was shorter even than she and walked like someone who thought carefully about every step he took. He had no hat, and his long black hair was slicked to his head with rain that beaded on it oddly, as if it were greasy as well as wet. Looking at him made Sienne uncomfortable, as if her own hair were greasy and her clothes soaked. She averted her gaze as he drew nearer. Staring at strangers never got you anything but trouble, in her experience.

His splashing steps grew louder. She risked a glance in his direction. His path was an undeviating line, not bothering to avoid the worst of the trash in the street. And he was headed directly for her.

Sienne's heart beat rapidly, urging her to flee. She told herself it was stupid, that this man, this total stranger, was unlikely to attack her in the middle of a busy street in the afternoon. But a quick glance told her the street was virtually empty, the heavy clouds made the skies as dim as twilight, and the man was getting closer and showed no signs of changing his path. Sienne backed away from the protection of the doorway, turned, and ran.

For the first few moments, she thought she'd overreacted. Then, over the sound of her own panicked footsteps, she heard the man's heavier ones, accelerating toward her. She clutched her spellbook to her stomach to stop it shifting and took the first left, praying she could outrun the man. She needed to find shelter, fast. She turned right, toward Master Tersus's house—she thought. The houses on this street were made of fat gray stones that gleamed with rain, not small brown bricks. She was lost.

She slowed and cast a glance over her shoulder and shrieked involuntarily when she saw her pursuer only a dozen yards behind. Pushing herself, she took another left, hoping to work her way back to safety. The new street was no more familiar than the last. She ran harder, scrambling to keep from slipping on the wet cobbles, and made several more turns. It was hopeless. She was just making herself more lost.

She gripped her spellbook again. Its hard edges gave her an idea —but she would need to outdistance the man, if only for a few moments.

She started looking for a tavern, or an inn, or any business that might still be open during this storm. There. A wooden loaf of bread hanging above a door. She flung herself toward the bakery and turned one last time, terrified of what she might see but helpless not to look. The man was only yards behind her. She threw herself through the door and slammed it behind her. "Someone's chasing me," she gasped. "I need your back door."

A slim older woman blinked at her. No doubt Sienne's disheveled appearance made her look disreputable. A spotty-faced boy said, "Back door's that way."

"Martus!" the woman exclaimed. "She might be a thief!"

"Thank you," Sienne told Martus, and bolted for the back room just as the door began to open.

The back door was unlocked, for which Sienne thanked any avatar who might be listening. Beyond it was an alley piled high with refuse. Sienne grabbed a barrel that was still mostly intact and hauled it to block the door. Then she whipped out her spellbook, threw it open, and gabbled out the syllables of *imitate*.

She was too well trained to let her panic affect her voice, but when it came to shaping the spell to give herself a new appearance, she found herself having to force the spell into performing properly. Three inches extra height, black hair instead of chestnut, and—yes— a male body, just to be sure. Now she looked like the rosy-cheeked launderer.

The barrel thumped as the door hit it. Sienne stuffed the spellbook into her shirt and ran for it again. She might not look like herself anymore, but unless her pursuer was truly stupid, he'd put it together that the stranger just outside the bakery had something to do with Sienne vanishing.

Once back on the main street, she hurried along without running, just one more person looking for shelter against the rain, which was dwindling. She recognized this street as one she'd run down moments before, though that still made it unfamiliar as far as returning to Master Tersus's house went.

She trotted across the intersection and saw, with a jolt of horror, the greasy man headed her way. *He doesn't know it's you. Stay calm.* She kept striding along, pretending she didn't notice him. Running might give away her game. So long as she stayed calm, the confusion spell would last, and—

Footsteps grew louder. The man was running toward her. Sienne half-turned to watch him approach, gripped by indecision. Run, and be safe for certain? Stay put, and brazen it out? Maybe this was a madman, intent on accosting anyone roaming the streets during the storm. She kept walking, her heart hammering a terrible rhythm.

The running footsteps were almost on top of her. She closed her eyes and prayed an unfocused prayer, her mind skipping over all six avatars and ending up on Averran: *O Averran, you cranky old avatar, protect me in my hour of need.*

The footsteps passed. Out of the corner of her eye Sienne saw the greasy man running away down the street. Her chest was sore from running, her legs ached, but she felt so relieved she didn't care. Now she just needed not to be lost.

She decided to maintain the confusion spell, just in case. She hoped she'd spun a good one, because she still looked normal to herself. At the end of the street, she turned right. She'd been here before, too.

Rapid footsteps came up behind her. She turned to see the greasy man barreling down on her, his hands outstretched to grab her. Terror made her confusion spell unravel. She shrieked, turned, and ran.

The rain was letting up, and the storm clouds had lost the battle with the sun, sending wan yellow light down on the streets. Sienne took more turns at random. She was only outpacing her pursuer because she was taller and lighter, but he seemed to have unlimited stamina, his pace never faltering. Her whole body hurt from keeping up the punishing pace, and she faltered, then dug deep for reserves she'd never tapped before. "Help me!" she shouted, but the few people venturing into the street ignored her. That was the drawback to the big city; people rarely got involved in other people's problems.

She turned a corner, and after a few steps, recognized the end of Master Tersus's street. Sobbing with relief, she flung herself up the shallow incline and through the side door. She slammed it shut and leaned against it, breathing heavily.

The bath house door opened. Dianthe poked her head out. "Sienne? What in—you're soaked! Why were you out in the rain?"

"Someone chased me," Sienne panted. "Didn't fool him. He—"

Someone pounded on the door once, making it rattle like a

sledgehammer struck it. Sienne shrieked and pressed against it harder, willing it to stay shut.

Thunderous feet on the stair heralded Alaric's appearance. "What in Sisyletus's name is going on?"

"Someone's after me," Sienne said. "He followed me, I don't know why, but he's out there."

Alaric swore and moved Sienne aside. "What do you think you—" he shouted as he opened the door.

No one was there.

Alaric stood with his hand on the knob and looked up and down the street. "I don't see anyone."

"There was someone!" Sienne shouted. "I'm not crazy!"

"I didn't say you were. I meant he seems to have run away." Alaric shut the door and put a hand on her shoulder. "You're terrified. What happened?"

Sienne tried to calm her breathing. "I went to the launderer," she began, and recounted the story, leaving out how frightened she'd been when she was lost. "He wasn't fooled by my confusion spell," she finally said. "He knew who I was regardless of my appearance."

"Are you sure it was enough of a deception?" Dianthe asked.

"I'm sure. I've done that spell more times than I can count." She laughed and hoped it didn't sound hysterical. "It's gotten me into trouble about as often as it's gotten me out of it. But I'm sure I looked nothing like myself."

Dianthe and Alaric exchanged glances. "That's not good," Dianthe said. "Why would anyone be after you? More to the point, what about you were they following? Are you carrying anything special? An artifact?"

"The only artifacts I have are the ones we retrieved from the keep, and I don't have any of them on me. I'm not even carrying the coin." Dianthe had given her one of the six coins for a keepsake, and she intended to have it drilled so she could wear it around her neck.

Alaric frowned. "Go get cleaned up," he said, "and let's go see Master Fontanna. If someone is after you, I hope he tries to reach you while we're around. It sounds like he has some questions to answer."

Sienne climbed to her room, feeling as weary as if she'd run—but then, she had run miles, hadn't she? She changed her soaked shirt, brushed off her damp trousers, and returned downstairs. Alaric and Dianthe were talking quietly when she appeared, a conversation that cut off when she arrived. That disappointed Sienne, because she had a feeling, based on how they looked at her, that they'd been talking about her.

"Stay close," Alaric said, and pulled the door open.

15

Master Fontanna's house was one of the palatial buildings of gray-streaked white marble on the hill above the palace. It backed on the Vochus River, which, at that point in its course, flowed too fast for bathing or boating, two things Sienne associated with riverfront property. With the many manors between the road and the river, they couldn't see the water, but they could hear it, a constant rustling, roaring sound like a storm wind over a forest. The noise must be unbearable for those living near it. Or was that something one became accustomed to? Sienne was glad she wasn't in a position to find out.

She thought they might go around the side, to the servants' entrance, but Alaric, box in hand, went straight to the front door, up the pathway of white quartz pebbles bordered with obsidian that had probably cost more than the expensive leaded glass windows. There was a pull chain with a smooth ebony handle next to the door. Alaric pulled it, producing only silence. Whatever bell it was attached to would ring deeper in the house, summoning a servant.

After half a minute, during which time Sienne tried not to watch in every direction at once for the greasy man, the door opened. A man wearing violet knee breeches and a violet waistcoat over a gray shirt with bloused sleeves examined them. "Please come in," he said, exactly as if they'd been nobles instead of scrappers.

The cold marble of the manor's façade extended to the entry hall, where an iron chandelier hung low enough for Alaric to touch, shedding its light over the floor and walls. A staircase of more marble ascended out of sight to the floor above, and closed doors to the left and right made the room look even more forbidding. No carpet or tapestries softened the effect.

"Master Fontanna is quite busy," the servant said. "You will wait in the library." He crossed the entry hall to the right-hand door and opened it, bowing them in. Sienne smiled at him as she passed and got only an impassive stare that made her want to laugh. Why was it servants were sometimes so much more stiff and correct than their masters?

The library smelled of dust and disuse, a smell that annoyed Sienne. She wasn't fond of books for their own sakes, not like her younger brother Alcander, but so many of them contained spells, or instructions for casting spells, that she felt they all deserved to be treated with respect. The room was tall and narrow, with shelves on all four walls that reached a good twenty feet high. Two ladders on rails gave access to the upper shelves, their wheels well-greased, as Sienne discovered when she gave one a little push. Alaric frowned at her when she did so, and she put her hands ostentatiously behind her back. There were a couple of leather armchairs with high backs in one corner, but no table or desk. This wasn't a working library. It was a library for show.

Sienne prowled the shelves, looking for familiar titles. "Oh, I've read this," she said, touching its spine.

"Sienne," Alaric began.

"I'm not touching it! Well, yes, I'm touching it, but I'm not going to take it off the shelf." Her fingers came away grimy. "I have to say I don't think much of his household staff, if they've let the books come to this condition."

"This is the only room he ever lets us enter," Dianthe said. "I don't think he cares much about it."

"Have you worked for him often?"

"A few times. He's very thorough in his research about the ruins, and usually has a specific item he's after. And he pays us whether or not we find it—pays us more if we do, obviously, but he respects our efforts."

"I guess not every client is as generous."

"Not even close," Alaric said. "Some of them hire scrappers solely for the salvage, for exclusive rights to whatever they find, and expect the scrappers to fund the expedition expenses. Others will pay a pittance up front and then stiff you if you don't come back with anything they like."

"So how do you know which jobs are likely to have...what you want? Rituals?" She felt nervous about broaching the topic in what could technically be considered a public place, but Alaric didn't shush her, so she guessed it was all right.

"We do our own research," Dianthe said. "Talk to other scrappers, when they're willing to talk. We're a close-mouthed lot, really, because of the need to protect our finds. But often what we want is in places that have been cleaned out, supposedly. And then sometimes we get lucky on an unrelated job."

Sienne opened her mouth to ask, *And have you found anything, ever?* but was interrupted by the door opening. A tall, handsome man of middle years, his black hair swept back from a widow's peak to brush his collar, entered with his hand outstretched. "Alaric," he said, his voice rich as coffee and cream. "Dianthe. And...who's this?"

"This is Sienne. She accompanied us on our excursion," Dianthe said.

Sienne took the man's offered hand. It was surprisingly cold and clammy, not at all as attractive as the rest of him. "Vincentius Fontanna," he said with a smile. "Very pleased to meet you."

"Likewise." Sienne managed not to wipe her hand on her trousers when he released it.

Master Fontanna's attention fell on the box. A broad smile spread across his face. "You found it."

"We did," Alaric said. He pressed two fingers against the center of the box's lid, and the iris opened, revealing the gold sheet and the styli. Master Fontanna drew in a sharp breath.

"It's amazing," he said. "And...Kitane's right eye, it still works!"

"Not perfectly," Sienne said. "The magic is erratic."

Master Fontanna glanced at her. "You're a wizard?"

"Yes."

He turned his sharp gaze on Alaric, but said nothing. He removed one of the styli from the clasps that held it and turned it over in his fingers, like spinning a baton. "Do you know what this does?"

The question seemed directed at her, so Sienne said, "No. Sir." Belatedly, she remembered she wasn't living as a noble and ought to address this man with greater respect. But he didn't seem to notice her gaffe.

"It's intended to direct the distance-viewer's gaze, as it were." Master Fontanna tapped the sharp tip of the stylus against the gold plate. A chime rang out, and the plate went briefly invisible. From where she stood, Sienne could see moving blobs of color, nothing discrete, but Alaric's eyes widened.

"Yes, and that's what it can do when it isn't fully functional," Master Fontanna said, a little smugly. He put the stylus back and took the box from Alaric. "Excellent work. You've more than earned the rest of your pay, and the bonus."

More pay? Sienne was about to protest when she remembered the day she'd met Dianthe and Alaric, how Alaric had objected to Sienne receiving fifty lari up front, and guessed if Dianthe hadn't taken pity on her obvious impecuniousness, she'd only have gotten twenty-five.

Master Fontanna pulled a rope hanging near one of the ladders. "May I ask if you found anything else?"

"A few things," Dianthe said. "Some coins. We stumbled across a hidden cache with what appear to be six lenses, some of them still magical. A pendant."

"I'm interested in anything that came from that keep. I can make it worth your while."

"Sorry, these are spoken for. But if our buyer doesn't want them, we'll come to you."

"I think, as your sponsor, I have right of first refusal on your salvage."

"That's not in the contract," Alaric said. "We're sorry, but we've given our word."

"I see." Master Fontanna's demeanor grew cold, but his voice, when he spoke next, was as warm and rich as ever. "Hermia will see to your payment. Good day to you."

"Good day," Alaric said. Master Fontanna smiled pleasantly at Sienne, then left the room.

"Wonderful. He's upset," Dianthe said. "Maybe we should have sold him the artifacts."

"We need Neoma's goodwill more than his," Alaric said. "He's not the only person we work for."

"Yes, but he's our best client."

"We can't afford to be exclusive." Alaric let out a deep sigh. "Maybe we can offer half of the artifacts to Neoma and bring the rest to him."

The door opened. A short, gray-haired woman wearing half-moon spectacles rimmed in gold entered, carrying a carved wooden box about the size of the artifact they'd given Master Fontanna. She set the box on one of the chairs and opened it, revealing several white bags of varying sizes. "Your payment," she said. "One hundred fifty lari, plus one hundred for the artifact."

She handed Dianthe two fist-sized bags and one about half their size. Dianthe tucked them away in the pack she wore slung over her shoulder. "Don't you want to count it?" the woman said.

"You've always been honest with me before," Dianthe said.

The woman nodded and shut the box. "Good luck to you." She held the door open for them.

Outside the manor, Sienne said, "Will we go to...Neoma...now?"

"Yes, and if she buys everything, we can divide the proceeds, you can take your share, and then you're free to find another contract," Alaric said.

Sienne hoped she didn't look disappointed. "Good."

Neoma's shop was in a quiet, run-down part of Fioretti. It wasn't quite a slum, but it had the air of a neighborhood that was headed that way. Still, it was clean, and lacked the loitering, aimless, hard-eyed men of the streets surrounding the pub where they'd met Perrin. It seemed like ages ago they'd ventured there. Only six days. No wonder Alaric and the others didn't feel compelled to stick together. Six days wasn't enough to build those kinds of bonds, even if they did include facing danger together.

Bells jangled as Dianthe pushed the freshly-scrubbed door of the shop open. Sienne gaped. Tall wooden bookcases, their shelves filled with all manner of items, blocked her view of the store's interior, giving it a claustrophobic feel. It took her a moment to realize there was organization to the mess. One shelf held nothing but boxes, mostly carved wood, but also metal and ivory and even a couple made of stone. Another shelf was filled with toys, some of them artifacts that worked on their own. Trinkets Sienne had no name for cluttered a low trunk that might be valuable all by itself.

"She's not a...fence, is she?" Sienne said in a low voice.

Alaric shook his head. "Just a dealer in miscellaneous goods from all over the world. Neoma has a good eye for what will sell."

"She needs to relocate, find someplace where the foot traffic is better," Dianthe said, "but she likes this area."

"That's right," a deep voice said. "And I notice you never have any trouble finding me."

A tall, broad-shouldered woman came around the end of a shelf containing old-fashioned scroll cases decorated with bronze and copper studs. She had hair as short as Alaric's, but dyed bright crimson, and her arms looked as if she could lift one of the shelves without breaking a sweat. She smiled at Sienne. "Who's the babe in arms?"

"Sienne," Sienne said. "I'm a wizard."

Neoma's eyebrows went nearly to her hairline. "You are not. And in company with the Ansorjan Mountain?"

"Times change," Alaric said, in a tone of voice that suggested that line of conversation was a dead end. "We have some things for you to look at."

Neoma gave him a narrow-eyed stare. "Oh, I think I want to hear the story first."

"We needed a wizard to access our last scrapping job," Dianthe said. "That's all the story there is."

"I'm sure it's not, but you're entitled to your privacy." Neoma shrugged and turned away. "Come on back to my office, and let's see what you have."

Neoma's "office" was a small space divided from the rest of the store by three bookcases, their shelves full of miscellaneous items that weren't organized at all. A tall table made of ash and an equally tall stool were wedged into one corner. The table held a brass lamp with bright white magical lights illuminating its surface and a magnifying glass on a matching brass frame that screwed into the table top. Neoma settled herself on the stool and crooked a finger at Dianthe. Dianthe opened her pack and removed one of the glass and metal artifacts, setting it in the precise center of the table.

"Interesting," Neoma said, prodding it with one long finger. "What does it do?"

"We don't know. It has a little magic still on it, but not enough to make it work properly. At least, we assume not. If you press the gems, some of them move."

Dianthe had cleaned all the artifacts free of soot, with Sienne's assistance creating water. They hadn't wanted to submerge the things, so they'd used the ends of Dianthe's lock picks to get at the crevices where the gems were attached to the metal cuffs. Neoma picked up this one, studded with round, smooth lapis lazuli stones. She pressed one of them, and it made a tiny click. White light ran across the engraving. Neoma drew in a startled breath and raised it to her eye to look through. "Interesting," she said again. She held it out to Alaric. "Recognize this?"

Sienne craned her head to look over Alaric's arm. A tiny picture of a grass hummock surrounded by worn flagstones, its detail as fine as if they were actually there, showed in the circle of the glass. A squirrel loped across the middle distance from left to right and disappeared.

"That's the ruin where we found these," Alaric said. "Looks like... the view from the northwest tower."

"Some kind of watching device," Neoma said. "Keep an eye on the place while you're gone. You found more of these?"

Dianthe laid them out on the table. Three of them were dark. One, studded with pearls, showed darkness that shivered when the gems were pressed. The fifth showed a view none of them recognized. "These three might be really valuable," Neoma said, nudging the ones that still worked, more or less. "If they can be reset to show new locations, they might be very valuable indeed. The other three are pretty enough, so a collector who doesn't care about the condition of his artifacts might want them. I'll give you a hundred for the lot."

"Ninety for five. I think we'll keep this one. Our client expressed an interest, and we'd like his goodwill," Alaric said, plucking the partially-working one from the lineup.

"Eighty-five, then. I have to make a profit."

"Done."

Dianthe shook the coins out onto the table. "Very good condition," Neoma said. "They're not uncommon, but the condition should make up for that. Fifteen for the set."

Sienne felt more excited about this than she had about the lenses. Her first find! True, it wasn't worth much, but that only made her feel less guilty about defacing one of them as a keepsake.

"Then there's this," Dianthe said, removing the bluestone pendant. It glittered brilliantly in the lamp's light. "It's not magical, just pretty."

"And big. The shape's odd."

"Is that a problem?"

"I doubt it. Makes it unique. I know a couple of people who'd pay well for this. Pair it with the right chain, and it will make quite the statement." Neoma held it up to the light to watch it glitter. "Sixty."

"That's acceptable." Dianthe pushed the coins into a little pile and slung her pack over her shoulder.

Neoma reached beneath the table and brought out a locked box about the length of her intimidating forearm. It flexed alarmingly as she set it down. Sienne had never seen a wooden box treated with invulnerability before. It looked deceptively flimsy. Neoma leaned down and breathed heavily on the lock, humming a low note as she did so. It clicked open, and the lid popped up.

Inside were a couple of white sacks, much larger than the ones Master Fontanna's steward had given them, and some loose faceted gems, and a diamond necklace that made Sienne gasp. Neoma grinned. "Don't get any ideas, young wizard," she said. "This box can't be gotten into by anyone but me."

"I wouldn't steal from anyone," Sienne said, lifting her chin in defiance.

"Don't make promises your scrapping jobs won't let you keep," Neoma said. She opened one of the sacks and dug around in it, counting out gold and silver coins into piles. Finally she pushed the piles toward Dianthe. "All square and proper."

"Our thanks," Dianthe said. "Business doing well?"

"As well as ever." Neoma tossed the bluestone pendant a couple of times, then dropped it into the box and closed it. The lock clicked shut. "Had an attempted break-in the other day."

"You ought to move uptown," Alaric said. "You won't always be around to fend off burglars."

"I have protection. And my family's been at this location for three generations. But thanks for your concern."

"Scrappers have to stand by one another, don't they?" Alaric saluted her in a funny way, right hand to left shoulder in a resounding smack. Neoma returned it, grinning again.

On the street, Sienne said, "Is she a scrapper?"

"Was," Dianthe said. "One of the best. She took me and Alaric under her protection back when we first came to Fioretti, six years ago. Taught us how to keep from being cheated by clients and other scrappers. Then her father died, and she retired to run the shop. It's some of why we take our finds to her first. We owe her more than we can repay."

"She's a firm believer in helping others without looking to profit," Alaric said. "Says there's better coin in goodwill and favors."

"And speaking of coin, there's fifty-two lari coming to you," Dianthe said. "We'll divide it up back at the hostel. It's a bad idea to show your money on the street corner."

"I'm in no hurry," Sienne said, then regretted it. Suppose they took that to mean she was desperate for their company? "In fact, could we walk by the jobs board on the way back?"

"Sure," said Alaric, "but you can do better than that. The best jobs are had from word of mouth. I'm sure we can find you something."

Dianthe shot him a sharp glance Sienne was sure she wasn't supposed to have witnessed. "We should be looking for something ourselves," she said. "Those lari won't last forever."

Alaric shrugged. "Plenty of time for that."

The jobs board was as unpromising as the last several times Sienne had looked at it. Alaric regarded it with the stern appraisal of a man sizing up his daughter's latest suitor. "Don't ever work for this woman. She's notoriously slow to pay out, and requires all salvage to be turned over to her for sale—and you get a bare commission, not full value. Oh, by Sisyletus, is this man still hiring? He's been trying to wring salvage out of that site east of town for two years and hasn't found anything."

"What about this one? The pay is good," Sienne said.

"The pay is good because it's dangerous. That place might as well be the Empty Lands for all it's crawling with monsters. I don't recommend taking jobs like that unless you know and trust your companions."

"Oh." Sienne wished Alaric and Dianthe weren't along for this. True, she appreciated Alaric's guidance, but it felt like cheating on them to be looking for a different team. Though apparently she was the only one who thought so.

None of the jobs passed Alaric's scrutiny. Sienne tried not to feel relieved at this. "Don't worry," Alaric said, "we'll ask around, see what we can find."

"Thanks, but you don't have to—"

"Helping others without looking to profit, remember?" Alaric smiled and squeezed her shoulder. "Who knows? We might need a favor from you someday."

They strolled back to the hostel in the late afternoon sun, which was doing its best to burn away the water that still slicked the cobbles. The air was clean and fresh, if a bit muggy, and the distant sound of the surf made a soothing counterpoint to the rumble of the city as thousands of people went about their business. Sienne trailed behind Alaric and Dianthe, content to let the big man break the crowds. She needed more work, and so what if it wasn't with them? She needed not to let sentimentality rule her life.

Traffic increased as they neared Master Tersus's neighborhood until the street was thronged with people no doubt headed home to their dinners. The idea cheered Sienne. Leofus was taciturn, but he was a good cook, and since he disliked preparing more than one meal for dinner, the scrappers got the same thing he prepared for Master Tersus. She'd had one of these dinners already and it had been excellent.

They turned the corner and trudged up the slope toward Master Tersus's house. Sienne felt a shiver of fear at remembering how she'd run up this street in terror only hours before. She'd almost forgotten the greasy man. Now she glanced around, wishing there weren't so many shrubs and trees giving cover to any madman who might happen by. There, by Master Tersus's side door. If she didn't know better, she'd swear—

Sienne grabbed Dianthe's arm. "There's someone by the door."

Alaric strode ahead, accelerating until he was running. Dianthe and Sienne followed more slowly. "You!" Alaric shouted. "What are you doing—"

The figure stepped out of the shadow provided by the bushes sheltering the door. It was Kalanath. A streak of blood ran down his face, his red hair was a mess, and his clothes looked as if he'd gone to the harbor and rolled around on the docks. He gripped his staff in both hands, preparing to fight, but relaxed when he recognized Alaric. "By Kitane's right arm, what happened to you?" Dianthe exclaimed.

"I was attacked," Kalanath said. "By someone who followed me far too well. I beat him off, and he fled. When I gathered my senses, I realized I was close to where you said is Master Tersus's house, and I came to you."

"Why here?" Alaric said.

"Are you badly hurt?" Dianthe asked.

Kalanath shook his head. "It is not much. I do not know why here, except..." He shrugged. "It did not feel like a normal attack, and I wished to tell someone. I did not think the city guard would care. I am a foreigner, and suspect."

Sienne's uneasy feeling at seeing Kalanath had grown. "What did he look like? Your attacker?"

"He was Rafellish. Very short. Wearing wet clothes as if he had not had the sense to come in from the rain." Kalanath blotted his face and looked surprised to find blood. "Small eyes, a blunt nose...and long black hair that shone with grease."

16

"But that sounds like the man who chased me!" Sienne exclaimed.

Kalanath looked her over. "You were not hurt?"

"I outran him. Barely. When was this?"

"Some fifteen minutes ago." Kalanath touched his head again. "He looks much worse than I. He got in one lucky blow before I make him realize attacking is a bad idea."

"Come inside," Dianthe said. "You can clean yourself up, and we can talk about what to do."

She showed Kalanath the bath house door. He hesitated before it, then extended his staff to her. "You will watch it?"

"Of course." Dianthe took it gingerly, as if it might come to life and attack people of its own volition. When the door was shut, Alaric said, "What's there to talk about? Kalanath scared the man off."

"You don't think it's suspicious that Kalanath was attacked by the same man who chased Sienne?"

"We don't know that it's the same person. We shouldn't jump to conclusions." But he looked uncertain.

"It's a little much for coincidence," Dianthe said. "And if Kalanath only scared him off instead of killing him—"

"You think Kalanath should have killed him?" Sienne said.

"No. It's like he said—he's a foreigner, and as cosmopolitan a city as Fioretti is, the guard looks more closely at Ansorjans and Omeirans when it comes to crime. That Kalanath was defending himself might not matter to them. My point is, if the man is still out there, he might still be a threat."

The door opened. "I wish to know why this man attacked me and also Sienne," Kalanath said. He'd washed the blood off his face and finger-combed his hair into a semblance of order. "That is also not good for coincidence."

Alaric sighed. "Let's go into the kitchen," he suggested.

Leofus looked up when they all tramped in. "I don't feed extras," he said, waving his spoon in Kalanath's direction.

"We're not hungry," Dianthe said.

"*I'm* hungry," Alaric said.

"Fine. Our friend isn't eating with us, so don't worry about him." Dianthe sat at the head of the scarred trestle table and gestured for the others to join her. "All right," she said. "Sienne was attacked by this stranger and outran him. When she returned to this house, the man disappeared. A few hours later, Kalanath was attacked by what seems to be the same man. I think that's cause for alarm."

"He saw past my confusion spell," Sienne said. "Or...that's not quite right. He passed me the first time. It was almost as if he was tracking some quality of mine that the confusion didn't disguise."

"He followed me for some minutes before attacking," Kalanath said. "I tried to trick him and failed. It is not a thing I am bad at, either. He was too good at following."

Alaric leaned back as Leofus put a large bowl of thick mutton stew in front of him, with a hunk of bread beside it. "What could do that? If he really was following something unique about you—both of you—is there wizardry for that?"

"No," Sienne said, accepting her own bowl and bread. The smell rising from it was divine, but when she took a small bite, she discovered it was too hot. She stirred it and added, "There's no spell language that can encompass finding things. You'd need a priest for that. So either he was a priest, or he had some kind of blessing that let him follow us."

"Priest," Dianthe said. "Perrin could be in danger."

Alaric took an enormous mouthful of stew, apparently unconcerned about how hot it was. "Then why didn't he come after the two of us?"

"We haven't been off alone since coming back to Fioretti." Dianthe broke off a piece of bread and absently dipped it in the stew without eating it. "And I honestly don't feel like heading out into the growing dark on my own to test the theory."

Alaric took another bite. "Eat up, and we'll go find Perrin," he said.

Dianthe slugged his arm. "We don't have time to eat! Perrin's no fighter. If that man catches him alone—"

Alaric sighed and picked up the bread. "All right. We go now. But I bet we find him safely inside a bar, drinking himself under a table."

The crowds had dispersed in the few minutes since they'd arrived back at Master Tersus's house. Sienne reflected on her uneaten stew and envied them, safe and cozy in their homes, eating their dinners. Then she remembered the man who'd come after her, how frightened she'd been, and her appetite dwindled. She hoped Alaric was right, and Perrin was safe somewhere, completely unconscious of the danger his former companions had faced.

The tavern Perrin had mentioned, Pasotti's, was near the docks and was a good deal more reputable than the one they'd first met him in. It was a low single-story building with plank siding that, while in need of fresh paint, had no gaps or shattered boards anywhere. Warm, ruddy light gleamed behind its many windows despite there still being an hour until sunset. A water barrel positioned under the corner of the roof brimmed with rainwater, its meniscus catching the last of the sunlight like a soap bubble near to bursting. Men and a few women dressed in the rough clothing of dock laborers passed in and out of its doors, and the merry music of a fife and tambour escaped the doors whenever someone opened them.

No one paid them any attention when they entered, which

surprised Sienne. By now she was used to either Alaric or Kalanath or both drawing stares. But this was the harbor, and sailors of all nationalities came and went regularly, so even a giant Ansorjan was likely no rarity. Alaric led the way to the bar and addressed the middle-aged woman standing there, drawing off a pint for a patron. "We're looking for Perrin Delucco," he said. "He said to ask after him here."

The woman kept her attention on her pint. When it was full, she slid it neatly down the bar to its owner. Wiping her hands on her apron, she said, "Perrin's not here."

"We're friends," Dianthe said, which told Sienne she'd had the same impression, that the barkeep might be protecting Perrin's privacy. "We have some money we owe him."

Now the barkeep looked up and took in Alaric's height and breadth for the first time. "Ah. He said a mountain of an Ansorjan might come looking for him. He's just stepped out for a moment. Have a seat."

"Stepped out?" Sienne said.

"To relieve himself," Alaric muttered. Sienne blushed. Sometimes she was forcibly reminded of how ignorant she was of the world outside her father's estate.

They found an unoccupied table big enough to fit all of them and waited. Sienne looked around without bothering to disguise her interest. The fife and tambour players occupied a corner far from the door and had quite an audience of toe-tapping, knee-slapping listeners. One of them stood and shouted, "Let's hear 'Oak and Ashes,' all right, boys?"

A mighty cheer went up from the crowd as the fife player struck up a new tune. Sienne found her own toe tapping to the rhythm, even though she didn't know the song. Apparently, neither did the listeners. Sienne heard at least three different sets of lyrics, each shouted at top volume as if it were a contest to see whose favorite would come out the winner.

"They do this every night," Perrin shouted, drawing her attention away from the singers. "I fear no one has been able to stop them, nor would they, as they all spend a great deal of money to become extremely drunk afterward." He looked unsteady on his feet himself, his smile relaxed and his eyes glassy. He clapped Dianthe on the shoulder and half-fell into the chair next to her. "I did not think I would see you all so soon. Let me buy the next round. I feel I am not drunk enough yet."

"You might want to reconsider that," Alaric said. "Has anything strange happened to you this afternoon? Seen anyone unusual?"

Perrin's smile wavered. "No one *unusual*," he said, with a strange emphasis on the final word. "More to the point, they did not see me, as is my sad fate." Sienne opened her mouth to ask what he meant, but he overrode her with, "I take it I should have done?"

"Maybe," Alaric said. "Sienne and Kalanath were both accosted by the same strange man. We thought he might have gone after you as well."

"But if you were here—were you here all afternoon?" Dianthe asked.

"I was not. I went for a walk in the gardens until the rains fell, then I came here and set about drinking myself senseless. For a priest of Averran, that is a difficult proposition." Perrin's hand, resting on the table, closed into a tight fist. He looked as if he wanted someone to fight. Then he smiled that lazy, relaxed smile again. "At any rate, I have not seen your fellow."

"When the rains fell, he was after Sienne," Dianthe said. "By the time we chased him away, Perrin was probably here. So he'd have been safe."

"Why are you so certain this man would have come after me? I admit it strains credulity that a single man might choose to attack at random two people who know one another, but surely stranger coincidences than this have happened."

"I don't believe in coincidence," Alaric said.

The barkeep approached with a double handful of mugs. "I'm sure you were going to order something," she said with a sweet archness that embarrassed Sienne, as if they'd come to Pasotti's under false pretenses. She accepted her mug and took a long drink. It was good, if darker than she usually liked.

Perrin drank off most of his in a single draught. "Then if it is not coincidence, Alaric, what is it?"

"I don't know." Alaric took a drink and stared into the contents of his mug as if he expected to find the answer there. "But this person went after two of us and was capable of following them beyond reason. I don't like it."

"So what do Sienne and Kalanath have in common?" Dianthe said.

"We were both on the same job," Sienne said. "We both handled the artifacts. But neither of us had one on us."

Kalanath said, "And the attacker did not simply follow anyone leaving Master Tersus's house, because I did not go there until after I was attacked."

Alaric's brow was furrowed in thought. Then he dug in his belt pouch and slapped down a few coins. "Let's go pay a visit to Master Fontanna."

The volume rose over his last words as the song, if one could call it that, came to an end. "Did you say Master Fontanna?" Sienne asked.

Alaric nodded and pushed back his chair. Sienne held back any further comments until they were outside, where the noise became a distant hum. The sun kissed the horizon, sending old, tired light slanting across the harbor and turning the waves gold. The sea salt odor of the breezes tickled Sienne's nose into a sneeze, which she stifled.

"That artifact we brought back, the distance-viewer," Alaric said, "was valuable enough for the Giordas to try to take it from us."

"Yes, but they were opportunists. They couldn't possibly have known what we were after," Dianthe said.

"Nevertheless, I think we should see if Master Fontanna has seen any unsavory types lurking around his manor this afternoon." Alaric set off in the direction of the hill. "It's unlikely, but I have a feeling there's more going on than simple assault."

Sienne trudged along after Alaric and tried not to feel relieved that they were all together again. It was only temporary, but she couldn't help imagining this was another job, one that demanded all their skills. *You're being stupid,* she told herself, and willed away the excitement that threatened to bubble up inside her.

Dusk had fallen by the time they reached Master Fontanna's manor. The river seemed louder than it had been that afternoon, as if darkness freed it to be as noisy as it liked. Alaric pulled the bell chain and they waited. It was most of a minute before the door opened. "Yes?" the same servant said, looking them over. His voice was as placid as ever, but his face betrayed bewilderment at seeing them again.

"Two of our companions were attacked by someone this afternoon," Alaric said. "We believe it had something to do with the artifact we retrieved for Master Fontanna. Would you ask if we might have a moment of his time?"

"Master Fontanna is entertaining guests," the man said, his posture relaxing fractionally. Sienne thought it likely he was on more comfortable grounds when dealing with importunate hirelings at dinnertime. "You may call again in the morning, and I am certain he will see you."

"Wait," Dianthe said. "Maybe you can help. Has anyone been lurking around the manor? Someone unsavory-looking, with long stringy hair?"

The man looked at her as if she were an unsavory type. "No one of that description has approached the manor," he said, "nor would they dare. Now, please return in the morning."

"Thanks," Alaric said, but the door was already shut.

"Now what?" said Kalanath.

"It was unlikely your attacker would come here, if he didn't try to go after Perrin in the tavern or the two of us in Master Tersus's house," Dianthe said, "but we had to try. I don't know what to do next."

"Let's move away from the manor. I don't want to be rousted by the guard for loitering with intent," Alaric said. "Whatever intent they think we have."

They walked down the gravel path to the bottom of the slope, then around the corner, where Alaric came to a stop. "Perrin," he said, "if you wanted to locate a person, what would you do?"

"I take it you do not mean in the traditional way, in which one inquires at the person's usual haunts." Perrin's gaze turned inward. "When one asks Averran for a blessing that will allow one to find a person...well, Averran is somewhat erratic on the subject. Two times out of five, he will deny the request without explanation. When the blessing is granted, it is in the form of a glowing stone, perhaps thumbnail-sized. One swallows it, and it imparts a sort of tug that grows stronger as one comes closer to the desired individual. Or so I am told."

"So what exactly is it drawn to?" Sienne asked. "How does it know what person out of all the thousands of people in Fioretti to find?"

"Ah, that depends on the nature of the blessing one requests," Perrin said. "Since God knows each of us by name, Her avatars naturally have no difficulty in identifying one individual out of those thousands. But it is possible to make a more general request. The guard, for example, often ask the priests of Kitane, who are the most experienced at such blessings, to locate people based on their physical features, or their location at a given time, or even those in possession of a particular item. It is far more difficult, naturally, and I understand the guard cannot rely on such blessings to catch every criminal in Fioretti, as none of the avatars are consistent in granting them. But it can be done."

"So it's possible this attacker used a blessing to locate Sienne and Kalanath based on something they have in common," Dianthe said.

"We don't have that much in common," Sienne pointed out. "We both traveled together. We both retrieved those artifacts. We both fought the splinterfolk. I guess we ate the same food for a while..." Her voice trailed off. Remembering what they had in common gave her a pang of envy that it wasn't going to happen again.

Alaric turned away and paced to the end of the street a few steps away, where an as yet unlit lantern hung, then returned to the rest of them. "Something in common," he said. "You both handled the artifact. What else?"

"I did not touch the lenses," Kalanath said.

"We both touched the pendant, though," Sienne said. "We all did. I remember passing it around."

"Hmmm," Alaric said. "It's worth investigating." He headed for the end of the street again. "Let's see if Neoma is still open."

As the sun set, the lights of Fioretti came on, one flickering lantern, one magical light after another. Sienne stared in awe at the ruby and white lights of the palace that turned it into a confectioner's dream. As they crossed the Vochus, the rushing water took the lights' reflections and churned them into ribbons of white and red. Sienne slowed to look at them and had to run to catch up when Dianthe called her name.

Fioretti by night was a different city, the men and women thronging the streets committed to pleasure. Every tavern had someone at the door calling a welcome to anyone who might enter. Sienne's face grew hot when she received a proposition of another kind from a brightly-lit brothel. She stuck close to Perrin's side, hoping the presence of her companions might fend off other advances. Perrin wasn't walking nearly as unsteadily as she'd expected, but the smell of alcohol coming off his breath confirmed that he'd been drinking for a few hours.

His behavior that evening puzzled her. It sounded as if he'd seen someone he didn't like, or at least someone he didn't want to think about, and had turned to beer to rid himself of the memories. Sienne didn't know much about religion, but she was certain that wasn't the kind of alcohol use Averran expected of his priests. She glanced at him, but his attention was on Alaric, striding along at the head of their procession like someone intent on getting his way. If they were real companions, she'd have felt comfortable asking Perrin about it. Just one more sign that they weren't.

The crowds were heavier on the street where Neoma's shop was, and the air was full of wood smoke coming from somewhere up ahead. Sienne moved closer to the center of their group and let them sweep her along like a bit of fluff caught in a draft. It meant she couldn't see much, so when Alaric came to an abrupt halt, she bumped into him. "Sorry," she said.

Alaric didn't answer. Dianthe said, "By Kitane's right arm, what happened?"

Sienne ducked around Alaric and gasped. A gaping, burned-out hole lay where Neoma's shop had been just hours before. Two guards stood sentry in front of it, though no one seemed interested in approaching too close. There might as well have been an invisible barrier keeping everyone at bay, the line of onlookers was that well defined. Sienne took a step forward and Alaric put a hand on her arm, restraining her.

"Was this our destination?" Perrin said.

"It used to be," Alaric said. "I don't see Neoma anywhere."

"Maybe she wasn't here when the fire happened," Sienne said.

"Maybe," Alaric said, looking grimmer than before. "But I have a very bad feeling about this."

17

A couple more guards, one wearing the red knot of a lieutenant on his left shoulder, emerged from the hole, stepping high over what was left of the brick façade. Dianthe said, "Give me a minute." She stepped forward and crossed the short distance to where the man and woman stood. The woman made a dismissing motion with both hands, but the lieutenant shook his head. They were too far away for Sienne to hear what he said, and automatically she pulled out her spellbook and opened it to *sharpen*.

A heavy hand came down on hers. "Bad idea," Alaric said. "With all the noise out here, the odds of you picking out one conversation are virtually nonexistent. You'll just deafen yourself."

She gaped. "How did you know—"

"Either you're predictable, or I'm coming to understand how you think," Alaric said with a grin. "Just wait. Dianthe will tell us what she learns."

The lieutenant had taken Dianthe to one side and they were having a conversation that, by the look of the gestures Dianthe was making, was rather intense. Sienne continued to watch Alaric, whose lips were moving soundlessly as if he were taking part in the conversation. Dianthe gestured at the shop, then made a motion with her hands Sienne couldn't understand. Alaric grunted in comprehension. "What is it?" Sienne asked.

Alaric made a quelling gesture with one hand. "Just wait."

Sienne was bad at waiting. She put her spellbook away and tried to read their lips, with no success. Finally, Dianthe gripped the lieutenant's shoulder in a friendly way and said something that made him laugh. He leaned in and whispered in her ear something that made Dianthe blush, visible even in the low light. She nodded, and returned to Alaric's side.

"We have to get out of here," she said. "Someplace quiet where we can talk." Her face was still red, but so were her eyes, as if she were suppressing tears.

Sienne stifled her questions as Alaric turned and pushed his way through the crowds. She hoped he didn't plan to go all the way back to Master Tersus's house for a private conversation, because she wasn't sure she could stand the strain of not knowing. But Alaric took them down a different alley, one that was mostly narrow houses with common walls, and stopped under a street lamp. "What did Renaldi have to say?"

Dianthe swiped a hand across her eyes. "She's dead," she said. "They don't know if...if she burned to death, or if she was killed first —" She drew in a sobbing breath. Alaric put his arm around her and hugged her tight. Sienne risked a glance at him. His face was impassive, expressionless, but she had the feeling it was the kind of impassive that concealed an explosion waiting to get out.

Dianthe breathed in again and wiped her eyes once more. "Sorry. She'd have hated it if I got maudlin over her."

"It's all right to grieve," Alaric said. "But now is the time to plan vengeance for her. She'd have loved that."

Dianthe choked out a laugh. "True. Well. The fire burned Neoma's shop and left the shops on either side untouched. That means magic, and more, it means arson. Denys said they're bringing in a couple of priests, one to determine cause of...of death, and one to identify the bastards who did this. He promised to let me know what they find."

"Never thought I'd be grateful to Renaldi for anything," Alaric muttered. Dianthe slugged him in the chest, not very hard. "What else?"

"I asked him about her box. He's not from around here, so he didn't even know it existed. They didn't see it inside."

There was a pause. Kalanath, who'd been unusually silent, said, "Then it was destroyed. I do not know why it matters."

"It was invulnerable," Sienne said. "It couldn't be destroyed, even by magic. Are they sure it wasn't just buried in the rubble?"

"Very sure. There's not a lot of rubble left." Dianthe sighed. "It's a damn waste is what it is. How many thousands of lari worth of merchandise did those bastards destroy? Her box never had more than about five hundred lari in it."

"And the gems, and that beautiful necklace," Sienne said.

"Also not worth much by comparison to the stock."

"And one more thing," Alaric said. "The pendant."

They all stared at him. "She paid us sixty lari for the pendant. Are you saying someone killed her for a trinket worth sixty lari?" Dianthe said.

"A trinket that came from a hidden cache from the before times," Alaric said. "A trinket each of us handled."

"The body I found was clutching it tightly, like it was his, or her, most treasured possession," Sienne said.

Perrin shook his head. "This is all supposition," he said. "Linked by the barest of threads. You, Sienne, told us yourself it was not magical, and magic is the only thing that would make such a bauble more valuable than its intrinsic worth."

"But it is one thing all of us, and this poor dead woman, have touched. *You* said a blessing might locate someone with such a...I do not know the word," Kalanath said.

"Qualification," Perrin said. "That is true."

"But if someone wanted the pendant, why not ask for a blessing that would track it directly?" Dianthe said.

"Possibly because they could not," Perrin said. "Either their avatar rejected the request, or they did not know the object well enough.

One cannot, for example, simply ask for the location of a diamond necklace. One must have a specific necklace in mind. No one has seen that pendant for hundreds of years."

"And yet they came looking for it now," Sienne said. "That frightens me, that someone knew we'd retrieved it and came after us for it. And now Neoma's dead."

"Then we must get it back," Kalanath said.

It was his turn to be stared at. Alaric said, "How does that follow?"

Kalanath shrugged. "I dislike being a target," he said, "and I dislike more that someone is dead because of a thing we found. Anyone who is willing to kill to have it will not stop at one death, and though we do not know why the pendant is special, it is certain the thief does. It feels like our responsibility to stop him."

"It's not our fault they killed Neoma," Dianthe protested. "You can't think like that."

"It is not about fault." Kalanath stopped and appeared to be searching for words. "It is that we are capable of stopping more evil from happening, and in my home, my mother—" He stopped again, closed his eyes briefly, and said, "I was taught that if you can stop evil, you should stop evil, because you cannot know if you may be the only one who can."

"But we know almost nothing," Perrin said. He ticked off his words on one hand. "We don't know what the pendant really is or why someone might want it, we don't know where it is, we don't know who stole it, and we have no idea where to begin looking for it. And the thieves may already have begun whatever wickedness they intend."

"Why thieves? Kalanath and I were attacked by one man, alone," Sienne said.

"But the destruction of the shop, and Neoma's murder, couldn't have been pulled off by a single person," Dianthe said. "He must have had accomplices."

"Well, they're not getting into that box any time soon," Sienne declared. "It can't be burned, cut, chopped, or *force*-blasted open. And the lock—Neoma breathed on it to open it, which means they'd need her living breath to get into it. Even a blessing can't get around that."

"That is true," Perrin said. "Unless one of them is a priest whose avatar can offer them an alternative, that lock will remain, well, locked to them. But we cannot count on that being true."

"Yes, and suppose they forced her to open it before they killed her?" Dianthe said. Then she shook her head. "No. There'd have been no need for arson if they had what they wanted. The arson was to conceal the fact that the box was missing. They knew someone might come looking for it."

"I think we should act as if we still have time," Alaric said. "Perrin, how likely is it that Averran will grant you a blessing to locate the pendant?"

Perrin shook his head. "I give it better than even odds," he said. "Averran is not fond of granting location blessings, as he believes a true search sharpens the wits and polishes the soul. But I am familiar with the object, which is something in our favor, and I believe the fact that we seek it for altruistic reasons will incline him to our aid. But I cannot do it until tomorrow morning. After eleven o'clock, by preference. I think I should not pester him unduly."

"It can't be helped." Alaric looked away down the street. "I think, now that our enemies have the pendant, we're no longer in danger, but we should escort you to your lodgings, just in case."

"That seems unnecessary," Perrin said. "I would not put you to the trouble."

"It's no trouble," Dianthe said. "I'd rather not take the chance."

Perrin shrugged. "Then I will not argue further. And I admit to feeling better for the company."

"I as well," Kalanath said. "But where will we meet tomorrow?"

"My lodgings are...uncongenial...to large gatherings, and by 'large' I mean 'more than two people,'" Perrin said. "We will need a place large enough to allow for my devotions."

"I have something in mind," Alaric said. "Now, where are we going?"

Perrin's lodgings turned out to be around the corner from the tavern where they'd first met him. The slums were darker by night than they should be, as if a mist hung over the streets, choking out the few lanterns hanging from poles. Perrin strode along with an air of graceful unconcern, nodding in passing to a few of the men and women loitering on the corners. Sienne edged closer to Alaric and tried not to meet anyone's eyes. She had never felt so out of place as she did then. But Perrin was, if not noble, at least from a wealthy family and technically no less out of place than she, so how did he manage to fit in? He made no sense.

Perrin paused at the door, which was an ill-fitting slab of planks held together by rusted iron nails. "Do we have a plan for if Averran chooses to grant my petition? Because a location blessing only lasts a few hours."

"Working on it," Alaric said. "We'll come for you in the morning."

"Not too early," Perrin reminded them, and shut the door.

They had to cross most of the city to reach the inn Kalanath was staying at. It was a large hostel that catered to scrappers, and light and music poured out of its ground floor windows. Sienne caught a glimpse of Kalanath's face; he looked mildly disgusted, as if he'd just witnessed someone belch. "It seems…exciting," she said.

"I do not like noise," Kalanath said. "It is not what I am used to, in my youth. I thought I would grow to like it because it is what scrappers do, but I have not."

"Not all scrappers entertain themselves this way. The hostel where we stay is very quiet."

Kalanath shrugged. "I try because they are all very kind, but we are not the same."

He sounded very young, and very lonely, and Sienne burst out, "Why don't you take a room at our hostel?"

"Sienne," Alaric said.

"Well, why not? It's quiet, and there are extra rooms, and it has to be better than this place. It's a wonder anyone gets any sleep at all."

"It's not a bad idea," Dianthe said. "Master Tersus said he wished he could rent out more of the rooms. I think he's feeling the need to expand his scrimshaw collection again and could use the money."

Alaric's brows were furrowed in a frown. Sienne couldn't figure out why. It wasn't his house for him to make the decision, was it? "You're right," he finally said. "It's not a bad idea."

Kalanath said, "But I will intrude."

"You can't intrude. You'd have your own room, and it's certainly less invasive than sharing a tent. Which you didn't mind doing on our expedition." The idea had taken hold of Sienne to the point that she could already picture the four of them sitting down to breakfast together. She suppressed the feeling that this was one step closer to being a team again.

A tentative smile crept over his face. "Very well. I get my things and we will go."

While they waited, Alaric said, "Why do I feel like I've just adopted a stray puppy?"

"That's unfair. Kalanath is a grown man. And it's not like it's your house." His words stung, as if he'd chastised her for some wrongdoing. Kalanath probably wasn't more than nineteen, but that still counted as grown, given how long he'd been on his own. How dare Alaric be so condescending?

"Don't get snippy with me. Dianthe and I—" Alaric began, a trifle hotly.

"Are not the owners of the hostel," Dianthe said, glaring at Alaric. "Wouldn't you rather share lodgings with people we like instead of whatever total strangers Master Tersus might rent rooms to?"

Alaric opened his mouth, then closed it without delivering whatever retort he had in mind. After a moment, he said, "Well, he is quiet, I'll give him that. And at least he's not a wizard."

Sienne felt as if he'd slapped her. "How dare you—" she began. Then she saw his eyes twinkling at her, and she subsided, feeling embarrassed. "I'm surprised anyone is willing to put up with you," she said instead.

"Ah, that is Sisyletus's own truth, right there," Alaric said.

Kalanath approached, staff in hand, a large rucksack over one shoulder. "I am ready," he said.

"Then let's away," Alaric said. "Master Tersus goes to bed early."

———

KALANATH WAS AT THE BREAKFAST TABLE WHEN SIENNE CAME DOWN the next morning, eating porridge and staring out the kitchen window. Sienne looked in that direction and saw only the hedge, and above that the wall of the house next door. "Something interesting?"

Kalanath startled. "I am just thinking," he said, taking a bite of porridge. "I need a place to fight. That is, to practice with the staff." He gestured at it, leaning against the wall next to the door.

"I guess the bedrooms are too small for that. What about the side of the house? There's space in the garden. Or on the other side—" she gestured at the window—"there's not as much space, but it's more private."

Kalanath nodded. "I will speak to Master Tersus. He may not wish for an Omeiran to practice in his garden where all may see."

Sienne privately thought Master Tersus would just charge him a couple of centi for the privilege, but said only, "That's a good idea."

Heavy footsteps on the stairs preceded Alaric's entry into the kitchen. "Ah, bacon," he said, fetching a plate from the sideboard and piling several pieces of crisp bacon on it. "I can't believe you two are eating porridge when you have better options."

"I like porridge," Kalanath said. "We say, *prakrhuti bhagyar khem donakhoti*. It means the same as what you say...it sticks to your ribs."

"Well, I'd rather have delicious bacon than anything sticky, first thing in the morning," Alaric said. He scooped up a large helping of scrambled eggs from the skillet on the back of the range and carried his plate to the table. "What's your excuse?"

"I don't like anything rich, first thing in the morning," Sienne said. "I do, however, like lots of sugar." She used the little hammer to break off a chunk of sugar and stirred it into her hot bowlful of porridge, where it slowly dissolved.

"I'm not sure how that's not rich," Alaric said, biting into three pieces of bacon at once.

"You have terrible table manners."

"I know how to behave. But I doubt either of you want me to impress you."

Rapid steps sounded on the stairs. "I overslept," Dianthe said. "Why didn't anyone wake me?"

"You need to come to terms with the fact that you're not a morning person," Alaric said.

Dianthe fell on the coffee urn in the corner. Sienne watched her in some amusement as she fumbled with the cup, the cream, and finally the sugar hammer, then sank onto a chair and drank deeply. "Ah," she said. "What I need is coffee before I've had my coffee." She set the cup down and glared at Alaric. "I can quit any time I want."

"Sure you can," Alaric said. "I think we should start at the amphitheater."

The abrupt change of subject left Sienne briefly stunned. She'd forgotten, in the pleasant comfort of breakfast with friends, that there was a murderer and thief out there in possession of a mysterious artifact that was worth killing for. "Why there?" she said.

"That's the center of Fioretti, or as near to as makes no difference." Alaric took another bite of bacon and chased it with a forkful of egg. "That ought to put us on the shortest route to wherever the pendant is."

"What if they took it out of the city? Perrin said the blessing only lasts a little while," Sienne said.

"Then we'll either ask for the blessing again, or use our heads," Alaric said. "It's a chance worth taking."

Kalanath rose and took his bowl to the pump, where he rinsed it and set it to dry. "I will speak with Master Tersus," he said, retrieving his staff and leaving the room.

"Why does he need to talk to Master Tersus?" Dianthe asked.

"He wants a place to practice." Sienne hoped he'd do it where they could watch. She'd seen his morning exercises while they were in the wilderness, and they were beautiful, all flowing leaps and kicks. It was hard to picture those movements being used to attack anyone, even though she'd seen that too.

Dianthe rose and served herself eggs and one small strip of

bacon. She took her seat just as Leofus came back into the room with a silver serving tray he set on the sideboard. "Can't believe we're letting space to an Omeiran," he muttered.

"Do you have a problem with that?" Alaric rumbled, dangerously placid.

Leofus shot him a nervous glance. "Don't like making allowances for their heretic faith," he said. "Master Tersus just told me mutton's off the menu for the future, unless I feel like cooking two meals. What's wrong with mutton, I'd like to know?"

"Nothing," Dianthe said. "Unless you're Omeiran, I suppose."

"Well, he's being awfully accommodating, is all I can say. He never cared this much for Kitane's name day celebrations, and he's worshipped her all his life." Leofus took up his spoon and gave the porridge a fierce stir. "I asked him, what next, no beef for High Winter, and he told me not to be a fool. I just want to know what to expect."

"That seems reasonable." Alaric got himself second helpings of everything. Sienne cleared her bowl and retreated upstairs.

She still didn't have bedding other than her blanket, but she made her bed as best she could, brushed out her hair, and tidied her things. It didn't take long. She'd grown up never needing to do those things for herself, even in Stravanus where she'd shared a maid with the five other girls on her floor of the boarding house. To her surprise, when she was finally on her own, she'd found tidying soothing and even cheering, like a daily accomplishment no one could take from her. Dianthe, on the other hand, was a slob. Sienne didn't like cleaning enough to offer to care for Dianthe's room.

She sat on her bed and set her brush on the windowsill above its head. With Kalanath living under the same roof, it felt as if they were almost a team again. Which was a dangerous feeling. This, too, was a temporary crisis, and she needed to stop daydreaming like a lovesick schoolgirl.

She closed her eyes and made herself think of other things. If she was going to be of use to a scrapper team, she'd need more spells. She should make an effort to find wizards willing to trade, or sell, more likely, since most of the spells she had were common. Which meant she should probably make a list of spells she was interested in. *Force*, and the *fit* spell for objects, even if that last one was self-indulgent rather than essential. *Cat's eye,* true night vision. *Open,* the more powerful version of the small magic that let her open her spellbook to whatever page she wanted. Probably there were more she'd never even heard of.

She took her spellbook and stood in front of the small oval mirror hanging on the wall over the chest of drawers. Willing it open to *shift*, she read off the syllables with deliberate precision and let the spell wrap itself around her. Blonde hair. Hazel eyes. A straight nose. She didn't need *imitate* to resemble her sister Felice, since they already shared many of the same features, just a couple of small changes. Sienne altered her earlobes a tiny bit and glared at herself. Felice glared back. She really was beautiful, unlike Sienne, for whom the same collection of features produced only an ordinary prettiness. And now she had Sienne's lover. Looking at her reflection, Sienne could hardly blame Rance for choosing Felice over her.

She released *shift* and let her features return to normal. "Who was that?" Alaric said from the doorway.

Sienne spun around, startled. "I didn't know you were there."

"We're ready to go. Were you practicing a disguise? I can't say I approve of that one."

"Oh? Why not?" Sienne wasn't about to admit to jealousy of her stupid sister and risk looking bitter or spiteful.

"Too self-consciously pretty. You'd draw attention wherever you went. That kind of negates the purpose of a disguise."

It made Sienne feel instantly better. "It was just a whim," she said, tucking her spellbook into her vest. "I don't want to look like that."

"I knew a scrapper wizard," Alaric said, stepping back for her to leave the room, "who hated the way he looked so much he kept a more or less permanent disguise up. More or less meaning he kept changing it, looking for the perfect face."

"That seems like a lot of work for vanity," Sienne said.

"It was. Cost him his life, in the end. He spent so much of his magical reserves on the disguise, he couldn't cast spells at a key moment. Some of his companions died too."

"That's awful."

"Just one more reason to be wary of magic."

"I would never do that."

"I didn't mean that as a criticism. I trust you."

It was so unexpected it left her groping for something to say. "I... hope I'm worthy of that trust."

Alaric shrugged. "It doesn't mean I like wizards in general any better. You're a special case."

"I'll take that as a compliment," Sienne said.

18

S ienne had heard of the Kondylus Amphitheatre, named for a long-dead king of Rafellin, but had never visited. This was mostly because she'd been warned about how dangerous it was. Once it had been a popular venue for open-air theater, where the rich and powerful of Fioretti promenaded. They ostensibly went to watch the plays, but Sienne was sure they'd been more interested in being seen, since she doubted human nature had changed much in the last century. Now, however, the popular entertainment in the big city was small, intimate salons with good conversation, a trend her own mother had imported to Beneddo, and the amphitheater was an over-grown stone pavilion no one used anymore. No one, that is, but homeless men and women who took over the many sheltered alcoves when night fell, and hard-eyed criminals who made unsavory deals in the bright light of day. Sienne hadn't needed more than one warning to stay away.

But entering the amphitheater surrounded by her friends was quite different from going in alone. Alaric strode confidently past the many hedge-bounded booths, some of which were still occu-pied even at eleven o'clock in the morning, and headed straight for the back of the stage. Its floor of aged oak beams hadn't been varnished in eighty years, but no rot had set in, and they didn't so much as creak under his weight. Sienne took a few steps to the side and tried to imagine declaiming blank verse to an audience of thousands, or being lowered from the high ceiling to portray an avatar of God.

"Holla, girlie. What are you doing here?"

Sienne turned to see three men approaching from the side of the stage. They were unshaven, their clothes unkempt, and all three had nasty smiles that said they were interested in making her life unpleasant. "It's a public place," she said, but took a step backward toward her companions. More loudly, she said, "Isn't that right? It's a public place?"

"What?" Alaric said. She didn't dare take her eyes off the three men to see if he'd noticed them. "Oh. We're not going to have any trouble, are we?"

"Not if you leave now," said the same man. One of his eyes moved in a funny way, and Sienne realized it was glass. "We have business to attend to."

"It's a big amphitheater. We'll carry on here and you can take whatever other spot you like." Alaric took a few steps to put himself between the men and Sienne. She was just as happy not to have to look at them.

"We was here first."

Sienne had heard somewhere that the myth of the criminal mastermind really was more or less a myth, because most criminals were stupid, hence their becoming criminals. These men seemed to be proof of that statement. They were outnumbered, facing down someone who could probably crush their heads with a squeeze of his massive hands, and they still wanted to brazen it out? Sienne thought about pulling out her spellbook, but decided that might make things needlessly complicated. Sometimes you had to let the fighters take charge.

Kalanath and Dianthe came forward to flank Alaric on either side. "Who are these?" Kalanath said.

"Just some businessmen who are leaving now," Alaric said.

Sienne heard the rasp of a sword being drawn. "I think it's you who'll be leaving," a different man said.

Faster than thought, Kalanath whipped his staff around in a complicated maneuver. There was a ringing sound as the man's sword hit the floor, and a thud, and a groan. "I think it is not," Kalanath said. "I do not like bullies. You will take yourself to another place now."

Sienne peeked between Alaric and Dianthe. Two of the men were helping a third rise. He reached for his sword, and Dianthe kicked it neatly out of the way, sending it skittering across the uneven oak flooring. "Fetch."

The three men glared. One of them said, "You—" He looked at Alaric, whose face Sienne couldn't see, and changed his mind. The three men turned and walked away, stopping only to retrieve the sword.

Slow applause from behind her made her turn. Perrin was clapping, a wry smile touching his lips. "Very bracing, to begin our little adventure with a near-foray into fisticuffs," he said. His eyes were squinted nearly shut as if the light hurt them. Sienne had smelled stale brandy on him when they'd arrived at his lodgings half an hour before and suspected he'd continued getting drunk after they'd left him that night. She tried not to think uncharitable things, but it was hard not to worry, even though she guessed if she expressed that worry, he'd become sarcastic to fend her off.

"Sorry about that," Alaric said. "I didn't think anyone would be so bold as to come after us. Is this too public a place? We can find somewhere else. Maybe we should start at Neoma's shop instead."

Perrin waved a dismissive hand. "Averran would say it is the drunks and scoundrels who are closest to the divine wisdom. Personally, I think Averran was having everyone on when he said that, as wisdom is not something I believe those three thugs are conversant with."

He turned in a wide circle, scuffing the planks with his toe, then settled into a cross-legged position and laid a handful of rice papers in his lap. "Please do not hover. You may sit near, or stand afar, but in either case I will need your silence. This is not a prayer I have made before."

They all backed about ten feet away. Perrin nodded and closed his eyes, resting his hands loosely on his knees. For a few moments, all he did was breathe deeply, in through the nose, out through the mouth, his chest rising and falling in slow rhythm. Sienne gripped the edges of her spellbook through her vest to keep her hands still. She'd never realized she was a fidgeter until she'd seen Perrin pray.

Perrin drew in a deep breath. "O mighty Lord of crotchets, it is your servant again. This morning I have only one request, and it is an exceptional one. Perceive, if you will, the pendant I envision now. It appears to be at the center of a widening circle of death and deception. My companions and I are responsible for returning it to the world, and we feel a further responsibility for repairing the damage those who possess it have caused, and likely will continue to cause."

He paused, as if he was listening to a voice none of them could hear. "I know it is not your way to provide answers when it is the pursuit of the question that makes us better people. Did you not say, 'It is for man to find the path, and when there is no path, to forge one'? I do not wish for you to put the evildoers into my power. I simply ask for guidance to locate the pendant. A trail to follow, as it were. I know not what may be at the end of the trail, but I assure you, o Lord of pestilential bad humor, that I will do my utmost to make of your blessing what I may. As always, I leave it to you—"

He went silent. Then he swayed as if he were about to pass out. Dianthe took a step forward, but halted when Alaric put a hand on her arm. A trickle of blood ran from Perrin's nostril, and his jaw was locked tight. "My Lord, it is for you to decide," he murmured through clenched teeth, "but you have always said persistence leads to wisdom, and wisdom leads to God, so by your leave I will ask again until—" He gasped. "Until I am satisfied." Tears leaked from beneath his closed eyelids, and he clenched his hands tightly enough that his knuckles showed white. Sienne's chest ached from holding her breath.

The papers in Perrin's lap sizzled and smoked with a white smoke that reeked of jasmine and sharp mint. Perrin opened his eyes. "Thank you, Lord," he said, and sagged, not quite fainting. Sienne and Kalanath rushed to support him. "I am well," he said. He wiped his nose with the back of his hand, smearing blood across his cheek. "I do not think I have ever pitted my will against an avatar's before. I cannot recommend it."

"Did it work?" Alaric said.

"I think so." Perrin sorted through the charred papers in his lap. "Healing...protection...Averran seems to think we are setting out on a scrapping expedition. Another healing. One similar but not identical to the blessing that revealed the ritual in the keep, very interesting. Something I do not recognize." He held out one that was, by contrast to the usual complex sigils of his blessings, a simple curved shape like half a crescent moon from which depended an angular, irregular shape like a warped bean. "And one location blessing."

Dianthe let out a relieved sigh. "So how do we use it?"

"It is as I have said. Invoking the blessing produces a stone one swallows, and then one is guided in some way to the object or person of one's desire." Perrin folded the other blessings away into his pocket. "I have never done it before, so that is as specific as I may be."

Alaric checked his watch. "It's half past eleven. Is there any reason we can't do it now?"

"We will have no time to stop for a meal. The location blessing lasts for no more than three hours."

"I don't think I could eat, I'm too eager," Dianthe said.

"Nor I," said Kalanath. "Better we do this now."

Sienne nodded agreement.

"Then...whenever you're ready," Alaric said.

Perrin nodded. He held the rice paper by one corner over his cupped hand, bent his head, and murmured, "Stop being a cranky bastard and be useful for once." The paper flared into blue flame, but instead of disappearing, it shriveled into a compact wad of fibers crackling with fire. Then the fire went out, and something small and blue dropped into Perrin's hand. He displayed it to the others. It was a round, faceted stone, pale blue and milky like the true summer sky, and no bigger than his pinky nail. Perrin took out his flask. "Fortune favors the foolish," he said, and popped the stone into his mouth. Swiftly he drank from the flask, wincing. "Very bitter."

They stood watching him for nearly a minute. "Don't you feel anything?" Sienne asked.

Perrin shook his head. "But it can take a few minutes to become effective." A strange, reflective look crossed his face. "I feel rather warm."

"It's a hot day," Alaric said.

"It is not that kind of warmth. It is...as if I had a live coal in my chest. But that would be painful, and this is not." Perrin took a few steps toward Alaric, who stepped aside, looking alarmed. "I think..."

"Yes?" Dianthe said.

He paced around the stage in a wide, irregular circle, his brow wrinkled. "The heat fades when I am *here*, and grows when I am *here*," he said, coming to a stop near the western edge. "I believe I have a trail."

"Then let's follow it," Alaric said.

Perrin had already leaped the short distance off the stage and was striding away through the low-walled alcoves. A furtive figure crawled out of one and scurried away at his approach, but Perrin ignored it. After a moment's startled pause, the others ran after him. "Slow down," Sienne said.

"I feel if I slow, I will lose the thread," Perrin said. His voice was distant, abstracted, as if half his attention were elsewhere. "It is... quite the compulsion."

The amphitheater was surrounded by public parkland, not as seedy as the amphitheater but still not a place Sienne would have felt comfortable walking in alone. Perrin crossed it in a direct line, ignoring the gravel paths and once coming up short against a high shrubbery wall. He looked at it in surprise at its very existence.

"Around," Alaric said, grabbing Perrin's arm and steering him to the right.

"I hope this is not a mistake," Perrin said. "Averran might consider it a denial of his gift."

"Averran can't expect you to walk through walls," Dianthe said. "We can only stay as close to the path as possible, and hope that's good enough."

The detour did not destroy whatever link Perrin had to the pendant; he picked up the trail immediately. After a few minutes, they left the parkland behind for the same run-down district Neoma's shop was in. Perrin walked half the length of one of the quiet, well-scrubbed streets before stopping. "The path is in a direct line that gives no heed to buildings. We will have to detour frequently."

"You walk, and we'll steer," Dianthe said, taking his arm.

"Very well." He crossed the street, ignoring the oxcart that rumbled toward them. Sienne, at the end of their procession, had to dart around it and, cursing, ran hard to catch up.

She lost track of where they were and had to work at not losing sight of her friends. If they were separated, it would take her forever to find familiar territory again. The impoverished district gave way to the industrial sector, where all the smelly and noisy businesses a city depended on were tucked away out of sight. The smells of the tanneries and abattoirs made Sienne grateful they hadn't stopped for a meal. Perrin seemed to be rapt in a world of his own, because once he attempted to walk through a slaughterhouse yard and was only deterred by Dianthe hauling back on his arm. Kalanath turned his back on the sight, looking unexpectedly squeamish. Alaric nudged Perrin. "Left, or right?"

Perrin closed his eyes. "Left," he said, and they were off again.

After about an hour of following Perrin's erratic trail, Alaric said, "We've been heading gradually uphill, through increasingly wealthy neighborhoods."

"Yes, and I don't like the way these people keep looking at us, like we're criminals casing their estates," Dianthe said. "Are we getting any closer?"

"I have felt neither increase nor diminution in the strength of the pull," Perrin said. "I fear we will know we have found it only when we are atop it."

"That is a problem," Kalanath said. "It is likely the thieves will be with the pendant."

"I don't see a problem," Alaric said, flexing his fists.

"It's a problem if the thieves are working for someone else who isn't there," Dianthe pointed out. "If—watch it!" She stopped Perrin from crossing the street directly in the path of a carriage going faster than was strictly safe. "If we burst in on them, we might not learn who's really responsible."

Perrin continued across the street, his eyes half-lidded against the sun's brightness. "Walk as if you had business here, and we will be unmolested."

"That only works most of the time. We're not dressed right for this neighborhood," Dianthe said.

Alaric looked around. "This is not good."

"We just have to keep moving," Dianthe assured him.

"That's not what I mean. This street is familiar. We're almost to Master Fontanna's home."

Dianthe brought Perrin to a stop, provoking a cry of rebuke. "You don't think…"

"He was upset that we wouldn't sell him the other artifacts," Sienne said.

"If it is Master Fontanna, we will know soon enough," Perrin said, wrenching away from Dianthe and proceeding rapidly up the hill.

They trotted after him. Sienne soon recognized the gray-streaked white marble of Master Fontanna's manor. Perrin's path took him directly toward it. Sienne's heart fell. She'd liked Master Fontanna, clammy hands aside, and she couldn't imagine how Alaric and Dianthe felt, having worked for him many times before.

Alaric strode ahead of Perrin and put his hand on the gate to the manor. Perrin ignored him and kept walking. "This isn't it?" Alaric said.

Perrin glanced at the manor. "The pull is from somewhere ahead."

Alaric and Dianthe looked relieved. Sienne only felt confused. If not Master Fontanna, who?

They continued walking. Sienne's legs burned from climbing. "We're almost out of street," Alaric said. "Could they have gone into the hills beyond the city?"

They were passing a manor surrounded by a shoulder-high yew hedge, trimmed off sharply across its flat top. Perrin suddenly turned left and tried to walk through the hedge. "It is near," he said. "I felt a pulse as of a heartbeat."

They all looked across the estate grounds, which were covered with more hedges in irregular patterns, fruit trees heavy with unripe apples and plums, and the occasional white marble bench. The manor of the estate dominated the property, three stories of well-polished granite that glinted here and there with bright mica inclusions, topped with a roof of a peculiar greenish-gray slate. "Let's circle around," Alaric said, "and verify that it's in there. I pray Sisyletus it's not."

They followed the hedge past a wide iron gate to where it turned a corner. There were no other estates north of this one, and the road itself came to an end a few yards farther on in a gravel circle suitable for turning a carriage around. The hedge on the northern side was much taller, at least eight feet, though not as thick. There were plenty of gaps for looking through.

"The pulse continues strong, and is directed toward that house no matter where I stand," Perrin said when they'd gone a few feet along the northern hedge. "The pendant is there."

"Wonderful," Alaric said. "Even if we could get in, by the time we did, the location blessing will have worn off, and we'll fumble around that enormous house looking for the box."

"I don't know *vanish*," Sienne said. Alaric shot her a sharp look, and she stammered, "It...it might not be the best option, though, because we'd be invisible to each other as well."

"I'll have to go in alone," Dianthe said.

"I hate that plan," Alaric said. "It's a terrible plan."

"It's the only option."

"Possibly not," Kalanath said. He stood near one of the gaps in the hedge, looking at something. "That is interesting."

Sienne found her own gap and looked. "The Giordas!" she gasped. "Why are they here?"

"And walking out the front door, no less," Alaric said, his face pressed to another gap.

"They could have been hired by whoever owns this estate," Dianthe said.

"Whoever owns this estate is probably thigh-deep in this mystery. And I don't believe in coincidence." Alaric stepped back. "We follow them."

"But should we not investigate the estate for the pendant?" Perrin said.

"I doubt it's going anywhere. The Giordas look like they've got something on what passes for their minds, and I want to know what it is."

"Wait," Dianthe said. "We can't go rushing out after them. They'll see us, and we'll never find out their business."

"We'll have to stay far behind. It's risky, but there's no other option."

"Actually," Sienne said, pulling out her spellbook, "there is."

19

It was likely, Sienne thought, they hadn't needed *shift* at all. Not that she intended to mention this to Alaric, who'd voiced a short but strenuous objection to her plan. The Giordas crossed the city boldly, without looking around to see if they were being followed. Her estimation of their intelligence dropped. Conn's unseasonal cloak billowed around him in the afternoon breeze, which was probably why he wore it. Her estimation of his vanity rose.

She'd disguised her companions as quickly as possible so they wouldn't lose sight of their quarry, so they mostly still resembled themselves in height and build. All except Alaric, whom she'd used *imitate* on to give him the image of a man six inches shorter, so he wouldn't stand out. They walked along in silence, keeping about fifteen feet back from the Giordas and lagging farther occasionally to avoid looking like they were following anyone. Sienne touched her spellbook for reassurance. She had no idea how they'd know when to jump the Giordas, or what to do when they had them captive. Well, she didn't have to know. That was down to Alaric and Dianthe. She hoped *they* knew what to do.

They'd entered streets Sienne was vaguely familiar with, but it wasn't until they passed the burned-out husk of Neoma's store that she realized where they were. The street was as thronged with passersby and travelers as ever, which made Sienne irrationally angry. Of course life shouldn't stop just because one woman died, and it wasn't as if Sienne had known her as more than a passing acquaintance, but it just felt wrong, like denying Neoma's vibrant spirit.

Alaric slowed. "Watch it," he said. The Giordas had turned a corner onto a much smaller side street. "Dianthe?"

"Sienne, will the confusion spell last if you're not within sight of us?" Dianthe asked.

"Yes. Just don't stay in contact with anyone for very long."

"Kalanath, stay with me," Dianthe said. "The rest of you, keep going and turn at the next right. Follow Alaric." In a few steps, they reached the corner, and Dianthe and Kalanath strolled along down the new street. Sienne, Perrin, and Alaric kept going.

"That street cuts across Lupin and Farrier streets," Alaric said. "We'll go around and pick it up again on Farrier. Keeps us from being a noticeable bunch of five."

No one paid them any attention. At least they were dressed for this neighborhood as they had not been for the wealthy estates, though Perrin stood out in his embroidered vest and expensive, if worn, boots. Sienne's nerves were keyed to the breaking point. If the confusion dissolved...if they ran into the Giordas, and were recognized despite the confusion...being separated from the others only made it worse. A pack of small children raced past, screaming with delight at some game, and Sienne clenched her teeth at the noise. Perrin looked as tense as she felt. He watched the children go and kept his attention on them even after they rounded a corner and were nothing but a trailing banner of sound.

Alaric turned the corner away from where the children had gone and slowed his pace. "We should see them pass," he said, pointing at another cross-street some distance ahead. "We don't want to get ahead of them."

Sienne slowed to match him. A couple of carriages lumbered past, then a young couple holding hands, followed by a scrapper team on horseback. No Giordas in sight. Suppose they'd already passed? Sienne didn't think they wanted to fall too far behind them, either.

They reached the cross-street and Alaric looked both ways. He grunted, and led them down the new street, back the direction they'd come, to where Dianthe and Kalanath stood in the lee of a tall wooden house, shabby but well cared for. "Back this way," Dianthe said in a low voice, though the sound of passing traffic made it unlikely anyone farther than five feet away could hear her.

They backed into the space between the house and its neighbor until the street was mostly invisible. "The Giordas went into a building across the street," Dianthe said. "It's one of those big ones with lots of one-room apartments."

"This isn't where they live," Alaric said. Sienne wanted to ask how he knew that, but held her tongue. "Let's watch and see what they do."

Dianthe nodded. "We'll need to be careful not to be noticed. In a neighborhood like this, people generally know their neighbors. We can't get away with loitering too obviously. How long will the confusions last?"

"Another half-hour, and then I'll have to do them again." Sienne had a feeling she was going to test her reserves on this.

"You could do different disguises each time," Alaric said. "Make it look like we're each five different people."

Again Sienne marveled at how someone who despised wizardry could come up with such clever uses for it. "That's a good idea."

"Then let me show you all where to stand," Dianthe said.

Dianthe positioned them all in places where they had a good view of the building she indicated without being immediately visible. Then she disappeared, saying she would scout out the rear of the building for back doors.

Sienne ended up two buildings down from their target, on the same side of the street, where she could barely see its front door. None of her companions were visible but Kalanath, directly opposite her, but she knew where they were. She would have to approach each of them in a short time to renew the confusions. Someone passed her and entered the building, and she managed not to cringe or, she hoped, do anything else guilty-looking.

A small sound behind her made her turn in alarm. "There's no back door, thank Kitane," Dianthe said. "You remember what I told you?"

Sienne nodded. "Walk casually, as if I'm going someplace familiar. Try not to catch anyone's eye, but don't avoid eye contact. Smile if the other person does. Does this really work?"

"Surprisingly, yes. Most people are so caught up in their own troubles, they don't generally take notice of anyone behaving like an ordinary person. Sneaking around stands out."

"I'll remember that."

Dianthe grinned. "We'll make a thief of you yet. Well, not a thief. I don't expect you to break the law."

"So how did you get to have all these skills if you're not a thief?"

It was the wrong question. Dianthe's smile disappeared. "Long story," she said. "One for another time." Her tone of voice said that other time would be "never."

"Sorry," Sienne said. "Um...I should go now."

"Walk lightly," Dianthe said.

Sienne walked up the street to the next intersection, crossed, and casually made her way back. There wasn't much traffic at this hour of the day, on this quiet side street, and she renewed the confusions on the three men without causing a commotion. Alaric, positioned almost directly opposite the building's front door, barely looked at her when she pulled out her spellbook. "I hate the waiting," he said. "Too easy to get lazy, waiting."

Sienne whispered the words of *imitate,* and Alaric's form shivered, then became a different nondescript Rafellish man. "And we don't know how long we might have to wait," she said.

Alaric shook his head. "Has anyone paid any attention to you?"

It was so odd hearing his Sorjic accent coming out of that stranger's mouth. "No one."

Alaric grunted in acknowledgement. "Be careful."

Sienne returned to her original position. It was getting late.

People should be returning to their homes soon, which meant either that she and her companions would blend in to the crowds better, or they'd be noticed as loitering strangers. Sienne decided to leave that for Dianthe to worry about.

The afternoon turned to evening. More people, not very many, went in and out of the houses on both sides of the street, including the building Sienne tried to keep an eye on. The sky darkened from pale blue to rose and then to dusky violet. The number of people entering the houses increased. From her awkward position, all she could tell was that no one had come out of her target yet. She couldn't see Kalanath anymore and wondered if he'd moved to avoid being spotted.

She was about to make another round to renew the *shift* spell when the building's door opened and four figures came out. She pressed against the side of the house shielding her from view and craned her neck to see better.

"It's them," Dianthe said from behind her, startling her heart into one terrified pulse. "Follow me."

Sienne stayed close behind Dianthe, gripping the edges of her spellbook through her vest. To her surprise, they turned right instead of left, away from the building and, presumably, the Giordas. "Just a quick detour, to throw them off the scent," Dianthe whispered, and in a few more steps turned and went back the way they'd come.

The street was virtually empty now except for Sienne and Dianthe and the four figures they trailed. Who was the fourth person? It was still light enough that Sienne could make out Conn in the lead, with the mystery man behind him and Milo and Alethea flanking him. Something flashed silver—a knife, held close to the fourth man's back. They were herding him, whoever he was.

Quick steps behind her announced Kalanath's presence. "We should attack before they enter the main streets," he said.

"We have a plan," Dianthe said. "Wait for the others."

As they passed an alley, Alaric stepped out of its shadows and fell into place beside them. "Where's Perrin?"

"Here," Perrin said, crossing the street toward them. "This is rather more good luck than I usually look for. They seem not to have noticed us."

"Let's hope so," Alaric said, "at least for now."

Perrin was right; once again the Giordas seemed oblivious to anyone following them. Dianthe made them spread out a little, just in case, but Sienne thought it was unnecessary. Not that she would argue with experience. This time, the Giordas took an indirect route, sticking to the less-trafficked streets and giving a wide berth to anyone they passed. The man they "escorted" was only a little taller than Conn, and pudgy, dressed plainly in laborer's tunic and trousers. He wasn't bound in any way, but by the way he stood, Sienne was sure the knife was as good as fetters.

They were coming up on a main thoroughfare, one still thronged with pedestrians and carriages and brightly lit despite its not being full dark. The Giordas turned to one side and entered an alley running parallel to the main street. Alaric and Dianthe exchanged a glance Sienne caught the edge of. It conveyed a conversation's worth of meaning. What would it be like to know someone that well?

"Sienne, come with me," Alaric said. "Perrin and Kalanath, follow Dianthe and do exactly as she says."

"Wait," Sienne said. "I have to renew the spell."

"Not necessary," Alaric said. His Rafellish form shivered, then dissolved. "We want them to see us."

Sienne, mystified, nodded, then had to trot after Alaric as he sped up, heading straight for the alley. "What am I supposed to do?"

"You're the decoy," Alaric said. "You just have to stand there. And *don't* go for your spellbook even if Conn does. If this goes wrong, and it turns into a public fight, you need to be clearly innocent of any aggression. Understand?"

"All right. But—"

They entered the alley. It was clean, mostly, piled here and there with broken furniture and empty barrels but free of human or animal waste. Barred cellar doors lay to the left and right. The Giordas still hadn't noticed them. "Giorda!" Alaric shouted. "I want a word with you."

All three Giordas jerked and whipped around to stare at Alaric. The fourth man turned more slowly, his hands held stiffly at waist level. Since Milo had a knife to his side, Sienne wasn't surprised by his stillness. Conn made a jerky motion as if to raise the spellbook tucked under his left arm, then subsided. "Ham-fist. What do you want?"

"An apology," Alaric said, "for attacking me and mine. You meant us to die out there, didn't you?"

Conn's mocking grin grew wider. "It would have been an unfortunate accident. Things like that happen all the time in the wilderness. There's nothing for me to apologize for, even if I were inclined to do so."

"And poaching? You've got an excuse for that, too?"

"Poaching?" Conn's eyes widened in mock innocence. "I made the whelp an offer and she refused it. Why she'd have such loyalty to *you*, I have no idea. You're not banging her, are you?" He assessed Sienne with his eyes. "Not that I'd blame you."

"You disgusting little rat—"

Alaric put a quelling hand on Sienne's shoulder. "She was paid fairly, just like the rest of my team, which is more than I can say for the people you work with."

"Do you have a point?" Conn drawled. "I have things to do."

"Looks like kidnapping is on that list." Alaric indicated the knife. "Let him go."

"What do you care? Did you develop a sense of civic duty overnight?"

"I enjoy interfering with your plans."

"What, you and the whelp? She's not even prepared." Conn's spellbook popped open and the pages riffled in an invisible wind. "I offered you a chance. You should have taken it," he said to Sienne. Behind him, Alethea drew her sword, while Milo kept the knife pressed to the man's side.

"You're a pig. I wouldn't work with you if it was a choice between that and a life of indentured servitude," Sienne said.

Conn smiled, dismissing her as he turned his attention on Alaric.

"Ten lari to your one says I can blast you before you draw that sword of yours."

Alaric smiled back. "The same bet says you'll be out cold before I lay a finger on you."

Conn's smile went confused. "What?"

Kalanath came flying out of the darkness behind the trio, followed by Dianthe. Conn turned just in time for Kalanath's staff to smack him hard behind the ear. His eyes rolled up comically in his head, and he folded. Dianthe's blade clashed with Alethea's, but Dianthe had the advantage of surprise, and pressed the woman hard against the alley wall. Alaric, moving swiftly for someone his size, darted past the falling Conn and advanced on Milo. Milo squeaked and stepped backward. His captive surged backward and ran for the far end of the alley. "I don't think so," Perrin said, stepping forward to grab the man's arm.

Sienne rushed to Conn's side and snatched his spellbook out of his limp hands, then backed away. She'd never handled anyone's spellbook without their permission before, and it felt vaguely illicit, like breaking a minor law no one knew about to enforce. But since he was already beginning to stir, she felt taking his weapon away was a smart move.

A clang and a clatter signaled the end of Dianthe's duel, as she knocked Alethea's sword out of her hand. Alethea sprawled against the wall, arms and legs outstretched, head turned away from the knife in Dianthe's off hand that was pressed against her cheek. Alaric shoved Milo, limp and unresisting, in Kalanath's direction. "Nicely done," he said. "Perrin, bring him here."

Perrin still had hold of the man's arm, but his "captive" wasn't resisting. As he came closer, Sienne saw how still and miserable his face was, as if he was sure he'd just traded one set of kidnappers for another.

"I wish I had rope," Dianthe complained. "Why do I ever go anywhere without rope?"

"As you told me the last time I suggested it," Alaric said, "it's heavy, it's scratchy, and you never need it." He drew his sword and strolled over to where Conn lay twitching, casually laying its edge against his throat. Conn stopped moving. "Now, where should we start?"

"Please just let me go," Perrin's captive said. "I don't know what you want from me."

Dianthe gasped and swiveled her head to look at him. "*Padget?*"

His mouth fell open. "Dianthe? What are you—why did you kidnap me?"

"We rescued you, Padge. Perrin, let him go, he's not going to run. Alaric, haven't you met Padget Tachonus?"

"I don't think so, sorry." Alaric scratched his head. "Tachonus?"

"Alaric, come on. He's Neoma's brother."

"Neoma's—" Alaric looked down at Conn, who had his mouth set in a stiff line. "More coincidences that probably aren't. Padget, tell us what happened."

Padget wiped sweat from his forehead. "They were waiting for me when I came back from the market. In my own home! They told me I was coming with them, and I said I wasn't, and they threatened to kill me if I didn't do exactly as they said. Then we waited for a while—*he* —" Padget pointed a shaking finger at Conn—"said it needed to be darker, so nobody would notice they had a knife to my back. Then they made me follow him. And then you attacked us." He sounded so much like Neoma, despite the differences in their size and sex, it was eerie.

"Hmm. They didn't say anything else? No details about why they wanted you?"

"Nothing like that. No, that's not true. The skinny one—" He pointed at Milo. "He said I didn't look anything like Neoma, and the one in charge said looks weren't what mattered."

"Interesting. Care to elaborate, Giorda?" Alaric leaned on his sword a little more heavily. Conn stared stonily at the sky. "Nothing? Well, I didn't expect you to talk. Sienne, go ahead and see if there's any spells you want in his book. Might as well profit from this."

Conn's mouth opened, but no words came out. Alaric grinned. Sienne, uncertain as to whether he was serious or not, opened the book. Conn groaned. Sienne turned the stiff, sharp-edged pages. Conn knew a *lot* of spells. There was *force*, and *open,* and *scorch* and *ice* and half a dozen evocations she'd never even heard of. That was before she even started on the summonings. "This is *amazing,*" she said. The book trembled in her grip as Conn tried to use his invisible fingers on it. She closed it and tucked it under one arm to prevent him grabbing it. "Maybe later," she told Alaric.

"Kalanath," Alaric said. Kalanath had Milo Giorda in a complicated lock Sienne was sure would dislocate his shoulder if he tried to break it. Kalanath released him only to swing him around and slam him face-first into the wall. Milo let out a weak groan. Alaric said, "All right, Milo. Why did you kidnap Padget?"

"Not telling you anything," Milo said, his voice muffled by the bricks.

Kalanath reversed his grip on Milo's arm, making it go stiff and hyperextended. Milo yelped in pain. "You've worked with Kalanath before," Alaric said. "You know he's familiar with all sorts of exotic Omeiran fighting techniques. I'm sure you've seen him use them. The question is, do you want him to use them on *you*?"

Milo was silent. "I just want a simple answer, and you won't have to suffer at all," Alaric continued.

"Shut up, Milo," Conn grated.

Alaric nodded to Kalanath. Kalanath did something that made Milo squeal. "Stop!" he shrieked. "Lord Liurdi sent us after him!"

"Shut *up*, you idiot!" Conn said.

"Is Lord Liurdi the owner of that estate we saw you coming out of this afternoon?"

"Yes! He needs this man to open a box! Let us go!" Milo was standing on his toes, trying desperately to get away from Kalanath. Sienne hoped Alaric and Kalanath were bluffing. Torturing a pathetic louse like Milo felt wrong, like using Alaric's sword to cut butter.

Alaric glanced at Sienne. "Would that work?"

"I...don't think so. Did they say why he could open the box, Milo?"

"Some prophecy or other. Let us go! You can have the little creep!"

"You'd better pray he doesn't let me go, Milo, because so help me, I'm going to crush your spine, if I can find it," Conn said.

Alaric ignored him. "So they have a priest, and a prophecy."

"We knew they had a priest, because the greasy man had a location blessing," Dianthe said. "Perrin, how could a prophecy tell them to go after Padget?"

"Sorry?" Perrin came forward from where he'd been staring at one of the low cellar doors lining the alley. "A prophecy is serious business. I would not attempt to direct Averran's will in that way— were I to ask for a prophecy, I would leave it entirely to him what response to make or, in fact, whether to respond at all. That our enemy dared ask for a prophecy on a specific matter...he, or she, must be well advanced in the worship of their avatar."

"But is it really as straightforward as asking for the answer to the question 'how do we open the box?'"

"In theory, yes. Though the answers one receives to a prophecy are always oblique. Delanie, for example, delivers all her prophecies in rhyme, or so I am told. So it is unlikely our enemy was simply told the name of this man. At any rate, the priest's interpretation led her, or him, to conclude kidnapping Master Tachonus was the solution to the problem of the box."

"Which leaves us with more questions," Alaric said. "And no way to get answers that I can see."

Sienne looked at Conn. He was glaring at her as if daring her to open his spellbook again. It was too bad they weren't friends, because she would love to trade for some of his spells. That was beyond unlikely, even if he weren't the man he was.

"We have to move quickly," Dianthe said. "At some point, they're going to wonder why their pet thugs haven't returned." She shoved Alethea harder into the wall as the woman made an attempt to break her hold.

"That's true," Alaric said, looking down at Conn. "Unless..."

"Unless what?" Dianthe said, when Alaric didn't immediately finish his thought.

Alaric closed his eyes and let out a sigh. "Unless their pet thugs return as scheduled."

"You surely do not intend to let them go?" Perrin exclaimed.

Alaric looked at Sienne. "You," he said, "are a very bad influence. I would never have considered this a week ago."

For a moment, Sienne was mystified. Then light dawned. She smiled at Alaric. "Don't worry," she said. "We won't tell anyone you've gone soft."

"Will someone tell me for the love of Kitane *what is going on?*" Dianthe said.

"I've lost my mind, that's what's going on," Alaric said. "Let's do some wizardry."

20

Alaric slammed the heavy cellar door shut and dropped the bar into place. "They won't get out of that easily." One of the captives pounded the door, making it rattle, but the bar held firm.

"Nevertheless, I believe I will give us some extra security," Perrin said. He tore a blessing from the riffle of papers and knelt before the low door, pressing it flat against the worn wooden surface. Bowing his head, he muttered an invocation. Pale yellow light spread outward from his palm, filling the grain of the heavy wood like melted butter. The wood soaked it up until it dimmed and finally vanished. Another blow struck the door, but this time, the wood didn't so much as tremble.

"Is that what that's for?" Sienne said.

"I believe it is actually for constraining a mud or rock fall, but it works to hold a door closed as well." Perrin stood and dusted off his hands. "And with that cellar opening only to the outside, they will be there for a long time."

Sienne nodded and crouched by the door. "I'm no thief," she called out, her voice still strange in her ears. "I'll leave your book here by the door. Probably no one will steal it." She didn't much care if they did, but Conn would want revenge on her if *she* stole his spellbook. Well, he was likely to want revenge regardless. She just knew she couldn't take his book, however much she might want the spells it contained.

"You're sure?" Alaric said. Sienne nodded again. "Then let's go. Stay close together, and I'll do the talking. Dianthe?"

"I'll meet you there. Don't worry, I'll find you," she added as Kalanath looked about to protest. Surprisingly, he'd been the one to object to Alaric's unorthodox plan, primarily on the grounds that he'd have to leave his staff behind. Dianthe would return it to Master Tersus's house, then join them at Lord Liurdi's estate.

Sienne cast her eye over all of them, checking her work. *Imitate* was simple when you had the subject of your image in front of you to work from. Conn, Milo, and two Padgets looked back at her. The Padgets were identical except for their expressions. One of them looked calm. The other looked confused and afraid. Sienne was glad the latter wasn't going with them.

"Conn" cleared his throat. "How long will these disguises last?"

"The confusions will last six hours, unless something happens to disrupt them," Sienne said. "Specifically, prolonged physical contact with another person will break the spell. The vocal transforms will last four, and those will simply revert when the duration is up. So I'm afraid you're going to sound like Conn for a while."

"Better than having this fall apart on us while we're in that place," Alaric said in Conn's voice. "Padget, go with Dianthe. You'll be safe at Master Tersus's, just in case we're wrong and someone lets Conn and his motley crew out sooner than later."

"I still don't understand what your plan is," Padget said. "And why did they want me?"

"I'll explain it as we go," Dianthe said. "Good luck." She saluted them with Kalanath's staff and ran off, Padget trailing behind her like a mournful dog.

Alaric gestured for them to form up the way the Giordas had been when they accosted them. Kalanath, who now looked and sounded like Milo Giorda, took up a guard position next to Perrin/Padget. Sienne flanked him on the other side. She couldn't see her own image, but the others had assured her she looked exactly like Alethea. She tried to remember the woman's swagger and copy it. *Imitate* had been popular in the amateur theatricals in Stravanus, with young wizards copying the portraits of famous men and women in history, but Sienne had never been very good at mimicking mannerisms. Now she wished she'd practiced more. Their lives might depend on it.

She watched Alaric, who strode along exactly as Conn did. How unexpected, that he'd not only thought of this plan, but championed it. For someone whose people were enslaved by wizardry, he'd come to accept having magic cast on him very quickly. Was his faith in her really that complete? After only a few days? Or was he just sensible enough to realize magic was as good or evil as the person casting it? She resolved to ask him about it later. Much later, probably.

It was now twilight, and music and laughter filled the air. There was some sort of festival going on in the center of Fioretti, and masked revelers rushed past, tugging at Sienne's sleeves to urge her to join them. She drew closer to Perrin, at the center of their lopsided triangle, and hoped they wouldn't be separated. On the other side, Kalanath did the same.

Alaric led them around the loudest and busiest streets, making good time despite the delay. Sienne tried not to fidget, or move too fast. She was conscious of time slipping past, of her fear that one of them would startle, or be jostled too hard, and the confusion would disappear. She was confident in her ability to generate a good *imitate*, even if she was bad at aping the mannerisms of the person she resembled, but things happened, and there was always a chance of failure. So she fretted, and willed the images to stay put, and composed a quick prayer to whatever avatar might be listening that this would succeed.

After a time, she realized the streets were quieter, and she had not heard music for some time. They were headed steadily uphill again, past the estates of the wealthy, and Sienne looked back and saw the lights of the palace below and to the left, candy-colored and exquisite. She'd wondered, back when she first arrived in Fioretti, whether the king disliked having some of his subjects looking down on the palace from their estates higher in the hills. Now, looking at the brilliantly lit palace, she realized the king's ancestors had likely chosen that spot specifically to remind the nobles and gentry who was the true power in Rafellin. No one could look at it and doubt the authority of the man who ruled it.

Lights lined the road, clean white magical lights that drew clouds of insects just as lanterns did. Scatterings of dark specks beneath them showed what happened when those insects came too close to the light. More lights illuminated the estates they passed, and their gates were open, admitting gaudy carriages filled with beautifully dressed people. They paid no attention to Sienne and her friends, trudging along the side of the road. Sienne averted her face, fearing recognition—there was always a chance one of these people knew her—then remembered she didn't look anything like herself, and stepped out more boldly.

They neared the end of the road, and the low hedge beyond which lay Lord Liurdi's manor. Unlike the others, it was not well-lit, with only a few magic lights hovering to either side of the heavy front doors. More lights scattered throughout the grounds only gave the gardens an eerie, haunted look, as if they were wisps frozen in place, waiting for a victim to stroll by.

"We're here," Alaric said in a low voice. "Remember, I'll do the talking. We want as much information as we can get before we snatch the box."

"What if we have to give ourselves away to get it?" Kalanath asked.

"We'll worry about that when the time comes. Watch for my signal."

A few more steps brought them to the front gate, which struck Sienne as a token more than anything else, given the height of the hedge. Alaric rapped on the bars with his knuckles. A man in forest green and cream livery under a heavy leather jerkin approached. "We're back," Alaric said. The guard looked them over just long enough to establish dominance, then unlocked the gate and pulled it open. Alaric gave him Conn's best sneer and walked past at a pace

Conn, with his shorter legs, would have found impossible to copy. The image shifted minutely around the hips and knees.

"Slow down, *brother*," Sienne called out. Alaric didn't turn to look at her, but slowed his gait. The image shifted slightly again, then settled down, and Sienne breathed more easily.

They crunched along the gravel paths, not as fancy as Master Fontanna's but still gleaming white where the magic lights struck them. The manor loomed over them, its windows dark. It looked uninhabited, but not deserted—more as if its owners had gone out of town for the summer, leaving it to the care of the servants. Sienne felt a sudden horrible fear that they'd gotten it wrong, that the pendant was not here, that she had to quash. The guard wouldn't have let them in if there were no one home, and he wouldn't have let them in if they hadn't been expected. This was all according to plan. She shifted her weight so she could feel her spellbook press against her stomach. It was comforting to know it was there, even if she couldn't use it.

There was a bell rope with a heavy brass handle hanging by the front door. Alaric pulled it with a firm yank. They waited. Finally, the door creaked open, unnerving Sienne further because it sounded just the way a haunted manor in a melodrama would. "We're back," Alaric repeated for the green and cream-clad servant who appeared in the doorway. She held a candle branch in one hand that lit her face with flickering shadows. The woman nodded and opened the door further.

"Wait here," she said, and walked away into the darkness, trailing candlelight with her.

"Why doesn't she expect us to find the way ourselves?" Sienne whispered.

"What, and let scum like the Giordas wander free through this lovely manor?" Alaric whispered back. "Besides, we want them to give us a guide. I'm lost and we've only just stepped into the entry hall."

The entry hall was only about twenty feet wide, but several times that longer, extending deep into the manor. It was as poorly lit as the outside of the manor, with candles rather than magic lights providing the illumination. They cast deep, almost tangible shadows over the farthest corners of the room and made the portraits lining the long walls seem to be laughing at them. Nearest them, doors to the left and right stood firmly closed, offering no hint as to what lay beyond them. Sienne nervously checked everyone's confusion spell. Still good.

The woman returned, emerging from the shadowed depths of the hall like a swimmer coming out of dark water. "You will follow me. You know the rules."

Sienne's heart gave a panicked thump. Rules? There were rules? Alaric remained perfectly calm. She wished she knew how he did that. Beside her, Kalanath prodded Perrin, who jerked away exactly as if he were a prisoner. Everyone was playing their parts except her, and she was giving in to fear. She stiffened her spine and glowered at the servant woman's back. She wasn't going to give the game away.

They followed the bobbing candles down the interminable hall. More doors loomed out of the darkness, flanked by more gilt-framed portraits of people whose eyes followed the interlopers. Where was Dianthe? How on earth could she get inside to find them? Sienne stomped down her fear again. Dianthe was a professional, and she and Alaric had been doing things like this for years. Everything would be fine.

The servant opened the last door on the left and stepped back. Alaric, ignoring her, entered the room, followed by Perrin and Kalanath. Sienne risked a glance at the woman and caught an unexpected expression of...was that pity? Who did she pity? Sienne felt another flash of fear. This one felt rational. If the woman felt sorry for Perrin/Padget, or even for the Giordas, it could mean their lives were in danger. She wished she could warn Alaric that the theoretical danger was rather less theoretical than they'd thought. She shifted her weight to feel her spellbook again, this time to get a sense for where it lay in case she needed to get at it in a hurry. She might only have the one offensive spell, but as Alaric continued to teach her, there were all sorts of sideways approaches to wizardry.

The room beyond was a study, at least as far as Sienne's experience went. To anyone not raised in a duke's household, this might look like a library, but there weren't enough bookcases and the desk occupying the far side of the room was far too large. Tall windows curtained in forest green velvet that matched the servant's livery flanked the desk. An empty fireplace still smelling of ash sat opposite it. In the far corner, a white iron staircase spiraled up out of sight through a square hole in the ceiling, through which came a slightly brighter light than that of the candles illuminating the study. Though the room was sizable, it felt hot and close and stuffy, and Sienne wished she dared throw back the curtains and smash open a window, since she doubted the ground floor windows were made to open.

Alaric went immediately to the staircase and began to climb. "You there," he said to Perrin, "stop dawdling. I warned you what would happen if you crossed us, didn't I?"

"Sorry," Perrin whined. Sienne mentally applauded.

She once again took her place at the end of the procession, as there was room on the staircase for only one at a time. Her feet rang dully on the metal treads, and the sound echoed with her companions' footsteps until it made her dizzy. She hoped it was the sound that caused her dizziness and not the frequent casting of spells. She hadn't reached her limit, but four *imitates* and four *voices* was pushing it. Out in the cool evening air, she hadn't felt it, but the warmth of the room and the echoing footsteps made her long for a place where she could sit down and put her head between her knees.

The staircase went up a very long way, through a narrow space like a chimney, and Sienne tried not to think about all the ways in which this might be a trap. Kalanath's legs filled her vision, and she noticed, to her chagrin, that his boots were featureless, lacking the creases actual boots might have. She prayed no one would notice the missing detail.

Kalanath stepped off the stairs, and Sienne followed him. The air was cooler here, and it took her a moment to realize this was because the room was open to the outdoors. She looked up and suppressed a gasp. It was an observatory, its domed roof painted with a replica of the summer night sky at solstice. Faceted gemstones, blue, red, yellow, and white, took the places of the largest stars. The lines of the constellations were traced in gold paint that glimmered in the light of the candles placed on candle trees around the room. Some of the dome's panels were missing, and the gaps were the sources of the cool, apple-scented breezes that brushed Sienne's face.

A grouping of four leather armchairs, their sides high and winged, stood between candle trees at the far side of the room. A strangely blocky table draped in blue silk sat at its center, like a focal point. Two men and two women occupied the chairs, their attention on Alaric and Perrin behind him. They sat stiffly, their hands gripping the armrests, as motionless as if they were mannequins posed for a still life. Sienne had to look carefully to determine whether they were living, noting finally the slow blinking of one, the measured breathing of another. It was unsettling.

Something else odd about the room niggled at her. That was it. There was no telescope taking pride of place at the center of the room, or even poking through one of the many gaps through which Sienne could see the gardens and, beyond that, the rest of Fioretti. This would not be the best location for stargazing, what with the hills blocking the view to the north, but surely anyone with access to an observatory this beautiful would take advantage of it?

One of the mannequins stood and moved forward, gliding as smoothly as if he were on wheels. "What took so long?" he said.

"We had to wait for dusk so we wouldn't be noticed," Alaric said.

"He's not bound."

"That would be noticed, if we hauled a struggling body through the streets. Not even Fioretti is that blasé about kidnapping."

The man drew nearer, and Sienne got a good look at his face. It was unpleasantly fleshy, though his body wasn't overly fat, with a thin brown mustache and beard outlining his mouth. His lips were large and pink and moist, making Sienne think of worms on a wet pavement. He was dressed finely in a velvet tunic too warm for the true summer weather and matching leggings, his dark-haired head was bare, and his shoes were an old-fashioned style with long, narrow toes and heels that gave him perhaps two inches in height.

"So this is he," the man said. Sienne guessed this was Lord Liurdi. She'd never heard of him, but there were a lot of nobles who didn't move in the same circles as her family. "You're certain?"

"I wouldn't try to pass off some stranger as the right man," Alaric said.

Lord Liurdi glided forward and examined Perrin. Sienne held her breath. If Liurdi touched him, the confusion would fall apart, because Perrin was five inches taller than Padget and much slimmer. But Liurdi had the expression of one regarding an unpleasant insect, one that smelled of intestinal gas. "You needn't fear," he said. Sienne was pretty sure he was lying. "I have a simple task for you. Complete it, and you may leave."

"Why didn't you just ask me? You didn't need to kidnap me!" Perrin whined.

Liurdi shrugged and turned away without answering. Two of the others, male and female, rose from their chairs and came to join him. The woman was beautiful, her dark blonde hair contrasting nicely with her dusky skin, her gown a rich blue Chysegaran silk in the latest fashion. The man was nearly as tall as Alaric, but painfully thin, the skin drawn tightly across his face like a skull wearing a flesh mask. He held a spellbook loosely in one hand, its wooden cover painted matte black and adorned with a bas-relief of a pile of skulls. Sienne watched him closely. The wizards who decorated their spellbooks with overly dramatic images were usually poseurs, but she had a feeling, looking at his gaunt face, that it would be a mistake to underestimate him.

The woman said, "Then what are you waiting for?" She turned back to address the other woman, still seated in her armchair. "Is there something we haven't done yet? Some other clause of the prophecy?"

The second woman crossed long, thin hands in her lap. "Delanie has given us all the help to which she is inclined," she said. Her hair was nearly black, parted sharply in the middle to fall straight on both sides of her face. The stark look combined with the dark red of the lip rouge she wore made her look undead, though of course no undead creature would be so articulate.

Liurdi walked past the armchairs to a cabinet under one of the missing panels. Wind blowing through it disordered his hair, but he didn't bother pushing it back into place. He opened the cabinet and withdrew Neoma's box, which flexed slightly under his hand. "You," he said to Perrin, walking back toward him, "open it."

Perrin gave him a look of bewilderment. Really, Sienne's friends had all missed their true calling on the stage. "Open it? I don't have the key."

Liurdi rolled his eyes. "Callia, what was the prophecy?"

The woman in the chair, the priest, tilted her head back and closed her eyes.

"'Let the blood of her blood
speak with her living breath,
his voice as her voice
to open the chest,'"

she intoned, sounding very bored.

The gaunt wizard said, "That seems very straightforward. Have the man breathe on the lock."

"Is that what it means?" Liurdi said. He shrugged again. "Then breathe on it."

He held the box up to Perrin's face. Sienne took a step back and, while all eyes were on Perrin, carefully extricated her spellbook. She held it close to the side of her leg and hoped no one cared enough about her to watch her. Perrin certainly wasn't blood of Neoma's blood, and even though his voice was Padget's at the moment, that wasn't going to be enough to open the box. When Liurdi and his friends discovered that, everything was going to fall apart. She watched the gaunt wizard. Disarming him of his spellbook would be her responsibility. She had a plan, a slightly ridiculous plan, but if it worked, it didn't matter how ridiculous it was.

Perrin swallowed and leaned in close to the box. He drew in a breath, then released it in a huff. Everyone tensed. Nothing happened. Perrin pursed his lips and blew hard, keeping his eyes on Liurdi. Liurdi said, "It's not working. Why is it not working?"

"If you people hadn't been so careless, none of this would be necessary," the wizard said to Alaric.

"It said 'blood of her blood,'" the elegant woman said. "Maybe we need blood."

"Maybe we do," Liurdi said. He reached for Perrin, who sidled out of reach. "Hold still, you fool, we're not going to kill you. We just want a little blood."

"I didn't agree to that," Perrin said. "Let me try again." He reached for the box.

"You, cut him," Liurdi said to Kalanath, who was still holding the knife. Kalanath hesitated. He couldn't hold Perrin without breaking the confusion spell, and Sienne was sure he didn't want to cut his companion.

"Don't be stupid, do as he asks," Alaric said. "Just *grab him*, all right?"

Sienne held her breath. Alaric wouldn't have forgotten, would he? This must be part of the plan.

Kalanath switched the knife to his left hand and reached for Perrin with his right. He took firm hold of Perrin's collar, and the image of Padget shivered and dissolved, followed a second later by Milo Giorda's figure disappearing to reveal Kalanath.

There was a moment in which no one moved. Liurdi's fleshy lips hung slack with astonishment. The elegant woman drew in a sharp breath. The wizard looked confused, as if he'd just heard something he couldn't comprehend. He showed no signs of going for his spellbook.

Sienne brought her spellbook up and willed it open. "Conn" moved toward Liurdi, reaching over his shoulder for the sword that became visible as he grasped it. Alaric seemed to explode upward out of Conn's smaller form.

The wizard's stunned incomprehension began to fade. Before he could react, Sienne spat out the short, curt, painful words of the summoning *slick*.

21

A silver, jelly-like substance glimmering with oily rainbows oozed from the surface of the wizard's spellbook. As he raised it swiftly to eye level, it shot out of his hand with momentum that carried it three feet away. The wizard shouted in alarm and dove after it, fumbling and trying to get a grip on its greasy surface. Sienne spat blood and grinned. That put him out of commission for a while.

She looked around and saw, to her astonishment, that the fight was over. Alaric had Liurdi backed against a wall. Kalanath stood threatening the beautiful woman, who stared at him disdainfully but made no movement. And Dianthe—wait, where had Dianthe come from?—had her knife against the throat of the priest as Perrin removed a riffle of bright blue rice paper squares from her hand. Sienne walked over to the wizard, still scrabbling at his spellbook trying to make it open, and used her invisible fingers to lift it away from him and toss it out one of the open panels. The man stared up at her, his fine linen shirt stained with silvery grease. "You bitch," he snarled.

"Watch it," Alaric said. "She's got no sense of humor and an excellent grasp of transformations. So unless you feel like being a frog—"

"Not possible," the man said, but he looked uncertain. Sienne made a show of opening her spellbook, and he sat back, mulishly silent.

Alaric picked up Neoma's box from where Liurdi had dropped it in the scuffle. "This doesn't belong to you," he said. "But you know that."

"You have no need of it," Liurdi said. "Who hired you to steal it? Was it Fontanna? Mossino? They have no idea what it is."

"You utter bastards," Dianthe said. "Why didn't you just buy it from Neoma? You didn't have to kill her."

Liurdi didn't look away from Alaric and his enormous sword, so very close to his heart. "That was a mistake. The Giordas are—were—overenthusiastic in their zeal to retrieve it. I don't suppose you killed them?"

Sienne spared a glance for Dianthe. She was crying. Alaric said, "Do you care?"

"Not really. They were hired help, and not very good at that. But you...I'm impressed. We were all completely taken in, I'm not ashamed to admit it. Come now, let's be reasonable people. We just want the key. You can have everything else in the box. Just bring us the man to open it—I swear we won't hurt him."

"The box isn't yours to trade away," Alaric said. "As for the key... no, I don't think so."

"It does you no good without the trunk. You know that." Liurdi smiled. "Very well. You can have an equal share in its contents."

"Gregor, stop talking," the elegant woman said urgently. "You're giving everything away."

"Raene, it's past time we acknowledge we've been defeated. It's only fair." Liurdi's smile was like a snake's, narrow and mirthless. Sienne hoped it was as obvious to Alaric that he was lying as it was to her.

"Not interested," Alaric said. He glanced at Dianthe, who widened her eyes and shrugged in a gesture that to Sienne meant she was out of ideas.

"If I may," Perrin said, tossing the blue riffle of blessings out the window after the wizard's spellbook, "I have an idea for preventing them from making our retreat an unpleasant one. If you would all gather here in the center of the room, and sit with your backs to one another? Yes, exactly, thank you."

Dianthe guided the undead-looking woman to join the other three, who glared at Perrin. Perrin was unmoved by their hostility. He shooed his companions toward the stairs, then tore a blessing from his own riffle of paper and placed it on the floor near where the four sat. "We should go with alacrity, nonetheless," he said, then murmured an invocation. A glimmering gray dome sprang up around the four, through which Sienne saw the blessing paper go up in flame. Liurdi and the elegant woman, Raene, leaped up and began pounding on the dome. The other two, Sienne saw, looked too despondent to move. Then Dianthe took her arm and guided her down the first steps.

They pounded down the stairs as quickly as possible and ran, not trying to be silent, down the long hall to the front door. As they neared it, the servant woman emerged from the left-hand door. "What in Delanie's name—" she began, but Sienne didn't hear the rest of it, because she was through the door and pelting across the gravel paths toward the gate. Ahead of her, Alaric ran with sword in hand, a terrifying juggernaut bearing down on the gate guard. The guard, turning at the sound of their approach, barely had time to bring his weapon up before Alaric swept it aside and punched him hard enough to knock him back a few paces. Perrin was already opening the gate, Kalanath leaped at it and bore it open under his momentum, and Dianthe and Sienne raced through.

It was a beautiful, clear night, and the stars shone more brightly than had the gemstone ones in Liurdi's observatory. Sienne threw back her head and laughed in sheer relief. They'd done it, no one had been hurt, they hadn't had to kill anyone. Dizziness aside, she felt as if she could run forever.

"How did you find us?" she gasped to Dianthe, running nearby.

"I saw the lights in the dome and decided to try there first," Dianthe said. "Got lucky."

"You make that kind of luck," Alaric said. "Keep running. I want us all off the hill and mingling with the crowds, just in case."

The celebrations were still going strong when they reached the city center. The cacophony of half a dozen musicians playing half a dozen different songs became unexpectedly melodious in Sienne's ears. A handsome young man danced past, extending a hand to Sienne, and she almost took it before remembering the job wasn't finished yet. She smiled and ran on.

Finally, pain stabbing through her side, her lungs aching, the world whizzing past her face, she slowed and bent over, gasping. "Give me a minute," she said to Alaric, who stopped beside her.

"We can walk from here," he said. "It's only a few more streets." His voice, somber and deep, quelled her high spirits.

"Why sound so despondent? We won," Perrin said, sweeping Alaric a deep noble's bow.

"It was too easy," Alaric said.

"You had the advantage of surprise," Dianthe pointed out, "and someone on the outside. I don't see how that qualifies as too easy."

Alaric shook his head and walked on in silence. Sienne and the others followed him. He was right, Sienne thought—it had been too easy. True, Sienne was fast, but the wizard had been unexpectedly slow to react, and so had the priest. And their disguises had caught the conspirators off guard, but surely Liurdi and his friends weren't so confident that they weren't at least a little paranoid? Sienne didn't know what it meant, but it seemed Alaric had some idea, and he wasn't happy about it.

The lights were on in the ground floor of Master Tersus's house when they arrived, tired and footsore. Sienne had wondered if they would detour to see if the Giordas were still trapped, but Alaric hadn't deviated from his path at all, and she supposed it didn't really matter. Would they dare return to Liurdi's manor after failing so spectacularly? Again, not something that mattered, but part of her wished she could be a fly on the wall for that conversation. She followed Alaric and Dianthe to the side door and into the kitchen, where

Padget and Leofus were having an animated conversation over a pot of soup.

Leofus paused long enough to acknowledge them with a nod. "Food's cold," he said, "but the soup is still hot. Even if this fool thinks I'm wrong in using chicken stock."

"Fool? *I'm* the fool? I've been cooking for twenty years and I say chicken stock—" Padget began.

"Just give me a bowl, I'm starving," Alaric said.

"What about the box?" Dianthe said. "We should open it immediately."

"I admit to some curiosity as to the efficacy of Delanie's prophecy," Perrin said.

"So...Padget just has to breathe on the lock?" Dianthe approached Padget with the box.

"That, and hum a note. At least that's what I remember Neoma doing," Alaric said.

Padget eyed the box dubiously. "I thought Neoma was the only one who could open it."

"Just breathe on it, and let's find out, all right?" Alaric said. "And if not, we'll figure something else out."

Padget leaned over, drew in a deep breath, and let it out in a warm puff against the lock, humming a low tone. Nothing happened. He drew in a breath to try again, and with a click, the lock sprang open. "It worked!" Padget exclaimed, and opened the lid. Sienne found herself in the middle of a cluster of people, all peering into the box. The contents were exactly as she'd seen them last, bags of coins, loose gems, the beautiful necklace, and the bluestone pendant, shimmering like cloth of gold dyed to match the night sky.

Alaric picked it up and held it up to the nearest lantern shedding a golden light over the kitchen. "A key," he said. "Liurdi called it a key."

"That woman, Raene, was right. He gave away too much," Dianthe said. "He clearly believed we knew what it was for."

"He said it would do us no good without the trunk," Perrin said. "A trunk he no doubt possesses."

"Then we must find this trunk, and open it," Kalanath said. He'd repossessed himself of his staff when they entered and looked more comfortable than he had in hours.

"Should we?" Dianthe said. "If he's the owner of the trunk, we'd be stealing from him if we used the key. If he hadn't had Neoma killed, if he'd just bought the pendant like a sane person, we wouldn't be involved at all."

"Somebody who's willing to commit murder, even by proxy, is no one whose ultimate goals are noble," Alaric said. "I have a feeling we've come in at the end of a long chain of crimes this man has committed in pursuit of this key."

"He killed Neoma?" Padget said.

They all went silent. Sienne had forgotten there was someone in the room for whom Liurdi's crimes were personal. "He hired the Giordas to get the pendant," Alaric said in a kinder voice than Sienne had thought him capable of. "They murdered Neoma to do so."

Padget's face was red and angry. A tear slid down his cheek. "I want them brought to justice. They should pay for what they did."

"The investigation will reveal the truth," Perrin said. "The guards will have a priest divine their identities—"

"I wish we'd known about it when we had the Giordas in our power," Alaric growled. "We might have taken more direct action."

"There wasn't time," Dianthe pointed out. "Padget, the guards will figure it out."

"Will you tell them what you learned?"

"It won't matter. It's just hearsay, if we tell them something Liurdi mentioned to us. But..." Dianthe's voice trailed off in the face of Padget's misery. She put an arm around his shoulder and hugged him.

"I think we need more information," Alaric said. "Perrin, could Averran tell us what's important about this trunk? Or where it is?"

"I know where it is," Dianthe said. "It's in the observatory. I saw it when I came through the window. Liurdi's got it next to those armchairs, like a funny table."

Sienne remembered seeing the table when she entered the observatory. "How do you know it's the trunk he was talking about?"

"It's an informed guess, really, but I feel confident about it. It's old, maybe a couple of centuries old, for one. For another, when I captured their priest, she had her blessings out and was getting ready to invoke one of them, but she wasn't looking at us, she was looking at the trunk. Then, when Liurdi mentioned the trunk, the other woman, that Raene, looked right at it."

"All right, so we know where it is," Alaric said. "Going after it will be difficult. I'd rather not do it unless we know what it contains, or whether Liurdi's plans are as sinister as I believe."

"I can ask," Perrin said, "but I am not certain it is a good idea."

"Why not?"

Perrin pushed his bowl away and leaned his elbows on the table. "Averran has been unusually helpful on this...I suppose one must call it a quest. He has given me not only the blessings I have asked for, but others that have turned out to be remarkably and unexpectedly helpful. That blessing that allowed me to bind the door behind which we locked the Giordas, for example. It was not something I asked for, and from that I conclude Averran smiles upon our venture."

"That sounds as if you *should* ask for more of his help," Dianthe said.

"But then we must consider the nature of our opponents," Perrin went on. "Specifically, that one of them is a priest who has received blessings from her avatar that will aid her and her fellows. In other words, God in Her guise as Delanie supports our enemy, while God in Her guise as Averran supports us."

"I do not understand how God can fight God," Kalanath said.

"It is a complexity I do not fully understand myself. I was taught that God in Her infinite wisdom and goodness may act at odds with Herself to teach humanity great truths, and that, when two avatars conflict, there is something else beneath the contention. In this case, Averran seems...perhaps 'eager' is not the correct word, but my instincts say his interest in our quest is beyond merely, mmm, interested. For whatever reason, Averran wishes Delanie's followers not to possess this key. It is very likely he expects us to make of this fact what we will, and not trouble him for details."

"So...it's up to our ingenuity and instincts," Alaric said.

"Even so."

Alaric set the pendant down on the table. They all stared at it, even Leofus, who'd let his spoon sink down into the pot. Sienne leaned over to get a closer look without touching the stone. "I could try..."

"Try what?" Dianthe said.

"Well, it doesn't look like a key. Maybe if I tried opening it like I do my spellbook?"

"Is that safe?"

"It won't destroy it." Sienne glanced at Alaric. She'd developed that habit fast, hadn't she? But he was looking at the pendant, too, so she picked it up and focused her will on it. For a moment, she felt it quiver, and its color deepened, the tiny sparkles dimming. Then the moment passed, and the pendant looked just as it always did. "No luck."

"That reminds me. I do have one more blessing like the one that revealed the ri—the location of the pendant," Perrin said, glancing swiftly at Leofus and Padget. Talking about rituals in front of people not of their company was a bad idea, Sienne agreed. "I might see if Averran is willing to give a hint, since he granted me this blessing without my asking for it."

"Do it," Alaric said.

Perrin laid the blessing on the table and, after a moment's thought, set the pendant on it. He stepped back, bowed his head, and whispered the invocation. Bright purple light traced along the lines of the sigil, sending up a whiff of jasmine and mint. The focused light drew the dark inverse of the scorched sigil on the ceiling, with the dark irregular shape of the pendant a shadow in the middle. The pendant itself sparkled more brightly, each of the tiny glittering specks shining enough to cast a second shadow on the table. Then the blessing went up in flame, causing Leofus to cry, "My table!"

"It is not that kind of fire," Perrin assured him. The fire went out, leaving no scorch marks on the table. For a moment, the pendant pulsed with purple fire. Then that, too, went out. Perrin picked up the pendant and turned it over in his fingers. "There are small marks here," he said. "I believe they are letters, but the language is not Fellic."

"May I?" Sienne asked. Perrin handed her the pendant. She scrutinized it closely. "The alphabet is Fellic, but it's not in any of the languages that use that script, and it's not transcribed Ginatic or Meiric. I think it's a code."

"Could you break it?" Alaric said.

"Possibly. But it will take a while. I haven't had much experience with codebreaking."

"And even if you break it, we still don't have the trunk," Dianthe said.

"So let's consider the possibilities." Alaric held up a finger. "One. We give the key to Liurdi on the condition we are present for opening the trunk, and deal with what's inside then. Two. We sneak in and open the trunk ourselves. Three. We steal the trunk and open it at a place of our choosing. And four. We bury or destroy the key so Liurdi can't ever have the use of it."

"I don't like number one because I don't trust Liurdi not to double-cross us," Dianthe said promptly. "Though that's really the easiest way to access the trunk. It did not look light, and it also had the same look the beams in the keep had. The ones that were indestructible."

"Do you think it came from the keep?" Kalanath said. "It would make sense."

"It might have, though that doesn't help us now," Alaric said. "If it's indestructible like the box, it can't be shrunk, right?"

Sienne nodded. "The *fit* spell won't affect invulnerable things."

"So we can't have you sneak in and make it small enough to smuggle out easily."

Again Sienne marveled at Alaric's sudden readiness to use wizardry. "I'm not good at sneaking, either."

"I find myself curious as to the contents of this trunk," Perrin said, "so I am reluctant to pursue option four."

"Same here," Alaric said, "but I think it may be more important to prevent the trunk being opened by the wrong person than to satisfy our curiosity."

"I don't know," Dianthe said. "It's late, and it's been a busy day. I say we sleep on it and make a decision in the morning."

"That is a good idea," Kalanath said. "Maybe we see a path in the morning that we cannot see now."

"But what about Neoma?" Padget said. "You're just going to let them get away with killing her?"

"Padge, it's not that simple," Dianthe began.

"It *is* that simple. You know who did it. Go and drag them to the guards, or...or kill them yourselves! You're scrappers, isn't that what you do?"

"We don't kill people," Dianthe said, "and we're not guards."

"It could have been accidental, if we'd known," Alaric said darkly. Dianthe glared at him.

"I can suggest to Denys that he look carefully at the Giordas," she said, "but I really think the priest they bring in will figure it out. Padget, it will be...I mean, Neoma will have justice. But we aren't it. I'm sorry."

"You were her friend, Dianthe," Padget said. "She depended on you." He turned and abruptly left the kitchen, and they heard the door open and slam shut. Leofus, looking uncomfortable, fished his spoon out of the pot, set it on the counter, and mumbled something about bedtime before slipping away.

"*Is* there anything else we could do?" Sienne asked, her heart aching at the stricken look on Dianthe's face.

"No," Alaric said with finality. "Dianthe's right. We should go to bed and see if things look different in the morning."

"Good—no, wait," Dianthe said. "Suppose that priest does another location blessing and sends that greasy man after us again? We need to protect ourselves."

"I have no protection blessings left," Perrin said. "I could pray for assistance, but I truly feel Averran will be unlikely to answer, and if we are to have his help on the morrow, I would prefer not to anger him tonight."

"Then we'll have to do it the old-fashioned way," Dianthe said. "I can rig something that will set off an alarm if anyone tries to get into the house."

"I think you should sleep here tonight," Alaric said to Perrin. "If Liurdi and his fellows come after us, and you're on your own, we wouldn't know you were in danger until it was too late."

"I had been about to make that suggestion," Perrin said. "If your Master Tersus does not mind."

"Not as long as you can pay." Alaric turned to Dianthe. "Do you need any help?"

"I just need to know that everyone's in for the night. I'll go explain to Master Tersus, if you want to come along, Perrin?"

When she and Perrin were gone, Alaric said, "This is not at all the way I expected this job to go."

"Are you disappointed?" Sienne asked, feeling unexpectedly anxious for his answer.

"Not yet. The idea of a treasure trove from before the wars is exciting. If we can figure out how to get at it." Alaric smiled. "We've certainly met some interesting people."

"It is the most interesting job I have ever had," Kalanath said with a smile.

Sienne almost said *So why don't we do this again?* But it seemed the wrong time to be talking about future jobs when the current one was unfinished. So instead she said, "Will Master Tersus mind that we're turning his house into a fortress for the night?"

Alaric shook his head. "One of the side benefits to hosting scrappers is you're pretty much guaranteed protection from criminals. Master Tersus has some very expensive art collections, and more than once Dianthe and I have deterred thieves. If this were a serious danger, we'd leave rather than expose him and Leofus to it, but Liurdi has no reason to attack anyone but us. And I doubt he still has the Giordas on his payroll, given their colossal failure, so there's little chance of collateral damage the way there was with Neoma." His expression grew briefly bitter. "At any rate, Master Tersus will likely see this as an adventure."

Dianthe reappeared. "Perrin is getting settled upstairs, and I suggest you all do the same while I set my traps."

Sienne nodded and trudged up the stairs, remembering to skip the loose treads this time. Soon she probably wouldn't even think about it. She returned to her room and changed into her nightdress, tucking her spellbook under her pillow. It made her feel silly and paranoid, since none of her companions were likely to steal it, but she wasn't going to let that deter her from taking precautions.

Someone knocked on the door. "Just checking in," Alaric said, poking his head around the door frame. "I don't like having this pendant where it isn't protected. It makes me nervous."

"I don't think anyone's getting in here tonight."

"Even so, I've learned to trust my instincts. If anything happens..." He shook his head. "Sleep well."

"Good night."

She extinguished her magic light and settled in to sleep. Her spellbook was a hard, angular lump under her pillow, not very comfortable, but she shifted into the best position she could find and tried to sleep. After the day she'd had, relaxing seemed impossible. She rolled onto her back and started tensing and relaxing her muscles one set at a time, beginning with her toes and working her way up her legs. She closed her eyes and focused on her muscles, not letting herself think of anything else, and felt herself drift into a peaceful heaviness of body and mind that was next door to sleep.

Something grabbed her and *yanked*, hard, pulling her sideways off the bed. She yelled, and tensed, but she never hit the floor. She opened her eyes to bright light from dozens of candles and hands grabbing her, rolling her on her side and jerking her hands behind her back. Sienne thrashed and bucked, trying to get free, but there were too many of them.

She blinked away the too-bright spots until her vision was clear. The first thing she saw was Liurdi's beautiful companion, Raene. She had Sienne's shoulders in both hands and was pressing her cheek-first against something soft that might be a sofa. Sienne twisted to look behind her. Liurdi had her hands pinioned, and the priest held a length of rope ready to tie her. Sienne looked about wildly for something her invisible fingers might throw, but everything was either too heavy or fastened down. The rope went around her wrists tightly enough her real fingers began tingling immediately. Raene released her and stepped back. Liurdi came to stand beside her.

"How did you—let me go!" Sienne exclaimed.

Liurdi smiled. It wasn't a pleasant smile. "Welcome back," he said.

22

The gaunt wizard appeared in the corner of her vision, just closing his spellbook. "You were lucky before," he said. "But you're too young to be very skilled, or to have many spells. Have you even heard of *tragoven*?"

Sienne automatically translated the Ginatic in her head. "Trade? No."

"The plebeians call it *castle*, like the chess move. Switch the places of two people. Bypasses all those neat little protections you people put up." His smile was as nasty as Liurdi's. "Batagli's getting the key as we speak."

"And then you'll send me back?" Hope sprang up, hope that she wasn't at their dubious mercy.

Liurdi said, "I'm not one to pursue revenge. You fooled us, true, and stole our property, but we care more about the contents of that trunk than we do about you. *Tragoven* a second time, once Batagli contacts us, and we have the key and you have—nothing." He squatted to put himself at eye level with her. "But tell your companions not to try attacking us again. You won't catch us unprepared twice."

Sienne tried not to wince at the smell of onions coming off his breath. This was twice in four days she'd been captured. She was turning out to be more a fainting maiden in a melodrama than a scrapper. "Why me? Do you think I'm nothing without my spellbook?"

"*Tragoven* requires something of the target's, when you can't see her," the wizard said. He removed a handkerchief from his sleeve and displayed a brownish smear on one corner. "You spat blood after casting *sepolisya*. Very careless. Saliva and blood are more than enough to make a connection with you."

Sienne wished she could spit in his face, show him what she thought of his dismissive attitude, but he was too far away. She settled for glaring at him instead. His nasty smile widened.

"Is Batagli done yet, Callia?" Liurdi asked.

"Have patience," the priest said. Her pale, undead face was very still, and her eyes were closed as if she were concentrating on something not in the room.

"It's been barely a minute," Raene said. "Even Batagli needs time."

The priest, Callia, made a tiny face of disgust. "This is the last time I will allow myself mental contact with him. His mind is a sewer. Even Conn Giorda was less offensive."

Sienne struggled to sit up and was pushed back down by the wizard. "No, lie down," he said. "You may not have your spellbook, but I don't think that makes you helpless. Using *sepolisya* on my spellbook was clever. Fortunately Callia was able to rid the book of the magic, or I might still be struggling with it."

Sienne lay still and assessed what she could see of her surroundings. The sofa she lay on was near the spiral staircase, facing into the room. If she craned her head, she could barely see the grouping of four armchairs Liurdi and his conspirators had been sitting in the first time. Ahead of her, near the center of the room, stood the boxy table now clearly identifiable as an old trunk. Sienne wasn't sure how Dianthe could tell its actual age, but it was very old. Someone had removed the blue silk it had formerly been draped with. Its lid was deep, and from Sienne's position she could see the heavy black iron hinges, shaped like upside-down bat wings. As Dianthe had said, the wood had that same slightly greasy look the beams in the keep had had. More invulnerable objects. Liurdi must be heartily sick of the spell by now.

The wizard turned away and crossed the room to sit in one of the armchairs, setting his spellbook on the floor next to it. After a moment, Raene went to join him. Liurdi crossed behind Sienne, and she arched her back to watch him. He was closing the gaps in the dome with huge folding shutters that blocked out the rest of the starlit sky. No one was paying any attention to her. Well, she wasn't going to lie there waiting to be returned to Master Tersus's house. She wiggled her fingers and managed to touch the rope binding her wrists. She was barefoot, so she had no helpful boot knife to cut herself free, but she'd been able to move it with her invisible fingers without seeing it, so maybe...

She focused on the rope, trying to picture how it went around her wrists, and envisioned hands plucking at it, loosening its knots and sliding it free of the loops. Her actual fingers were growing numb, and she had no idea how successful her attempt was until she felt something thin slither across her hand. It was working! She controlled her excitement and focused on that loose strand. Up and around, back through a loop and under. She shifted her position slightly to hide her hands between the sofa and her back. She felt the other end of the rope free itself and join the first in its slithering dance. She flexed her wrists and the rope gave, just a bit, but enough that she could work feeling back into her fingers.

"It's taking far too long," Liurdi complained. Sienne froze. The rope was looped loosely around her wrists now, not binding her at all, but it might be good enough for a cursory glance if Liurdi was inclined to look. Her arms ached from holding this position and her mouth was dry.

"Batagli says he has worked out where the key is kept, and will retrieve it now," Callia said. "I can see very little because it is dark where he is, but I think he is in the big man's room."

"We're so close," Raene said. "Just think of what treasures the trunk might contain!"

Sienne wondered why they hadn't had Callia do some kind of blessing to reveal the trunk's contents, and almost asked the question before remembering she didn't want them paying too close attention to her. She looked around for something else she might do, anything to spike their plans. It was probably futile, but she wasn't going to be a helpless victim.

Her eye was drawn to the spellbook lying on the floor, right at the limits of her vision. Sienne had been taught to treat her book with care, which included not putting it face-first on what was probably a dirty floor. The wizard might know more spells than she, but he certainly wasn't respectful of them. Idly, just to see if it was possible, she worked the complicated clasp that held the spine to the pages with her invisible fingers, and saw the book's back cover flex once as the latch disengaged. She glanced at the wizard. He had his attention on Liurdi, closing the final pair of shutters, and hadn't noticed.

The room felt stuffy already, but closing it off made it feel even warmer. The candlelight reflecting off the shutters made the room brighter as well. The shutters were painted to fit the rest of the night sky, filling in the gaps and completing some of the constellations picked out in gold paint. Directly across from Sienne was the Weaver, his right arm raised high above his loom. It was one of the constellations Sienne felt required the most imagination to perceive.

Callia cursed and opened her eyes. "The fool," she said. "He's been caught."

Sienne stifled an exclamation of excitement. The others groaned. The wizard and Raene left their chairs to join Callia and Liurdi near the trunk. "It's not a disaster yet," Liurdi told them. "We still have the girl. We can offer an exchange."

"Batagli says he hasn't told them anything yet. We need to give him instructions," Callia said.

Sienne stopped listening. The wizard's spellbook lay alone and untended on the floor. Swiftly she opened it, leaving the binding exposed and the pages loose. With her invisible fingers, she whisked the topmost page—technically the last one in the book—away from the others and sent it gliding along the floor in a curve that kept it away from the conspirators. It slid neatly beneath the sofa she lay on, perfectly silent. She took the next page, and the next, and the next, slipping them to join the first beneath her.

"Then that's what we'll do," Liurdi said. Sienne quickly shut the spellbook and engaged the latch. She probably should have been listening to their plan, but the idea of giving that wizard a metaphorical slap to the face was too tempting to ignore.

Liurdi and the wizard came to stand beside her. "Why don't you send me back? Your man's failed, hasn't he?" Sienne said.

"Batagli is more valuable where he is," Liurdi said. "Just as you are now significantly more valuable to us here."

"Alaric won't exchange the key for me. He doesn't like wizards. He only kept me around because Dianthe made him."

"Alaric? The Ansorjan madman?" Liurdi's eyes lit with interest. "Callia, tell Batagli to say nothing more until we give the word." He crouched to bring himself nearly to eye level with Sienne. "Is it true he searches for rituals?"

Sienne thought about saying nothing, then decided there was no harm in confirming what everyone seemed to know. "Yes."

Liurdi's nasty smile returned. "Then I have something he will want far more than he does a useless key. More than he wants you, apparently."

"You killed his friend to get that key. He won't give it to you. That would be a betrayal of her."

"We'll see. Callia, tell Batagli to offer Alaric a trade."

"He doesn't know who Alaric is."

"The Ansorjan. Tell him to say I'll give them the Dardel Contract in exchange for the key."

Callia shrugged and closed her eyes again. It was fascinating to watch her, Sienne thought, because her every emotion and every thought was clear on her face. There was puzzlement, irritation, and disgust, probably at having to make mental contact with Batagli. How did it feel, speaking mind to mind with someone? Did you know all their thoughts and feelings, or was it more like a spoken conversation without sound? It certainly sounded intimate, which would be unpleasant if you didn't like the person you were talking to.

Once again the other three focused on Callia, and Sienne took the opportunity to untie the ribbon cinching her left sleeve to her wrist and loosen it. With her invisible fingers, she squared up the pages she'd stolen from the spellbook and carefully brought them up over the armrest near her feet. They slid smoothly between her legs and the sofa back without drawing any attention. Holding open the wrist of her nightdress, she curled the pages into a half-tube and slid them up around her wrist and forearm, their sharp edges scraping her skin painfully but not drawing blood. The tube fell open when she released it, constrained only by the sleeve, and she quickly tied the ribbon tight to keep the pages from sliding back out. It would be obvious something was there, but she didn't intend to let her captors get a good look at her arms.

"—have to come here to get it," Liurdi was saying, and Sienne realized that in her concentration she'd missed yet another probably important conversation. What was the Dardel Contract, and why was Liurdi sure Alaric would think it valuable enough to exchange the key for it?

"If he's smart, he'll want a neutral location for the exchange," the wizard said.

"He doesn't have a reputation as a smart man," Liurdi said. "I understand he's rather obsessive in his quest. We can use that." He turned and strode to the staircase, disappearing down it.

Sienne wanted to laugh. Alaric, not intelligent? Just because he was big and well-muscled? She wondered if he traded on that misperception often, to have such a reputation.

Callia closed her eyes again. "They've shut him into a closet while they deliberate. This could take a while."

"I hope not," the wizard said. "I'm tired of waiting. You, girl, what's your name?"

Sienne realized he'd addressed her and once again debated the value of staying silent. "Sienne," she finally said.

"Sienne. Why are you working with this fool? You're clever, you have potential."

"That's what Conn Giorda said, right before I spat in his face," Sienne said.

Raene laughed. The wizard's smile was genuinely amused now, not at all cruel. "And perceptive," he said. "So, again, I have to ask—why do you associate with this Alaric? I assume you're a scrapper. You may be a beginner, but I can't imagine you couldn't find other work."

"It paid well," Sienne said.

"I see. I imagine that's important to someone in your position, just starting out."

"What makes you think I'm just starting out?"

The wizard chuckled. "*Sepolisya* was clever, but not something an experienced wizard would have gone for if she had access to anything better. You were just lucky."

Sienne wanted to say *And you were slow*, but didn't think it was a good idea to antagonize her captor. She said nothing. The wizard added, "It's almost too bad this is all over, or we might have work for you. You're certainly more qualified than the Giordas, and less personally repugnant than Batagli."

"What is 'this'?" Sienne asked.

The wizard's lips thinned, and he went silent. Feet sounded on the iron staircase, and Liurdi appeared, carrying a folio the size of his chest. It was bound in black leather with silver fittings at the corners and a strap locking it shut. "Go ahead and tell her," he said.

"I'd rather not. It's your venture, ultimately."

Liurdi gestured at the trunk. "I bought this from a scrapper team five years ago, retrieved from a ruined keep north of here. Only the ancients were able to make anything this size invulnerable, and I knew immediately it contained something valuable. Callia's divinations revealed it was heavily warded, requiring the key to open it without destroying the contents. So we began searching for the key."

"Should you be telling her this?" Raene said. "We haven't succeeded yet."

"What can it hurt?" Liurdi's eyes blazed with excitement. He had the look of someone who'd been dying to share his genius with the world for far too long. "Most of our searches went down false paths. We...acquired...any number of items we wrongly believed to be the key. We tried to send more scrapper teams to the ruin, but no one was interested once it had been stripped bare. Then the Giordas came to us. They'd heard of our interest in the ruin and proposed to search it for us."

"By way of ambushing another team," the wizard said sourly. "Typical."

Liurdi waved this off. "However they went about it, they uncovered the key and then lost it. Apparently the other team turned their ambush on them."

Sienne wanted to leap to her feet and tell them what had really happened. Outrage nearly propelled her upright before she remembered she was pretending to be a captive. Besides, it sounded as if they didn't know Sienne's team was the one that had discovered the pendant, and that was the sort of information she didn't need to share. "And you killed Neoma and took the pendant," she said.

"We didn't kill anyone. That was the Giordas," Liurdi said.

"But you were responsible for sending them after her. That still makes you guilty."

"Not according to Rafellish law." Liurdi's smug expression made her wish she could hit him with something. "It's not our fault if our subordinates have been somewhat...overenthusiastic in their interpretation of—"

"Batagli's back," Callia said. Liurdi strode to her side. "He says... they're willing to make the trade. The book for the key, and Batagli for the girl."

The book? The Dardel Contract was a book? Of course. The folio. Sienne almost sat up, and wriggled more deeply into the sofa instead. "Did they name a location?" Liurdi asked.

Callia smiled, her eyes still closed. "The fool is coming here. No neutral location, no guarantees of his safety. But he wants to see us open the trunk."

That sounded wrong. Alaric was too smart to walk back into the lion's den, and he didn't give a damn what was in the trunk. He must have some other plan. The edges of the spellbook pages dug into the inside of Sienne's elbow, but she couldn't shift position without drawing attention to them, because the four conspirators were all looking at her. "I suppose, if she's his companion, even temporarily, it would look bad for him not to redeem her," Raene said.

"Or maybe he just doesn't like losing," Sienne said. They all laughed.

"If he gives up the key in exchange for that worthless book, he's already a loser," Liurdi said.

"So you've lied and cheated to get this key, and probably stolen and murdered as well," Sienne said through her teeth. "I hope the damn thing is empty, and you get nothing."

"Delanie assures us what is inside will more than compensate us for our trouble," Callia said.

"But she won't tell you the details? Are you sure you're asking the right questions?" It came out before Sienne could shut herself up. She really couldn't stay quiet in the face of injustice, could she? But no one struck her for her insolence, or grabbed her to reveal her unbound wrists or the stolen pages.

"Delanie prizes knowledge, and the search for knowledge," Callia said. "She knows the joy of discovery. Telling us the contents would ruin the surprise." She closed her eyes, frowning. "They've blindfolded Batagli. Stupid, since it's not as if he doesn't know the way to this place. He says they're on their way. He and the Ansorjan."

"Batagli is a liability," the wizard said. "He bragged too much. If they link his crimes to us—"

"Alaric is too obsessed with his personal quest to care about our crimes," Liurdi said. "But you're right, we should dispose of him. Of both of them."

"I can make him disappear like I did the Wrathen thieves," the wizard said.

"Shut up, you fool, the girl's listening," Raene said.

"As if she can do anything about it. I think—"

"I know what you think, and I agree," Liurdi said. "But Alaric is a powerful fighter, even if he is a madman. We'll give him the book, take the key, then do away with him."

"What about the girl?"

Liurdi turned to Sienne. "She'll have to go, too. Pity, since she's not guilty of anything but choosing the wrong side."

The wizard looked like he wanted to argue, but subsided. Sienne realized she was holding her breath and let it out slowly. Alaric was taking an awful risk. He didn't even know if she was still alive, didn't know if they meant to be honorable, and now he was walking into their center of power. Maybe she was wrong about him. Maybe he was so obsessed with finding ritual he'd lost his common sense. They were both going to die if that was the case. She closed her eyes. *O Lord Averran,* she prayed, *if Perrin is right, and you care about our success, please don't let Alaric walk into a trap.*

They waited. Sienne started to need to relieve herself. She stayed quiet. If they planned to kill her, they probably didn't care about her physical comfort. The wizard settled in a chair, tilted his head back, and went to sleep. Callia sat near him, flicking through her riffle of blue blessing papers. Liurdi and Raene sat at a table and played cards, though Sienne couldn't tell what game it was. Sienne distracted herself from her fears by wondering what spells she'd stolen from the wizard. If he organized his spells by language, then in order of difficulty, she might have some very powerful spells indeed. If he was more typical and just added them in as he got them...well, if he was as experienced as he seemed, they might still be powerful spells. In either case, it was unlikely they were ones she already had. Not that it mattered, if they killed her. What time was it, anyway? Surely after midnight.

Metallic footsteps sounded on the stairs, gradually growing louder. The woman servant who'd let Sienne and her friends into the manor a few hours earlier emerged through the hole in the floor. "My lords and ladies, there is a person here to see you," she said, managing to make "person" sound equivalent to "scum."

"Show him up, then leave us," Liurdi commanded.

Sienne tried to relax, but her heart was beating painfully fast and it was harder to keep her hands concealed behind her back. The woman's footsteps receded. The impulse to race after her, to find Alaric and warn him it was all a hoax, was so strong Sienne had to shut her eyes against it. Alaric wasn't stupid. She just needed to be alert, because if he had a plan, she was surely a part of it, and she had to pay attention to find out what part that was.

A hand descended on her shoulder. "Sit up," Raene said. "And don't say anything." The point of a dagger pricked Sienne between the ribs. Sienne struggled to sit without the use of her hands and felt one of the rope's coils slip down. She pulled her wrists close against the small of her back to prevent any more movement, but Raene didn't notice; she had her attention on the stairs, where the sound of footsteps came once more. Two sets of feet, one heavier than the other. Sienne made herself breathe calmly. All right, she was in her nightdress, barefoot, and surrounded by enemies, with no spellbook and a knife to her side, but that didn't make her helpless. Whatever came next, she was ready.

23

A head appeared in the hole in the floor. The greasy-haired man, Batagli, came fully into view. He was indeed blindfolded, but seemed to have no trouble finding his footing on the iron stairs. Behind him, Alaric emerged, one hand on Batagli's lower back as if guiding him. His enormous sword was slung across his back, making Sienne wonder if the servant woman had even bothered asking him to disarm. It didn't matter, because Alaric could probably beat all four of the conspirators senseless with his fists alone. The sword was just intimidating. Sienne hoped it worked.

Nobody spoke. Alaric gave Batagli a little shove. The man stepped away from him and removed the blindfold as casually as if it had been an intentional part of his attire. Alaric surveyed the room, his gaze lingering briefly on each of the conspirators before coming to rest on Sienne. His pale blue eyes showed no hint of interest in her, and it chilled her despite the stuffiness of the room. *All part of the plan*, she told herself. She wished she knew what the plan was.

"Your companion is alive and unharmed, as promised," Liurdi said.

Alaric shrugged. "She's no companion of mine, but I told Dianthe

I would see her returned," he said, his deep voice sounding a dark counterpoint to Liurdi's tenor. "You have the book?"

"You have the key?"

"Book first. Let's see what I'm trading for."

Liurdi handed over the folio. In Alaric's giant hands, it almost looked normal-sized. "It's locked," Alaric said.

"Just an ordinary lock. I'm sure you have associates who can deal with it. You recognize it?"

"By its description, yes." Alaric sniffed along its spine. "All right. Here's the key." He dug in his belt pouch and removed the pendant, holding it up to the light. All four conspirators sucked in a simultaneous breath. It would have been funny if Sienne hadn't been so conscious of the mortal danger she and Alaric were in. What was he doing? How could he actually give them the key?

She untied the ribbon around her left wrist and gingerly gave her arm a little shake. The prick of the dagger grew more painful briefly, a warning from Raene. One of the stiff pages slid out of her sleeve into her hand. Sienne risked a glance at Raene, whose attention was on the key. It would have to do.

"So take your prize, and the girl, and go," Raene said.

"That wasn't the bargain," Alaric said.

"You don't really care about what's in this trunk," Liurdi said.

"I'm curious. Indulge me. I brought you the key, after all."

Sienne caught the edge of the glance Liurdi threw the wizard, and it chilled her further. The wizard stepped away from the group as if making room for Alaric near the trunk. Alaric approached, still holding the key, and the spellbook flew from where it lay by the chair to land, open, in the wizard's hands.

Sienne threw herself away from the dagger's point, swiveling in her seat to bring both feet up to kick Raene hard in the chest. *"Alaric!"* she screamed.

Alaric was moving before the last syllable left her lips. He turned on the wizard, who'd begun speaking the sharp, hard-edged sounds of an evocation, and backhanded him across the face. The wizard stumbled, tripped over a chair, and went down hard. Sienne rolled off the sofa and lunged for his book. He saw her coming and pulled it close to his chest. Sienne dove atop him and slashed his face with the sharp edge of the spell page. The wizard screamed and dropped the book, clutching his face. Blood seeped between his fingers. Sienne grabbed the book and ran.

Something thin and invisible wrapped around her head, covering her nose and mouth and cutting off her air. She choked and scrabbled at it with her free hand, trying to peel it away. Not the wizard— Callia, with some blessing Sienne had never heard of. Desperate, she twisted the page she held so its edge faced her and drew it in a quick slash across her open mouth. Pain stung the corners of her lips, and she tasted blood, but the membrane parted, and she gulped in warm, stuffy air. She grabbed the severed edge and pulled the caul off over her head, flinging it down and resisting the urge to stomp on it.

Alaric hadn't drawn his sword. He'd knocked Liurdi down and had Raene in a headlock. With his free hand, he grabbed her dagger-wielding hand and forced it open so the knife fell with a clatter to the floor. His eyes met Sienne's briefly, and he shouted, "Look out!" just as a pearly gray dome popped into being around him.

Hands came down on her arms and spun her around. "I'll take that," the wizard snarled, reaching for the spellbook. Sienne tried to back away, but he'd already taken hold of it and was pulling hard. She wrapped her arms more tightly around it, certain if he wrested it from her, she and Alaric were both dead. The wizard wasn't strong, but neither was Sienne, and for a few moments they wrestled in silence, both snarling at each other like a couple of wolves fighting over the last piece of deer meat. *This is stupid*, Sienne thought. She needed a different approach.

She let go, making him stumble back a step. He regained his balance and smiled at her, changing his grip on the book. It flew open. "You deserve this," the wizard said.

Sienne darted forward and grabbed, not for the book's cover, but for the latch underneath the spine. Swiftly she released the latch and with her invisible fingers snatched hold of the pages, tugged, and flung them into the air. They scattered like leaves in dead air, fluttering in all directions. The wizard shrieked and tried to gather them up, bloodying his fingers. Sienne turned and ran at Callia, who stood with her mouth open in shocked amazement. Sienne shoved her and knocked her down, then snatched the riffle of blessings out of her hand and tore the papers in half.

A silent explosion knocked her halfway across the room. Sienne screamed as her fingers caught fire and stuck her hands under her arms to put it out. Shaking, she sat up and examined her hands, but they were unmarked, and the pain was disappearing. The three remaining spell pages had caught on the hem of her sleeve, tearing it, but hadn't fallen out.

Someone ran across the room to kneel at her side. "You're all right?" Alaric said. Sienne nodded. "It's almost over. We just have to wait a little longer."

"Wait for what? Alaric, they're going to kill us!"

Alaric grinned. "I know. Perfect, isn't it?"

She started to tell him he was insane, but was interrupted by Liurdi saying, "You think you've defeated us? You come into my home, attack me and my associates, destroy our property—I'll have the guards on you for daring to—"

"Funny you should mention the guards," Alaric said, helping Sienne rise. "I think I hear them now."

There were a lot of people coming up the stairs, Sienne realized. Callia was just getting to her feet, and Raene knelt by the trunk, breathing heavily. The wizard, sobbing tears of what Sienne judged to be rage rather than sorrow, scrabbled the pages of his dismembered spellbook together, smearing blood everywhere. Liurdi leaned on the trunk, a lump forming on his left temple. "Good," he snarled. "Saves time all around."

Men and women in leather jerkins and the odd round helmets of the Fioretti city guard came pouring up through the hole in the floor. Two of them came to flank Alaric and Sienne, others took places near the conspirators, and one took Batagli—who had, oddly, sat the fight out—by one arm. "What," Sienne began, and Alaric shushed her.

A man wearing a lieutenant's knot on his shoulder came through the hole. Sienne recognized him as the man Dianthe had spoken to outside Neoma's shop. Denys Renaldi. "Would somebody like to explain this?" he said. His voice was deep and pleasant, and he sounded genuinely interested in an explanation. He wasn't at all how Sienne pictured a guard lieutenant.

"Of course, Lieutenant," Liurdi said, stepping away from the guardswoman flanking him. "These two invaded my home and attacked us. I demand you take them into custody."

"You're Lord Gregor Liurdi?" The lieutenant sounded polite, but not overly respectful.

"He is," Batagli said, startling Sienne.

"Alaric?" Renaldi said, turning his way.

"Liurdi kidnapped Sienne, hired the Giordas to steal from Neoma Tachonus, indirectly causing her death, and attempted to kill both me and Sienne." Alaric might as well have been reading off a shopping list for all the emotion he displayed. "You have his other crimes from Master Batagli there. All four of them were in on it."

"What? That's—*lies,* all of it, lies!" Liurdi sputtered.

"I don't think so," Renaldi said. "You've been at the periphery of a number of mysterious deaths in the last five years, Lord Liurdi. It's difficult, in this city, to arrest a nobleman, but you've just given me everything I need to do so. Sarran, Wylter, take him into custody. All of them."

"I am a personal friend of the *king!*" Liurdi shrieked. "Your career will be over when I speak with him!"

"I'll take responsibility for that." Renaldi smiled. It was a pleasant, unthreatening smile, but there was steel behind it. "And I seriously doubt he wants anything to do with this mess."

"No!" the wizard shouted. He pointed a bloody finger at Sienne. "She stole my spells! I demand you arrest that thief!"

Renaldi looked at Sienne. She resisted the urge to draw closer to

Alaric's comforting bulk. Renaldi turned his attention on the scattered spell pages. "I can't see how you can tell anything's missing in this mess," he said. "You should be more worried about what she'll say when she brings witness against you for kidnapping. Careful with them, fellows, they're nobility."

Sienne tied her sleeve closed again, feeling the stolen pages burn against her skin with imagined heat, and watched the guards shepherd Liurdi and his associates down the stairs. Batagli was the last to go. He gave Sienne a nod, Sienne thought of apology, but it was hard to tell. Eventually she and Alaric were alone with Renaldi, who removed his helmet and spun it in his fingers.

"Well?" he said. "I'm curious."

Alaric pulled out the pendant and walked over to the trunk. Sienne and Renaldi followed him. The front of the trunk bore a many-sided irregular hole just the diameter of the pendant. Alaric inserted it and gave it a push with his finger so it went all the way in. Sienne braced herself for bright lights, or an alarm, or the ground shaking. But there was only a small click. Alaric took hold of the lid and tugged upward.

The trunk had no lining, just the same slightly greasy-looking wood it was on the outside. Inside lay a jumble of assorted objects, none of which were magical. Several daggers in plain leather sheaths were scattered across the top of the pile, along with cloak pins, jeweled combs, and a couple of slim copper arm rings. There were metal goblets, some plain, some of gold or silver studded with gems, all of them inscribed with letters too small for Sienne to make out words. Two silver platters engraved with abstract designs lay at the bottom. Alaric went very still. "Artifacts," he said. "Are they magical?"

"No." Sienne's heart fell. "They're just...I don't know. I suppose someone might want them, but they're not anything special. Certainly not worth the trouble Liurdi and his friends went to."

"Unfortunately, they're now the property of the city," Renaldi said. "I'm sorry, but I can't hand it over to you. It belongs to Lord Liurdi, and with him going to prison or possibly the hangman's noose, I have to confiscate it."

"Understood," Alaric said. "But—just one, maybe? In recognition of services rendered?"

Renaldi matched him gaze for gaze. Then he deliberately turned his back on the trunk. Alaric swiftly snatched up one of the goblets and tucked it away in his shirt. "We're free to go?" he said.

"You'll need to testify, but that won't be for a while yet. Lord Liurdi and his friends aren't getting away with anything. I'm doing everything by the law on this one."

"Don't you always?"

Alaric and Renaldi exchanged the kind of sneers only old acquaintances and sometime enemies can manage. "Stay out of trouble," Renaldi said. "Dianthe would hate it if I had to arrest you."

"I still don't know what she sees in you," Alaric said. "Good luck."

Sienne let Alaric steer her down the stairs and through the manor to the front door, where she hesitated before the sharp-edged stones of the path. "I'm barefoot."

"You are indeed," Alaric said, and swept her up into his arms. "Fortunately, you also don't weigh much more than a half-drowned cat."

"So—did you have that all planned? Why didn't Batagli help them? What—"

"Too many questions. Let me start from the beginning." Alaric strode through the open gate. There was no sign of Liurdi's guard. "When we caught Batagli trying to lift the pendant from my room, we were busy enough that we didn't immediately realize you'd been taken. Once we figured that out, we convinced Batagli that his master would be arrested for kidnapping and he might want to think about whether he wanted to take that fall as well. Batagli isn't a nice person, so I don't imagine we appealed to his soft side. More likely the opportunist in him saw a chance to get away with most of the crimes he's committed on Liurdi's behalf. To give him credit, I don't think he's ever killed anyone, so I didn't mind letting him turn king's evidence, since it meant getting the real criminals."

"But he was connected to Callia, that priest. I know she saw through his—oh, the blindfold."

"Oh, the blindfold, exactly. The communication blessing she used gave her a mental link to his thoughts and his vision, but not his hearing. We took him to the guards and Dianthe convinced Renaldi to listen to our rather garbled account. Perrin was invaluable there. He knows how to string words together in a way even guard lieutenants can't help but respond to. Once we explained the situation, and what Batagli knew, Renaldi agreed to bring his men to make the arrest. As he said, he's been watching Liurdi for years, but never had enough evidence to bring him to justice. Knowing that the Giordas, whom a priest of Kitane had positively identified as the arsonists who burned Neoma's shop, were hired by him made him even more eager to help."

"So why weren't they with you when you arrived?"

"It took them some time to collect themselves, and I had to move quickly so Liurdi wouldn't be suspicious at how long it took me to reach his manor."

Sienne gasped. "The book! You left it behind!"

Alaric chuckled. "I found the Dardel Contract three years ago. It's worthless except as a conversation piece. I didn't sell it to Liurdi, so I imagine he bought it from someone who cheated him shamefully. It warms my heart to think of it."

"I'm just sorry we didn't get to keep all that salvage. Which one did you take?"

Alaric pulled the goblet out. Sienne's brow furrowed. It was one of the plain ones, made of hammered brass and engraved with Ginatic script around the rim and the outer edge of the base. The letters were too small for her to read in the dim light from the lanterns. "It's...not very valuable. Is it?"

"Wait and see," Alaric said. "Hmm, what else...I'm glad I was right that you wouldn't be helpless when I reached the manor. I was counting on having your support during the fight. We had to hold them off long enough for Renaldi's men and women to reach us. I assumed Liurdi would try to kill us, and figured his guilt would be even more convincing if he'd clearly already tried to do so. He—ow! What *is* that?" He shifted his arm away from hers.

"It's the wizard's spellbook, three pages of it, anyway."

Alaric threw back his head and laughed. His laughter echoed off the brick walls of the dark buildings, startling a stray cat into hissing at them before fleeing into the night. "I have to say, you're the most deceptive person I've ever met, and I've been Dianthe's friend for eight years. You look as innocent as a newborn lamb, but there's steel behind that wide-eyed smile."

Sienne blushed. His regard made her feel uncomfortably exposed, as if he'd seen past her façade all the way to her soul. "Is that a compliment?"

"Of course it is. You won't sleep until you've ferreted out what spells those are, either."

"So not all wizards are awful, is that what you're saying?"

Alaric swung her down to deposit her on Master Tersus's doorstep. "You're still a special case."

The kitchen was well-lit despite the late hour, and the smell of soup lingered in the air. Sienne stopped in the doorway as Dianthe swooped down on her for a warm hug. "Your face is bloody," she exclaimed. "You both look like you've been in a fight. Didn't it work? I *knew* we should have come along!"

"We're fine, just a few bruises," Alaric said. "Sienne, how did your face get cut?"

"I did it to myself." Sienne took a seat at the table. "It's not much."

"Nevertheless, as I have these healing blessings," Perrin said, "I should perhaps show gratitude to Averran by using them."

The healing felt warm and tingling and just the way it smelled, sweet and minty. Sienne worked her mouth gingerly and found it no longer stung at the corners. She pulled the spell pages out of her sleeve and spread them on the table. "Whose are they?" Kalanath asked, leaning over her shoulder.

"That wizard's. Well, they're mine now." Sienne traced the spells, one sharp and hard-edged, one made of staccato lines and abrupt dashes, and one flowing and full of vowels. "This is *force*. This one, I think, is the one he used to kidnap me—*castle*. And this...it's a transform called *sculpt*. It lets you shape stone."

"That does not sound useful to a scrapper," Kalanath said.

"Maybe. But I'm starting to think usefulness is what you make of it. I'll copy them out tomorrow. Tonight I'm exhausted."

"Not too exhausted for another explanation, I hope," Alaric said.

That woke Sienne up. "Of course not!"

Alaric seated himself at the head of the table and gestured for the others to sit. He pulled out the goblet and set it on the table, where it caught the light like gold. "I'm afraid this is all the salvage we got from this job," he said, "if that's what you'd call it. And I owe all of you an apology. I had a chance to choose one thing, and I selfishly chose this. Selfish, because it's worth nothing to anyone...but me."

"I did not expect to gain more than I already have," Perrin said. Kalanath nodded agreement.

"So what is it?" Sienne asked.

Alaric spread his hands flat on the table and let out a deep breath. "I told you I was looking for something that would free my people. It's more complicated than that. The wizard who created the Sassaven tried to make them utterly loyal to him, but the best he could do was make them vulnerable to a particular ritual. The binding ritual. It makes it impossible for a Sassaven to betray him in any way, starting with not turning on him and continuing with not working directly against him, obeying his every order, not running away...you get the idea. It also opens a Sassaven to his full potential as a magical creature."

"You mean, like breaking the *force* spell on those stones?" Sienne asked.

"No, more than that. A team of full Sassaven unicorns could have levitated the entire fallen tower out of the way and maybe even rebuilt it, using just their magic. Even the non-unicorns have access to magic." Alaric's left hand closed in a loose fist. "The binding ritual would have happened to me on my sixteenth birthday, but I ran away a few weeks before that. Anyway, the point is, the Sassaven need that part of the ritual to become their true selves. They just need it without the binding. If I could find that, I could become...complete, really."

"How can that happen?" Kalanath asked. "You are not a wizard."

"The thing about rituals is you don't have to be a wizard to perform some of them," Dianthe said. "Necromantic rituals, for example—most necromancers are ordinary people, if you take my meaning, since raising the dead isn't exactly ordinary. The rituals are lists of instructions on what to do, what to say, what items to use, even what time of day to perform them."

"I've been looking for information on rituals for the last ten years," Alaric said. "I've seen parts of what the wizard called the coming of age ritual done a couple of times, so I know some of what goes into it. Not much. I wish I could remember more, but...well. What I have learned, mostly from studying necromantic lore—"

"Alaric!"

"I didn't raise the dead, Sienne. Don't tell me they didn't teach the fundamentals of necromancy at your fancy school."

"Point taken. Sorry."

"Anyway, what I've learned is that reversing, or inverting, the effects of a ritual require you to know the original form of the ritual. Laying the dead to rest uses a variant on the ritual that raises them."

"That is also the province of a priest, Alaric. And I believe we are more efficient at doing so."

"True. But that's not the point. The point is that it's true of every ritual, not just the necromantic ones. If I could find the complete coming of age ritual, I could theoretically invert it to negate the binding while still giving the Sassaven their full magical potential. I just haven't found it in ten years of searching."

Alaric fell silent. Dianthe said, "None of that explains the goblet."

"The goblet." Alaric smiled. "I should have said, I haven't found anything in ten years of searching—until tonight." He picked up the goblet and handed it to Sienne. "How much of that can you read?"

Sienne squinted at the half-uncial lettering. "This isn't the best light, but... it says 'heart' of something... I think this says 'closed'..." She gasped. "*Sa'asava.* Faithful. Sassaven!" She rotated the goblet. "And the bottom has... 'accept the offering' and 'by my hand.' It's like the lines around the rim are directed at the one drinking, and the ones around the base are written for the one offering the cup. Like a bargain."

"Or a command," Alaric said. He extended his hand to Sienne, and she gave him the goblet. "I recognized this because I'd seen its twin in the wizard's castle. It's the only part of the ritual I've found in ten years, and when I had the chance, I snatched it up. It didn't occur to me until later that I owed it to you all to take something more intrinsically valuable. I apologize."

Sienne gaped at him. Perrin said, "And give up on your quest for the sake of mere money? I could not have accepted gold at that price."

"We do not mind," Kalanath said. "I am certain of this for all of us."

"Thank you," Alaric said. "But I'm prepared to compensate you for your loss."

"Don't you dare," Sienne said. "And cheapen what all of us went through to get it?"

"She has said it exactly," Perrin said. "But I wonder now about the rest of the items in the trunk. Could they, too, have been ritual items?"

"That makes sense," Sienne said. "They were all locked away where nobody could easily get at them, but none of them were magical. And most of them, like the daggers, were the kind of thing you could use in a ritual. At least, most of the necromantic ones I've studied require daggers. For bloodletting, you know. What *I* want to know is, if this wizard uses the ritual to bind the Sassaven, and he created the Sassaven, what is a ritual cup with their name on it doing way south of the Pirinin Peaks?"

Alaric opened his mouth, then shut it again, his brow furrowed. "That's a very good question. I was so astonished at the find it didn't occur to me to wonder that."

"But it doesn't say Sassaven," Dianthe said. "It says whatever the Ginatic word for 'faithful' is. Suppose this wizard used a ritual that existed for some other purpose in the before times? Or corrupted a perfectly innocent ritual to his purposes?"

"Can I see that again?" Sienne asked. Alaric handed her the goblet. "I might be able to work out the full translation, given a few days and...damn. I can't."

"Why not?" Alaric sounded alarmed.

"Because I'd need access to the University of Fioretti library, and I can't get that unless I tell them I'm Sienne Verannus. *That* would get back to my parents, and they'd...I don't know what they'd do. Drag me back home kicking and screaming, probably."

"There are other scholars who work with scrappers," Dianthe said. "We could ask around. Do you need, I don't know, a dictionary or something?"

"Something like that. If I had access to the right materials, I could work out the full translation. That might give us some idea of what else the ritual requires, or even if it was originally intended for something else." She set the goblet down and glared at it. "It's a start."

"This is more than I had yesterday," Alaric said. "And...honestly, I didn't know how relieved I'd feel, finding part of the ritual. I guess I felt, deep down, I really might be mad. Like I'd made up an entire race to explain away my other self."

"That would be quite a delusion, to cover more than a ton of magical equine," Perrin said with a grin.

Alaric smiled and shrugged. "People do stranger things to avoid facing the truth."

Sienne opened her mouth and found herself yawning. "What time is it?"

Perrin consulted his watch. "It is nigh on two o'clock. Well past a sensible person's bedtime."

"We all deserve a good night's sleep," Alaric said.

Sienne trailed along after him up the stairs, followed by Perrin, Dianthe, and Kalanath. She'd been surprised at Perrin joining them, having forgotten he'd arranged to spend the night. It seemed like that had been ages ago.

Safely in her bed, with the spell pages tucked neatly into her own spellbook for safekeeping, she lay on her back and stared up at the ceiling. Her mind still fizzed with plans for the morning. Copy out the stolen spells. Find some way to translate the Ginatic script. Buy bedding—the mattress was scratchy. She went through her relaxation routine again, but sleep eluded her. Finally, she squeezed her eyes tight shut and told herself, *They'll all still be here in the morning.* On that thought, she drifted off to sleep.

24

Sienne loosed the band from around her left arm and pressed a cloth against the cut vein inside her elbow, bending her arm to hold the cloth in place. She wiped the blood from her forearm and moved the shallow metal bowl out of the way so she wouldn't accidentally spill any of the carefully collected fluid. It was awkward, doing this at the chest of drawers in her bedroom, which was just a little too high for the kitchen chair she'd hauled upstairs, but she'd been taught never to collect blood at a table where people ate. That sounded disgusting enough she hadn't needed the warning.

With her right hand, she took a pinch of ground cinnamon from the container open in front of her and sprinkled it over the surface of the bowl. It settled in a thin layer over the blood. She took a slender steel rod and stirred it slowly counterclockwise, careful not to slop any over the sides. It took forever for the spice to blend, and she'd had to learn patience in preparing this ink, but she used the time to focus her mental energies inward, on scribing the spells to come.

When no trace of the cinnamon remained, she wiped the rod on the cloth in the crook of her elbow and set it aside. She picked up her pen and flicked the freshly-trimmed nib with her finger. Then she angled a clean sheet of paper just so, drew the spell page containing *force* toward her, and began the laborious process of scribing the spell.

It really did take forever this way, she reflected, what with having to switch her attention between the two pages, and forgetting where she was if she was too slow. But the end result was the same as if she'd had someone read it off to her. She probably could have waited until after breakfast, but the urge to add these spells to her book was overpowering.

It was hard not to be excited about the prospect of gaining new spells, two of which were far more powerful than anything she currently had. If her experience with summoning spells like *slick* was any guide, *castle* would rip shreds out of her mouth. It was still worth it. *And,* she thought, *once I'm done I can sell these pages in the market, or trade for others!* She felt like a real scrapper—but then she'd felt like a real scrapper from the first night she'd fallen asleep in Dianthe's tent, all those days ago. Only eight days ago. It felt like a lifetime.

She finished *force* and set it on her bed to dry. You never blew on spell pages to hasten the drying process; that could ruin the spell. No, you had to, again, exercise patience. She switched pens—always use a fresh nib for each spell—and started on the staccato lines of *castle*. She was saving *sculpt* for last because she loved the swooping peace of scribing a transform.

Someone knocked on the door. "Are you—oh, you're busy," Dianthe said.

"It's all right. We were expected to be able to scribe amid distractions," Sienne said, dotting another short horizontal line.

"Kalanath is going to talk to someone who might have a library we could use. He asked if you wanted to come."

"That's all right. I want to finish this. If he doesn't mind."

"No, I think he was just being polite. He seems to prefer to work alone."

Sienne paused a little too long as Dianthe's words sent a pang through her heart, and had to read the summoning twice to find where she'd left off. "I suppose he'll be leaving soon."

"I suppose. I thought...but he never stays with a team long."

Sienne came to the end of the summoning and laid her pen down. "Is that what we are? A team?"

Dianthe smiled. "Don't tell me you're looking to leave, too."

Sienne shook her head. "No, I...no. But I don't want to impose."

Dianthe leaned against the door frame. "It may take some convincing to get Alaric to believe it. He really—"

"—doesn't like wizards, I know. I'm a special case, he says."

"He's also never told anyone the truth about himself before. I think..." She shook her head. "Perrin's still asleep. He's even less of a morning person than I am. I'll see you downstairs when you're finished." She shut the door quietly behind herself.

Sienne laid the second page on her bed and gave the blood ink a little stir to keep it from congealing. She didn't have time to sit around woolgathering if she didn't want to waste the blood, but it was suddenly hard to focus. Dianthe thought they were a team. Kalanath didn't. Alaric was in denial. And Perrin...he was as independent as Kalanath, in a different way. So why couldn't they all see what was obvious—that what they had together was greater than anything they could dream of separately?

She sighed and picked up a new pen, hoping the transform would calm her mind. She could almost taste the honey-sweet flavor of the spell as she scribed the flowing lines. She could have stayed home, studied confusions and transforms, made political connections, and learned to live with Rance and Felice's marriage. Could have done all those things, and shriveled and died inside. The six weeks since she'd left home had been anything but peaceful, and nothing she'd endured made her wish she'd given them up.

She laid aside the third sheet and stretched. The cut in her elbow had mostly clotted, and she wouldn't even have a bruise this time. She was getting better at drawing blood, and better at estimating how much she'd need—there was barely a splash left in the bowl. She summoned a tiny glob of water that turned pink immediately when it hit the bowl, swirled the water around, and then dumped it in the chamber pot.

She dried the bowl, burned the pens and the cloth, and put all her supplies away in the little case that usually lived at the bottom of her pack. She checked the pages and discovered they were dry, focused her will, and turned them invulnerable. They shimmered briefly and took on the pale brownish tint typical of invulnerable paper. Carefully, she laid them in her spellbook, then latched it closed. She would have to experiment with making that latch more secure. If she could think to break open that wizard's spellbook, somebody might think to do it to her.

She left her spellbook in her room and went downstairs, hoping for a late breakfast. The kitchen was empty, with even Leofus gone, but a pot of porridge bubbled on the back of the stove. Sienne helped herself to that and a big chunk of sugar. Stirring idly counterclockwise in memory of preparing her ink, she sat at the table and thought of nothing in particular.

"Good morning," Kalanath said, startling her out of her reverie. He propped his staff against the wall and sat next to her with his own bowl of porridge.

"Good morning. I thought you were going to talk to someone."

He shrugged. "I have decided it is better to wait and go together. Then I do not have to return and go again."

Sienne nodded. "That...makes sense. I—"

Dianthe entered the kitchen and poured herself a cup of coffee. "Is Alaric not back yet?"

"I didn't know he was gone."

"He said he had something he wanted to investigate." She drank deeply and sighed. "I can quit any time I want."

"Sure you can," Sienne and Kalanath said in unison. They looked at each other in surprise. Sienne laughed.

"Whoever said laughter is medicine for the soul never heard it at...dear Averran, is that the time?" Perrin said, stumbling into the kitchen and aiming directly for the coffee urn. "Please, I beg of you, silence until I have had some of this bitter, life-giving nectar."

They sat in silence watching him pour himself a cup and drink it down, black and unadulterated. He let out a sigh and finally opened his eyes. "Ahh. Truly a gift of God to us poor mortals."

"And you, too, can quit any time you want?" Kalanath said with a smile.

"Blasphemy! Why on earth would I want to quit? Averran does not need competition for the title of most cantankerous being, which I assure you I would challenge him for were it not for glorious coffee, first thing in the morning." Perrin poured himself another cup, sipping this one.

The outer door banged open, and Alaric appeared in the kitchen doorway. "Oh, good, you're all here," he said. "I had an idea—go ahead and sit—" He took his seat at the head of the table. Sienne scraped up the last of her porridge and pushed her bowl aside. "Is that all there is for breakfast?"

"Eat it and be grateful," Dianthe said.

"I'll pass, thanks." Alaric settled back in his chair. "I went to talk to Sabinia Pelegrus just now. She's hiring scrappers to investigate a ruin south of here, along the coast. It's half-submerged even at low tide, so it's hard to get into, but she wants stones from the ruin itself as salvage. I told her no two weeks ago, because it requires a team of at least five, but the pay is good, and..." His voice trailed off, and he looked at each of them in turn, his expression slowly growing impassive. "I don't know what I thought."

They sat in silence for a moment. Then Kalanath said, "You thought we are a team."

"I was wrong to make assumptions," Alaric said.

Kalanath shrugged. "It is not wrong to assume truth," he said. "But I cannot go with you."

"Why not?" Alaric demanded. "Are we, or aren't we?"

"Because I must first speak with this woman who has a library Sienne may use. We should not forget what is the important thing, and that is your quest." Kalanath nodded to Sienne. "You will come with me?"

"Yes, because I still have to translate that goblet. Oh, and we have to go to the market so I can sell those spells," Sienne said, solemn in the face of Alaric's growing surprise. "And it sounds like we'll need a water breathing spell. If you can bring yourself to let me cast it on you."

Perrin cleared his throat. "As to that...I have been thinking about what you said last night, about being unable to remember much of the ritual you seek. Averran has been gracious—well, I say 'gracious,' but in truth he was rather testy—at any rate, he granted me a blessing that enhances the memory, and perhaps this afternoon we might test its efficacy?"

"A memory...blessing?" Alaric said.

"Indeed. Aside from that one request, I failed to specify in my morning prayers what blessings I needed for the day. To my surprise, based on what I received, Averran seems to think I am embarking on yet another scrapping adventure. But if that is what we intend, who am I to desert my team?"

Dianthe poked Alaric, who looked stunned. "Don't look so surprised," she said. "We were a team the moment you revealed your other self. You just needed time to accept it."

"As do I," Kalanath said. "I do not make friends easily, but you are all...I do not know the word."

"Congenial? Sympathetic? Harmonious?" Perrin suggested.

Kalanath shook his head. "It is when you support each other. To want to make the others better. That is the word."

Family, Sienne thought. After eight days? Stranger things had happened.

"I agree," Perrin said, "whatever word you use. And now I believe I will accompany Kalanath and Sienne to this woman with the library. You may need my charming tongue to convince her of our sincerity and well-meaning."

Alaric's stunned look was fading. "Well," he said, cleared his throat, and went on more firmly, "Well. Then Dianthe and I will go to Mistress Pelegrus and confirm the details of the job. I've been thinking we may need to bribe someone to let us look at the contents of the trunk, if there are more ritual items there, and this job will go a long way toward paying for that."

"Bribery? Is that something we do?" Sienne asked, pushing back from the table.

"Welcome to my world," Dianthe said. "Just so Denys doesn't find out. He thinks I'm completely respectable."

"He's handsome. *I* can see what you see in him," Sienne said, making Dianthe blush and Alaric laugh.

She ran upstairs to fetch her spellbook and bumped into Alaric, coming the same way, as she left her room. "What changed your mind?" she asked impulsively.

"About what?" Alaric said.

"About using magic. I know it frightens you a little, and after hearing your story I can't blame you. So why did you suddenly embrace it?"

"Aside from your sheer manic exuberance in insisting on using it for absolutely everything?" His eyes twinkled at her, and without thinking she punched him lightly on the arm. "Ow. Truthfully?" His amused look vanished, replaced by a seriousness that made her uncomfortable with its honesty. "My relationship with magic is inconstant. On the one hand, my people are slaves thanks to a magic that removes their ability to choose for themselves. But I'm also a creature of magic by nature. I've spent years dwelling on the former and trying to forget about the latter. Having to change my shape to get us out of that keep...I couldn't stop thinking about how that magic saved our lives. Or how determined you were to use your magic to protect all of us. And I thought...I shouldn't have to deny what's good about magic just because one evil man twisted its nature to his own ends." He smiled, and the somber look vanished. "But I still don't like wizards."

"And I'm still a special case," Sienne said, putting her hand on his arm.

Alaric put his hand over hers. An unfamiliar expression crossed his face, an inward-turned, probing look as if he were reaching for a memory just beyond his grasp. Then it vanished, and he smiled at her and turned away. Sienne went down the stairs behind him more slowly than she'd ascended, skipping the broken treads automatically. For a moment, she'd almost thought— She shook her head to clear it. He was her companion, even if for the briefest moment she'd seen him as something more.

Alaric held the back door open for her and for Dianthe. Perrin and Kalanath waited outside, Perrin squinting against the sunlight. "We meet again at noon?" he said.

"Agreed," Alaric said. "Don't get into trouble."

"We make no promises," Sienne said.

They strode off into the bright Fiorettan morning together.

SIENNE'S SPELLBOOK

Summonings:

Summonings affect the physical world and elements. They include all transportation spells.

Fog—obscuring mist

Slick—conjure grease

Evocations:

Evocations deal with intangible elements like fire, air, and lightning.

Scream—sonic attack, causes injury

Confusions:

Confusions affect what the senses perceive.

Camouflage—disguise an object's shape, color, or texture

Cast—ventriloquism

Echo—auditory hallucinations

Imitate—change someone's entire appearance

Mirage—visual hallucinations

Mirror—creates three identical duplicates of the caster

Shift—small alterations in appearance, such as eye or hair color

Transforms:

Transforms change an object or creature's state, in small or large ways.

Break—shatters fragile things

Fit (person)—shrink or enlarge a person; temporary

Sharpen—improve sight or hearing

Voice—sound like someone else

The Small Magics

These can be done by any wizard without a spellbook, with virtually no limits.

Light

Spark

Mend

Create water

Breeze

Chill/warm liquid

Telekinesis (up to 6-7 pound weights)

Ghost sound

Ghostly form

Find true north

Open (used to manipulate a spellbook)

Invulnerability

ABOUT THE AUTHOR

In addition to *Company of Strangers,* Melissa McShane is the author of more than twenty fantasy novels, including the novels of Tremontane, the first of which is *Servant of the Crown;* The Extraordinaries series, beginning with *Burning Bright;* and *The Book of Secrets,* first book in The Last Oracle series. She lives in the shelter of the mountains out West with her husband, four children and a niece, and four very needy cats. She wrote reviews and critical essays for many years before turning to fiction, which is much more fun than anyone ought to be allowed to have.

You can visit her at **www.melissamcshanewrites.com** for more information on other books.

For news on upcoming releases, bonus material, and other fun stuff, sign up for Melissa's newsletter at http://eepurl.com/brannP

SNEAK PEEK: STONE OF INHERITANCE (COMPANY OF STRANGERS, BOOK TWO)

The cloudy gray light before the storm dulled the white marble façade of the Tombrino auction house to pearly dimness. Its many arches and spires gave it the look of a temple of the avatar Gavant instead of a temple to worldly wealth. White statues topped the small round arches lining its roof, too far away for Sienne to make out details or identify who they were meant to be. She guessed long-ago rulers of Fioretti, or possibly representations of divine virtues, monitoring the activities of anyone who dared go within.

A gust of freezing wind snatched her cloak from her hands where she gripped it closely around herself. She grabbed it and wrapped it more tightly to her. Winter clung to the city despite having supposedly been evicted by first summer. Rain was imminent. Sienne was grateful they were far enough south that it wouldn't be snow instead. Snow was pretty when you were indoors looking at how it covered the gardens and drinking spiced wine, but less pretty if you had to be out in it.

"Was this always an auction house?" she asked Perrin, who strode along beside her. His long dark hair was windblown, and the tip of his nose was as red as hers no doubt was.

"It was the home of a minor noble, some hundred and seventy-five years ago," Perrin said. "Someone who plotted against the queen of that era. His fortune and lands were confiscated, his family driven into exile, and his life forfeit. I am certain it was a far more tragic story at the time, but now it is simply a cautionary tale. The Fiorus family have ever been canny when it comes to protecting their rule."

"I don't know. That still sounds sad, at least for the family. I suppose it was generous of the queen not to have them all executed."

Perrin took a drink from the flask at his hip. "Indeed. And daring, to leave alive any who might seek revenge for their father's death."

Sienne eyed the flask, but said nothing. After nearly nine months of being Perrin's companion on their scrapper team, she was used to his near-constant state of mild to moderate inebriation. The priests of the avatar Averran, whom Perrin worshipped, were expected to be a little drunk when performing their devotions, but Sienne couldn't help feeling Perrin took it too far. She'd overheard enough of his side of the prayer conversations he had with his avatar to suspect Averran didn't like it either. But any time she brought it up, even obliquely, Perrin sidestepped the issue with steely grace, and after four months she'd given up even the most subtle queries.

The entrance to the auction house was an open arch with no door, through which men and women bundled up in cloaks against the cold scurried like so many drab gray or black beetles. Perrin and Sienne followed the trickle of people through a short hall where the wind blew briskly and into a larger antechamber with a domed roof. There was no indication as to what it had originally been meant for, but the fine frescos on the walls and the doors beneath them suggested some kind of reception chamber. Scuffs on the parquet floor, which had not been waxed in some time, told Sienne this was a place of serious business that didn't have time for niceties like polished floors. Though the room was sheltered from the wind, it was still bitingly cold, and Sienne wished her magic for heating water applied to air as well. Though it was unlikely she could heat a volume of air this size.

There were only about twenty or twenty-five people in the room, standing in knots of two or three, all of them huddled into their cloaks or coats as she was. Sienne surveyed the frescos. They depicted a series of familiar fairy tales featuring talking animals that walked on their hind legs and dressed like humans. It was subject matter she would have expected to see in a nursery rather than a noble's reception chamber. Nobody else seemed to notice. "There's not many here," she said in a low voice. "That's good, right?"

"It's not bad," Perrin said. "Though we are counting on no one wanting the rather pedestrian lot we are here to bid on. But we should not discuss it in public. It may be a pedestrian lot, but we do not want to give any hint that it matters to us more than that."

Sienne nodded. Perrin was right; the knives they were here to bid on shouldn't matter to anyone but themselves, but no sense giving the game away, and possibly encouraging someone to bid against them.

It had been a long nine months leading to this point. At first, their newly acquired quest to free their companion Alaric's people from the wizard who had them in thrall went nowhere. Perrin's blessing enhancing Alaric's memory of the wizard's binding ritual had given them plenty of information, but no clues as to where to look for more. Then, three months ago, Alaric had been successful in bribing someone to let him look at the confiscated possessions of Lord Liurdi, from whose property Alaric had originally taken one of the ritual pieces, a brass goblet. According to Perrin, the city treasury made good money off letting prospective bidders do this, so it wasn't that spectacular an achievement, but it had been progress all the same.

Alaric's enhanced memory identified one of the knives in Liurdi's trove as companion to the goblet. Warned in advance by Perrin, who refused to explain why he knew so much about city policies, Alaric didn't try to buy the knife outright. Instead, he found out when Liurdi's possessions would be auctioned off. And now Perrin and Sienne were going to bid on the knife. The lot of knives, actually; there had been five knives in the ancient trunk the team had found the key to. Sienne still felt annoyed that they hadn't been allowed to keep the salvage, since they'd essentially found it, but Denys Renaldi, the guard lieutenant who'd arrested Lord Liurdi for kidnapping Sienne and a host of other crimes, had refused to break what was city custom, if not law. So bidding it would have to be.

Perrin abruptly turned away from Sienne and swore under his breath. "What's wrong?" Sienne asked.

"There is someone here I would rather not encounter," Perrin said. "Fortunately he is just as loath to meet me, but his companions might decide to force the issue. Better if they simply do not see me."

"Who—"

"It is unimportant. Someone I knew once. Someone who took exception to my conversion." Perrin raised the flask again, stared at it, then put it away with a grimace. "I must keep my wits about me, however much I would prefer to lose myself in a gentle fog of brandy. Damn him."

Sienne knew little of Perrin's past except that his family had cast him off when he converted from the worship of Gavant to that of Averran and, to make matters worse, became a priest of that avatar. She casually scanned the crowd, looking for anyone who might be paying close attention to them. Was it a relative? Another noble associated with the Delucco family?

She met the gaze, briefly, of a short, slim man wearing an old-fashioned jerkin over a bell-sleeved white linen shirt and hose. He appeared to be scanning the crowd as she was, and she wondered what he was looking for. Sizing up the competition, perhaps? A nearby woman dressed in a long gown of heavy chartreuse brocade looked warmer than everyone else, and for a moment Sienne envied her the gown. Then she thought about how awkward gowns were, and the moment passed.

A high-pitched bell rang out, a single tone that stilled the already quiet conversations. A woman dressed as Sienne was in fine linen shirt, close-fitting wool trousers, knee boots, and a form-fitting vest emerged from one of the side doors. "The auction will begin in five minutes," she said in a clear, carrying voice. "Please follow me."

Perrin hung back, Sienne guessed to avoid whoever it was he didn't want to meet. They went through the door nearly at the rear of the group, giving Sienne plenty of time to observe the others. Most of them were men wearing the colors of various Fiorettan guilds: carpenters, watchmakers, chandlers, and a few Sienne didn't recognize. There was the woman in chartreuse, and the slim man in old-fashioned clothes. A group of two men and a woman, dressed more finely than the others, might be a rich merchant's representatives or even those of a noble house. And finally, a young woman, probably in her late teens, clutched a purse to her side in both hands as if fearing thieves. Her thin nose was red-tipped as Perrin's was from the cold, and she kept her gaze focused straight ahead on the backs of those in front of her. Sienne couldn't help wondering what all these people were after. How many of them had, like Alaric, bribed their way to an early showing of the merchandise?

They passed through the door, and Sienne had to control a gasp. The enormous room beyond had once been a ballroom, though one at least twice the size of the ballroom at her father's ducal palace in Beneddo. More frescos, these of dancing nobles in the dress of two hundred years earlier, covered the walls and the high, arching ceiling where chandeliers still hung, dark and cobwebby. The light came not from the disused chandeliers, but from lanterns on poles scattered throughout the room. This floor was also scuffed and scored with deep scratches where merchandise had no doubt been dragged over the years. It was almost criminal that they'd treated such a magnificent room so.

But what had startled a gasp out of Sienne was not the beauty of the room. It was its contents. The ballroom was packed with furniture, tables and chairs and armoires and chests and all manner of household furnishings. Wooden crates with their lids removed lay here and there, some with packing straw sticking out of the top, others gleaming with unidentifiable contents. Sienne's eye was drawn to a blocky, antique trunk atop which were piled furs, probably minks if Sienne had to guess. They weren't interested in the trunk, though it had come from the same ancient keep that had started their quest in motion, but Sienne was tempted to bid on it, for nostalgia's sake. Men and women in the uniforms of the Fiorettan city guard stood at attention around the room, armed with the traditional sword and knife and looking willing to use them. Sienne didn't need their deterrence to keep her distance.

The auction house employee walked to a spot near where the goods were piled most heavily and said, "Bidding will proceed as follows. An item will be presented and an initial price declared. I will call for bids, and the highest bidder will be the purchaser. All items must be paid for at auction's end. If the highest bidder lacks the cash to pay, the second highest bidder will be given the chance to purchase. Items not purchased at the end of the auction will remain the property of the city." She waited as if expecting questions, then said, "The first lot is a dining table and sixteen chairs. Bidding will start at one hundred lari."

Sienne scanned the room again. This was going to be a *very* long day.

She stood, trying not to fidget, as Lord Liurdi's possessions were auctioned off. She hadn't gone to the man's execution—none of them had—and the last she'd seen of him had been when she testified to his kidnapping of her. When she'd first met him, he'd been vibrant and confident, if unattractive. At the trial, he'd looked as if all the life had been sucked out of him. Sienne felt no pity, because he'd murdered and schemed to get the key to open that trunk, but she did feel awkward, as if she'd seen him naked and not just beaten. She'd also felt angry that the Giordas, who'd been his accomplices in murder and theft, had been given prison sentences rather than death simply because they'd testified against him. Prison was awful, true, and it was possible they wouldn't survive the term of their sentence, but it was just wrong.

The bidding proceeded. It was boring, actually, with most items going for their first asking price and some items not bid on at all. Sienne couldn't see a pattern to the order in which things were presented for auction. A sofa—a familiar sofa, she'd lain bound upon it while she listened to Liurdi and his friends plot her death!—was followed by a set of silverware, followed by porcelain bedroom utensils Sienne prayed someone had cleaned thoroughly. She let her mind drift, thinking about what Leofus might make for dinner. They were almost certainly going to miss the midday meal, the way things were going.

Perrin put up a hand, startling her. Surely she hadn't missed the knives being presented? But no, it was the pile of minks on the trunk he'd bid on. A few bids were exchanged, and Perrin was outbid. "Why did you do that?" she asked.

"Camouflage," Perrin said quietly. "And there are a few items we could use or resell at a profit."

"But what if we don't have enough for the knives?"

"This is not my first auction, Sienne. Have faith."

Sienne subsided. Perrin knew what he was doing. She was just there to keep him company and, she now thought, provide magical backup if necessary. If he bought an armoire like the one they were selling now, he'd only get it back to Master Tersus's house if she cast *fit* on it.

"Next lot," the auctioneer said. "Five artifact knives recovered from an ancient ruin, non-magical, but in excellent shape. We will start the bidding at twenty lari."

Perrin raised his hand. "Twenty lari, do I have twenty-five?" the auctioneer said. The young woman with the thin nose let go her purse long enough to raise her hand high in the air. "Twenty-five, I'm looking for thirty." Perrin bid again. "Thirty. Thirty-five?" The young woman's hand shot up again.

Sienne examined her more closely. She was plainly dressed, but in clothes that screamed bespoke and a pair of boots Sienne recognized as coming from the bootmaker she and her companions patronized, a woman whose wares were as expensive as they were high-quality. Her hair, unusually light for a Fiorettan, hung loose to her waist in mouse-colored waves. Sienne's hands closed into fists. What was her game?

The bidding continued to mount. Perrin looked as calm as if this weren't crucial to their plans. Sienne didn't know how much money Perrin had brought. Surely it would be enough. She resented the young woman and her stupid intrusion into their plans. They needed that knife, damn it!

"That's two hundred lari," the auctioneer said as Perrin lowered his hand. She was trying to maintain her calm, but her wide eyes gave away her astonishment at the turn the bidding had taken. "Two hundred fifty?"

One of the merchant's representatives raised a hand, outbidding the girl. Sienne's heart sank. The unusual activity made it look like Perrin and the girl knew something about the knives' value, and now others wanted in on it. She wanted to scream, snatch the knives, and make a run for it. How far could she get before the guards tackled her?

"Two hundred fifty," the auctioneer said in a faint voice. "Three hundred?"

"One thousand lari," the girl said. Her voice was thin, but clear. The woman in the chartreuse gown gasped.

"The bid is three hundred," the auctioneer said. Her hand by her side was shaking.

"I'm prepared to pay one thousand," the girl said. "This just saves time."

The auctioneer considered her. She looked at the merchant's representative and at Perrin. Perrin's jaw was rigid. Sienne was sure they didn't have a thousand lari. "One thousand lari," the auctioneer said. "Do I have one thousand and fifty?"

No one moved. The merchant's representative shook his head. "One thousand, then," the auctioneer said. The girl came forward to accept the numbered chit, then merged back into the crowd.

Perrin stared at nothing. His hand came to rest on the hip flask, but didn't take it. Sienne couldn't think of anything to say. They'd lost, and to a girl who...what? Believed the knives had a value they didn't? Or was she an unknown enemy who wanted them to suffer? But how could she have known they'd be there? Sienne stared at the girl, who was turning the numbered chit over in her hands like it was a precious jewel. Maybe they could reason with her. Maybe they could offer her money for just the one knife. Would that sound like desperation, and make her inflate her price further?

"Should we—" she began.

"Let us talk later," Perrin said. "When there are fewer prying ears."

Sienne nodded.

More lots came and went. Perrin half-heartedly bid on a kitchen table, and won. "Leofus has been complaining about the old table we use now," Perrin said as he accepted the chit showing the lot number he'd purchased. "I thought this would be a nice gift for him."

"He'll be thrilled." Sienne felt empty. Of course there was no point conserving their money now the knives were out of reach, but it was so *pointless*. She didn't know how Perrin managed not to despair. Or maybe he was despairing, and concealed it well.

It was hours before the auction was over, and by the end Sienne's feet hurt from standing so long, her stomach was empty, her bladder was full, and her hands were numb from cold. The announcement of the last lot energized her, until she remembered they still had to pay for the table. After what had happened, she resented the table for keeping them one moment longer than necessary, but she waited more or less patiently with Perrin to present their chit and hand over the money. "Will you arrange for delivery?" the man who took their money asked.

"My companion will handle the details," Perrin said, walking over to the table. Sienne followed him, pulling out her spellbook and opening it to *fit*. She'd had the spell for six months and still wasn't tired of using it. Slowly she read out the syllables of the transform, envisioning the size she wanted the table to become, and savored the honey-sweet taste that filled her mouth. As the last sound left her lips, the ten-foot-long table vanished, replaced by a doll-sized table no more than a foot long. There was never any transition between the two states; objects went from one size to another with no intervening stages. Sienne closed her spellbook, ignoring the stares and whispers of the onlookers. Perrin picked up the table. "Our thanks," he said, and strode off toward the exit.

Sienne began to follow him, but a hand on her arm stopped her. It was the girl who'd outbid them. She held a bulky leather bag larger than Sienne's spellbook in her other hand. "I have something you want," she said in the same thin voice.

"How dare you taunt me!" Sienne said, jerking away.

The girl was unmoved by Sienne's anger. She dipped into her belt pouch and brought out a rectangle of pasteboard. A calling card. Sienne had once had ones just like it. She extended it to Sienne, who took it without thinking. "Be at that address at nine a.m. tomorrow. All of you." She tucked the leather bag under one arm and turned to go.

"Wait!" Sienne said. "Why—"

"Tomorrow," the girl said, and kept walking.

Perrin hadn't stopped walking, and now he returned to Sienne's side. "Sienne," he said, "why were you talking to her?"

Sienne looked at the card. It bore the name *Odela Figlari* and an address on the east side of Fioretti. "I think," she said absently, "we've just been had."

Made in the USA
Middletown, DE
10 June 2022

66940636R00176